sources say

LORI GOLDSTEIN

RAZORBILL

With all my love to Mom and Dad

RAZORBILL

An imprint of Penguin Random House LLC, New York

First published in the United States of America by Razorbill,
an imprint of Penguin Random House LLC, 2020

Copyright © 2020 by Lori Goldstein
Screen Queens teaser text copyright © 2019 by Penguin Random House LLC
Interior illustrations copyright © 2020 by Mallory Heyer

Visit us online at penguinrandomhouse.com.

LIBRARY OF CONGRESS CATALOGING-IN-PUBLICATION DATA
Names: Goldstein, Lori (Lori A.), author.
Title: Sources say / Lori Goldstein.
Description: New York : Razorbill, [2020] | Audience: Ages 12+.
Summary: When ex-power couple Angeline, a social influencer, and Leo, an injured athlete, face off for student council president, Angeline's sister, school-newspaper editor Cat, and an underground newspaper editor also compete.
Identifiers: LCCN 2020020353 | ISBN 9780593117408 (hardcover)
ISBN 9780593117415 (ebook)
Subjects: CYAC: Elections—Fiction. | High schools—Fiction.
Schools—Fiction. | Newspapers—Fiction. | Sisters—Fiction.
Classification: LCC PZ7.1.G652 Sou 2020 | DDC [Fic]—dc23
LC record available at https://lccn.loc.gov/2020020353

Printed in the United States of America

1 3 5 7 9 10 8 6 4 2

Design by Theresa Evangelista

Text set in Minion Pro

sources
say

Acedia Confronts Its Inner Sloth:
Controversy Surrounding Student Council
Unprecedented in Charter School History

A SPECIAL REPORT

by Cathleen Quinn, senior

Editor of Acedia Charter School's The Red and Blue

Some say it started with the vegan bacon. Others claim it was the election of 1800. And some trace it all the way back to the dummy with an astounding likeness to Principal Schwartz perched in a lawn chair on the roof of the school. But everything that occurred during the student council election at Acedia Charter School started with a party.

"I was ripped, man," Josh Baker, junior, said. "Three, four of those apple pie balls, and *whoosh*! See ya! Wait, you quoting this? Yeah, so, yeah, hundred percent, thought it was apple juice. Vodka? Shocking, man. Shocking. But I saw. They were there. Both of 'em."

The "they" to whom Baker is referring are seniors Angeline Quinn—a popular lifestyle YouTuber—and Leo Torres—who's been romantically linked to Angeline and whose mom regularly makes headlines as a vocal progressive candidate for Congress. The party at senior Maxine Chen's was three weeks before school started.

"The house is up on the cliffs," junior Natalie Goldberg said. "It has a hot tub and a screening room. You know, like, with seats that recline? Not old-people recline but movie-theater recline with cup holders and personalized popcorn tubs. Her parents are in tech. So, you know."

Acedia Charter School has the distinction of being set upon land both rich in history—with a past of defending its shores against the invading British—and blazing with the future, thanks to its proximity to Boston with its elite schools of Harvard and MIT and influx of tech firms of the old guard (Amazon and Microsoft) and the new (BotBurgers—fast food cooked by robots—and BugBites—snacks made from ground-up crickets). Which means Acedia Charter School, nestled along a picturesque coastline in a small town on the South Shore, has as many students with parents at the upper levels of income, like Maxine Chen's, as it does below.

"I heard she did it for the cash," junior Andreas Costa said.

"I think it was the dude running against Torres's mom," Baker said. "Bribed Angeline with stocks or some shit. But what the hell do I know? I was off my ass. *Off . . . my . . . ass.*"

While reports differ, one thing is certain. The fight that ended a three-year romance, sparked a political rivalry, and left Angeline Quinn in tears and Leo Torres with a busted shoulder happened in that screening room at Maxine's party.

Click for more: 1 of 6

Comments (295)

BakedBaker24/7 *2 hours ago*

Dude look at me! I'm famous! Apple pie ball people: Available for all spokesman opportunities. DM me!

Like 👍 45

SlothsArePeopleToo *3 hours ago*

We . . . don't . . . appreciate . . . *(yawn)* . . . the insul— . . . zzzzzzzzzzzzzzzzzzzzzz

Like 👍 145

NatGberg *4 hours ago*

I have nothing against old people. I swear. Some of my favorite grandparents are old.

Like 👍 0

AskanAngel *5 hours ago*

Look at those wings flutter.

Like 👍 60

1

When Cat's Buttons Are Pushed

The assault on Cat's nose was quick and painful.

"Manure," she said, buckling herself into the passenger seat.

"I know." Angeline sighed. "First day of school makes me want to curse too, though less like a farmer."

"I mean the smell. In my car."

"Our car."

"Gramps gave it to me last year."

"With the intention of sharing it with *me* this year."

Angeline finished the last *over, under, over* of her long braid and secured it with a black elastic, nearly the same color as her roots and Cat's blunt bob. Twenty minutes it had taken Cat to flatten her light-socket cowlicks, and yet her sister perfected the black to brown to honey to gold ribbons of her ombre side braid while behind the wheel of the silver hatchback that had been their grandfather's until the eye chart said otherwise.

Cat nuzzled into the familiar leather, slippery and smooth from wear. "Well, the car—"

"Our car." Angeline turned the key, and the hatchback sputtered to life. She backed out of their apartment building's assigned parking spot with the barest of glances in the rearview mirror. She'd had her license for all of five minutes, but already she was a more confident and skilled driver than Cat, who'd had her license for nearly a year.

"Fine." Cat wrinkled her pale nose. "But it smells."

"That unscented lotion you insist on using isn't so much unscented as reeking of antiseptic. Seriously, Cat, a little mango-lime wouldn't kill you."

"It's not me." Cat swiveled her neck, spying first her sister's tanned thighs peeking out of her dress-code-violating skirt and then something gold and shimmery on the floor of the back seat.

"Another one of your freebies?" Cat said. "Don't tell me. It's some lipstick—"

"No."

"Dry shampoo—"

"Stop."

"Yoga pants or corset revival—"

"Enough, Cat."

Right. Cat reached behind the seat and picked up the gold bag. Another half-baked test product from some "women-empowering"—definition loosely applied—startup. The single demeaning word "better" was written in minuscule lowercase letters across the front and inside—

"My God!" Cat flinched at the stench. "I think I'm going blind." She gingerly removed the gray cylindrical package, stamped with "bigger is better" in the same tiny font whose irony she'd bet had been lost on the perky female founders. "What is this?"

"Facial rejuvenator. Says it works best when heated naturally by the warmth of the sun."

"So you're leaving it in my car?"

"Our car."

"Which now smells like a rest stop on 95 during an August heat wave."

"They added essential oils." Angeline extended her long neck and sniffed. "Don't you get the lavender?"

"No. The only essential I get is shi—"

"Night soil," Angeline corrected.

Cat dropped the cylinder. "As in . . . ?"

"Waste matter. Recycled."

"That you put on your *face*?" Cat rubbed her fingers on the side of her khaki cargo skirt—two inches below the knee, one more than required by the student handbook. "Please tell me it's not human."

Angeline rolled her eyes. "Obviously."

"Right. Of course. *Obviously*." Cat tied the bag shut. She held it between two fingers and eyed the open window.

"Don't even think about it," Angeline said.

"Your funeral, which is a very real possibility if you use that." Cat tossed the bag behind her seat and zipped open her backpack. She squirted half the container of hand sanitizer into her palm.

"It's approved . . . ish," Angeline said. "Elephant mostly, I think."

Cat groaned as she smeared hand sanitizer on her nose. "Because 'bigger is better.' That's disgusting. You really have no line."

"What I have are two hundred thousand subscribers and the chance to turn that into two million. Ten times my current ad revenue. *Ten*. Mom could retire. Let Dad suck on that."

"Sure. Thanks to YouTube voyeuristic weirdos, who you cater to."

Angeline shifted her hazel eyes from the road to Cat. "Have you even watched recently? Seen the likes from Evelyn's Epic Everyday? Read the comments?"

"Do you want me to?"

Angeline faced front again and shrugged with the grace of a princess bending in her thousandth curtsey. A shoulder lift and fall that Cat knew every muscle twitch of. She and her sister shared a room and a grade but little else.

Cat twisted toward the open window, breathing in air heavy with the smell of the ocean and donuts from the lone chain store in town. Angeline had taken the scenic route, chauffeuring them from their apartment complex at one end of the five-block stretch of the harbor to the other. Since their unit faced the back, they didn't get a glimpse of the deep blue waters along Frontage Street that defined the town and everyone in it.

They passed the aging grocery, well-stocked hardware store, and two-screen movie theater with gum from the seventies cemented to the seats. Sprinkled in between were more ice cream stands than a stretch of real estate this small could normally sustain, though half would shutter before the first frost, hibernating until spring. The requisite Irish bar and hipster gastropub nestled in among the year-round clothing, home decor, and accessories shops that, like the harbor itself, somehow managed to fall on the right side of cute versus cheesy—a rarity in towns that wouldn't be towns without the ocean drawing people to them. All these businesses were potential advertisers for *The Red and Blue*. Cat had made her pitch to most of them over the past couple of weeks.

She glanced at her white plastic digital watch, and Angeline huffed.

"What?" Cat said.

"We're not late. And if we were, it'd be your fault not mine. I was the one waiting in the car for you."

Because you hit stop instead of snooze on my phone's alarm so you could drive.

Cat took a steadying breath. "I just wanted a chance to stop by—"

"The newsroom, I know. Your second home."

She said it as if it shouldn't be. As if the time Cat spent there could be better allocated elsewhere. As if it didn't matter. Which, by extension, meant neither did Cat.

They drove in silence up from the harbor, the landscape shifting from boats, docks, and sand to towering oak, birch, and maple trees. Lush green leaves lined the winding streets where clapboard homes from the 1700s mixed with mini McMansions in subdivisions. This town wasn't exactly small, but being in it beside Angeline made it feel like a coffin.

Only two traffic lights guarded intersections along their seven-minute ride. At the second one, Angeline flicked the blinker to take the next left into Acedia Charter School's parking lot.

Three stories high with rows of slender windows lining the red-brick front, Acedia gave the optical illusion of being narrower than it actually was, like its architect had implemented one of Angeline's "Five Closet Tricks That Shed Pounds Instantly!"

Angeline paused and glanced at Cat. "Be different with them gone . . . Stavros and June."

Cat swallowed. "Jen."

"That's what I meant."

"Mmm . . . sure." Stavros and Jen had graduated last year, leaving Cat as the sole remaining editorial member of *The Red and Blue* and with a friendship count of zero. She'd been too embarrassed to tell Gramps that the empty masthead was how she'd nabbed the editor in chief role.

"So, yeah," Angeline said, "you can sit with us at lunch if you want."

"Us? You and Leo are back together?"

"No." Angeline bristled. "I meant us—Maxine, Sonya, and Riley, you know."

"I'll probably be in the newsroom."

"Right."

"Right."

"Well, that's done then."

"Done? Wait, did you promise Mom you'd extend a pity invite to your pathetic *older* sister?"

"Gramps, and the wording was different but close enough."

Cat clamped her jaw shut. She barely waited for Angeline to put *her* hatchback into park before escaping it. Lately, Angeline had been pushing Cat's buttons more frequently, and the sensation of her head about to explode was becoming all too familiar.

She eased the clench on her backpack, preparing to start her senior year alongside the classmates she barely knew.

Out of the corner of her eye, Cat caught sight of a distinctive lime-green sweatshirt. On anyone else the bright zip-up would've looked silly, but the combination of Leo's tawny skin, thick black hair, and unwavering confidence made it work. He loved that sweatshirt almost as much as he loved Angeline—though presumably it got top billing now.

Cat remembered the first time she'd seen him in it, freshman year when Gramps had insisted on meeting the boy stealing away his granddaughter. He'd arrived with a loaded beach tote: flowers for their mom, a potted pink beach rose for Angeline, and chocolates filled with hazelnuts that his grandmother had brought from Venezuela on her last visit to the States. Leo's parents were both Venezuelan, first-generation, and though Leo lacked a sweet tooth, the rest of his family—and now Gramps—couldn't get enough of that Toronto candy. But Leo also had something for Cat: a spiral-bound notebook with *Editor in Chief* handwritten on the cover. She still had it. She'd waited, as if opening it before the role was hers would jinx it.

They'd had to use Cat and Angeline's desk chair as the fifth seat at the dining room table, but Leo fit in instantly. He'd watch the Red Sox with Gramps, listen more attentively than either Cat or Angeline when their mom delved into stories from the law firm where she worked, and came ready with a new obscure fact to every dinner—he was obsessed with this podcast that uncovered the unusual in everyday things. Over the past three years, he'd become an everyday thing for the Quinns. He'd become family.

And Angeline being Angeline meant he no longer was.

Leo met Cat's eye, and she smiled weakly at seeing his left shoulder cradled in a sling, hoping he wasn't hovering on the fringes of the parking lot just to get a glimpse of his ex, especially after what she'd done to him.

It was their breakup that had made her sister more antagonistic than usual. At least, Cat suspected as much. She and Angeline didn't talk about that stuff. Angeline had her friends. And Cat, well, Cat didn't need to talk about that stuff because Cat never had time for that stuff. School and homework and studying for the SATs took Cat double the time it took Angeline. Leo ending things with Angeline was the first time in her sister's life that things hadn't gone her way.

Cat hit the path that wound around the side and to the front entrance of the school. Most everyone else opted for the short-cut across the lawn, under the WELCOME BACK, ACEDIA! marquee and past the concrete island with the statue of town founder Major Mushing that attracted the pigeons and doves and feathery beasts that kept Cat far away. Her classmates' heavy, shuffling feet would grind down the pristine blades, leaving nothing but a muddy trail come October, same as every year.

2

When Angeline Is Here for It

It was the same as every year, except in the ways it wasn't.

The one colossal way.

Angeline's heart clenched as her eyes settled on the bright green of that mangy old sweatshirt that smelled like seaweed and sunshine even direct from the wash. She strained to meet Leo's gaze across the parking lot, to see if he'd been looking for her—waiting for her—but he dropped his Ray-Bans over his eyes and fell in step beside his little brother, Sammy, a shorter, skinnier version of Leo, wearing his own favorite article of clothing: a red plaid shirt perpetually tied around his waist.

The idea that Sammy was starting his freshman year seemed as ridiculous as Angeline starting her senior year without Leo.

She'd known Sammy since he was eleven. *Eleven*. They'd devour Mr. Torres's homemade arepas—corn cakes stuffed with whatever they had in the fridge: queso blanco or deviled ham or eggs or even just plain butter. Delicious no matter the filling. Then she'd sit on the couch next to Leo, pinkies entwined, pretending to do homework and providing cover so Sammy could sneak clips of *Saturday*

Night Live, which his parents had said he was too young for.

And now Leo was escorting Sammy through the front door of high school.

She should have been beside him. Them.

Angeline hugged her tote tight to her chest and forced air back into her lungs.

"Good summer, Angeline?" said a girl she didn't recognize.

"Loved the last vid," said the girl's friend, whose strappy sandals cost as much as a smartphone. Angeline knew because she'd been trying to land a promo gig with the brand all summer.

Angeline donned her Ask an Angel smile and shifted to showcase her better side. "First day. Embrace it and don't forget, flut—"

"Flutter your wings!" the girls cried in unison.

Her signature phrase.

The one she ended every video with, the one that brought out the corny she loved in Leo, who'd flap his arms like a seagull on speed when she said it in front of him.

In front of him now in her place was Tad Marcus, singlehandedly the offensive line for the football team, who strutted up to Leo and high-fived his good hand—the one not in a sling. Guilt and remorse rose inside her like bubbles in a shaken bottle of seltzer, and she fought to shut it down, blinking away the burning behind her eyes. Before anyone saw. Before anyone videoed Ask an Angel losing it in the Acedia parking lot.

She moved slowly, giving Leo time to enter the school and put distance between them. But Tad, whose white skin had gained a layer of freckles thanks to the summer sun, stood before him, gesturing wildly. Probably telling a joke she was the butt of or that her butt was in. Knowing Tad, probably both.

Tad was the king of "tics": narcissistic, misogynistic, and

anticlimactic (at least according to Riley's intel from Tad's girlfriend, Tamara). He towered over the Torres brothers, and when his voice rose as if coming to a punch line, he slapped Sammy squarely between the shoulder blades, knocking him forward about a foot. Leo's dimple disappeared along with his smile as he set a hand on Sammy's forearm and gave a quick squeeze that Angeline swore she could almost feel.

The group was blocking the doorway, and Leo stepped back to allow others to pass, including Emmie Hayes, shoo-in for valedictorian, lover of causes and fundraisers, and student council something or other. Her strawberry-blonde hair skimmed her shoulders with each purposeful step of her no-nonsense flats. She'd paired them with a wrinkle-free, short-sleeved blouse and straight-legged trousers (*on point only for working an afternoon catering job at the yacht club*).

Right before Emmie reached the door, Leo pressed his hand against it, opening it, just like he'd done for Angeline a thousand times. Car, house, school, movie theater. Riley said she wasn't supposed to let him. Feminism and all. But Angeline saw it less as him thinking she was weak and more that he wanted a way to show everyone, not just her, how much he cared.

Emmie gave Leo a curt nod as she entered the school.

Tad pursed his lips and tilted his head to check her out from behind. He shoved a thumbs-up in Sammy's face, and Emmie whipped her head around just as Leo clamped his fingers over Tad's, pushing them down so she wouldn't see.

Typical.

Angeline had never liked him. But Leo being Leo meant he gave everyone the benefit of the doubt. Even Tad Marcus.

Which said a lot.

Which said everything.

About what Angeline had done.

Too much for even Leo to forgive.

Angeline nervously spun the silver claddagh band on her right hand. A traditional Irish ring, it had belonged to her grandmother. Angeline liked to think the two hands winding around weren't just holding the heart topped with a crown, but were her grandmother's hands also holding her. The symbols represented love, loyalty, and friendship, and the ring was a centuries-old way of defining one's relationship status. Married women wore it on their left hand, unmarried on their right. And the unmarried had a choice: the point of the heart facing toward the hand meant the wearer's heart was taken and she was in a relationship, away, the opposite. Angeline slipped off the ring and reversed direction, returning it to her finger with the tip turned out.

She swallowed hard and aimed for the side door.

As her open-toed bootie (*see the official Ask an Angel review in my "Boot Up!" video*) landed on the sidewalk, a beanpole of a kid with ghostly white skin barreled into her. He lifted his head of dark curls from the phone it had been buried in.

"And that's news to you" spilled from the speaker—the catchphrase from one of the local Boston news stations that made Cat's eyeballs roll so far back in her head, she risked losing them.

"Sorry," said the obvious freshman with an unfortunate first-day-of-school pimple on the end of his nose. "Cousin." He held up his phone.

"Your aunt, the tablet, must be so proud," Maxine Chen deadpanned in that strong, dry tone Angeline knew as well as her own.

The kid cocked his head, studied Angeline, and his eyes widened behind his gigantic, black-framed glasses. "Aren't you—"

15

"Flutter your wings!" Maxine motioned him along with a twiddle of her fingers.

He frowned, and Angeline gave a weak smile before he walked away.

"I do have an image to keep up," Angeline said.

"Not for a freshman."

"For everyone. I'm everyone's best friend, sister, and girlfriend all rolled into one."

"Definitely the first two for me. For the third . . ." She tapped the ocean wave pendant on her necklace and gestured toward Tad Marcus and his girlfriend across the front lawn. "She's more my type."

"Of course she is," Angeline said. "She's an 'a.'"

"An 'a'?"

"Tamara," Angeline said. "Lana, Zoya, Pamela . . . you do realize you only date girls whose names end in an 'a'?"

"Huh." Maxine's forehead creased, and she ran her tongue across the "oh-so-berry" gloss on her lips—an Ask an Angel favorite. Maxine was Chinese American, third-generation, and she had her dad's wide smile and her mom's smooth black hair, whose ends she dyed a different color every three months. She'd traded in the summer pink that matched the stripes on her surfboard for a bright electric blue. "We've both got a thing for vowels, then? Since you've only dated boys with names ending in 'o.' Well, *boy*, singular." Angeline winced, and Maxine quickly switched gears. "How about we both shake things up this year? Now that the administration's finally stamped yes on my Girl Coders Club, maybe we'll develop an Acedia dating app?"

Under the marquee, Tad hugged Tamara while simultaneously checking out a pair of freshman girls nervously shuffling to the entrance. Tamara had light brown skin and short, dark hair that let all the focus be on the petite features of her face. Too pretty, too nice, too everything for Tad.

"Or maybe we concentrate on us," Maxine said. "And make our every day epic."

"Here for that." Angeline tucked her arm through Maxine's and headed into school for the first day of senior year. "Bring it."

3

When Cat Comes Down with Election Fever

Cat flicked on the lights of the supply closet turned newsroom.

Poorly ventilated with not a single window to let the outside in, the room could double as a sauna. The stale air invited dust mites to take up residence. They clogged the keyboards and coated the monitors with a haze of dirt. Just inside the door, someone had left a used plunger and a chewed-up broom, which she hoped weren't used for the same purpose.

Still, instantly, Cat's mind calmed. Her sister was wrong. The newsroom wasn't her second home. It *was* home. The place she dreamed of escaping to when her actual one brimmed with so much Angeline, she couldn't breathe.

Okay, so days like today, breathing brought a sneeze or two, but Cat could fix that. Here, she could do anything, be anything, become something. Someone. Someone who'd leave this small town behind and enter a world she'd report on, like her grandfather had done.

She relished these few minutes before the first day of her senior year officially began. The solitude let her think, let her plan, let her wrap her head around what was to come. She set her backpack beside the chair that had been Jen's, the one with "EIC" spelled out on the back in masking tape. She drew the seat toward her and hesitated before lowering herself into it.

A nervous smile spread across her face. She pressed her feet into the floor, kicking herself into a spin. But as the chair slowed, the emptiness of the room settled deep in her chest: the three other computer stations, the printer stocked with its last toner cartridge, the physics lab table she and Stavros had snagged from the dumpster. It'd been missing a leg, and the two of them had brought it back to life thanks to a roll of duct tape and two old ski poles Stavros had convinced the team to donate.

This year she'd be alone. Just her and Ravi Tandon, if he came back as the paper's designer. He'd been flirting with moving on to yearbook at the end of last year. She could hardly blame him if he did.

Her hand dropped to the stack of last year's undistributed newspapers, piled on the floor beside her chair almost as high as the seat. Jen had tried, Stavros too, but neither of them had been able to make *The Red and Blue* something anyone wanted to read.

Cat's investigative reports hadn't helped. She grabbed the top newspaper with her byline on the front page. It had been good journalism to uncover the source of last January's daily fire alarm—hotboxing in the server room. She thumbed through the stack and found another: this one exposing the perpetrator selling the password to the school's unblocked Wi-Fi.

Then there was the series that began with her report on the notorious spirit week incident, in which the hard work of the cheerleading squad—who'd gone to state for the past four years, unlike the football team—was rewarded with the sexist "cupcake" being scrawled across their uniforms. The series continued by asking why such pranks seemed rampant at Acedia. Whether weak investigations by the administration fostered an environment that gave pranksters license to act and to amp up their stunts, which had begun to reflect a sexist and intolerant culture that no one wanted to talk about. There were even rumors that students, namely male students, had been caught in various acts but let go with barely a warning after parental pressure on the school.

Turned out, such articles didn't endear her or *The Red and Blue* to student, faculty, or parental readers. By the end of last year, it'd been practically impossible to get anyone to even agree to be quoted in the paper.

She might be riveted by Gramps's stories of reporting on everything from the war in Vietnam to the attacks on 9/11, but she knew the media of his day was not the media of hers.

One look at her sister giving a tutorial on "identifying your good side" to the delight of two hundred thousand followers on YouTube told her that.

The only places doing the type of reporting her grandfather had done were the best of the best: *The New York Times*, *The Washington Post*, *The Atlantic*. Cat needed every advantage to get there, starting with the Fit to Print award for best high school newspaper in the state. Without it, she'd be just another eager but undistinguished applicant to Northwestern. Without it, she'd be stuck here. With Angeline.

She rolled the chair under Jen's old desk and pulled out the notebook Leo had given her three years ago. She ran her fingers along the words he'd written, now in the position he'd predicted she'd have.

She carefully set it to the side and opened the accounting ledger. The newspaper was responsible for funding itself: equipment, repairs, printing costs. Issues were distributed in school and at the grocery store, post office, and town hall—if they could afford the larger print run. The amount left in the account would barely cover the first issue, and Cat's efforts to recruit new advertisers from the local businesses had gotten her nothing but blisters from those damn loafers Angeline swore were as comfortable as clouds. Perhaps the way they tore at her skin was karma for borrowing them without her sister's permission.

Cat needed a story that people cared about. Stories led to readers, which led to advertisers. Without them, *The Red and Blue* would fold, like so many newspapers were doing. She wouldn't let that be her legacy.

She pressed the power button to bring the ancient iMac to life. The whirring of its hard drive was interrupted by a knock on the door. A woman with medium-brown skin and a straight, layered pixie cut cradled a box in her arms. Written across the side in neat, blocky letters was FOR ACEDIA!

Cat stood. "Can I help you?"

"Sure can," said the woman, who looked to be in her early twenties. "You can make me proud."

"Uh, I guess I can try?"

The woman grinned, shifted the box, and held out her hand. "Ms. Lute, adviser to *The Red and Blue*."

Cat met her at the door and awkwardly shook her hand. The paper hadn't had a real adviser since she'd started freshman year. Mr. Monte technically oversaw, but he'd never once stepped inside the newsroom. She doubted he'd ever read an issue, which was fine with Cat. "Oh, okay. I mean, great. And I'm Cat."

"And you're in charge here?"

Cat nodded, anxious Ms. Lute's presence might change that.

"Ah, deer in headlights! No worries, this baby is yours."

Relief spread to Cat's fingertips.

Ms. Lute added, "I won't interfere, but I'm here if you need me. I edited my own high school newspaper before jumping into the political ring."

"You're teaching government?"

"Yup. One-stop shop for all things politics and media. I hope you'll be in my class?"

"Yeah, I think it's required for juniors and seniors."

Ms. Lute frowned. She set the box on the floor, a stack of makeshift ballots with the names of the two candidates running for president in November on top. "I wish it didn't have to be. But this is too important. My goal is for every student to understand why the whole country's swept up in election fever. My first year of teaching, and it's like I won the lottery. No better time for a government class to focus on the power of the vote."

"I guess, but the students—"

Ms. Lute talked over her. "Especially since I hear the full student council is to be elected, and I get to be the adviser of that too. Signups will run through this first week, and then we're off to the races—or race, singular, in this case. The student council election will be the centerpiece of my course this semester."

"StuCo? Sorry to have to tell you this, Ms. Lute. But no one cares about student government here. You know the school mascot's a sloth, right? Total self-fulfilling prophecy."

Ms. Lute arched an eyebrow. "Life lesson for you, Cat: people care when someone makes them. Couldn't be a teacher if I didn't believe that."

She grabbed her box and confidently strode down the hall, her red, white, and blue heels clicking on the tile floor.

Election fever. Accessorized.

But she wasn't wrong. Local and national news, talk shows, podcasts, radio, Twitter, Facebook, Instagram—the race for president was everywhere.

The whole country *was* swept up in election fever.

Including, without a doubt, the Fit to Print judges.

But this was Acedia. *The Red and Blue*'s most-read issue ever featured Cat's article on the previous year's senior prank—the one that had turned Principal Schwartz's normally fake-orange-tanned complexion Hot Tamale red. An unknown group of seniors had somehow reached the roof of the school, which was well above the height for any standard ladder. They'd glued down a lawn chair, and in it, they'd plunked a surprisingly lifelike doppelgänger dummy of the principal holding a sun reflector in one hand and a three-foot-tall sloth in the other. They set up a webcam that live-streamed "Schwartz" and "Slothy," as he came to be known, on YouTube.

That's what got Acedia engaged.

Cat leaned against the doorjamb. Down the hall, Ms. Lute carefully pinned a stars-and-stripes streamer around the edges of the bulletin board outside her classroom. She was officially the most committed teacher at Acedia, and she'd barely started. If anyone stood a chance of drumming up interest in student government, it would be her.

Covering the election, with in-depth candidate profiles and extensive campaign-platform analysis, would give *The Red and Blue* a focus, a purpose, one entirely timely and relevant.

Cat pulled her phone out of her back pocket. The last text she'd received was a dorm-room selfie from Jen the day she'd arrived at

NYU, where she'd only just made it in off the wait list despite her internship at *The New York Times* and a family legacy at the university. Cat had neither.

She searched her contacts and found a number for Ravi. She texted him, asking if he was returning to the paper.

Because if she did this, if she killed it, the Fit to Print award was hers for the taking.

"Please let me kill it," Cat whispered.

4

When Angeline's Every Day Becomes Epic

Angeline stared at the little blue dot at the top of her inbox. A new message. She hadn't changed the settings on her computer, but she swore the sender's name was bigger than usual.

She sat up straighter in the nubby tweed chair—the last thing she'd let her sister pick out—behind the desk they shared in their bedroom.

All those hours in front of her laptop studying every YouTube channel from GamerGirlz to Car Builderz DIY to Bette's Books to Bet On. Every grasshopper-topped sushi roll she ate, every chocolate laxative cleanse, every questionable and disgusting concoction she'd lathered on her body, all came down to this.

Her hand hovered over the mouse, but she couldn't bring herself to click. Instead, she kicked off the pointy-toed loafers she'd worn to school that day, wincing as the air hit the raw pink welt on the back of her ankle. She'd said they were comfortable.

They weren't.

But the endorsement had paid for her new laptop so . . . *trade-offs.*

She pressed her toes into the white carpet she'd freshly steamed before the school year began and fixed her eyes on her computer screen.

"Ask an Angel" leapt from the subject line, the YouTube channel Angeline had grown into a brand over the past two years. Influencer? *Please.* She was so much more. Part advice giver, part counselor, part confessor, she served her viewers by listening to and answering their daily dilemmas—even if that meant boots-on-the-ground research.

Okay, so truth?

She'd never admit it to Cat, but that elephant dung *had* nearly made her pass out.

Her sister thought it was easy. But had she ever tried to squeeze herself into the trifecta of compression underwear?

High-waisted capri britches . . .

Tummy cincher . . .

Hip slimmer . . .

After eating two pints of caramel gelato.

Angeline had come *this* close to dialing 911. But her lack of circulation had surely prevented others from asphyxiation.

Turn blue, and the followers would come.

She hadn't read that in any influencer guide. But it had worked. As had a modest display of cleavage and pink lipstick. Pink, not red. She'd lost ninety followers before she'd realized that mistake.

Now she had more questions than she could answer, and her ad revenue crushed whatever she'd make working round the clock as a barista. But she was determined to take it to the next level.

Evelyn's Epic Everyday: Make Every Day an Epic Day.

The pinnacle of lifestyle YouTubers, promoting positivity,

following one's dreams, and making each day an extraordinary one. An extraordinarily profitable one. Evelyn had raked in half a million dollars from her YouTube channel alone last year—a pittance compared to what she'd snagged from endorsements and book deals. Her second book, *Girl, Talk like Everyone's Listening*, hit the bestseller list, joining her first, *Girl, Match Your Bra and Underwear and Other Life Secrets*, which had never dropped off.

And here she was: Evelyn's Epic Everyday in Angeline's inbox.

Angeline took a deep breath and clicked.

Her heart stopped.

And jump-started.

"Bring! It!" she screamed, and Tartan, Gramps's orange-and-white cat, sprang from her lap.

She'd gotten the invite. *The*, all caps, underlined, circled, highlighted, *invite*. When Evelyn's Epic Everyday had given her video on "5 Ways to Know He's Interested" a thumbs-up over the summer, Angeline had known what it meant.

Evelyn was watching her.

Her.

Ask an Angel.

Which meant she had a shot.

At this.

And she got it.

> *Hey girl!*
> *Evelyn's Epic Everyday has her epic eye on you!*
>
> *As you may have heard (wink, wink), she's putting together her very first YouTube up-and-comers boot camp.*

Invitation only!

Those she thinks are ready to break out big will make her annual "Top 10 to Get Behind or Be Left Behind" list. And you know what that means! But still, I'm gonna tell youuu! Because it's that freaking fantastic: every single previous lister has gone on to be a Star of the Super sort. Think: a million subscribers, two, three . . . five?

Not yet, but you could be Evelyn's first!

So welcome, Ask an Angel, to your every day being an epic one. But remember: keep it hush-hush! We'll be doing a big reveal in the lead-up.

See you in December!
Don't forget to send in that deposit!
(Nonrefundable!)

Kiss kiss!

Angeline vaulted out of her chair and pumped her fists in the air.

"Evelyn's!"

"Epic!"

"Everyday!"

She spun around and snatched her phone off the bed. She had her messages open to her last text with Leo before she remembered.

They were broken up.

He had broken up with her.

Because of all this.

The one person she wanted to share this with was the one person she couldn't.

Is this what they call irony?

She sunk back into her chair, staring at the pink roses on the plant that Leo had given her freshman year. They'd repotted it together since, four times, always here on the balcony off the living room, its small size still more comfortable than being at Leo's, where his mom's scowl awaited around every corner.

Besides, Angeline was the one who knew how to cultivate and trim and fertilize. Her grams had loved gardening. Leo's contribution had been keeping her company, sharing stories of his family. Like how they always celebrated Christmas on the eve, not the day. How on New Year's Eve, they'd run around the house outside, in the freezing cold, carrying a suitcase and wearing yellow underwear, traditions passed down from his grandparents to bring travel and fortune in the new year. And how his mom would immediately feel a sense of home when her foot hit the floor of the airport in Maiquetía. Striped with red, blue, yellow, and black, the floor was famous, with its own Instagram hashtag. As he'd spoken, his eyes had been both happy and sad, for so many of their family traditions had waned as his mom's career had grown.

Other times, he'd simply entertained her with one little-known fact after another. Like how rose hips were a good source of vitamin C and how one of the oldest fossils of roses discovered in Colorado dated back thirty-four million years.

He always had one ready, his memory for random tidbits fueled initially by his mom's requirement that he be able to engage with anyone on anything. It had made them a good team on Ask an Angel; she didn't have his patience for passive research or his speed at typing—his former speed.

She'd seen the sling.

The rumors were true.

No lacrosse.

No leading the team to state.

Leo being Leo, letting down his teammates would be tearing him up more than not playing himself.

One moment of distraction, and good-bye MVP. He'd been biking home from Maxine's party when he'd flipped over the handlebars.

Guilt crept in, and Angeline elbowed it aside in a move she'd been perfecting since they'd broken up. She'd like to think she'd done a good job of successfully avoiding him, but she was pretty sure that was only because he was the one excelling at avoiding her.

But really, he had been her boyfriend. Who supposedly believed in her. Shouldn't he have *wanted* to help her?

And, technically speaking, hadn't she stayed true to her word?

Semantics.

Whatever, so maybe her literal interpretation didn't give her a total pass, but how else was she supposed to keep Evelyn on the hook? Leo's charisma was second only to her own. She'd needed him.

Now she was here.

Here with an invite to Evelyn's Epic Everyday Boot Camp.

Here without Leo.

"Heard the call," Gramps said, poking his head into the room. "Though the specifics on what exactly needs to be brought elude me."

Cat smirked behind him. Sardines had to snuggle to be as close as those two. Same way Angeline had been with the grandmother she was named after. Grams had died a few years ago, about the same time as her dad had flaked, bolted, and *his* dad had moved in to take his place. A total upgrade.

"What's up?" Cat said. "Get a new ad from a women's mustache remover?" She flopped on her bed—or, rather, on the clothes and newspapers and old scrapbooks of Gramps's articles on her bed.

Angeline cringed.

This was her studio. The backbone of Ask an Angel.

A perfect square, their bedroom was divided as equally as the Ikea furniture in it: two white dressers, two twin beds, two squat nightstands. While Cat's side got the desk, Angeline's had the teal faux-fur, bowl-shaped chair, courtesy of an Ask an Angel sponsor. Their mom had mandated that they agree on the common space, so there were no posters on the walls, no flashy paint colors, no constellations on the ceiling, despite how hard Angeline had pushed for that last one.

Angeline's side was flawless, with her crisp white comforter, pink-and-white diamond curtains, and quirky Edison bulb lamp she'd found on Etsy.

But Cat's side . . . threadbare comforter with a juvenile print that looked like a newspaper front page, a cheap plastic blind, and three LED lamps clipped to her bed frame. Books were strewn on the floor like a quilted rug, and pens and notebooks and highlighters poked out from under her pillow. Her sister kept her newsroom neat and orderly, yet she couldn't even be bothered to clear peanut butter cup wrappers off her nightstand. Not passive-aggressive. Aggressive-aggressive. And gross. Not to mention unhealthy.

Gramps sat on the end of Angeline's bed and let Tartan knead into his side. "Now, granddaughter, enlighten me."

"I'm in."

Cat's head jerked up, and she almost seemed to smile before a look of indifference won out. "Mom'll never let you go."

Angeline squeezed her phone as if the Evelyn in her inbox could give her an encouraging hug back. "She has to."

"She won't," Cat said.

"Unless . . ." Angeline ignored the eye roll Cat directed at their grandfather and focused on him. "Just hear me out. She trusts no one more than you. So you could maybe sorta help convince her?"

Gramps scratched Tartan behind his ears. "Flattery appreciated but not necessary. Because for you, my angel, I'll do my best. Now go ask, and I'll provide backup."

Angeline frowned, but it was entirely fake, and they both knew it. He had a pass for life for stepping in to help her mom—his daughter-in-law—raise her and Cat. Especially since all her own father had managed to raise was a spoiled cockapoo with his new wife. He'd been remarried for four years, but she would always be new thanks to the Botox she infused by IV.

Botox Wife subscribed to her channel. *Seriously?* She was into barre and hashtagged half her spoken words and wore headbands with daisies on them to match her purse-sized pup. It was like having a unicorn for a stepmom. Not that Angeline saw her much. Or her dad. They'd moved to Los Angeles not long after the wedding to pursue his lifelong dream of being a famous musician and hers of being a famous musician's wife.

"Okay. Let's do this," Angeline said, and her heart sank at channeling Leo. It was natural that they'd pick up a thing or two from each other after three years.

Three years, gone in one night.

All she had now was her future.

She squared her shoulders and headed down the hall toward her mom's bedroom.

Bedroom slash law library slash PTA headquarters slash booster club mission control. Which, right now, was buried in glitter.

Her mom had thrown herself into two things after Angeline's dad left: her paralegal job by day, and everything and anything associated with Angeline and Cat by night. She'd hand-sewn their *Toy Story* Halloween costumes even though they'd preferred something store-bought like everyone else. She'd belted out off-key "sun'll come out tomorrow"s with Angeline to help her rehearse *Annie Jr.* And she still sat beside Cat, reading all three Sunday papers her sister had delivered every week.

It was as endearing as it was suffocating.

Angeline watched her mom glue a photo of last year's casino night onto a piece of cardboard. Her bedroom door was always open—literally, her mom wanting to be available at a moment's holler. Not that anyone needed to shout to be heard, what with the thin walls of this apartment they'd downsized to after her dad left.

Angeline prepared herself and said breezily, "Hey, hey, Mom."

Her mom's head popped up. "Well, hey there, yourself." She propped the cardboard on its end. "How's it looking? Brag board for back-to-school night." The center photo was of Angeline and Leo, both modeling the new uniforms—her cheer, him lacrosse—that her mom's fundraising had secured the previous year. Her mom followed Angeline's gaze and smiled softly. "You know . . . it's okay to admit you miss him, Ang."

Her mom thought this would help. Getting Angeline to open up about Leo.

It wouldn't.

As her mom tucked the board under one arm, Angeline considered the best strategy for asking about Evelyn's Epic Everyday. The previous conversations, though hypothetical, had all ended in a real no.

"So," Angeline started. "Want to grab dinner? Just the two of us?"

"Sorry, honey, but I can't. Booster meeting." She shouldered her grubby canvas messenger bag and made her way through the combination living room–dining room and into the galley kitchen, where she grabbed a protein bar. "This is all I have time for. I'll split it with you, if you want."

"I'm good," Angeline said. "Actually . . . I'm great. You know that boot camp I was talking about?"

"No."

"The one with Evelyn's Epic—"

"That's not what my 'no' means."

"But it's over winter break and—"

"No."

Angeline laced her long fingers together in front of her stomach and regrouped. "It's totally safe. Lots of kids my age."

"Well, lucky for them I'm not their mom."

"But it'll make me skyrocket!"

"That's what I'm afraid of."

"But . . . wait, what?"

"Angeline, is this really what you want your life to be?"

Angeline eyed the sequin border of the brag board and the gray streaking her mom's dark brown bob.

Is this yours?

"Look, sweetheart," her mom said, "you're smart. Talented, obviously. But you need a real future. Not one you define by how many people click a thumbs-up symbol next to your picture."

"This is a real future, Mom. Do you have any idea how much I could be earning?"

"And what do you have to give of yourself for it?"

"Don't." Angeline shook her head.

"I'm just saying . . . Leo—"

"No, Mom, just, no."

"Okay then."

"Okay then I can go?"

"No."

Gramps cleared his throat from behind Angeline. "Might an ole fella have a say?"

Her mom sighed. "And he trots out the Irish accent. Why do I feel a gang-up coming on?"

Gramps winked. "I prefer 'mediation.' Now, Marie, is there something you'd like from Angeline in exchange?"

Her mom eyed the two of them and finally said, "In all the ways you've talked about this boot camp—"

"So, so, so many ways." Cat slunk past Angeline and Gramps and entered the kitchen.

Her mom flattened one of Cat's persistent cowlicks and said to Angeline, "One thing's been missing. How much?"

"I've got it covered," Angeline said. "I've been saving."

"You've got enough?"

Angeline nodded. "I told you I was doing well. I could be doing better. For all of us."

Cat snorted, and Angeline bugged her eyes at her sister. *How does she think she'll pay for her precious Northwestern, exactly? Not Dad and Botox Wife, that's for damn sure.*

Conflicting feelings of pride and embarrassment shone in her mom's eyes even though she worked her ass off at that law firm. It wasn't her fault money was tight. Her dad should have helped more, but why would he now when he barely did then?

"And you won't miss any classes?" her mom asked.

"Holiday break. She knows a lot of us are still in school."

"Uh-huh. So preying on the young?"

"Mom—"

"All right, you can go—"

Angeline pumped her fist.

"On one condition." Her mom trained the hazel eyes they all shared on Angeline.

"Anything!"

"You're still applying to college, so you need to get an extra-curricular—"

"Done, I can go back to cheer—"

"No. One with more of an academic bent." Her mom's eyes spanned from Angeline to Cat and back again. "Maybe Cat could use some help—"

"No!" Angeline and Cat cried in unison—well, almost in unison. Cat's preceded Angeline's by just enough for them all to notice. "Now, Cat . . ." her mom started.

"It's just that the student council election's coming up. Ms. Lute thinks it'll be a big one, and the paper's reporting will require total focus."

And of course, Angeline, who pumped out three videos a week, didn't have focus.

Whatever.

She ran through the options in her head for something re-spectable but that wouldn't take too much time away from Ask an Angel. She was on the verge of moving up to the next level of influencer, which was why she'd given up all her extracurriculars last year—cheerleading and drama club and swim team.

But wait, what had Cat said? StuCo? Big? Student council was one of the most ignored activities in school. Angeline had never voted in any of the elections. Not once. Did it even meet?

All the reading, watching, and talking about this year's tight presidential race with Gramps and their mom had made Cat delusional.

And yet . . . her mom *was* riveted.

"Student council, huh?" Angeline said. "My video on best apps for note-taking couldn't be more on point." She twirled her hand above her head. "Meet StuCo's newest secretary."

Her popularity meant she'd totally win, and if the council actually held any meetings, she'd pop in via video once or twice, then transition out. Done and done.

Her mom smiled. "Excellent. I like how you're broadening your horizons. But don't underestimate yourself, hon. You are presidential material."

What?

"Her? President?" Cat cried. "But I've got all this election coverage planned! I'll have to . . . to, like, interview her."

"Even better," her mom said. "Give you two a chance to spend some time together. Everything will be different next year."

"Thankfully," Cat said.

Angeline's jaw clenched. "Finally something we agree on." She spun around to head for her room when she realized their deal lacked one key element. "What if I don't win?"

"Only way you don't win is by trying not to. Which means . . ." Her mom winked at Cat. "I need an inside woman."

Cat flipped back the bangs that Angeline would have cautioned

37

against since they only accentuated the roundness of her face. But Cat hadn't asked her advice.

"I don't really have time to spy," Cat said.

"Not spy, keep tabs," their mom said. "You'll be covering it for the paper anyway, so you let me know if your sister's not hitting that campaign trail as hard as she might."

"Way to enlist an impartial judge," Angeline grumbled, to which Cat gave a smug smile, to which Angeline offered a "bite me" face. She then marched down the hall to her bedroom.

President.

Seriously?

Leo would never let her live this down.

Except Leo wasn't speaking to her.

Just outside her bedroom, Angeline unlocked her phone. Still on the screen was her last text to Leo:

Miss you.

It hung there without a response, not a like or a thumbs-up or even a thumbs-down. Just . . . nothing. Like it hadn't been seen. Like it didn't even exist. She closed her messages and opened her inbox. The email from Evelyn's Epic Everyday flowed in, and even though she'd already read it on her computer, seeing it a second time only added to her excitement.

President.

Okay then.

Let's do this.

Because if she did this, if she killed it, she might be the next Evelyn.

"Please let me kill it," Angeline whispered.

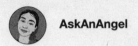 **AskAnAngel**

AskAnAngel Hey, hey, Angels! Ready to make a difference?

Start local. I'm tossing in my hat (a perfectly chic gray wool beret from Paris in Your Pocket, retail $49.99, but 20% off today only with the "AskAnAngel" code!).

Student council prez. Here I come.

Remember.
You're not standing unless you're standing out.
Flutter your wings, my Angels!

View comments

BakedBaker24/7 Something's fluttering, but it ain't my wings.

MaxineChenontheCliffs Go Ang! Oh, and suck it, Baker.

5

When Cat Becomes a Cartoon

28 DAYS TO THE ELECTION

Acedia Student Council Election Sign-Ups
DUE MONDAY! NO EXCEPTIONS!
(But if you can't make Monday, please see Ms. Lute in Room 116 ☺)

<u>Name</u>	<u>Position Sought</u>	<u>Grade</u>
Angeline Quinn	President	Senior
Jay Choi	President	Rocking Frosh
Emmarie Hayes	President	Senior
Leo Torres	President	The Big 1-2
Andreas Costa	Treasurer	Junior
Dipti Patel	Vice President	Junior

"She did it," Cat whispered to herself, staring at the bulletin board outside Ms. Lute's classroom.

She actually did it.

And Angeline would get what she wanted by taking away the same from Cat.

Because this election would now be nothing more than fodder for gossip about the breakup of the beloved "Angeo" or "Leoline" or whatever ridiculousness they were called. Cat could say good-bye to covering a real race that would impress the Fit to Print judges.

Reluctantly, she began to copy down the names just as a hand with perfectly polished coral fingernails appeared over her shoulder and ripped off the sheet.

"Hey, I was reading that!" Cat spun around to see . . .

Angeline.

"No freaking way!" Angeline cried. "I mean, how petty can he be! He can't do—"

"Breathe, just breathe," came the calm, soothing voice of Sonya Robins, one of her sister's best friends. Sonya had dark brown skin, natural brown curls that floated past her shoulders, and soft, caring eyes that encouraged Angeline to follow her lead as she added, "From the diaphragm," and then inhaled deeply, like she was sitting cross-legged on a mountaintop, breathing in the crisp scent of pine instead of lemon-infused bleach.

A giggle, followed by, "*Diaphragm.*"

Sonya tilted her head at Riley Donovan. "Again?"

"I can't help it, Sonya!" Riley, tall and thin and just as pale as a razor clam shell, stifled another giggle. "I swear, every yoga class you drag me to, even when my arms are shaking from a full two minutes in my handstand, I can't help but picture a cervix every time Amber says, *Breathe from your diaphragm.*"

Sonya rolled her eyes.

Angeline crinkled the sign-up sheet.

And Cat was outta there.

She nearly ran into Maxine, whose arrival completed the quartet that had been together since seventh grade, when they'd all started at the charter school. Of the four, Maxine was the one Cat could relate to most. Her drive was just as strong as Angeline's but for something real. While Angeline counted hearts and smiley faces, Maxine spent her time coding them.

Sonya's focus on "mindfulness" made Cat uncomfortable, like she was being judged for actually planning for her future instead of meditating on how a future could exist if everything was transitory. Her dedication to mastering thyself stood in sharp contrast to Riley's dedication to mastering the selfie.

Fingers splayed on jutted hip, center-parted blonde hair smooth as glass, a dozen different micro smiles at the ready, Riley existed in perpetual model mode. While she offended as easily as she was offended, her friends were secure enough in themselves to allow Riley to be the one thing she craved most: the center of attention.

Despite sharing a grade—and Angeline—Angeline's friends had never been Cat's friends. They were never meant to be. Eleven months older than Angeline, Cat should have graduated along with Stavros and Jen, but she'd been held back in fourth grade, infusing her with a drive that had helped her maintain a 4.0 GPA and a long-harbored resentment of her sister.

"All hail the queen of the humblebrag!" Maxine said, flicking Riley's ponytail. "And since when are you an expert on cervixes?"

"One of my best friends happens to have an informative YouTube channel celebrating the female body," Riley said.

"Thanks for the reminder." Maxine's response was heavy with sarcasm.

Riley nodded condescendingly. "The price I pay for being such a supportive friend."

Cat could literally feel her brain cells dying.

Angeline faced her friends, putting her back to her sister.

"Seriously, how can you be talking about anything else . . ." She pushed the sign-up sheet into Maxine's chest. "When *this* is happening?"

"First, my mom read some 'news'"—Maxine used air quotes—"online that said coffee's the road to female hair loss, and she flushed every last bean in the house. The morning after I was up all night debugging the code in the polling app you asked for. Which, by the way, also made me miss the best waves in weeks. So you need to take it down, like, a dozen notches." While Sonya was closer to Cat's height—a solid three inches shorter than Angeline—Maxine and her sister were near equals. Maxine met Angeline's eyes, flattened the crumpled sheet, and read. "Well, well, well, it's only fourth period, and you might actually have some competition."

"Emmie," Cat said reflexively. "She's really smart. And she's been on the council before."

Sonya perched on tiptoes to read over Maxine's shoulder. "I think she means Leo. Or maybe that Jay Choi . . . I'm getting a strong aura from the curves of his lettering."

"Leo, she means Leo." Angeline tore the paper from Maxine's hand and let it float to the floor. "Who's only doing this to get back at me. But thanks for the vote of confidence, sis."

Angeline looped her arm through Riley's and led them down the hall.

"Absurd as ever," Cat muttered under her breath, and yet she stood where she was, watching, until they disappeared into the girls' bathroom. Together.

📣 📣 📣

Cat leaned against the bulletin board, trying to pry loose the end of a roll of tape. The sauna that was her newsroom had dried it out to within an inch of its sticky life.

Angeline.

She cursed her sister as she attempted to spend her lunch period taping back together the sign-up sheet.

"Schwartz, nine o'clock," a girl's voice said.

Cat jerked her head up and looked in the wrong direction.

"The other way," Emmie Hayes said.

"Oh, right." Numbers had always tripped Cat up. As did instant recognition of spatial issues like left and right. It was a thing, a real thing; she'd googled it a couple of years ago. She couldn't read a clock with hands until she was twelve—and still now preferred her digital. Gramps had tutored her by understanding she thought about things differently. He'd not only helped ensure she wouldn't be held back again but had been the one to recognize writing might be a good fit.

Cat rotated her head and saw Principal Schwartz in a suit two sizes too big eyeing them from down the hall.

"Let me." Emmie slid the sheet out from under Cat's arm and pressed it against the bulletin board, matching up the two halves. "Look contemplative," she whispered.

"Got it." But Cat's finger traveled on its own and bounced against the side of her leg.

Northwestern wouldn't look kindly on a record that included her destroying school property. She wouldn't have risked being here now if it weren't for Ms. Lute stepping in as adviser to *The Red and Blue* as well as student council when no other teacher would. It certainly had nothing to do with protecting Angeline. She knew from experience that her sister wouldn't protect her if the situation were reversed—unless there was something in it for her.

Emmie bugged her eyes at Cat. "Contemplative, not constipated."

Cat scrunched her brows together, only relaxing them when a

wide smile overtook Emmie's petite face. She was shorter than Cat, with reddish-blonde hair that skirted her shoulders, a plain, business-y blouse, and ironed pants. Perfectly groomed like she'd followed every rule in the textbook given to female politicians, except for the red, white, and blue friendship bracelet on her wrist that had seen better days.

"So, why president?" Cat said casually as Principal Schwartz's shiny dress shoes clicked against the tiles.

Emmie's blue eyes brightened. "Change requires a top-down mandate, and so if one's desire is to effect change, there's no other option."

"And you want to do that here? No easy task."

"Neither was being so far ahead that I've all but secured valedictorian and hence early decision to Harvard. I'm prepared for difficulties. I also believe in the people. But you have to believe in yourself before you can expect others to follow suit."

Principal Schwartz slowed to listen.

"Lunch," Cat said to explain them being in the halls. His eyebrow lifted, and she realized he probably thought they were sneaking out to grab a slice from Frank's Pizza across the street. The "no off-campus lunch" rule had been instituted a couple of years ago. She pulled a pen out of her back pocket and handed it to Emmie. "Make sure you fill in your grade."

"Certainly," Emmie said, though she cringed as she accepted the pen.

Principal Schwartz nodded his balding head at them as he continued down the hall.

"Where was I?" Emmie gave the pen back to Cat and squeezed hand sanitizer out of the container clipped to her backpack.

Cat tried not to take offense, but it was a pen, not elephant dung.

"Oh, yes, the people," Emmie said. "I believe informed voters make the right decision. If there is fault, it lies with the candidates for not crafting their message in a way that engenders understanding."

"Nice work, but he's gone. You can stop now." Cat once again turned her attention to the tape. "Thanks for covering by making up that speech."

"I wasn't making anything up."

"So you actually . . . care?" A flicker of hope quickened Cat's pulse. This was exactly the type of candidate who'd make a real story. The opposite of Angeline and Leo.

"Why else would I sign up?"

As they put the sheet back together, Cat wondered if Emmie stood a chance. Honors classes, track, debate team—Emmie wasn't unliked, but she also wasn't *particularly* liked either. She was a bit of a loner.

Like Cat would be this year without Stavros and Jen.

"Thanks again," Cat said. "I'll try to keep my sister's claws off this for the rest of the week."

"Can I count on your vote?" Emmie said.

Cat eyed her sister's perfect cursive, signing the sheet like it were an autograph.

"*Thanks for the vote of confidence, sis.*"

"I should probably stay nonpartisan. Since I'm reporting on it," Cat said. "Speaking of, are you up for an interview?"

The iMac wheezed its last breath, and the screen went black.

"No, no, no, no, no!" Cat cried to herself in the newsroom after school.

She slammed her hand on the table. Miraculously, the screen lit back up.

"Whatever your superpower is, I want it." Ravi Tandon strolled into the newsroom, messenger bag slung across his chest, wearing the shorts he only traded for jeans when it snowed. And even that required a two-inch minimum.

"Ravi! I didn't know you were coming." Her relief almost matched that of seeing the iMac come back to life. "Did I miss your text back?"

"Nah, gave yours a like."

"Oh, sure, right." But a "like" to a yes-or-no question conveyed nothing. Was two more taps for a "yes" and one more for an identifiable "no" too much to ask?

"First issue on Tuesday?" Ravi dropped into the chair in front of the other large monitor in the room. "Anything special in mind this year?"

Ravi had light brown skin and wavy hair a shade or two darker than hers, though the summer sun had painted it with copper streaks. He'd let it grow longer. Actually, all of him had grown longer. His legs, torso, arms, which cradled his sketchbook as his graphite pencil flicked back and forth.

"Special? I'd consider it pretty darn special if everything kept functioning." She gingerly set her hand on the iMac. "No funds to replace anything this year since I couldn't land any new advertisers."

"So just the bowling alley? I swear Mr. Murphy relies on us and people hearing *clunk, thud, thud, thud* while shopping for screwdrivers to let the world knows it even exists."

"It is bizarre that the bowling alley's above the hardware store."

"Like a bowling speakeasy."

Cat hesitated. "Right."

His eyebrows drew together. "Wait, you haven't been? Not possible. It's like a birthday party ritual!"

Cat shrugged. "I'm not really into sports."

"Me neither. But my friends and I bowl. Total throwback, but thankfully retro's in."

"I'll have to try it then."

"Cool. Text me."

Cat smiled politely and continued her examination of the equipment in the newsroom. As she bent to check the printer, she tugged on the hem of her khaki skirt—a duplicate of the one from the first day of school. Her wardrobe was a clone of itself. Rotating the same basic three outfits saved time and brainpower.

And irked her sister.

She was counting how many sheets of paper they had left when Ravi approached. He carefully detached a page from his sketchbook and handed it to her.

In the drawing, a girl with a blunt bob and bangs wore a cape, a Clark Kent–style fedora, and a press badge on a lanyard around her neck. Except it wasn't a girl. It was her.

In the background, skyscrapers, including the Empire State Building, rose up around her. She balanced on a mountain of broken e-cigarettes, about to enter through an arched doorway labeled *The New York Times*.

"This is . . ." Words, her trusty sidekick, failed her. Cartoons had a tendency to exaggerate features, using humor to mock, but this was all about highlighting the best, not the worst. She was still on the shorter side but stood tall in her surroundings, thanks partly to the platform boots he'd sketched on her feet; her long eyelashes accentuated her otherwise average eyes; her life's dream, which she was surprised Ravi knew, was on the verge of becoming a reality.

"You did this just now?" she asked.

"Hence the bare bones," he said. "Though the concept's been in my head for a while."

The concept. *Her?*

"Um, thanks?" Her tone unintentionally conveyed the awkwardness she felt.

"So you like it?"

Like? She wanted to have it framed. But she simply nodded.

He rubbed his palms together. "Excellent. Because, and hear me out: How can a proper newspaper not have editorial cartoons?"

Oh, right . . . that *was the concept that'd been in his head.*

"Especially during an election year. There'd be no elephants for Republicans or donkeys for Democrats without a cartoonist: Thomas Nash back in 1874. Think of what *The Red and Blue* could do—what *we* could do, because you'd have total approval. I'm cool with that. And . . ." He tapped a drumroll on the paper still in Cat's hand. "To sweeten the deal, I'll get you an introduction to the owners of the bookstore where I work. I'm thinking they may be good for a half-page ad in the first issue."

"You're bribing me?"

"Negotiating. Do we have a deal?"

Whatever Cat thought of editorial cartoons, she didn't have a choice. She needed the ad as much as she needed Ravi. "Deal."

"Cool," he said.

But the decision being hers and hers alone suddenly made the absence of Stavros and Jen and the paper's existence now squarely on her shoulders seem especially pronounced.

"Excuse me." A lanky kid with a fading pimple on the end of

his nose appeared in the doorway. "I'm looking for Cathleen Quinn."

"Editor in Chief Cathleen Quinn." Ravi rolled his hand toward Cat and bowed.

"You're such a suck-up," she whispered, but her heart beat a bit faster. No one had referred to her as editor in chief out loud before. She liked it. A lot.

The boy bounced into the room, ran his hand through his dark curly hair, and then dropped it into his pocket. "Grady Booker, ma'am."

"Yeah . . . don't call me ma'am."

"Grady Booker, Chief."

Better. "Can I help you? Do you need directions or . . ."

"Freshman, nailed it! Course you did, Chief. But what I need is a job."

"The newspaper doesn't pay."

"The sorry state of journalism today, *amirite?*"

Cat and Ravi exchanged a look, the same way she and Stavros or Jen would have.

"But I worked over the summer, so I don't need money," he continued, barely pausing to take a breath. "Well, I'd *like* money, but what I need is to learn. To do this. From the best." He grinned, showing a mouth full of retainers. "I need to learn from you."

Sucking up, just like Ravi.

Didn't mean it wasn't effective.

Was this how Angeline felt all the time?

6

When Angeline Battles Vegan Bacon

25 DAYS TO THE ELECTION

Star-spangled overload. Ms. Lute's red, white, and blue ensemble matched her classroom, which looked like a clearance aisle after the Fourth of July. Angeline pushed her sunglasses tight against her face to block out the patriotic explosion as she slipped into a seat beside Sonya in her first government class of the year.

The weekend had passed in a blur of filming, splicing, and refining. She'd tackled questions on everything from whether to ombre at home, to the fairness of a ruling from a peer jury system at school, to how to tell your mom she was too old to be wearing a jumpsuit. All carefully crafted responses to enlighten but not offend.

This morning, Angeline's tote bag brimmed with freebies from current and prospective advertisers for use throughout the day. So far, no face mask or eye cream could conquer her puffy lids or the dark circles under her eyes. No energy pill or tonic could stop the yawns that kept creeping up. Not even the free codes to the meditation app she'd been punching in one after another to "find her center," as Sonya liked to say, had helped.

She was tired. Tired of listening to herself talk. Which never happened.

At least she'd lined up videos for the next three weeks. By then, this student council nonsense would be well behind her. She'd be wearing the crown as Madame President and could get back to what really mattered.

Wait, did she get a crown? When she was president, she could make an executive order that she get a crown. A cute little tiara with red and blue gemstones. That glittered. And glowed in the dark. She could light up the path to Friday-night football games and—

Holy smokes, was she punchy.

She sipped on the peanut butter, sweet potato, turmeric smoothie Riley had brought in that morning. Riley considered herself a flavor connoisseur, concocting weird drinks that usually tasted like a compost bin. This one a bit of an exception. Or maybe Angeline's taste buds were as worn out as she was.

As the last bell rang, Angeline noticed Emmie Hayes cleaning her desk with a sanitizer wipe and talking with Ms. Lute from her seat in the front row.

Wrong demographic, hun.

Angeline leaned over to say the same to Sonya, but the words stuck in her throat. Leo, his left arm in that sling, ducked into the room at the last moment. They hadn't spoken . . . hadn't been within three feet of each other . . . hadn't had a single class together. Until now.

His eyes met hers, and even though she was wearing her sunglasses, they punctured deep—right through her anger at him running against her in the student council election and to the reason why.

The only seat free was the one in front of her. He slid in without another glance, but the loop on his sling got caught. His body jerked back, and he winced.

"Are you all right?" The first words she'd spoken to him in weeks. She rested her hand on the back of his neck. The warmth of his skin met the coldness of hers, and they both stiffened. It was as foreign as it was familiar.

They'd do that, her perpetual chill cooling him and his heat warming her. On beach towels on the sand, sometimes under the sun, sometimes under stars they'd try to identify, the skin on the sides of their legs and arms meeting in an exchange of temperatures and a recognition of how comfortable they were with each other. To just be, not to be someone else or someone others saw or expected to see. That mutual sense of purely existing in the present time and place where the most significant thing to be done was temperature regulation might have been what she missed most about Leo.

Did he? Miss it? Miss her?

She pressed her hand deeper, her claddagh ring pushing into the flesh of his neck, but Leo slanted forward to wrench himself free. Angeline's hand fell along with any hope that he would forgive her. That this wouldn't be her senior year.

Sonya whispered, "Breathe, just breathe," which threatened to actually draw out the tears pricking Angeline's eyes.

And the truth that she only had herself to blame.

At the front of the room, Ms. Lute clapped. "And so we begin! Welcome, my virgin voters!"

Half the class cracked up. Ms. Lute gave a wry smile. It was exactly the reaction she was hoping for. Angeline sat up straighter and slid her sunglasses onto the top of her head.

"Some of you will be lucky enough to hit that big one-eight before November," Ms. Lute said. "And I fully expect to be leading an Acedia student parade right to the polling station!"

"We get a day off from school?" Josh Baker woke himself up enough to ask.

"Well, no, but—"

"Then count me out."

"Okay," Ms. Lute said.

"What now?" Josh rubbed the tanned skin around his eyes. "Aren't you supposed to, like, I don't know, tell me I'm wrong?"

"My job is to teach," Ms. Lute said. "You being wrong has everything to do with you, and very little, if anything, to do with me."

"Ooh"s and "damn"s echoed, and Ms. Lute held up her hands. "Oh, and Mr. Baker . . ." She tapped the top of her head. "Dress code."

Josh frowned and flicked his trucker hat off his head. "Bull. Especially since we were outta conditioner this morning."

Ms. Lute nodded. "Rules though. Which can only be changed by getting in the game—whether it's in here with your student council election or out there in the voting booth. If you're not turning eighteen before November, you'll be able to participate by joining the hundreds of thousands of your peers who have already preregistered to vote, so you're automatically enrolled when you do come of age." Ms. Lute grabbed a remote off her desk. "Now, when I set out to teach here at Acedia, one thing drew me in."

A picture of last year's student council, which included Emmie, flashed on the screen. A yearbook photo and still most of them hadn't bothered to show up. Entirely representative of how student council functioned at Acedia. Which was why it was the perfect extracurricular for Angeline.

"Unlike many schools, your student council is elected at the start of the year." Ms. Lute pressed the remote, and a calendar appeared. "In twenty-five days."

"*Leo!*"

"*Angeline!*"

Cheers rang out for each of them.

No one said, "Emmie."

Not that Angeline would have expected them to. Emmie had experience, but she'd used her time on StuCo to push blood drives and rolling backpacks and things no one at Acedia cared about. She had no real clique to speak of and the wardrobe of a schoolmarm. Emmie didn't worry Angeline.

"And to make sure this election provides the teaching moment that's so important this year of all years, Principal Schwartz has agreed to my proposed amendments." Ms. Lute clicked to the next slide. "Enter the Acedia Student Council Presidential Primary."

"What?" Angeline said. "We have to be in two elections?"

She didn't have time for this.

Ms. Lute leaned against the edge of her desk. "Only if you want to be student council president."

Is that a dare?

Or a threat?

"We're a microcosm," Ms. Lute said, "and our election will be no different. Though the primary system is a relatively new addition, only dating back to the 1970s. There's nothing about primaries in our Constitution."

Emmie raised her hand. "The framers didn't even envision two parties."

Ms. Lute pointed her remote at Emmie. "Exactly."

"*Exactly,*" Angeline mocked under her breath.

Leo glared at her. Angeline sunk into her seat.

"Aaron Burr and Alexander Hamilton left a legacy beyond a gazillion-dollar musical. It was the election of 1800 that gave us two parties. Aided by the media. The candidates and their supporters funded the newspapers, and they dictated what appeared in print. Personal attacks based on rumors were printed as truth. It wasn't just common, it was expected. But eventually that changed. And yet . . ." Ms. Lute pressed the remote until she landed on a picture of George Washington. "This guy was entirely opposed. He thought two parties would divide a country they'd fought so hard to bring together."

"He was right," Leo said.

Ms. Lute's eyes shone with concern. "Hmm, you are in the thick of it, aren't you, with your mother's bid for Congress? To think she started on the school board . . ."

Leo politely nodded.

"Then town selectwoman, a woman with Venezuelan heritage able to stand out in this traditionally strong Irish community. And then state senator and now . . . Congress." Ms. Lute crossed her fingers, starstruck. Proof that she didn't know Mrs. Torres personally. Ms. Lute lowered her voice. "I know her schedule must be overwhelming, but if she'd ever consider a school visit—"

Angeline watched Leo's body go rigid.

"I'll be sure to let her know," he said automatically. "If it were up to her and not her campaign manager, she'd love nothing more."

Respectful and diplomatic, just like the politician's son he'd been raised to be.

"Hush, little baby, don't you cry," someone sang in a soft voice from the back of the room.

Leo jerked his head around, searching, landing on no one but Angeline. She'd hoped the teasing would have died down by now.

She'd strong-armed everyone in their circle of friends and beyond into taking down the captured videos and screenshots of him. If it wasn't online, it didn't happen, right?

"They'll forget soon enough," Angeline whispered to Leo. Every part of her wanted to say more, to apologize again, but his firm jaw and dark eyes were like a brick wall.

He gave a cursory glance at her ring and the heart turned out, but his expression never changed. He faced front again, and she did her best to focus on Ms. Lute and the immediate problem at hand: the primary. Because if she didn't win, or prove to Cat that she was trying to, this would all be for nothing.

Ms. Lute flipped to her next slide: *A Primary on Primaries!* "We'll see our own primary in action on Friday at a school-wide assembly. Better get cracking on your speeches, my prospective nominees."

She swept her hand toward Emmie, Leo, and Angeline, who smiled her "Ask an Angel" signature smile while thinking: *Well, isn't this a kick in the ovaries?*

"If I'm elected, you're elected," Emmie said near the entrance to the cafeteria, where dozens of rectangular white Formica tables sat surrounded by metal chairs of red and blue.

Angeline stopped and tugged on Maxine's arm. They were on their way to get BLTs at the sandwich station—the only edible lunch all week. She missed going to Frank's, even though she'd only ever ordered a caprese salad.

"The primary's *Friday*," Angeline said. "We don't have to do anything for days." Three more students—freshmen, but still—gathered around Emmie. "What is she doing?"

"Campaigning," Maxine said. "The time you spent on Ask an

Angel this summer's probably the same as she's spent preparing for this. She's waited three years to go for president."

"But that's not fair."

Maxine laughed.

"What?" Angeline narrowed her eyes at her best friend.

"Have you met you?"

Emmie's voice could still be heard, but her small frame was easily swallowed by the few students around her. "Did you know the student council president used to serve as a liaison to the school board? Bringing concerns—your concerns—to the administrators who have the power to effect change. If I'm elected, I'll take up that mantle once again. My figurative door will be open to all of you. Tell me what you need. Tell me what's important to you. Tell me what I can do to effect change for you."

"Make them stop rejecting my happiness club!" someone cried. "Like, seriously, what's wrong with being happy?"

"Screw that!" Josh Baker yelled from across the room. "You need to do something about this." He lifted his sandwich in the air.

A screech, and Emmie's tiny head popped above those around her. From the blue metal chair she now stood on, she said, "What is your concern?"

Angeline snorted.

Josh peeled open his sandwich and let the slice of bread on either side fall to the floor, followed by the tomato and lettuce. He swung a piece of bacon with the end bitten off in front of his lower abdomen.

"What are the odds Joshie knows the image he's projecting?" Maxine said.

Angeline smirked as Emmie pressed on. "Is there an issue with the preparation?"

Josh trudged toward Emmie, the bacon pinched between two

fingers. "Clueless on how it's cooked. All's I know is how it tastes. Hundred percent like ass."

Emmie's lips screwed up, but Angeline's widened into a grin. Perfect attendance, valedictorian, rule-follower Emmie being forced to choose between defending the lunchroom staff or appealing to her constituents. *Nicely done, Baker.* Angeline couldn't have orchestrated something better.

Well, totally, she could have, but still . . .

Emmie smoothed down the front of her lace-fringed shirt that would make grandmas everywhere green with envy. "Well, maybe I can speak with—"

"Less talking, more tasting." Josh planted himself in front of her, still dangling the bacon. He leaned in, so close that his nose touched the bacon, and sniffed.

Emmie visibly recoiled, probably calculating how it would look if she slathered hand sanitizer on the bacon before taking a bite. And then Emmie opened her mouth and clenched her teeth around it.

What?

Emmie chewed and grimaced. A bulge of a swallow followed.

"Shocking, man, right?" Josh said. "It's vegan. Vegan bacon? On our BLTs? Sacrilege. Don't we have a say?"

Murmurs spread through the crowd, and the number of students around Emmie multiplied.

"What's happening?" Angeline said.

And then Emmie spoke. "We will have more than a say. We will have a choice. For those who want to eat"—she swallowed again—"*that*, they should be able to. Just as those of us—you, I mean—who want to eat traditional bacon should have the decision firmly in your hands."

Josh whooped and pumped his fist. "My girl, Emmie Hayes," he cried, drawing out her name.

"What's happening"—Maxine crossed her arms in front of her chest—"is that she's winning."

Angeline ground her teeth together. "Yeah? Well, bring it." She yanked a chair to an open space and hopped up. She separated the straps of her tote and pulled out a fistful of small packets. "Hey, hey, there! Vegan. Cruelty-free. Organic. Whatever you need, I've got."

She lifted sample after sample in the air just as Leo appeared at the end of the pizza line, struggling to balance his tray with two slices of pepperoni and a chocolate milk—the combination that always turned Angeline's stomach. At the cashier, he tried to steady the end of the tray on his hip and snake his good arm into his back pocket for his wallet. The tray started to tip, and a freshman girl, a doe-eyed blonde with sun-kissed white skin, rushed over. But not before a different freshman, a long-legged, brown-skinned girl with lush dark curls, beat her. Lush Curls cradled his tray while Doe Eyes tossed Leo's backpack over her shoulder.

With a sheepish grin and cheeks tinged pink, Leo extracted his wallet.

"All right, all right. Who's crying now? Milk it, Torres!" Tad Marcus strutted over and shot his arm up for a high-five. "And may the gods let me break something!"

Tad's hand hovered, waiting for Leo's.

Leo surveyed the room, eventually settling on Angeline. He held her gaze, and she could feel the entire cafeteria watching. Because they were running for student council against one another—Ask an Angel and Big Man on Campus Leo, former Acedia power couple whose breakup had been so very public, every step of the way. Angeline shook her head, gently, and Leo's attention left her, focusing somewhere behind her.

She turned to see Sammy in the cafeteria doorway. She was surprised to see him without the red plaid shirt tied around his waist. He looked smaller without it. Sammy had taken their break-up hard. She'd hurt and embarrassed the big brother he idolized.

She hadn't meant to. It just sort of happened. Partly because Leo used to help her. Not only with research, but also serving as her test subject on everything from beard softeners to best head angles for a first kiss.

His appearances in her episodes were sparse. Yet super effective, as hooking Evelyn proved. But running for Congress had made Leo's mom hyper image conscious, and she demanded Leo stop. He told Angeline she couldn't run any of the recorded footage she had of him. A request she technically honored by live-streaming him instead.

Unlike Angeline, Leo didn't do things without fully thinking them through. Her spontaneity was something he lived vicariously. But now, Leo's eyes traveled from Sammy to Angeline to the entire cafeteria to Tad's twiddling fingers.

Tad, who'd backed his truck into a telephone pole because he'd angled his rearview mirror to check out his abs while doing seated crunches behind the wheel.

Leo pushed his wallet back into his pocket, lifted his hand, and smacked it against Tad's.

"All right, all right, that's my man!" Tad said. "Feel good to not have that angel on your shoulder, Torres?"

Fighting dirty wasn't Leo's thing.

Yet he faced Tad and smiled until his stupidly cute dimple appeared. "Think you mean devil, don't you?"

A bunch of Tad's friends hooted, and a few girls eyed Angeline, realizing Leo really was on the market for the first time in his high school career.

Angeline's on-camera training helped to keep her expression neutral. "Shea butter." Her voice came out weaker than she'd like. She arched her back and projected, "Coconut oil, blemish blocker. And who's into yoga?"

Meanwhile her stomach churned, and all she wanted was to take everything back and for everything to be as it was, without Leo humiliated, without her standing on this chair fighting for something she didn't even want, fighting *him* for something she didn't even want. Something she was sure he didn't want either.

He hated politics—anything even remotely connected to it. They both loved this town, complete with its questionably poor taste (*see the abundance of shark-eating-swimmer Labor Day floats*) and high cornball factor (*see lobster and crab stencils at every crosswalk*). But he wouldn't even vote in the "Mayor for a Day" contest that was part of the Saint Patrick's Day parade. Politics had taken his mother from him. And opening up about how much that hurt was what had taken him from Angeline.

She'd wished she could take it back the moment it happened—*while it was happening.* How could she have known she'd be so successful in delivering the promise of "How to Get Him to Open Up"? She hadn't archived the video, and it was gone from her channel the same day. But not before thousands had seen and some had captured their own videos and screenshots.

Now he was here with Doe Eyes clinging to one arm and Lush Curls on the other. Seemed like maybe he'd found his silver lining.

Leo aimed for the table whose underside held their joined initials when he noticed Chelsea Anders. A junior, Chelsea had been in a wheelchair ever since a horseback-riding accident in eighth grade. Leo took his tray from Lush Curls, set it on the nearest table, and pulled out a chair to sit beside Chelsea.

Angeline tore her eyes from Leo and worked to compose herself as a string of girls flowed toward her, including ones peeling off from Emmie.

Natalie Goldberg led a group of the most popular junior girls. She styled herself like a walking Pinterest board, a different mood for every day. Today was boho chic with a loose, flowered skirt and gold scarf in her hair. "Are these, like, Ask an Angel certified?" she said.

"Not all of them." Pride swelled, confirming why Angeline had started her YouTube channel in the first place. Her viewers trusted her; they needed her. She was the big sister they never had—becoming what she never had herself. "But I could use volunteers to serve as a focus group."

A dozen hands shot up, and Angeline swiveled her neck, wanting to ensure Emmie was witnessing Angeline's reach. But Emmie was climbing down from her chair, helped by Ravi Tandon. Angeline's eyes darted around the room, looking for Cat. Of course she wasn't there. Her sister would be squirreled away, alone, in her newsroom, not here with her classmates, not here to see Angeline securing her position.

"You've got that facial rejuvenator from 'better'?" a girl with red hair and freckles said. "I've been dying to try it."

And die while trying it, you might.

"Here, take two," Angeline said.

"You've got my vote," the girl said.

Angeline smiled, but all she heard in her head was Cat: *"You really have no line."*

7

When Cat Struts Her Stuff

Cat perched herself on the edge of her chair in the center of the newsroom. With her pencil poised above her notebook, she asked, "Can you spell your name for me?"

Angeline rolled her eyes. "We squatted in the same womb."

"I'm a professional." Cat tilted her head toward Grady, sitting in the back, jotting down his own notes, just as she'd instructed. "I take my job seriously."

"Meaning I don't."

"I didn't say anything about you."

Angeline fidgeted in the hard wooden chair. "Why are we doing this here? Now? During lunch? With this stupid primary, Maxine and I need to use every free period to reach voters."

Grady cleared his throat. "Don't you mean bribe?"

Angeline sprang to her feet. "You little twerp. What are you even doing here?"

"Learning." Cat gestured for Angeline to sit and directed a warning glance at her new mentee. Grady had been more persistent than a seagull going after a bag of chips. He had a sixth sense for when Cat crossed the threshold into the newsroom, because about three minutes later, he'd appear, asking about number of sources, which layout program to use, *The Red and Blue*'s social media accounts, of which there were none. He'd been texting her four times a day, and she didn't even know how he'd gotten her number (something he pointed out as evidence of his investigative skills). He plain wore her down. The fresh scones he brought her every morning didn't hurt. But the two had come up with rules. Cat couldn't be slowed down by him, and she'd never risk her paper publishing anything less than her high standards.

"And," Cat said, "as someone who's learning, he's simply observing. Otherwise—"

Grady mimed zipping his mouth shut but pouted.

Cat had never felt her extra year of age so much.

"Now." She turned back to her sister. "Where were we?"

The arrangement of four chairs that Cat had set up, with her own in front, trapped Angeline. Exactly the claustrophobic feel Cat had wanted to create.

"This is a total fire hazard." Angeline tried to wriggle her way out of the semicircle. "Can't we do this at home?"

"Not unless you want Emmie Hayes, Jay Choi, and Leo in our living room tonight."

"But why do you have to interview us together?"

"Deadlines." True, though the real reason Cat had scheduled all the interviews at the same time was to encourage debate that would lead to the most authentic story she could get. And . . . maybe the tiniest part of her had scheduled them all together to show Angeline that she could, that she was in charge here.

Angeline freed one leg, then the other, and strolled the newsroom. She skimmed her fingers along the table with the finicky printer, and it was like she was drumming Cat's spine. She nudged the stack of last year's newspapers with the toe of her sandal, but it was Cat's body that felt rocked. Angeline sat her butt right on top, and the weight nearly crushed Cat.

As Angeline leaned over the old iMac and set her iridescent painted fingernail on Ravi's drawing of Cat, she rethought the decision to bring her sister here.

And then footsteps resounded in the hall.

"Welcome to *The Red and Blue*," Ravi said, ushering Jay Choi, Emmie, and Leo into the newsroom. "This here's our editor in chief, Cat. Though, careful, because she's a real shark when it comes to getting at the truth."

Leo looked at Angeline, whose lips ticked up into a hesitant smile.

"I'm so not doing this," Leo said.

Cat watched her sister's face pale, and something prickled beneath her skin. "But you agreed. It won't take long, I promise."

"No offense, Cat, but Quinns don't exactly have the most trustworthy track record."

Leo's words were like a slap. No matter the reason why. She waited for her sister to fling a gibe back, to save face in front of everyone in the room, but she remained quiet and simply claimed a seat on the end.

It was Ravi who spoke up, his eyes bright and friendly as always, but his tone expressing exactly what he thought of Leo. "Embrace it, I say. The ladies are looking for a man who's in touch with his feelings."

Across from Leo, Cat held the notebook he'd given her face out. Leo's eyes softened, and he took the only free seat, right beside Angeline.

8

When Angeline Watches Cat
Strut Her Stuff

24 DAYS TO THE ELECTION

3 DAYS TO THE PRIMARY

Angeline's hands were clammy. She didn't sweat. She'd trained herself out of it after having to refilm a segment where everything was on point . . . except for the rings under her armpits.

But all her hard work vanished the moment she was in Cat's newsroom by Leo's side, looking at him in that lime-green sweatshirt, taking in the buzzed sides of his dark hair, the sweep of long locks across the top, the slight sunburn on the tops of his ears . . . His arm had brushed hers. Twice. By accident? Maybe the first time. But the second . . .

Was it remotely possible he missed her too?

While Angeline stole glances at Leo, Emmie droned on like a robot. "Eligible voters . . . twenty percent . . . unregistered . . . voting . . . ingrained . . . microcosm . . . supporting Ms. Lute . . . preregistering initiative."

Angeline zoned in and out until, finally, the buzzing in her ear stopped, and she realized Emmie had finished speaking.

Cat nodded politely. "That's all very interesting, Ms. Hayes, but this is Acedia."

Emmie tilted her head ever so slightly. "I'm aware."

"Acedia," Cat repeated. "Where for the past three years student council hasn't actually completed a single fundraiser."

"Well." Emmie laced her fingers together in her lap. "That's why I'm running. I intend to follow through with every initiative I plan."

Another nod from Cat. "That's a commendable goal, Miss Hayes, but it's not that the student councils haven't planned a fundraiser, as you would know, having served as secretary. The failure has been in the participation by the student body. The sharing of the photo of Principal Schwartz's doppelgänger outnumbered actual ballots cast in last year's StuCo election by a factor of ten. And the Show Your Support Day you proposed last year led not to students engaging with one another but to thrift store bras being hung throughout the school. No one was held accountable, not even by their peers. A few girls challenged with 'slap on the wrist' emojis, but the outrage that should have been simply wasn't. How do you intend to combat the apathy that is Acedia?"

Angeline's eyes widened. Who knew her sister had this in her? She tried to catch Leo's eye, but he aimed his gaze straight ahead.

Emmie pursed her lips. "Like I said yesterday in the cafeteria, my platform centers on students having a voice in what happens here—all students, not just the ones on the student council."

Angeline leaned forward. "If students have a voice, what do they need us for?"

That was when freshman nobody Jay Choi piped up. "I'm thinking free shit. Like *that one* did but better." He pointed to Angeline, and the snort that came out of Leo jarred her. "Skins for Minecraft, bagels in homeroom . . . oh, and highlighters. Like, in every classroom. Always losing my highlighters."

Cat turned to Jay. "But student council doesn't have that kind of money or authority."

Jay snorted. "Off the record? Sheep don't know that." He tore open a bag of fried onion skins from the vending machine whose greasy scent made Angeline queasy. "All's they know is what I'm promising. So make sure you print all those as my campaign pledges. Frosh rule!"

Angeline and Leo burst out laughing. Looked at each other. And stopped. Him first.

Emmie recrossed her ankles, but otherwise remained stoic.

"Anyone else?" Cat asked.

Leo fanned himself with a back issue of *The Red and Blue*. "Straws. That's my thing."

"Excuse me?" Cat said. "Did you say 'straws'? Like drinking straws?"

"One and the same. The school yanked them last year. Have you tried to share a chocolate milk since?"

Leo's fingers cradling Angeline's, hers curled around a plastic straw. She sipped. He sipped. Under the lunch table, thighs touching, legs snaked together, unable to tell whose feet were whose.

Yesterday the tray Lush Curls carried had held a chocolate milk—the closest Leo got to eating sweets.

"Impossible," Leo said as an ache spread across Angeline's chest. "School needs to stop telling us what to do."

Emmie turned to face Leo. "So you hate fish? And birds? And coral reefs? Five hundred million straws are thrown away every day. We're not five-year-olds. To think I'd looked forward to seeing what the son of Eliza Torres would do." Emmie reset her heart-shaped jaw. "Well then, while you push straws, and he pushes highlighters, and she . . ." Emmie cocked her head at Angeline. "Skin care, is that about the sum of it?"

Angeline fumed, but Emmie continued, "I'm going to ensure that students have an avenue to share their daily concerns. And that those concerns make it to the appropriate channels. Because you are correct, Ms. Quinn, that the escalating antics at this school have not engendered sufficient outrage. I believe this is because students, especially female students, feel there is no point. While the 'cupcake no more' hashtag that began after that unfortunate stunt last year indicates a rise in students wanting change, I believe that will only happen if they feel they are being listened to."

She clasped her hands in her lap, and her eyes drifted across each of them. "What's interesting here is that there's often a misunderstanding about where real power lies. It's simply a numbers game. The jocks, the cheerleaders, the beautiful people . . ." She said it as if Leo and Angeline weren't all of those things and weren't sitting beside her. "They're the elite in this school for one reason: because their ranks are small. An asset if one is looking to be exclusive, but if one is looking to garner votes . . ." Emmie spread her hands wide. "The masses are who you seek."

Silence. And then . . .

"Damn," Grady said, echoing the only thought in Angeline's head.

Emmie might dress like someone three times her age, but she was wicked smart. She knew her stuff—this stuff. Stuff Angeline knew nothing about. She was outside of her comfort zone. If this wasn't just going to be a vote for the most popular, if Emmie made it something more, could Angeline actually lose?

What if she did?

Was running enough?

Would her mom really listen to Cat? Would Angeline have time to find another "respectable" extracurricular?

The boot camp suddenly felt like it was slipping from Angeline's grasp.

She hadn't paid the deposit yet. She should do it now. Her mom would have to let her go then regardless, wouldn't she?

Cat eyed Angeline warily, and Angeline plastered on a smile. She wouldn't let her see that Emmie had gotten under her skin.

Leo raised a finger in the air. "Cat, can I add something?"

"Of course," Cat said.

Leo shifted to address Emmie. "One hundred and seventy-five million straws. The five hundred million came from a nine-year-old who called three straw companies and made a guess that went viral. Fact-checking needs to make a comeback."

Emmie bristled. "Even if that's true, it's still a huge number."

"Admittedly. But the issue is much more nuanced. Do you know Chelsea Anders?"

"Not personally but—"

"She told me that straws provide a simpler, more accessible way for her to drink," Leo said, hints of his mom infusing his words. "But the school didn't think about that. Banned them outright without a replacement. Replacements, which have their own baggage, like the increased cost and pollution of manufacturing paper straws, temperature-regulation issues with stainless, allergic reactions with wheat-based. Not to mention compostable only work if there are facilities that accept them."

Emmie cocked her head. "Is this really your main platform? I wasn't aware you were an environmentalist?"

It wasn't that Leo didn't care, but his mom *really* did. He was

71

only biking home from Maxine's party because his mom was on a preelection green energy kick.

"My platform," Leo said, "is choice. Ours, not the administration's."

"There's a system," Emmie said. "Understanding it and working within it is the only realistic way to effect change."

Leo shrugged. "Maybe what we've been missing is a little imagination."

"And that seems like a good ending point." Cat set down her pencil. "I think I've got enough from Emmie and Jay." She gestured to Grady. "Photos?"

Grady grabbed his phone, and Cat shook her head. "An actual camera. With a lens that's bigger than my pinky." She pointed to a clunky camera that looked too heavy for Grady to pick up. "Try outside. The lighting's better than in here."

"But I've got all these filters," Grady whined.

Cat sighed and turned to Ravi. "Could you—"

"Sure thing. Two siblings got me well-trained in babysitting." He grinned at Cat, who, Angeline noted, reflexively smoothed down her cowlicks.

The group clambered over chairs and out of the newsroom, but before she left, Emmie thanked Cat. "It's nice to see someone else who cares."

"About what?" Cat said.

Emmie flicked her eyes to Leo and to Angeline. "Anything."

That's it.

If Emmie thought Angeline wasn't going to go on the offensive, she need just look at her track record.

Leo stood. "We done?"

Look at her collateral damage.

Angeline kept her mouth shut and let Emmie go.

"Just a sec," Cat said. "I need quotes from both of you as to why you're running."

Angeline had had enough. "Are you entirely mental? You know why I'm running. Mom won't let me go to Evelyn's boot camp unless I have something geeky to put on my college applications."

Leo's head drew back. "You got in?"

She'd forgotten he didn't know. He always knew everything about her.

Sharing secrets was one of the things she loved most about being in a relationship. Secrets like how she'd secured Maxine a last-minute lesson with a top surf instructor on her family's trip to Hawaii thanks to a *slight* exaggeration of her engagement rate. Like how she'd feigned a back spasm to be able to replace the flyer atop the cheer pyramid. Like how she'd asked her mom to send her to the public school instead of the charter just so Angeline could have distance from Cat.

"But then we'd have never met," Leo had said, nestled alongside her on the beach. They'd packed a picnic dinner and were babysitting Sammy, even though they weren't supposed to call it that since he was twelve.

"Thank fate," Angeline had said, burying her cold hands in the pocket of his sweatshirt. "And sibling rules. My number in the charter school lottery was higher than Cat's. She wouldn't have gotten in without me. Though we weren't even sure either of us would sneak through."

"Sneak? Why sneak?"

"Technically we weren't in the region yet. Dad had just . . ." A lump had hardened in her throat, and just as quickly, Leo had wrapped his arms around her. "Left. And we hadn't moved into the apartment yet. You know Mom though. She doesn't let anything get in the way of what she thinks is best for us." *Except letting Dad go*, Angeline remembered thinking. She'd then told Leo about the night she'd gone to her dad's before he married Botox Wife, the night she really knew her dad was gone.

That was the night Leo had told her that he used to be so shy in elementary school that he'd pretend he didn't know the answer rather than have to speak aloud in class. He fought his fears, became the outgoing, likable guy he was now partly because he didn't need more reasons to be different in this town where his Latinx family was already different. With his dad constantly mixing up lemons and limes, since in Spanish "lime" is "limón" and "lemon" is "lima," needing Leo and Sammy to remind him that limes were "the green ones." With their tradition to eat twelve grapes in the last twelve seconds of the year, making wishes, on New Year's Eve. With his parents insisting until sixth grade that he only speak Spanish at home—even in front of his friends. With the closeness of his extended family, who'd sleep on sofas and floors and triple up cousins in beds when they came to visit, as staying in a hotel instead of with family was unheard of. Differences he loved, craved, tired of, and, sometimes, was embarrassed by. And that embarrassed him even more. All of it, pulling at Angeline's heart for the boy he was and the man he was becoming.

Secrets had brought them closer.

Were all of hers now ammunition?

But then a smile brightened his face upon hearing about the boot camp, the smile he reserved for her.

Angeline wanted to say so much, but she only managed a nod. He knew how important this was to her. He'd see now, wouldn't he? That this was bigger than a little embarrassment at Maxine's party? "And you . . . Are you really running because of straws?"

His shoulders slumped, and he flinched in pain, and it was like a sucker punch to Angeline's gut.

"Mom," he said. "Good optics for her campaign to have a son active on student council. So I run and win, I get out of photo ops until election week. Then she'll trot me back out: the perfect son."

"Sammy too? Is his freshman year off to a good start?"

Leo's demeanor shifted. "Yeah, it's all a ride at Disney World. Schwartz telling Sammy he can't wear a shirt around his waist because it looks too much like a skirt, and the dress code doesn't let dudes wear skirts, which is bullshit, anyway. They take away his security blanket just when he's got so much crap to deal with at home what with Mom all over my ass because of what you pulled, and Sammy being Sammy, caught in the middle."

Whatever spell Angeline thought they'd been under vanished.

Because of Leo's mom. Again. She'd never liked Angeline, couching it under disapproval of Leo dating someone with what she dismissively called a "presence" on social media.

Course, Mrs. Torres had quickly turned any social media backlash after the live-streaming to her advantage; she'd never have gotten that TV interview—Leo and family at her side—discussing the difficulties all working mothers face had it not been for Angeline.

No one had thanked her.

Leo raked his hand through his hair. "Do this for me, okay? Don't ask about my brother again—don't ask me anything." He shoved a chair out of his way. "Cat, we done here?"

Cat tapped her notebook with the end of her pencil. "I don't really have a quote . . . unless you want me to use that."

Leo shook his head. "You two are more alike than you think." He addressed Cat. "All that was off the record, Katie Couric. But if you need a quote, here it is." He pointed to Angeline. "I'm running to save the school from her."

9

When Cat Enters a Maze

24 DAYS TO THE ELECTION
3 DAYS TO THE PRIMARY

The newsroom was so quiet, Cat swore she could hear the spiders spinning cobwebs in the corners. She welcomed the incoming text—even if it was from her sister.

> **Angeline:** So . . . get what you need for the article?

> **Cat:** Finishing now.

> **Angeline:** 👍

It really was an epidemic.

> **Angeline:** Just a check on where we landed . . .
> you're not printing why I'm really running, right?

Cat considered giving her sister's text a swift, one-stroke like and shutting off her phone. Instead, she pushed it aside and read over what she'd written about Angeline wanting to "make a difference." Nothing could have been more vanilla and predictable. Unlike

Angeline's true motivations for running for president, which would have made this story an actual story. Add in Leo's, and the whole school, town, and then some would read her newspaper. Maybe even look forward to the next one.

Angeline: It's just . . . I need this.

Cat sighed. *Right.* The Angeline show. With Cat and Gramps and Mom and even Leo as her backup dancers. It had been this way from the day they'd taken their first steps—Cat a late walker at seventeen months and Angeline an early one at eight. Two months. For two months, Cat had been ahead of her sister. She'd been playing catch-up ever since.

Angeline: Cat?

Printing the truth about Angeline might change that while simultaneously gaining Cat the readership she needed to secure new advertisers, keep her paper afloat, and give her a stellar submission for the Fit to Print award. But Cat only knew what she knew about Angeline because she was her sister. She couldn't print such privileged information without her source's consent. As for Leo . . . he'd said "off the record," but only after he'd spilled the truth. Technically she could use it. Give Emmie, who'd probably be a great student council president, a better shot at winning.

Nothing stood in Angeline's way: not rules, not morals, not anything—or anyone.

Cat: Don't worry about it.

Angeline: I'm safe then?

Cat: 👍

Angeline's ambition had ruined her relationship with Leo. For the past three years, he'd been as regular a fixture at their dinner table as their mom's garlicky mashed potatoes and—though Cat would never say it to her mom—a more welcome one. Cat liked him. And despite being sure he was better off without her sister, something inside Cat wouldn't let her say that either.

Cat: Leo too.

Angeline: Beat me!

Angeline: That was my next text.

Sure it was.

◁ ◁ ◁

An energy infused Cat's step the following afternoon as she walked through the harbor to meet Ravi.

Her first issue as editor in chief was in the can. Now she just needed to ensure she could pay for the next. For which she'd go full-on Nellie Bly. One of the few female reporters in New York City in the late 1800s, Nellie grew tired of only receiving arts and theater assignments. Instead of waiting to be given access to the big stories, she took it. She got herself committed to an insane asylum, where she lived for ten days undercover, inventing a new style of investigative journalism. Her exposé on the poor conditions and questionable treatment prompted more oversight and funding. She became a superstar. Cat had read her biography in a history of female journalists over the summer.

Though she usually pulled from Gramps's well-curated bookshelves, she looked forward to browsing Harbor Books, which sat at the opposite end of town from her apartment on a narrow street that led up from the main road. It was steeper than she re-membered, proving just how long it'd been since she'd gone inside. Probably before the new owners bought it, and that was more than a couple of years ago.

The incline stole Cat's breath, but she was rewarded with an expansive view of what made her town her town. The calen-dar's gentle flip into September meant the harbor remained full of boats, lulled and spun by the tide that came in from beyond the rock jetties. The harbor answered to the Atlantic Ocean, the draw for summer tourists, the lifeblood of sea-hardened fisher-men bringing in lobsters and striped bass, and the reminder of the power of Mother Nature for full-time residents.

At least up here Harbor Books wouldn't have to toss down sandbags during nor'easter floods.

She pushed open the door, and a seagull squawked.

Cat jumped. She hated birds. All birds.

"Realistic, isn't it?" Ravi appeared around the side of a book-shelf. "Owners grumble about it, but I think it's important to be in harmony with one's surroundings."

Her pulse notched back down. "How Frank Lloyd Wright of you."

"You know Frank Lloyd Wright?"

"Not personally."

"Seeing as how if you did, that'd make you look damn good for your age."

"My gramps . . . my grandfather once wrote a story about Fallingwater, the house he built that's—"

"Sinking." Ravi rested the box he'd been carrying on the an-tique desk with gargoyles carved into the legs that served as the register. "Which is why I'm not pursuing architecture. I want the freedom to draw without the paralyzing fear that my creations are going to collapse on people's heads." He spread his arms out to either side. "Down to business. Welcome to Harbor Books. If we don't have it, you don't need it. Actually, we'll order it for you. Indie bookstores gotta pay the rent."

Cat stepped deeper inside, taking in the bookshelves that reached to the ceiling, crammed together in a Tetris-like pattern. She walked between them, following the maze of endless rows of spines, having a hard time believing the store didn't have every book printed in the last ten years. Winding down one path, she faced a dead end and then a choice of left or right.

"Left," Ravi whispered from behind her, and the hair on the back of her neck stood up.

She weaved left and could feel the space in the converted house narrowing and widening as she went. The bookstore didn't only take advantage of every bit of real estate but fostered a mood that matched the contents of the shelves. Cozy and candlelit by the romance section, dark and claustrophobic for the horror books, bright and covered in trailing plants and succulents in the gardening how-tos.

"And now, right," Ravi said.

His directions took her past a shelf with a Life board game perched on top. *Clever*, she thought as she scanned the titles in what was the biographies section, running her finger along the spines, lingering on one of female journalists of the modern era that Gramps didn't have. Soon she entered a rectangular area with beanbag chairs on the floor and hand-drawn posters on the walls.

"Cartoons?" Cat eyed a band of colorfully decked-out superheroes.

Ravi slapped his chest. "How insulting."

Cat turned away from grotesque zombies and what looked like a rabbit girl in a red cape. "Am I missing something?"

"Graphic novels?" Ravi pulled a book off the shelf. On the cover, a girl with the wings of a wasp hovered in midair.

Cat shrugged sheepishly. "I don't read much fiction."

Ravi placed his hand on his heart and feigned the twisting of a knife. "Killing me, Quinn, killing me. So, what do you read?"

"Biographies. History of journalism, that kind of thing."

"A woman of singular interest."

She crossed her arms in front of her chest. "Guess it's a bit boring."

"Only in the way Yao Ming or Serena Williams or Stan Lee are boring. No shame in dedication. They say it takes doing something for ten thousand hours before you begin to perfect it. You're on your way."

"And you? Are you making a comic book?"

Ravi groaned. "Graphic novel."

"Ooh, sorry, is that like calling a newspaper a tabloid?"

"No, comic books are rad in their own right. It's just they're different."

"How?"

Ravi flopped into a purple beanbag chair and slid a few comics off the bottom shelf. Cat felt silly towering above him, so she sat down on the lumpy beanbag beside him.

"Okay, so first, comics are shorter," Ravi said. "Tons of issues. Graphic novels are longer, more complex, and usually wrap up in one book, maybe two."

"Is yours one or two?"

"One. Sequels are never as good as the original. A series of movie marathons with my friends prove the exceptions are *Empire Strikes Back* and *Terminator 2*."

"Don't forget *Toy Story 2*."

"Classic," he said.

"Angeline and I were obsessed. She switched from being Buzz Lightyear to being Jessie the minute it started. Wore a cowboy hat to bed for, like, three months."

"And you?"

"I was Woody."

"The responsible one."

Another word for "boring." A bean dug into Cat's left butt cheek, and she shifted. "What's yours about?"

"Fat Indian American kid at summer camp who discovers he's a shape-shifting rakshasa who ultimately uses his powers to save the asshole campers who made fun of him from an evil counselor who's descended from Lizzie Borden. Your basic autobiography."

Cat hesitated.

"Don't tell me," he joked. "You've read one just like it."

"No, you're good there." Cat smiled, but softly. Thanks to Angeline, she could relate. "But I am sorry if it's even a bit autobiographical."

"Well, I'm channeling it for good." He raised an eyebrow. "Or is it evil?" He gave an exaggerated villain laugh. "Anyway, got a tight group of friends now. Concentrating on it means you keep living it instead of learning from it. At least, according to our self-help section. Fully stocked, spread the word."

Now Cat let herself laugh. "Noted. But tell me, what's a rakshasa?"

"Like a demon with magical powers. Comes from Hindu mythology. Some are good, some eat the flesh of men. Let's just say my mom's bedtime stories forced us to go to bed with the lights on."

"Is your mom into books too?"

"Can't own a bookstore and not be into—"

"What did you say?"

"Oops." Ravi smiled sheepishly.

"Your parents own the store? This store?"

"Sorta why I figured the ad was a done deal."

Cat leapt to her feet. "You tricked me."

Ravi crinkled his brow. "How did I trick you?"

"You said you could get the bookstore owners to run an ad in exchange for me running your editorial cartoons."

"I'm fulfilling my end of the bargain. Come on, I'll show you."

"But . . ." Cat struggled for why Ravi's omission stung. Technically he was doing what he said he'd do. Yet anything with a whiff of manipulation reminded her of her sister.

She trailed Ravi back through the store to the gargoyle desk, where he handed her a check made out to *The Red and Blue*. The amount would cover the next two issues, easy. "This is too much. It's more than a half-page ad."

"Thank preorders for the final installment of *A Thorny Kingdom* and consider it my apology for bringing you here under false pretenses."

"That's not . . ." Cat felt bad about her reaction. Ravi wasn't Angeline. Not even close. "I didn't really mind."

"You didn't?"

"It's a short walk from our apartment."

Something flickered in Ravi's eyes that Cat couldn't make out, and an uncomfortable silence followed. Her gaze fell to the desk, where a sketchbook lay open, one side weighed down by an oblong green wish rock from the beach. Cat wanted to pick it up, something she never got the chance to do around Angeline.

When they were little, Angeline would search the beach for wish rocks, snatching up each and every one. She'd trace the white line around the circumference of the rock with her little finger, making a wish with her tongue sticking out between her lips, then drop it back into the sand. "One rock, one wish," she'd tell Cat, so Cat couldn't pick up the same one and make a wish. Angeline had an eagle eye for finding wish rocks. Cat could scarcely remember nabbing one first. Maybe that was why all of Angeline's wishes seemed to come true. She'd had so many chances to will them into being.

The one time Angeline had given Cat a wish rock, she'd flushed it down the toilet.

Cat left the wish rock in place and studied Ravi's drawing. A tall being that looked like a cross between a human, a tiger, and an octopus waved a gilded sword at a bunch of cowering twelve-year-olds in Lake Lookey Loo Camp T-shirts.

Cat was in awe of all the detail, from the texture on the rakshasa's skin to the large whites on the eyes of the terrified campers. "You really are talented. I'm so glad I came today."

"Me too."

"I wasn't convinced before, but I think your editorial cartoons are going to be a great addition to the paper. The Fit to Print judges will be impressed, I know it."

She smiled, but he wouldn't meet her eye. Was she not complimentary enough?

"Really," she said, "we're going to be a great team on the paper this year."

Squawk!

Cat flinched.

The door opened, and in came Natalie Goldberg in leggings

and a gauzy sweater, like she'd just stepped out of a yoga class.

"Hey, Ravi," she said. "Kate."

"It's Cat."

"Oh, of course. You're Angeline's sister?"

Cat nodded, her finger automatically striking the side of her thigh.

"Would you mind . . . could you let her know if she has any more 'bigger is better' samples, I'm up for the challenge. And she's locked up my vote."

Cat gave a polite tilt of her head. She turned to thank Ravi, but his eyes were squarely focused on Natalie.

Their business was done. Cat had gotten exactly what she'd come for. The paper—her paper—was no longer on life support. She tucked the check in her pocket, her mind focused on planning the spread announcing the primary winners.

Kate.

Really?

Well, most of her mind.

Cat headed for the door, but a yelp from Natalie made her turn back around. Natalie's phone was vibrating, and Ravi's was dinging, and the same look of confusion wrinkled their faces.

"Oh my God," Natalie squealed. "That's my right leg! But those so aren't my lips. Are you seeing this?"

"Uh, yeah, but what exactly am I seeing?" Ravi glanced at Cat. "Any ideas?"

"Me?" She checked her phone. "I didn't get any emails."

"Not an email," Natalie said. "One of our friends sent a link. Look!" She held up her phone, but before Cat could see, it erupted with another vibration, and Natalie snatched it back. "No! It's being retweeted! Kate, quick, check if it's on Insta yet."

Cat's shoulders rounded. "I'm not on Instagram. Or Twitter."

"What kind of photo is this anyway?" Ravi held out his screen, and this time, Cat wrapped her hand around it. An image of a girl with her legs, arms, hands, feet, eyes, lips, breasts, a dozen female body parts, all labeled.

She pointed to the caption. "The Acedia Perfect Tens. What does that mean?"

Natalie's jaw clenched. "It means our classmates have finally done it. Gone too far. Way, way too far."

Jon Bernwick @JonnybBad73 • 15m

What am I hearing about Frankengirls @AcediaCHSMA?

Reply 6   Retweet 2   Like 12

Show this thread

Tad Marcus @TadIsRad • 11m

Replying to @JonnybBad73

THIS. @AcediaCHSMA

<<Photo removed due to sensitive content>>

BakedBaker24/7 @Josh Baker • 9m

Replying to @JonnybBad73

Total BS, man! Show me my ladies! @AcediaCHSMA

Dipti P. @drp98 • 6m

Replying to @JonnybBad73

These are actual WOMEN, you pervs! @AcediaCHSMA

BrosAndBros @brosandbros • 5m

Replying to @JonnybBad73

Perfect women. See? @AcediaCHSMA

```
           _
        ( ( ^ ) )
       ( ( ' ' ) )
        ( \ 0 / )
        . ' .
      / ( Y ) \
      \ \ )   ( / /
       /         \
      /           \
       _____
        \ | /
        / | \
        \ | /
        / Y \
```

Acedia Charter School @AcediaCHSMA • 4m

Replying to @JonnybBad73

Please refrain from tagging the school, thank you.

Nat @NatGberg • 2m

Replying to @JonnybBad73

Why is there nothing about this in The Red and Blue?

Cat: Did you see—

Grady: Replying now . . .

Cat: No, don't! That's not professional.

Grady: But we look scooped.

Cat: Those are people on Twitter. An actual news outlet has to be reporting it for us to be scooped.

Cat: And I'm writing the article now. We'll have to use the website. Have it to you to post in an hour.

Grady: I can interview—

Cat: On it. Just waiting for Schwartz quote. Can you get visuals?

Grady: Social media blocking most. But I can try, Chief.

Cat: If you do, ask Ravi to mask faces.

Grady: But that's—

Cat: Professional. We're not Playboy.

10

When Angeline Stands Up and Out

22 DAYS TO THE ELECTION

1 DAY TO THE PRIMARY

Crackle . . . static . . . muffled voices . . . throat clearing . . . tap, tap, tap . . .

"*Attention Acedia students. This is Principal Schwartz. By now you are all aware that our school has experienced an unfortunate incident. We appreciate your understanding and discretion as the events of this morning remain under active investigation. Acedia Charter School maintains a strict sexual harassment policy.*"

"Pro or con?" Maxine shouted beside Angeline from their table in the center of the cafeteria.

"*What we have witnessed is not only disturbing but shocking to myself and all of Acedia's dedicated teachers.*"

"You want shocking? Step inside any boys' bathroom any day of the week," Maxine bellowed.

Angeline swatted her arm. "You're making a scene."

"I'm well aware. Those photos plastered all over the school are real."

"I know."

"Taken at *my* party over the summer."

"I know."

"So the question isn't why I'm making a scene, but why aren't you?"

"The perpetrator or perpetrators behind these so-called Frankengirls do a disservice to what we know is a decent and upstanding majority of our student body."

"Again, boys'—" Maxine started.

Angeline elbowed her. "We can't take sides."

"This isn't choosing blue or green eye shadow."

"Never wearing blue eye shadow's a total myth. It's really quite flattering. So long as you keep the rest of your makeup palette subtle, you can—"

"You can't be serious right now."

"What? The primary's tomorrow. I can't risk offending voters."

"You're offending me right now. I'm in those pictures. So are you."

"Rest assured, these 'Frankengirls' will not be seen again. We have reported this . . . transgression to the appropriate social media outlets, and seeing as how some of the . . . body parts labeled belong to female students under the age of eighteen, any and all images and moving pictures will be taken down immediately. We would request that if you have posted an image of these 'Frankengirls' . . ."

"Did he just use that word twice?" Maxine jolted out of her seat, her wave necklace bouncing against her chest.

Several other girls followed Maxine's lead, a few raising middle fingers toward the speaker in the ceiling.

". . . on your social media accounts that you remove it yourself. We will not tolerate such a brazen disregard for the rules that govern this institution."

"For the rules?" Maxine cried. "That's what you're talking about? Rules? Broken rules? To cover your own asses? What about the girls?"

"It's a joke!" Josh Baker shouted.

"Oh yeah?" Maxine said. "Then you won't mind stripping to your grubby tighty-whities and letting me take a pic?"

"Chill," Tad said. "It was a freakin' pool party. You all chose to be half naked. And hey, Maxine, you should be liking it as much as the next guy."

High fives at his table, and Angeline rested her hand on Maxine's and squeezed.

"Misogynistic assholes!" one girl cried.

"Homophobes!" another said.

Boos and yeses erupted throughout the room.

Maxine squeezed Angeline's hand back. "I'm fine. But you want to defend my honor, then get in the game. This is it, A. This goes beyond hanging bras in doorways and writing 'cupcake' on the backs of girls' shirts. You want to stand out, stand the eff up and do what you're always saying: *Bring it.*"

Angeline's heart beat in her throat. She had yet to prepare her primary speech. But everyone was here, listening, today.

But what should she say? Would being in the photos make people more or less likely to vote for her? She twirled her ring around her finger. Social media had taught her that backlash came like whiplash. And was just as unpredictable.

She scanned the room, lingering on Sammy, who stood under the football team's questionable SLOTHS GIVE A SLOW DEATH banner, and then on Cat, frantically scribbling in her notebook a couple of tables over. Angeline's eyes floated to the end of her own table, where Leo sat. Where she used to sit with him.

His expression was neutral, but the tightness of his jaw sent Angeline's mind spinning. Was he upset? About the Frankengirls? Generally or specifically? Specifically related to her ... *her parts* ... being a part of it? The former meant he was the boy she knew he was, the one she loved. The latter meant he might still love her back.

Angeline inhaled a breath and propelled herself out of her chair. "Frankengirls." Here, unlike at home, she had only one take. *One.*

"*Frankengirls,*" she said louder. "The name's almost as demeaning as the images themselves, isn't it?"

Murmurs of assent spilled from most of the female students, encouraging Angeline. "This morning, the walls of our bathrooms and locker rooms were plastered with photocopied images of female students in our school. Or should I say versions of female students in our school. Three of them. Someone took the liberty of designing their perfect physical specimen. They pilfered photos— real photos—off social media and Photoshopped them together like they were creating an avatar. A little of this, a little of that, and voilà! A composite picture. A composite *girl.*"

Her phone buzzed with a notification. Someone had tagged her on Instagram. She made a show of shaking her head, masking her quick unlock and swipe. It was a pic of her, from right then with a single #femaleempowerment as the caption, posted by Natalie, whose Pinterest look for today was Parisian girl with her nautical-striped shirt, perfectly tied scarf, and red beret. The comments were coming fast.

Angeline lifted her head. "Some of these girls—us, some of *us,* because I'm there too—wearing nothing but bikinis at a private party. Maybe we could live with that. Not like it, but live with it.

But what did this person do? They labeled us. Like we were meat. Shank, ribs, center cut, except it was torso Maxine Chen and right leg Natalie Goldberg and boobs Angeline Quinn." Maxine rapped on the tabletop. The adrenaline racing through Angeline's veins spurred her, and she climbed up.

Emmie stepped forward. But every pair of eyes was focused on Angeline.

And their phones.

Notifications were popping up on all of Angeline's social media accounts.

Screw the election, this will totally bump up Ask an Angel subscribers, she thought.

She projected, using the authoritative tone she'd honed from her YouTube channel. "'Vote for your Perfect Ten,' this sicko wrote on the bottom of those images. 'A multiple choice you can't get wrong,' this perv said. And what is our school doing about it? Filing a complaint with social media so the reposts of the pictures are taken offline? So it won't, what? Get sued? While we're objectified?"

With purpose but not haste, Emmie strode toward Angeline. She situated herself directly across from her, but Angeline literally and figuratively towered over her.

Emmie raised her palms in the air. "It's only been a few hours. I'm sure the administration is doing everything it can to identify the culprit."

"It's him!" shouted the redheaded girl with the freckles who had taken two of Angeline's samples. "String him up by his balls!" She thrust her finger at Josh.

"We can't rush to judgment," Emmie said calmly. "We need to let the investigative process proceed until it can determine fault."

"Traitor!" the redhead said, and Emmie transitioned through a dozen shades of red. Angeline actually felt a little sorry for her.

"I should say something," Angeline whispered to Maxine.

"Do that. After you win the primary."

Angeline hesitated.

"What?" Maxine said. "You want to win, don't you? Here's your chance."

Angeline thought of Leo, and a knot tightened in the pit of her stomach.

But Leo was gone.

Evelyn's Epic Everyday was here.

Angeline pictured a million, two, five million subscribers. And she pictured all of them hitting a thumbs-up beside her name.

She elongated her neck. "We can't just wait. We can't sit back and let our fates be determined by those who are not us—those who don't care as much as we do. Which is why, if I'm elected student council president, I'm going to . . . to . . ." Angeline's eyes flickered to Emmie, and she thought back to what Emmie had said about the power of the masses. And giving them a voice. "To create a system for you to voice your concerns—"

"This isn't the time or place for primary speeches," Emmie said, a vein pulsing in her neck.

"Didn't seem to bother you the other day," Angeline shot back. "Or is vegan bacon more *concerning* than the objectification of women? Than having a voice? Than . . ." Her mind seized on the question she'd just answered for her loyal Ask an Angel viewers. "Than ensuring justice?"

Justice . . . sure, but what really engaged was a rallying cry. #femaleempowerment, right?

Angeline swiveled her head to ensure everyone got a glimpse

95

of her good side. "But to have justice, we must have account-ability. And accountability starts with us. Bras were strewn all over the school, and we Instagrammed it. A few decried the spirit week cupcake stunt, but one defaced shirt sold on eBay for two hundred dollars. We need to stop. We need to demand responsibility. And we need to advocate for ourselves, every day, right here. One way we can do that is with a peer jury system where students investi-gate and determine consequences for acts like these committed by their classmates. We need more stringent guidelines for behaviors and sanctions for infringements—ones we collectively agree on. We create an environment where these Frankengirls won't happen again because they won't be tolerated, period. Because we know we must answer to one another as fellow citizens of this school." She wet her lips. "Hashtag #MoreThanOurParts."

Silence, and then a resounding "More Than Our Parts" echoed through the cafeteria.

Tad planted himself in front of Leo. "You seriously letting this chick lead a witch hunt, Torres? Your balls still tucked in a little velvet pouch in her purse? Or are they in your mommy's? Or do they share 'em like a custody agreement?"

Leo's eyes coldcocked Tad, but his hands remained pressed flat against the table.

"More *can't do*s, like, seriously?" Josh said. "Man, already I can't even wear a baseball cap."

"Abomination," Tad said, staring at Leo.

The redhead who yelled "traitor" set her sights on Tad. She pointed to his feet, which wore the newest, flashiest sneaker named after a player on the Boston Celtics.

"And you shouldn't be wearing those," the girl said. "They cost more than my car."

Tad snickered. "Remind me not to hitch a ride."

The girl remained unflustered, like she'd been waiting for this moment a long time. "They foster a divisive environment. We're here to learn, aren't we? Not to flash our credit cards. The dress code should have limits."

Extreme? Probably. But more agreement than Angeline would have expected rolled through the cafeteria. And so, even though it went against every pricey parka, every strappy sandal, and every prepaid prom limo offer that she'd used her talent—not a trust fund—to acquire, she said, "Damn straight. Ultra expensive clothes and shoes and limos to prom single out those whose parents don't work in tech." Beside her, Maxine muttered a "Jugular, huh?" but the nods and fist pumps encouraged Angeline. "School should be a safe space where what we have and wear doesn't create a hierarchy. It's hard enough, isn't it? So let our peers at it—figuring out what stays and what goes. From thousand-dollar backpacks to—"

"Dried fruit in the vending machine!" Natalie cried.

"And apples!" Lush Curls said.

"Why not?" Angeline said, surprised that healthy snacks trumped Leo's smoldering eyes and great hair.

Emmie once again tried to insert herself. "Those are all things to be taken up, but there is already a system in place to do so. Suggestions made to the appropriate teacher liaison using the forms readily available in the front office are filtered through to the administration and brought up—"

"In about a thousand years," Angeline said. "Screw bureaucracy. We form the world we want by taking action. Ourselves. We bring change. *We. Bring. It.*"

Tad scoffed. "By ramming things down our throats, more like it. What about you, Torres? Political dynasty offering us the same load of crap?"

Tad pounded his fist against the table, egging Leo to climb

up. But Leo's fear of heights meant even a step stool offered a challenge.

He took a stand but kept his feet firmly on the ground. "What am I offering? One thing that's easy to comprehend. Stop telling us what to do. We're here, expected to get top grades, lead our teams to state, drive a car, hell, vote for president. And yet we can't be trusted to wear whatever we want to school? Because a hat or a plaid shirt tied around your waist is distracting? We should be able to wear whatever we want."

"Got my vote, hundred percent," Josh said.

Leo gave a thumbs-up. "This school used to trust us. There was a time we could go off campus and grab a slice of pepperoni from Frank's Pizza for lunch. We should be able to go where we want." Agreement spread through the room. "They tell us what clubs we can have, what plays we can put on, what music band performs. Take away our hats, jerseys, our straws. They keep taking, and what are they giving? Nothing but an environment full of pissed-off kids. That's what makes something like these Frankengirls happen. Pure and simple misplaced frustration. She wants more restrictions? I want less. I want us to be trusted to make our own decisions—all of us, not some elite jury of what surely won't be all of our peers."

Emmie stood before them, waving her hand. But this wasn't class, and there was no teacher to call on her. Angeline and Leo were firmly in charge.

Leo held out his palms to calm the hoots of support, led by Tad. "These photos are unacceptable. But we can't have a bunch of vigilantes leading the charge."

Angeline gritted her teeth. They were both spewing BS. She just had to do it better. "And we can't have the administration enacting a cover-up to save face. This injustice will only be righted by us. We'll find out who did this together."

Maxine yelled from beside Angeline. "So vote your conscience! Vote for—"

"For . . . for . . . highlighters!" A breathless Jay Choi hurled himself into the cafeteria. "Who's . . . with . . . me?" He gasped, coming to stand next to Emmie, whose arms were tightly bound across her chest, but it was too late for both of them.

Angeline and Leo stared at each other across the expanse of the lunchroom table.

Welcome to Acedia's two-party system.

Acedia Confronts Its Inner Sloth: Controversy Surrounding Student Council Unprecedented in Charter School History

---

A SPECIAL REPORT

Part 2 of 6

In an effort to mirror the inner workings of the national election, first-year government teacher Ms. Jules Lute instituted the Acedia Student Council Presidential Primary. The election to narrow the slate of candidates down to two may have been held during a school-wide assembly in fifth period, but the results were locked up the previous day when the "Frankengirls" appeared.

Shortly after the images were discovered, Principal Jeffrey Schwartz glossed over the administration's "active investigation" and made what became seen as a controversial request for students to delete any social media postings depicting the composite photographs. Following this announcement, a spontaneous debate broke out among several of the candidates in the school cafeteria. Speculation as to who was behind the Frankengirls transitioned into a discussion that set each presidential hopeful's platform in stone and led to frontrunners Quinn, who proposed increased governance by their peers, and Torres, who advocated for trust and a relaxation of the rules.

On the day of the primary, each of the four candidates, which included Jay Choi, freshman, and Emmie Hayes, senior, gave five-minute-long speeches. Ballots were cast, and Quinn and Torres nabbed resounding wins, with Quinn in the lead by a strong twenty-five percentage points.

No one could have predicted then just how far the tentacles of the Acedia Student Council election would reach. Hashtags, angel wings, *The Boston Globe*, and the halls of Congress were all still to come.

The election engaged students in a way nothing at Acedia had before. Ms. Lute's government classes had the highest average grades of any course that marking period. A twice-weekly poll, created by Chen, who was also working on a voting app for the wider election, tracked each candidate's odds of winning. Yet the question remains as to why this election was the one to garner such attention. The facts are clear: Quinn and Torres are popular students at the school, each with visibility beyond its brick walls; their status as a former romantic couple piques a voyeuristic interest; and their campaign platforms embody a conflict core to the national presidential election. And certainly, the provocative nature of the Frankengirls, which only came to be thanks to that summer party at Chen's, created conditions primed for strong opinions and extreme outrage.

But Goldberg presents another theory as to why the student council election became so renowned: "If you ask me, it's all because of *The Shrieking Violet*."

Click for more: 2 of 6

11

When Cat's Words Are Read

20 DAYS TO THE ELECTION

The taxidermic bass on the wall above Principal Schwartz's desk stared at Cat. She tried not to move, even though her feet dangled uncomfortably above the blue carpet tiles. One shift and she feared the thing would come alive, that single glossy black eye the motion-activated trigger for it to break out into song.

"Naturally, we're investigating," Principal Schwartz said. His oak desk was barren save for a computer monitor, an inbox with neatly stacked folders, and the metal clipboard that had brought Cat here. "But with no proof of who's responsible, I'm afraid we can't take any disciplinary action."

Cat scooched forward, keeping her eye on the green scales surrounding the fish eye. With her feet firmly planted on the ground, she asked, "Can I . . ."

He frowned. "Go ahead, but no photos."

Cat rotated the clipboard and scanned the janitor's cleaning log, which marked when the bathrooms and locker rooms had last been seen free of the Frankengirls photos. She noted the time. "And the two students who first reported the photos in the west corridor bathroom—"

"Ms. Quinn, we've been through this. Those boys were cleared."

"Yes, but how, exactly?" She lifted her notebook. "For the article."

"We've spoken with them, their parents, and their cross-country coach. The students' early arrival was for extra practice. Nothing more."

"Right. Speaking of, I was hoping the exterior camera footage might be available?"

"I'm afraid not. We have a duty to ensure the privacy of our students and employees. I can assure you—and you can assure your readers—that no viable suspects entered the premises overnight." He stood. "Now, considering I agreed to this on a Saturday, if you'll excuse me . . ."

Cat held up one finger, pretending to need more time to scribble down notes as she formulated what would become the backbone of her story. "While finding the perpetrator is important, this incident has prompted reactions from the student council candidates. They have differing views regarding discipline and justice. Considering Slothy and 'cupcake' being written on cheerleader uniforms and the full history of attacks and pranks going unpunished, has this made the administration consider changes?"

Principal Schwartz lifted a Yeti cooler and a tackle box out from under his desk. "No."

"Right, then." Cat forced herself not to smile as she slid off her chair. She ducked below the fish and hightailed it out of his office, adrenaline quickening her pulse, for that "no" perfectly set up what came next.

📣 📣 📣

Cat didn't know where to look: the indigo of the Atlantic Ocean framed by the floor-to-ceiling windows in Maxine's living room; the three-foot-wide compass chandelier; the whitewashed rafters from which rustic kayak paddles hung. All deserved her attention, and yet her eyes couldn't stop jumping from Natalie's right leg to Maxine's torso to Dipti's left clavicle to Riley's nose to Sonya's left hand to Angeline's boobs.

All of the Frankengirls—all of the *actual girls* labeled in the Frankengirls photographs—surrounded Cat.

"No? *That's* what he said?" Maxine perched herself on the edge of her white linen sectional, which made the sofa in Cat's apartment feel like it belonged in a dollhouse. "Is Schwartz living in a different decade? Just because this is high school, this stuff can't just be allowed to go on."

Dipti, whose long, dark hair was pulled back into a bun, said, "I'm grounded for the entire semester. My parents thought I was bowling. *Bowling?* Like it's my fault they're gullible?"

"I got kicked out of regionals!" Tamara said. "Disqualified from the pageant because of 'inappropriate conduct.' My hand"— she held up her right hand and waved like the queen of England— "was holding a tequila shot."

Riley hopped up from her center couch seat to nab some of the spotlight. "Tequila, honey, and Dr Pepper. For accuracy." She looked at Cat, who tried not to grimace.

"I lost my car for two months," Maxine said. "My parents would have never found out about the party otherwise."

"Not fair" and "Can't keep brushing us under the rug" and more came from the girls' lips. They wanted to tell their story of injustice. And they chose to tell it to Cat. The number of views on that online article she'd written must have shown them how relevant *The Red and Blue* could be.

Out of the corner of Cat's eye, she saw Angeline sitting just back from Maxine's gleaming white surfboard on the bottom step of the staircase that led to the second floor, letting the focus be on everyone but her. Smart campaign strategy. These girls would leave here and tell their friends how Angeline supported but didn't outshine them. Her sister was always thinking about herself, even when she appeared not to be.

With the next pause in conversation, Cat asked the question that would allow the girls to directly respond to Principal Schwartz's "no." "Does this make anyone feel uncomfortable in school?"

Every hand shot up. Cat lifted the newspaper's camera and clicked.

📣 📣 📣

Cat sat at the lunch table two days later ignoring her grilled cheese and holding her newspaper in her hand. The last copy. In the entire school. Maybe even in town.

Grady had swung by the grocery store that morning and said the stack there was gone too. Every copy of the latest *Red and Blue* had been snatched up.

Her words were being read. Read by actual people.

A tingle traveled from the crown of her head all the way to her toes. Then she got back to business, grabbing her notebook and compiling her to-do list: increase the print run, pitch more advertisers, recruit another writer—at least one.

Battle of the Exes, the election had been dubbed—not by Cat. Though it was news, and she'd reported it as such. That it made Angeline twitch was simply a bonus.

She smoothed the front of the newspaper and slipped the issue between two plastic sheets in her portfolio, which thankfully had room for many more. Because this was bigger than just one story. The tentacles of the Frankengirls reached in all directions, and Cat would cover them all.

And the Fit to Print judges would get the chance to see it.

Cat grabbed her phone and plugged in the Fit to Print website.

She clicked through until she found the application. Her heart beat faster with each empty box she completed until she reached "Apply." She tapped the button, and that was it. *The Red and Blue* was officially entered for the Fit to Print award.

She exhaled a long breath.

"Is this seat taken?"

Cat looked up to see Emmie Hayes in a blue cardigan and pressed khakis holding a tray.

"Sure. I mean, no, it's free. I mean, sit, please."

Emmie lowered herself into the seat. "Great issue. Definite keepsake material."

Cat's face grew hot. "The plastic's maybe a bit much, but I picked up the habit from my grams."

Her grandmother had kept a scrapbook of every one of Gramps's stories from the small paper in upstate New York where he started to the *Portland Sun* in Maine to *The Boston Globe* and even an article or two in *The New Yorker*.

"You should be proud of it." Emmie squirted hand sanitizer into her palm. "You're a decent writer."

"Decent"?

"But the way you construct a story, it's engaging. You really bring everything to life. Impressive."

"Impressive" was better.

"You really think so?" Cat asked.

Emmie scooped up lettuce and nodded.

"Because . . ." Cat scooted to the edge of her chair. "Well, I'm thinking if the election continues to hold people's interest, then covering it like this—weekly, at the very least, maybe even twice a week until the votes are cast . . . I mean, it could change the whole way the school thinks about the paper. They'd be looking for it. And Grady wanted me to skip the actual printing and just publish this whole thing online. But Stavros and Jen never used our website. And the Fit to Print award has never been won by a digital paper. *The Red and Blue* has enough obstacles to climb, you know? But Grady's as persistent as an itch from a mosquito bite, so I did let him upload the stories—but only after they were in print. I gave in and let him set up Twitter and Instagram accounts too. He said they already have more than three hundred followers on each. Do you know, is that a lot?"

Emmie set down her fork with a clunk.

Cat cringed. "Oh, wow . . . that was really insensitive to be blathering on about covering the election you wanted to win. I'm really sorry."

So neutral was Emmie's expression that Cat wasn't sure if maybe she hadn't actually been paying attention, was on the verge of tears, or was about to lash into her . . . and then, Emmie gave a crooked smile.

"*Should* have won," she said. "But it's okay. I just thought you might need a reminder to breathe."

"Uh, yeah, I guess I don't have many people to talk to about this, except my gramps." Cat sounded like a six-year-old. She cleared her throat. "It's too bad you didn't win the primary. Your ideas were good. You seemed to know how to do this."

"Not well enough apparently."

"Welcome to the tsunami that is my sister." Cat jutted her chin across the cafeteria. "Just look at her. Flipping pancakes on an electric griddle. I've never seen my sister do anything in the kitchen except mix cucumber slices into coconut water, but here she is actually cooking at her 'Vote for an Angel' gluten-free, dairy-free, taste-free pancake breakfast."

"Branded as such with everyone repeating it. Even though it's lunchtime."

"The power of Ask an Angel." Cat felt guilty by association. She lowered her eyes and noticed Emmie was wearing that string bracelet again. "Good luck charm?"

"Reminder. Of the place I get to go to every summer—the place that isn't here."

"That must be nice," Cat said, a bit jealous. "Where's that?"

"Leadership camp. I've been going every year since I was ten and found my best friends there. We have a group chat to get us through the school year. Hopefully we'll get into the same poli-sci programs next year."

"Politics is really your thing?"

"Leadership is my thing. Don't think this is going to stop me. I know where I'm headed, and I know exactly what to do to get there." She picked up her fork and dug back into her salad.

So maybe Emmie did have that air of superiority that kept others away, but it was refreshing to find someone who cared about something so deeply.

Cat lowered her voice. "You're better off not getting drawn into the drama that is my sister."

Emmie's straight face faltered enough for Cat to see the hurt.

"Angeline puts Angeline first, always." Cat's throat closed around the words. "A race against her, with the crap she'd pull . . . it wouldn't be worth it."

Cat had fallen victim to trying to keep up with Angeline. Something that had ended in the fourth grade. That was the year she'd followed Angeline's lead and signed up for a starring role in the school play even though the idea of speaking in front of an auditorium full of people made her tremble worse than wading in the ocean after a shark sighting.

During the first performance, Cat froze. She had to be carried offstage. And Angeline, her sister, *her younger sister*, had cracked a joke: *"No worries, folks, even fraidy cats have nine lives."*

It was like something had clawed out Cat's heart. She ran to her mother, to her father, who'd both appeared backstage. She reached her dad first. Cat stood before him, tears and snot and saliva dribbling down her face. He bent down and wrapped a hand around each of her upper arms.

"Ah, Cathleen." He sighed. "Better to learn these things when you're young. Save you trouble when you're older. Some people's dreams are beyond their reality."

Cat hadn't known her heart could be ripped out twice.

Emmie studied Cat's face. "Certainly, you know your sister better than anyone."

They watched Angeline pose with a group of the Frankengirls who had stuck Post-it notes on every limb, torso, forehead, and butt cheek.

"Frankengirl this," they shouted together as their phones captured them.

Cat cocked her head. "Is that like a protest or something?"

"Or something," Emmie said. "Watch, it'll become a meme by tomorrow."

"Fulfilling one of her biggest bucket list items."

Emmie laughed. "Would you want to hang out sometime?"

Cat thought of Ravi and his tight circle of friends. Cat's were in college, Emmie's were online. Maybe they could fill in the gap for each other.

"Definitely," Cat said. "Have you been to Harbor Books?"

Win with Quinn!

Angeline means "messenger."
Trust that she will deliver.
And she will BRING. IT.

Vote Angeline and
vote for your FUTURE.

Hey, girl,

They say it takes seeing something

seven times for it to register.

You're welcome.

12

When Angeline Does the Math

Angeline jammed her foot on the brake, and the hatchback lurched. "No way."

Cat braced herself against the dash. "Did you almost kill something? Aside from me?"

"That has to be against the rules." Angeline slammed the gas pedal and careened into Acedia's parking lot, the three-foot-tall halo designed and installed by Sonya swaying on the car's roof.

"Angeline! That's it, I'm driving tomorrow."

"Whatever. Just look." Angeline could barely see straight. On the front lawn of the school, the ten-foot-high marquee that the previous day had advertised the Friday-night football game against Acedia's biggest rival instead cheered on Angeline's.

In like a Lion: Vote for Leo and Feel the Pride.

"Not the best slogan, I grant you," Cat said. "But 'A' for effort."

Angeline glared at Cat. "I'm reporting him."

"One, you can't even be sure it's him. Leo's whole campaign has Tad Marcus written all over it. Two, even Gramps could see that. Pretty safe bet Principal Schwartz is in the know."

"This isn't funny."

"Oh, come on, Angeline, we both know you'd be relieved if Leo won. No matter what I tell Mom, she'll give you a pass, like always."

"For as much as you wear it, martyr's still an unattractive look for you, Cat." Angeline left the car running and snatched her bag from the floor by Cat's feet. "But be sure to take a picture for your newspaper."

Who the hell did Cat think sent the Frankengirls to her stupid newspaper? People were reading *The Red and Blue* because Angeline had made it worth reading.

"Not even a thank-you. And I'm the selfish one," she muttered as she stomped past six-foot-high devil horns on Tad Marcus's truck and toward Leo's latest Battle of the Exes stunt. Leo's fear of heights meant this *was* all Tad, Leo had minions, or both. "Feel the pride, my ass."

Leo had taken his ridiculous stance about no rules just to be contrary to her.

Good grades, team captain, liked by everyone, without a mar on his record, and not even a beer at parties, Leo was the picture-perfect son. He embodied all the respectable qualities his mom needed to complete her image as a female politician who had it all. And image was all it was. Leo ranked at the bottom of her priority list, which was why he poured his time into making sure his little brother, Sammy, never felt the same.

Except now he had something else to do: get back at Angeline. And he was listening to Tad Marcus to do it.

Angeline put her back to the marquee and marched past the statue of Major Mushing. Her head deep in her phone, she clicked to Leo's Instagram feed.

A picture of his message on the marquee had nearly four dozen comments. She quickly divided that by his number of followers and—

No freaking way!

His engagement rate was off the charts.

Fake accounts?

Had to be.

Anger fueled her into the school. She scrolled through the comments on Leo's post, recognizing a lot of the male names: jocks. Football team, baseball, track, tennis, and, naturally, lacrosse. Even benched because of his shoulder, Leo had them.

The girls commenting on the post looked to be mostly freshmen. Fourteen-year-olds swooning over his dimple and Muppet hair.

Leo had found his base.

Whatever. She had hers. Her speech on the Frankengirls and her #MoreThanOurParts posts since had secured the girl-power vote, which meant her followers had to outnumber Leo's. Emmie had said whoever had the masses behind them would win.

Whether they—*whether she*—wanted to or not.

But she'd maybe, sorta already sent in the boot camp deposit so . . . *onward.*

Besides, being president *had* to be less time-consuming than this damn election, which was eating into the hours Angeline usually reserved for responding to comments on Ask an Angel. She'd skipped breakfast that morning to squeeze in a few "flutter your wings!" and now her stomach growled at her. She headed for the cafeteria, assuring herself that in just a couple more weeks, it would be all over, and she could go back to normal life.

Normal life without Leo, which wasn't yet normal life.

Leo hadn't spoken to her since the day of Cat's interview. Instead he'd been strutting around school in that sling she wasn't entirely sure he needed, letting Lush Curls carry his backpack and Doe Eyes feed him and for all she knew wipe his damn ass.

He was enjoying this.

Playing up the whole Battle of the Exes.

Humiliating her.

She deserved the breakup, fine, sure, whatever.

But he was making their entire relationship look like a joke. Like it wasn't serious. Like they hadn't been in love.

Like they weren't still.

Her rapid breaths slowed.

Because . . . because he wasn't.

With the person Leo was becoming, she shouldn't be either.

But she was. And that might be what bothered her the most.

She took a deep breath, from the diaphragm, knowing how proud Sonya would be.

Outside the cafeteria, a crowd had gathered by the table usually selling egg sandwiches and bagels. A sign hung from it:

TORRES CAMPAIGN DONUT BREAKFAST*

*Actually during breakfast hours.**

Dudes do math better.*

***Who do you want managing your student council budget?

Dudes do math better? What a hypocrite! She'd tutored Leo in calc all last year.

A fire now burning in her chest, she whirled around to capture both herself and the sexist sign when she saw Leo inside the lunchroom, talking to prospective voters. He'd traded in his lime-green sweatshirt for a white button-down and crisp navy shorts. The outfit they had bought together at the start of the summer.

Angeline had picked it out for him to wear to his mom's outdoor fundraiser in the harbor—one of the few times Angeline had accompanied him to one of his mom's events. He'd insisted it was a Saturday night in the summer and they were a package deal.

"I look like a snob," Leo had said when he'd exited the dressing room.

"Says the boy who plays lacrosse," she joked.

"But I get to carry a big stick." He had reached for her and erased the distance between them. "Well, two."

Angeline groaned but let herself relax into the one place that slowed her down. Leo's body was warm and smelled like the ocean they'd swum in that morning. With it being early summer, the water temperature had hovered around sixty degrees, but they'd dove in. They knew how to warm each other up when they got out.

Leo had curled his fingers into her long hair, tucking in the beach rose he'd picked for her. "You know why I play, don't you?"

"Your mom thinks the football team looks cliché."

"Fine for a Republican, but not a woman advocating to abolish ICE. Want to show the country deportation and immigration in a new light? A kid with Venezuelan grandparents playing lacrosse in a beach town? Let's all get together and roast marshmallows around the campfire. Eliza Torres brings us a better tomorrow!" He made light of something Angeline knew wasn't, out of a need to protect himself. He then swung Angeline so they both faced the three-paneled mirror. Him behind her, legs and torsos glued together, her brown hair, not yet ombre, a shade lighter than his. Angeline could see him from nearly all angles; she hadn't known to imprint it on her brain then. He'd brushed her hair back, rested his chin on her shoulder, and met her hazel eyes with his dark brown ones, the mixed feelings he had about his mom ever present. "So besides the fact that lacrosse happens to be the fastest game in the world to be played on two feet, no clue why I play?"

"You thought since it had a stick it was some form of baseball?"

"Nice try, but more Viktor Krum."

She drew her freshly threaded (*in an on-camera tutorial*) eyebrows together.

"Freshman year, I heard you telling Maxine about your crush on him. Seeing as how I couldn't conjure up a Quidditch field at Acedia . . . figured lacrosse was as close as I could get."

Angeline spun around. "You started playing lacrosse because twelve-year-old me once had a crush on a fictional athlete from Harry Potter?"

Leo gave a sheepish smile.

"But you're really good," she said. "You made varsity sophomore year."

"Fast learner," he whispered, nuzzling her neck.

She'd pushed him back. "Wait. You learned to play lacrosse for me?"

"See, Ang, the thing is, you inspire me to do things I thought I'd never do. Play lacrosse. Eat raw fish. Be supremely happy."

Was he *supremely happy* now?

Angeline positioned herself just inside the entrance to the cafeteria and snapped a photo of Leo's sexist donut sign.

She had a hard time imagining him agreeing to it let alone coming up with it. But he'd done one or the other. Both sucked.

A roar of laughter broke out at a table where Tad and a bunch of guys were huddled together.

117

"Hey, Leo, check it out," Tad said, stepping back to make room. A square donut box lay open like a stage backdrop.

"Frankengirls good enough to eat!" Tad lifted his hand to high-five Leo.

Éclair legs and cruller arms and donut hole heads and extra white icing glopped on the upper half of Boston cream pie torsos, like breasts topped with pointy pink sprinkles jutting out from the centers. One creation had a rubber band attached to a toothpick sticking out of its munchkin head—a halo. A croissant split in two made a pair of angel wings. It rested a giant scone foot on top of a pile of crushed strawberry-filled donuts, their red jelly oozing out like blood, and that fire burning in Angeline's chest exploded. Tad or no Tad, Leo was in charge of Leo. And he was turning this—*her*—into a joke.

She might not particularly want to win, maybe didn't even need to win, but she wanted and needed something: to beat Leo.

She snapped a photo just as Tad's hand met Leo's. Just as Leo faced her, recognition dawning . . . of Angeline, her phone, this moment . . . captured.

And about to go viral.

Sugar and Spice, All's Not So Nice
for Quinn Campaign

by Cathleen Quinn, Editor in Chief

A donut breakfast sponsored by student council presidential candidate Leo Torres backfired this morning when he was seen enjoying a re-creation of what's known in the school as the "Frankengirls."

"Sprinkle nipples," Maxine Chen, senior, said, holding up her phone. Displayed on her screen was the Instagram feed belonging to the second candidate for student council president, Angeline Quinn. At the top was a photograph taken before first period of donuts arranged to resemble the female form. "This is what Leo Torres thinks of girls at this school. How's this for something sweet, Torres: LGBTQIA+ Alliance and Girl Coders Club officially endorse Angeline Quinn for president."

When informed of the endorsements, Quinn was pleased but said bigger issues are in play.

"This is supposedly a new era for women, but still this 'boys will be boys' culture exists here at Acedia. As evidenced by the administration sitting on its thumbs and not reprimanding even a single person involved. Perhaps it has something to do with Friday night's game?"

Quinn's insinuation that no action had been taken against the male students clearly seen in the Frankengirls pastry photo because they are first-string football players has been gaining strength online.

With comments pouring in, Quinn's Instagram post has become a bastion of #MeToo versus male privilege.

Pigskin matters more than being in a woman's skin! #MoreThanOurParts

Playing with your food stopped being cute ten years ago, you sickos.

Can't these chicks—sorry, I mean, ladies—take it as it's meant: flattery, pure flattery.

Quick! Someone eat the evidence! I'm in for half a Goldberg!

Such comments continue to appear. For every outraged sentiment there is a matching one suggesting that not only are the girls in the school overreacting but that Quinn is pandering, taking advantage of the moment to secure votes.

"That's entirely wrong. This isn't just some Battle of the Exes game for me. How we're treated matters to me. How stereotypically sexist can you be? Dudes do math better? Ask Leo if he really thinks that's true."

Quinn appeared to want to say more on this but refused to elaborate. Instead she shifted direction. "To those who tell us to lighten up, I say, imagine how it feels to get up in class to write on the board or go to the bathroom and think: all these guys are checking out my [buttocks]. Sizing me up, choosing what donut hole makes the perfect boob. I know these guys, some are my friends, some are . . . were . . . more than that.

It's not just degrading but a total betrayal of those friendships. Two-faced. They should be ashamed of themselves, especially Leo."

Torres declined to comment, but one of the students involved in this morning's incident, who spoke only under the condition of anonymity, said, "Yeah, Torres laughed. Who wouldn't? It's a freakin' Franken-donut. But that's all he did. It was Marcus and the rest of us—them. I mean, them."

We reached out to Principal Schwartz, who gave us an unofficial statement declaring that while the administration is looking into the incident, it remains unclear as to what if any school rule had been violated. "That the donuts represented female students at the school is an assertion made solely by Ms. Quinn."

That may be the case, but the majority of those commenting on Quinn's post believe her, including a celebrity.

Evelyn Lee, *New York Times* bestselling author and founder of the Evelyn's Epic Everyday brand, wrote: "Well done. The only way one hears is if others speak."

Quinn is talking. The question is whether talk translates into votes.

13

When Cat Gets Lucky

Cat strode into the newsroom waving a check with a shamrock on the front. "How do you feel about pots of gold?"

Ravi spun his chair. "Pro, always."

"Luck o' the Harbor." Cat plunked the check down on the table. "Our new advertiser."

"Ah," Grady said. "Must have been all those scones I bought. Baristas there love me."

"Uh-huh." Cat raised an eyebrow. "Must have been."

"Then again . . ." Grady's tone lost its boasting edge. "Your article on the Franken-donuts got nice traction on Twitter. You really are doing a great job at drumming up interest in StuCo, Chief. Readers want a follow-up. Maybe something more multimedia this time?"

"No," Cat said.

"I'm ready," Grady said.

"Not yet."

His large eyeglasses fell down the bridge of his nose as he hung his head. "But, Cat . . . the big stories like the Frankengirls are the only ones anyone reads. If I don't write one, no one's going to know who I am to follow me."

"That's not why we're reporters. We cover the stories, we aren't the stories."

"Not according to my cousin." Grady showed Cat a picture of a tall, more fleshed-out version of himself next to Mark Wahlberg at a Boston movie premiere with *And that's news to you* written along the bottom. "His social's as big as what he's covering. People are following him for him."

Like Angeline. Who was the furthest thing from a reporter. "Your cousin runs social media for . . . what? Is that the local TV news? That's fluff. If that's your goal, you're in the wrong place."

"But there's no BuzzFeed equivalent here." Grady lowered his phone. "Don't you want more reach than this?"

Outside the newsroom, Angeline led a group of sophomore and junior girls down the hall. "Normally you'd have to submit a question like that via the appropriate form on my website," Angeline said. "But since you're my constituents and I know you're all fluttering your wings . . ."

That familiar prickling simmered under Cat's skin. Angeline was fluff, through and through. No wonder she weighed so little.

Accurate, fair, and thorough, Gramps always said. The core tenets of journalism. The opposite of everything Angeline did.

Clickbait headlines, incendiary posts, inflammatory trolls, Angeline as an influencer, anyone with an internet connection could post opinion as fact. The more salacious, the better. Truth had become secondary. With presidents gaslighting on Twitter and newspapers laying off thousands of journalists each year, real reporting was on the verge of extinction.

Someone had to care. Old-school journalism wasn't dead. Grady needed to see that.

"I want to run a story about the average Acedia voter in the next edition," Cat said. "You up for some student interviews?"

"On it, Chief." Grady saluted.

Cat fought the urge to roll her eyes. "Remember to record them, but ask permission first."

"On—"

"And remember, if you can't write worth a damn, the least you can do is spell the names right."

Gramps always said that too.

This time, Grady silently saluted and bolted out of the newsroom.

Instantly Cat second-guessed her decision. "Tell me I'm not creating a monster?"

"Creating, no. Feeding, on the other hand . . ." Ravi flashed a smile, and his lips formed a heart shape that Cat hadn't noticed before. "No shame in going after what you want, is there?"

An unfamiliar flutter in Cat's chest made her turn to the accounting ledger.

"I sure hope not because . . ." Ravi came up beside her, spreading out four freshly printed pages. "I've got my favorite, but you go first." Each was a different spin on the front page of the last *Red and Blue*. "I played with the fonts and sizes but also the white space."

Cat took in the changes. "And the column width." She pointed to one on the end. "Makes this one seem . . . bolder."

An eager head bob from Ravi. "Modern without being edgy. But the one next to it . . ."

"Razor-sharp," Cat said.

"A real risk, that one. So different from the current look."

Cat barely managed a nod, overwhelmed that Ravi had become so invested.

He misinterpreted and dialed back his enthusiasm. "Not that there's anything wrong with our current layout. These were just some ideas. I should get started on designing that new Luck o' the Harbor ad anyway." He pushed a lightness into his tone. "Question is, are leprechauns cheesy or retro? Never can tell with the kids these days . . ."

"Wait." The hairs on Ravi's arm tickled Cat as he reached for the pages, and goose bumps erupted despite the newsroom being as hot as an Arizona desert. "I, uh, haven't chosen my favorite."

"You have one?"

"Not exactly," she said, and his face fell. "The problem is, I have more than one. These are really good, Ravi. It's nice to have you here."

His hand was no longer gathering the printouts, but his arm had yet to move away from hers.

"To be honest . . ." Cat spoke slowly, unaccustomed to revealing any cracks in her exterior. "I was worried about going after Fit to Print without Stavros and Jen. Even with the student council election suddenly hot, nabbing the win is going to take every spare moment I have. But I feel so much better knowing you care about *The Red and Blue* as much as I do."

"No one cares about this as much as you, Cat."

Ravi shifted to the side, and Cat felt a coolness replace the warmth of his skin.

"Right then." She straightened her spine. "This one." She pointed to the modern but not too edgy redesign.

"You made a good choice," Ravi said.

Cat nodded, feeling like she had and she hadn't.

The locker room buzzed with chatter.

Cat traded her khaki skirt and black long-sleeve for gray knit shorts and a red Acedia athletic tee. Someone had set out vases with smelly sticks atop the three rows of lockers but hadn't coordinated the scents, and the place smelled like a grapefruit pine forest dipped in sugar cookies.

She rested her foot on the wood bench in front of her, just down from Sonya and Riley.

"Two hundred and fifty dollars a ticket?" Riley waved a set of stapled pages. "Perhaps my stellar math score on the SATs needs adjusting, because I can't even calculate something as basic as this. How could last year's student council have mismanaged funds so spectacularly that prom's going to cost as much as my last pair of jeans?"

"*That* we'll tackle later." Sonya brushed back her braids and removed the pages from Riley's hand.

Riley picked up a clear reusable bottle with fluorescent green liquid inside and turned to Cat. "Is this true?"

"Got me." Cat continued tying her sneaker. "Angeline's your prom expert."

"But isn't this yours?" Riley said.

Sonya waited for Cat to finish tying and then handed her the pages they'd been reading.

Council Needs Counsling: Send in the Shrinks, Stat!

Cat frowned at the glaring typo and scanned the rest of the 8 ½" x 11" sheet of paper, sloppily laid out in two columns, probably using Microsoft Word, with a heading that read, *The Shrieking Violet*.

"What is this?" Cat said.

Riley sipped her drink, which added a minty algae smell to the already nauseating room. "Isn't it, like, a special edition or something?"

"Of *my* paper?" Cat said. "Yeah, no." She leaned against the locker and skimmed the top story.

> *Two hundred and fifty smackers for prom?*
> *Gasp with me, Acedia!*
> *We hate to be the one to light a fuse with our*
> *breaking news (oh, who are we kidding, we love it!),*
> *but sources say last year's student council embizlled*
> *funds—your funds—and now we'll have nary a penny*
> *leftover for a single apple p,ie ball!*

Sources? Like who? Cat gritted her teeth and moved on to the next story.

Saving Cows, Sacrificing Guinny Pigs

> *When the rumors fly, we here at* The Shrieking
> Violet *make it our mission to catch! Word in the*
> *halls is that the whole vegan bacon fiasco comes from*
> *a certain female teacher trying to grease her way*
> *into early retirement on the Cape with an artisanal*
> *"beets not beasts" product line.*
> *"Us kids at Acedia are her guinea pigs," our*
> *mystery (even to us!) source said. "Which, like, goes*
> *against her whole 'save the cows' thing, doesn't it?"*
> *However many cows may be saved by eating vegan*
> *bacon aside, the decision of what to consume and when*
> *must remain an individual choice, many students*
> *believe, same as our student council presidential*
> *hopeful Leo Torres.*

Cows.
Cows.

"Bacon comes from pigs!" Cat tossed back the first page and read the second.

Hear Us: A Shrieking Violet Editorial

As if this whole thing weren't an editorial?

Prom, bacon, what's next?
The whispers tickling our ears tell of a planned live-streamed streaking event at homecoming that has the administration in hush-hush consideration of canceling the whole shindig.
Which makes us think . . .
Hmm . . . maybe we shouldn't say.
But maybe we *could* say . . .
If you pinky-swear promise to keep it just between us?
You do?
Okay then.
Go.
We mean now. Bend those little pinkies, Acedia!
Good job.
Now then, in a race where one candidate's saying "don't" and one's all about the "do," who do you believe will save homecoming?
The one with the better hair?
Us too.
Yes, yes, we'd all rather be lounging around, hanging upside down in our trees, but sometimes you gotta get on those long-clawed foots and stand! Tip for ya, dearies, the hard thing about doing nothing's that you never know when you're done. So take it from us and do SOMETHING.

Rise up, Sloths!

Student council is yours because your students.
You've got two things to do this semester: read The
Shrieking Violet *and vote (for Leo!)!!!!!!!!!!!!!!!!!!*
!!!!!!!!!!!!!!

One, two, three, four . . . twenty-nine. *Twenty-nine exclamation points?*

Cat's pulse nearly exploded out of her temples. She flipped through the stapled pages. No name. "Where did you get this?"

Riley shrugged and passed her bottle to Sonya, whose nose scrunched upon smelling it.

"You have to know where you got this," Cat said. "It didn't just materialize out of thin air."

"Oh, I see," Riley said, propping her phone in her lap.

"See what?"

"Nothing." Riley leaned toward Sonya and whispered, "Attitude. Angeline's totally right."

Cat gripped the edges of the . . . the . . . what the hell was this? "Riley . . . can you . . ." Cat forced a breath. "Would you mind thinking about where this came from?"

"Stacks in the lunchroom. Didn't you see?"

"I was in the newsroom."

Riley used her phone's camera app as a mirror as she wound her hair into a messy topknot. "Of course, all alone."

"I wasn't alone. Ravi was there."

"Ravi?" Riley's eyes widened. "The artsy dude? Angeline didn't say anything about a Mr. Cat. About time. Plus he's pretty cute in a dorky camp counselor way."

Sonya frowned at Riley.

"He's not dorky," Cat said.

"Way to defend your man," Riley said.

"He's not my man," Cat said quickly. "There's no Mr. Cat." *Did she actually say "Mr. Cat"?* "Lunchroom, that's where this was?"

The bell rang, and Riley and Sonya finished stowing their clothes and bags. Cat hung back and pulled her phone out of her locker.

Cat: Have you seen The Shrieking Violet?

Grady: Seen and read. Hilarious.

Cat: It's in the lunchroom?

Grady: Lunchroom, bathroom, locker room, hallway, where u been? Insta and Snap too. My bud texted me a pic before I snagged my own.

Grady: They're eating it up. This is the kind of newspaper we should be doing, Chief.

This? This printed-on-a-home-printer, photocopied, error-riddled . . . *thing.*

Cat: If you think this is a newspaper, you haven't been paying attention.

Cat shoved her phone in her locker and slammed the door shut.

Rumors, false statements, unnamed sources, inflammatory statements. This was no newspaper. This wasn't journalism. It was such a mockery of everything Cat had ever been taught. And students were devouring it? Snapping photos and sharing it on Instagram?

No freakin' way.

She crumpled *The Shrieking Violet*.

Those were *her* readers. She'd worked hard to get them. And they liked her paper. The town . . . the advertisers liked her paper.

But how could those same readers like this?

No, no, no, no, no, no. This wasn't just inflammatory, it was outright lies. Something done by Baked Baker or Tad Marcus or someone selfish enough to not care about what they said and who it hurt. She wouldn't let them. She'd find out who was responsible and have them stopped under the school honor code. Lying had strict consequences—it said so right in the student handbook.

Cat flung the wrinkled ball into the trash and marched past the row of lockers.

She paused inside the entrance to the gym and hurried back into the locker room. She pulled the pages out of the garbage and set them on the bench to be recycled later. *She* had standards.

14

When Angeline Becomes an App

Angeline's arm throbbed from holding her phone at such an awkward angle. But if she didn't, all her viewers would see she was filming alongside the outdoor track behind the school rather than in her room with her LED light wand that gave her videos their softer vibe.

"Hey, hey, that's all for today, my angels!" She ignored the bored look on Maxine's face. With all the time Angeline had been spending on the election, multitasking like this was the only option. "So the key fly-aways are to never mix a flowered print with plaid, listen when your BFF says you've been spending all your time locking lips with that new hottie, and never try to remove a pea from your little brother's nostril without wearing a full hazard suit. Until next time, flutter your wings, my angels!"

Maxine hopped up from the grass alongside the red track lane, where she'd been impatiently stretching her hamstrings. "Peas, Ang, really?"

"I barely have time for an exfoliating mask, let alone sifting through questions for the best ones." Angeline shoved her phone in the band around her upper arm and pushed off on the balls of

132

her feet. "Which that BFF one is. Do you need me to remind you of the whole 'Maxana' thing?"

Maxine sighed and fell in step beside Angeline. "I should have followed Lana to San Fran when her family moved. I miss her. I miss dating. I miss surfing. I miss doing *anything* other than working on your voting app."

"Yeah, nice try, but I know for a fact you're looking for a way to market it."

The blue tips at the end of Maxine's ponytail grazed her neck as the two of them picked up speed. "I'm expecting connections from that boot camp. Do you really think your mom would stop you from going?"

Angeline shrugged. Probably not.

She struck the ground, digging in deeper.

But that was no longer her motivation for winning.

She rounded the curve.

Beating Leo was.

Leo and Tad and donuts and . . . *he didn't even like sweets!*

She focused on her breathing and her heart hammering in her chest, and she drove her calves down and her knees up, picking up speed. She'd completed a full lap before she realized Maxine was no longer at her side.

"Sorry," Angeline said, when she met back up with her.

"So long as you got it out of your system." Maxine adjusted the wave pendant on her necklace as they started running again at a more sustainable pace. "Speaking of systems, your peer jury is polling well. Emmie thought it might be harder for the school to adopt than her original idea, not that you shouldn't keep pushing for it."

"Since when are you and Emmie Hayes friends?"

"We aren't really. Unlike her and your sister. I trust you've seen?" Maxine said, and Angeline nodded. "Anyway, Emmie came to me before the primary. Wanted to collaborate on a digital way for students to share their concerns with student council."

"Seriously?" Angeline jutted her chin toward the football field adjacent to the track, and she and Maxine crossed the manicured lawn to reach it. "Did you come up with something for her?"

"Um, hello, loyalty?"

"But you could. Come up with something."

Maxine snorted. "Please."

"Acedia Ask an Angel app, here we come." Angeline grinned. "I so love a good branding opportunity."

"For full functionality, time's tight," Maxine said. "Even for me."

"No worries. Appearances speak louder than reality."

They entered through the open metal gate of the football field and wordlessly headed for the bleachers, pounding the metal treads in unison to reach the top, where Maxine bent over, hands on her knees, to catch her breath. Angeline inhaled the scent of newly cut grass and looked out on the bright white stripes lining the field and the larger-than-life ACEDIA in block letters on both ends. She pulled out her phone, checking to make sure her video had uploaded properly before hitting the rounds of Instagram, Snap, and Twitter, which was where she saw it.

Keep Your Friends Close . . . Unless They're These Three!

She was tagged in a tweet. She clicked on the link, which took her to a new online issue of *The Shrieking Violet*.

Good leaders know they're only as smart as those in their inner circle. While it hasn't always worked in TSwift's favor, she was totally right about the power of a squad!

Fortunately for you, my Acedia pretties, Leo Torres shed a hundred-and-something-pound, ombre-haired parasite at the end of the summer, and such a smart move makes our lion the top dog in this cat fight. (Achievement unlocked! Four mammal animals in one sentence!)

And then there's Angeline Quinn, who has not a circle but a square. First off is Sonya Robins, who spends all her free time impersonating a pretzel. They say inversions are good for the brain, but hard to advise well when you're lightheaded from one too many downward dogs. Next up, is RILEY DONOVAN. RILEY is super SMILEY in her all-caps Insta, with 😎 and 😏 but nary a smidge of 🧠.
🥺

Which brings us to Maxine Chen. As attendees and envies of #LastSummerBlastOnTheCliffs know, BFF Maxie has the bank to roll out Quinn in the style her campaign doesn't want us to get accustomed to. Hmm . . . curious. Even curiouser? Is it any coinky dink that Chen's Girl Coders Club finally got programmed at the same time as sources say the administration got a hot tub (psst! parents in tech!)? Which was right before Quinn pushed a more restrictive platform, assuring those with the itch to club have fewer options? Collusion?! Conspiracy?! Overload of mixed metaphors?!!? Is this the cloth from which we sloths are made? Only you can decide, dear reader.

Keep visiting this site and get your SHRIEK on.

P.S. How's about we show that #LastSummerBlastOnTheCliffs what a real soiree looks like? #LightUpEggshell beach bonfire tonight!

"Oh my God," Angeline said.

Maxine, who'd been reading over Angeline's shoulder, pivoted to face her. "That secretary *bought* our old hot tub. She's got a bad back!"

"And Riley's the first to shout that her GPA lands her in the top ten percent."

"That thing will be eating its words when I'm running Sonya's IPO for her yoga franchise one day."

Angeline and Maxine fluttered their wings, their version of a fist bump.

"And parasite?" Angeline said. "Seriously? Which isn't a mammal, by the way. Besides, if anyone was riding anyone, it was Leo." Angeline watched as Maxine's eyes widened. "Oh, you know what I mean."

"It's not you." Maxine grabbed Angeline by the shoulders and spun her around. "It's that."

Taped to the bench of the top row of bleachers, as far as Angeline could see, were printouts. They alternated in a pattern of three around the entire oval of the football field.

"Now snap a pic and steal that shrieking thunder," Maxine said.

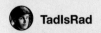 **TadIsRad**

They're back!!!! And who knew? Frankengirls like football!

Tad Marcus @TadIsRad • 10m
#Frankengirls in da house! Hit my Snap!

BrosAndBros @brosandbros • 5m
Replying to @TadIsRad
Now that's my OTP.

```
          _
       ( (^) )
       ( ( ' ) )
       (\ 0 /)          _  _
       -'-'-          ;(TIIIII|()
                      (_)___/_/
      / (  Y  ) \
      \\)   (//
       /      \
      /
       \ | /
      / | \
       \ | /
      / Y \
```

The Red and Blue Newspaper @TheRedandBlueAcedia • 3m
Active investigation under way regarding the reappearance of
photographs of what have been dubbed "Frankengirls." Reports
say images were taped to bleachers at Acedia's football field.
Follow for updates TK.

Grady: You forgot the hashtag.

Cat: I didn't forget. It's demeaning.

Grady: It's how people find us.

Grady: The Shrieking Violet's using it.

Cat: What? They printed another paper?

Grady: Gone digital. shriekingvioletacedia.com @shriekingvioletacedia, twitter and insta, no snap yet.

Grady: They just put out a breaking news alert that says the photos were planted by your sister.

Cat: What? By Angeline? She only discovered them.

Grady: Well, according to SV: "Sources say there's a chance a popular YouTube micro influencer's more involved than most think."

Cat: How unequivocal.

Grady: You think?

Cat: Joke.

Grady: ha

Cat: This isn't funny.

Grady: 😖

Grady: Need help with the story, Chief?

Cat: Yes.

Grady: 🏺

Cat: Stand by to post.

Grady: Oh

Grady: 👍

15

When Cat Goes Social

Notebook in hand, Cat pushed open the door to Frank's Pizza. The smell of yeast and a wood fire filled the space, leaving barely enough room for the two plastic tables and three chairs. A cracked fourth rested in the corner, home to a potted basil plant.

She ordered a plain cheese slice, her mouth already salivating. The homemade tomato sauce and crispy crust that made one believe in magic would have kept this place in business even if it weren't directly across from the high school. Which was why Cat was here.

She kept an eye on the likes on *The Red and Blue* tweet advertising her "to come" article as she waited. So far, those little hearts had barely ticked up. Unlike the ones on *The Shrieking Violet*'s absurd claim about Angeline.

How did anyone accomplish anything while logged in to social media?

Cat shoved her phone into the pocket of her skirt as the owner, who personally brought out every order, appeared.

Bald head, deep bronze tan, Frank carried her slice and three pizza boxes out of the kitchen. He set the pies on the counter and handed her a paper plate striped in the green, white, and red of the Italian flag.

"One plain," he said.

Cat nodded her thanks. Steam escaped the bubbling mozzarella and parmesan, and she had to force herself to let it cool. She was here for something more important. "There was an incident at Acedia. I'm not sure if you've heard—"

"Part of me wishes I hadn't." Frank stacked napkins and hot pepper packets on top of the pizza boxes. "One of my kids did that, I'd lock 'em up myself. Find out who did it yet?"

"Not yet, which is why I'm here. I'm writing an article for the school paper, and I noticed that your security camera is aimed directly at the football field. I was hoping I could take a look at your footage, if you still have it?"

"Smart thinking, but you're outta luck. Camera's just for show. Though maybe with all this nasty business going on there, it shouldn't be."

Disappointment weighed down Cat's limbs. Another dead end. If only Schwartz would have let her have just one of the Frankengirl pictures she could have at least dusted for prints.

She nodded politely and picked up her pizza just as a guy with fair skin and short brown hair opened the door.

"Just three deliveries?" he asked, reaching for the boxes.

"Devon!" Frank jutted his calloused finger at the kid's red sweatshirt. "You know we switched uniforms last month."

"New one washes out my complexion, Frank."

"Oh, really?" Frank covered his heart with his hand. "I'm so sorry. There's an easy fix for that."

"Yeah, yeah, unemployment line," the kid grumbled, which

caused Frank to launch into what sounded like a not-uncommon lecture.

Outside, Cat sunk her teeth into her slice, willing some of its magic to rub off on her.

Cat arrived home just in time to see Angeline coming out of their bedroom with her long hair in tight curls, wearing dark jeans, a white silk tank, and gladiator sandals. She had a cashmere blanket draped over her arm.

"Let me guess," Cat said, "big binge-watch planned?"

"Streaming's all yours tonight. I'm off to light up Eggshell."

"You really think there'll be a bonfire? Wouldn't call *The Shrieking Violet* the most reliable news source."

"Haven't you seen? Hashtag's got more followers than your newspaper." Angeline reached for the car keys in Cat's hand. "Can I?"

Cat clenched her fist around them. "And you're going? After everything it said about you?"

"Exactly why I have to go." Angeline's brow knitted. "And why you should too."

"Yeah, no, haven't quite perfected my keg stand. Maybe another time." Cat gave her the keys and started for the kitchen.

Angeline blocked her. "You know what speaks louder than words? Hashtags. You need to be seen." She grabbed her elbow, and Cat nearly tripped over her own feet as Angeline yanked her down the hall and into their room. "Just make an appearance." Hangers screeched as Angeline shoved one after another in her closet. "Show this shrieking farce you're not afraid of it. And anything with the election happens, you'll be there to report on it, firsthand."

Right. *That* was why Angeline wanted her to go so badly. But as

Angeline tossed her a light pink sweater and a pair of black jeans, Cat realized something. "You think they'll be there? *The Shrieking Violet*?"

"For sure." Angeline bit her bottom lip and traded the sweater for a cut-out-shoulder tee.

If her sister was right, Cat could use the party to narrow down her list of *Shrieking Violet* suspects. She'd ranked the biggest pranksters in order of most likely to least likely, but none seemed like the right fit. Gluing fake bloody fingers to lockers on Halloween and blocking the hallways with piles of desks weren't obvious lead-ins to this. Her best suspects didn't even go to the school anymore. *The Shrieking Violet* was on par with last year's seniors who'd pulled off the Schwartz/Slothy hoax or whoever had orchestrated the spirit week cupcake stunt. This #LightUpEggshell might be her best chance at a little bit of magic.

Angeline settled on a black tank with a short line of fringe along the hem. "You know who else might be there?"

"Who?" Cat gave in and changed into the top.

"Lots and lots of prom date potential."

"Like I have any interest in lots of prom date potential."

Angeline adjusted a clump of fringe. "Shame, because I'm pretty sure there's a bit of interest in you. Might try living a little, Cat in the Hat."

She'd said the same thing freshman year before the only other high school party Cat had gone to, incidentally also because Angeline had forced her. This time, Cat would be better prepared. She followed Angeline out the door, but not before grabbing her backpack with her computer inside.

The night sky flashed with a burst of red, triggering whoops and cheers down the beach. Cat trudged through sand still damp from the receding high tide, trying to note everyone who was here, but it was a lost cause—because who was here *was* everyone. As she watched a group of three guys and two girls—one of whom she was pretty sure was Maxine—in wetsuits paddle out for an ill-thought-out night surf, she had to concede that no one wanted to talk to *The Red and Blue*. Not during #LightUpEggshell, which half the school was achieving via sparklers, bonfires, or beer.

All three surrounded Angeline as she addressed a group of girls just beyond the yellow flames of the bonfire.

"Come listen," Riley said, gesturing for Cat to follow. As they walked toward Angeline, Riley handed Cat a red plastic cup. "I'm conducting a focus group. It's spiked green juice. Healthy *and* fun." When Cat hesitated, Riley said, "It won't kill you. At least I don't think . . ." Then under her breath, "Show that stupid *Shrieking Violet* I'm more than an Instagram all-caps smiley face."

Anticipation shone in Riley's blue eyes, and the unexpected glimpse into her need for approval threw Cat. She pretended to sip what smelled like seaweed coated in bubble gum, faked an "Mmm," and watched as Riley's demeanor shifted back to its usual narcissistic conceit.

The crowd around Angeline had doubled, and Cat stood on a rock to get a better view of her sister.

"It's becoming clear that the school can't get to the bottom of this," Angeline said, raising her voice to be heard over the crash of the ocean behind her. Cat pressed record on the app on her phone. "We need a voice. The peer jury system is part of the solution, but we need to be heard in the moment. After I'm elected, my Acedia Ask an Angel app will go live. Student council will be open to you twenty-four/seven. *I* will be open to you twenty-four/seven."

Angeline's spell left the girls in front of her enraptured. She posed for selfies and handed out more samples, plugging an Ask an Angel giveaway that'd go into effect when she racked up a hundred more subscribers.

Cat dumped Riley's drink and moved down the beach to where Leo sat in front of one of the smaller fire pits encircled by rocks, sounding very much like his mom's son, which Cat knew he'd hate to hear.

"With all due respect," Leo said, "my opponent, whom I hold in minimum high regard, is making counterproductive claims for how to handle this unfortunate incident. I won't go so far as to say she's disingenuous, but she's certainly found a way to use what these poor young ladies are going through in every aspect of her campaign platform. Almost as if it were designed that way. Ultimately it will be the voters who interpret these actions."

Leo's insinuation that Angeline bore responsibility for the Frankengirls might not have been clear to all the drunken, sparkler-twirling students of Acedia, but surely some would pick up on him furthering *The Shrieking Violet*'s claim.

Cat stopped the recorder and sighed at the pathetic "he said, she said" that this campaign had become. She searched for a spot by one of the less populated fire pits where she could work on her article and wait for Angeline. But before pulling out her laptop, an invisible force made her check Twitter.

Someone had retweeted her post about her upcoming story!

Not someone . . . Ask an Angel. The likes on Angeline's retweet had already surpassed those on the original *Red and Blue* tweet. And they kept on coming.

They went beyond students at Acedia. Though rationally it made sense, a twinge of surprise came at seeing the like from Evelyn's Epic Everyday. There were also a few from some feminist organizations, both local to Boston and beyond.

The quoted retweet had Angeline prefacing *The Red and Blue*'s post with: *Look for this article, my angels, for yours truly has a lot to say!*

When didn't she? She talked. People listened.

Another heart.

And another.

Angeline's followers dwarfed those of *The Red and Blue*, and once again Angeline was one-upping Cat, promoting herself more than Cat's article. Same as both she and Leo had just done in their speeches; they were advancing their campaigns at the expense of real commentary on the Frankengirls.

Cat needed a quote that would put this whole thing into context and prevent Leo and Angeline's shiny words and dazzling smiles from spinning this for their own agendas.

As Cat retrieved her backpack, a streak of light blinded her.

"You're it," Natalie screamed, waving a flashlight in the air.

"With pleasure!" was followed by a B movie maniacal laugh that Cat recognized. "Revenge will be mine."

Cat watched Ravi rise from a crouched position behind a group of freshmen on the opposite side of her fire pit. Natalie passed off the flashlight, and, slowly, three or four others joined, emerging from their various hiding spots along the beach.

"Ninety seconds," Natalie said before dashing off.

Ravi turned his back while his friends dispersed. He grinned at Cat, and the light from the fire picked up the auburn-colored streaks in his hair. She felt herself relax and tense at the same time.

"Flashlight tag," Ravi said. "Still time to play."

"Oh, thanks, but I've got a deadline."

"Ten thousand hours, right? Go for it, Cat."

Angeline would have made a joke or scoffed at Cat for working at a party, if she paid her any attention at all. But Ravi acted like it was the most normal thing in the world to bring a computer to a beach bonfire, which she suddenly realized it wasn't. She strained in the darkness to follow Ravi's friends as they disappeared behind rocks and fire pits and paddleboards. Part of her wanted to hide right along with them. See what it felt like to be found.

"Another time, maybe?" she said.

"Definitely." He smiled, and this time, Cat didn't just notice that heart shape—she was looking for it.

Back at home, Cat put a pillow over her head to drown out Angeline, who was video chatting with Maxine. A wink, half wink, toothy grin, their inane debate over which smiley face emoji to put beside Angeline's name in the voting app made Cat long for the days when she had her own room. She reached for her book on female journalists before remembering she'd let Emmie borrow it.

Before she overthought it, Cat grabbed her phone and sent Emmie a text.

> **Cat:** Read any biographies yet?

Emmie immediately started writing back.

> **Emmie:** Nellie Bly's. What a total badass. After reporting on mental institutions and zoo cruelty, she travels the world alone? Just to prove a woman can do it?

> **Cat:** 72 days, 6 minutes, just like Jules Verne's character.

> **Emmie:** Except she was real. Whose story should I read next?

Cat: Alice Allison Dunnigan. First black female correspondent to get White House credentials. President Eisenhower was so afraid of her tough questions that he avoided calling on her.

Emmie: Putting my bookmark in now. What are you doing? Studying?

As Angeline made her case for a monocle emoji, Cat replied.

Cat: Writing an article about the Frankengirls.

Emmie: Such a shame. Just like the candidates scooping up their cause and making it their own. Even if Angeline's in them, she's taking it too far.

Cat: Can I quote you on that?

Emmie: If you think it'll help. I still believe in the election. At least I want to.

Cat: I know. My sister makes everything about herself.

Emmie: And how does that make you feel?

Cat: Spectacular 😉.

Emmie: Not fun to talk about, totally get it.

Cat: It's just how it is. How it's always been.

Emmie: Makes me feel better that my dads decided I'd be an only child . . .

Cat: I can relate.

16

When Angeline Gets into a Scrap (or Two)

Suggestions, bitches!

A flowered tissue box with the words scrawled in permanent marker hung on the double doors to the cafeteria.

Leo's response to Angeline's Ask an Angel app. A campaign move. Just like the four dozen slices from Frank's, all individually wrapped, stamped with "sample, not for sale" and his smiling face, that he'd handed out while standing on a chair in the cafeteria. Entirely indicative of his own brand, which, near as Angeline could tell, was mocking hers.

She knew it.

Could see what he was doing.

And why.

It didn't make it feel like any less of a slap in the face.

Same as that last article of Cat's.

She separated the braided straps of her tote bag (*$99 with the 15 percent off Ask an Angel code!*) and plunged her hand inside. She lifted the issues of *The Red and Blue* she'd been reading. What was up with Cat including that quote from Emmie? *Scooping up the*

Frankengirls cause and making it their own? Angeline was giving them—*she was giving everyone*—a voice. Unlike Leo.

Angeline's fingers curled around her phone. She unlocked and swiped to Instagram. Her last post had garnered her most follower engagement ever. *See? A voice.* People were touting her as an advocate for young women with her #MoreThanOurParts. Which honestly had never really been her brand.

She stiffened at the smiley face from tone-deaf Botox Wife and moved on to the rest of the comments. The female empowerment tags ran deep. If she kept this up, she could expand her base.

Angeline held up her phone to take a picture of Leo's "suggestions box." That "bitches" might have been plural, but it felt squared directly at her.

On the way to her locker, Angeline passed three *Finding Nemo* stuffies dangling from the ceiling, each being strangled by a straw. Her supporters' response to Leo's campaign platform. She smiled wide, keeping an eye on her comments until she heard two girls deep in conversation outside Ms. Lute's classroom.

"I can't afford two hundred and fifty for prom," one of them said.

"Right? Ridic. Guess we better rise up."

"Vote for Leo, then?"

"He does have a mom in politics. And that good hair. Seems like the right choice?"

What? Angeline whirled around, but the girls had already disappeared into the classroom. That was all *rumor* printed in *The Shrieking Violet*. And suddenly Angeline disliked the rival paper as much as Cat.

She turned back around and collided with someone's chest.

Sammy.

Her breath caught in her throat. Sammy was less stocky than

150

his brother, but the buzzed sides of his dark hair matched Leo's. He trailed his hand through the long pieces on top that fell toward his ears as he fixed his brown eyes on Angeline. More intense than Leo's in color and attitude.

"Sorry," she said.

He bit down on his bottom lip and sidestepped around her.

She shifted to block him. "So, taking world history like we talked about? Did you get Mr. Monte—"

"Nice, right?" Sammy gestured down the hall to the tissue box. "Tad's a kick-ass campaign manager."

Her relief that it had been Tad's idea matched her anger at Leo for allowing it.

She tried to focus on this boy in front of her wearing an ill-fitting coat of bravado. "Listen, Sammy. What happened with me and Leo doesn't have to affect us."

Sammy sniffed. "You smell that?"

She wrinkled her nose. "No. Should I?"

"Guess it's the same way smokers don't smell tobacco anymore. Hard to smell bullshit when you're always knee-deep in it." Sammy strutted off without a glance back.

This wasn't the Sammy who reenacted *SNL* and did stand-up routines in eighth grade. She and Leo had sat in the audience in place of his parents, giving him a standing ovation, Leo shouting "¡Felicitaciones!" the way their dad would have when Sammy won the talent competition.

And now he thought she was a bitch.

"Nice move, Ang."

Leo's voice made the hairs on her arms stand up. He circled in front of her wearing that sweatshirt she'd been trying to get him to replace for years.

"I just ran into him. I wasn't looking for him." As if she didn't have a right to. She'd rip into Maxine or Sonya or Riley if they sounded as meek as she did. Would tell her Ask an Angel viewer to stand up for herself. She squared her shoulders.

"Good, and keep it that way, but that's not what I meant." Leo's tone was flippant, but his eyes looked the same as always. *How can that be?* "I was talking about the Frankengirls. Don't know why I'm surprised; you know how to make things explode. Or is it implode?"

"My campaign has every right to address this injustice."

"Again, not what I meant. Address is one thing. Invent, an entirely different one."

Confusion jumbled Angeline's thoughts. "Wait, you really think I did this?"

"If the torso fits."

"Those are my friends in those pictures."

"Hence your abundance of photos to choose from."

"Nice try, Leo. I pride myself on being flexible, but that's way too low for me."

"You forget, I know you."

That snide look on his face seemed as uncharacteristic as the angry one on Sammy's. Yet instead of it making her sad, it ignited something inside her veins, and the blood that rushed through screamed *enough*. What she did to Leo didn't define her. No matter how much he wanted it to.

"You know what I think?" she said. "This reeks of Tad Marcus and the rest of those guys who are suddenly attached to your hip. And instead of owning up to it and apologizing, they're keeping it going. For fun, for this ridiculous campaign of yours, because they think they can get away with it. And you're following so closely you're about to be crushed by their heels."

The muscles in Leo's jaw tightened.

"You want to get back at me, Leo? Fine, whatever, run against me—win, if you can. But just leave everyone else out of it, okay? Enough with the photos."

"It's not me and—"

"Save it." Angeline clutched the straps of her bag so hard that her claddagh ring dug into her skin. "Whatever you want to think, hurting you was never my goal."

"I didn't think it was."

"Then why—"

He jammed his hands into his pockets. "Because barreling toward your goal eclipses everything else. I'm tired of being roadkill."

Angeline leaned in. "It was one mistake, Leo. *One*. You may be sick of being roadkill, but the truth is, only one of those tire treads belongs to me."

17

When Cat's Weekend's Jam-Packed

"Leo's going to abolish finals? Leo's going to bring in a Food Network chef for lunch menu consultation? Leo's a descendant of George Washington and a third-generation twice-removed cousin of Jennifer Lawrence? *Three sources, people! Three named sources!*"

On the couch in their living room, Cat read *The Shrieking Violet* to her grandfather, her temper at a rolling boil. "How is anyone believing this?"

And preferring it to her own?

"I think you may be missing that this is a prime example of a little-known technique called satire." He gingerly extracted the tablet from her tense fingers. "Let's keep this in one piece. I've got me a date with an away game tonight. And I'd rather not borrow your sister's computer since that comes with strings of agreeing to join some mixer they call a dating app."

"Wow, she's always working it, isn't she?"

"Your sister's intentions come from the right place even if the execution needs jiggering. Your grams was the same way."

Cat looked dubious.

"Ah, you remember her with hair always curled and feet always in heels when she was actually a woman who would hide my passport in between cake pans to stop me from going on foreign assignments."

Cat smiled. "She wanted to keep you safe. It's actually kind of sweet in a warped way."

"Same as your sister."

"Uh-huh, sure."

Tell that to the "Fraidy Cat" moniker that had stuck through most of fourth grade. By the time the kids had found a new bull's-eye, Angeline had disappeared into her friends. Cat had clung to her own from fifth until the jokes she missed and the homework they had and the recess she didn't share began to put distance between them.

Cat threw herself into following in her grandfather's footsteps, reading every one of his articles, begging him to tell her stories, flipping through that passport and learning about all the places he'd been, imagining going to them herself. She threw herself into being what her sister wasn't: focused on something other than herself.

Not to mention proving her father wrong. Her dreams would become her reality.

"You trust me, Cathleen?" Gramps asked.

"More than anyone, you know that."

"Then listen when I say that life needs lightness as much as it needs the truth. A balance."

Cat tried to focus on him, but all she could see was the new ad at the bottom of *The Shrieking Violet*'s page: Luck o' the Harbor. The first of what had become a handful of new advertisers for Cat. Ones she was going to lose if things kept going like this. Because no one was reading this thing as satire; they were swallowing it whole. She half expected *The Shrieking Violet* to edge her out for the Fit to Print award.

On the coffee table in front her, her phone buzzed. Seeing Ravi's name, she swiped and immediately began typing.

Cat: Everything okay with the print run?

Ravi: 👍 I double-checked.

Cat smiled, feeling a surge of the camaraderie she'd had last year. She wrote back: Thanks. See you Monday. Then she shut off all the notifications on her phone and got back to work.

The next day, Cat burst out of her apartment building, her mind still consumed with *The Shrieking Violet*. She tromped down Frontage Street, her heels striking the sidewalk with its inlay of seashells. Ravi had said he worked most Saturdays. Maybe together they could figure out a plan.

Though the day checked a near equal number of boxes between the end of August and the beginning of October, the weather clung to summer. She headed toward the frozen yogurt shop, opening her messages to see if Ravi could meet her on a break. That's when she noticed the text he'd sent the previous day.

Ravi: Monday or . . . tomorrow? Few of us heading into Boston for an exhibit on editorial cartoons at the BPL. Interested?

Her feet cemented to the sidewalk. He'd invited her to hang out with him and his friends at the Boston Public Library. He'd tried again, just like he said he would after her no to flashlight tag.

And she hadn't even responded. She'd been so obsessed with *The Shrieking Violet* that she'd left her notifications off. Missing his text stung more than she'd have expected.

Maybe they hadn't left yet. Maybe she could meet them at the train station. She started typing:

> BPL sounds fun.

She hit backspace.

> BPL sounds fu

> BPL sounds f

> BPL

> BPL?

> BPL? What time train?

> BPL? What time

> BPL? BPL? BPL? BPL?

Crap. She erased everything and instead logged in to *The Red and Blue*'s Instagram account. She clicked on Ravi's profile—on Ravi, smiling, on the steps of the Boston Public Library. He wore his green cargo shorts and carried his same sketchbook. His caption read: "'Editorial cartoons move the discussion forward.' From stellar exhibit at BPL. Swipe for more."

So she swiped. There were three photos of editorial cartoons on the wall inside the library. The last photo was back outside: Ravi surrounded by his friends, including Natalie, dressed like an urban street musician.

If Cat were there, would she be calling her Kate?

But Cat wasn't there.

She clicked out to the overview of Ravi's feed. A mosaic of tiny squares, each filled with images of art, of Ravi with his art, of Ravi with his friends, siblings, parents. The most important things in his life for the past few months, maybe years?

If Cat had an Instagram account, how many squares would she have? And what would be inside them? Would they represent the life she had or the one she wanted? Which Cat had never before felt might not be the same thing.

She was no longer hungry.

As she turned to head home, she glanced through the window of the frozen yogurt shop. Despite the warm weather, most of the tables were empty. A lone girl sat in the corner with her laptop, wearing a VOTE TORRES tee.

Emmie.

Cat pocketed her phone, wrapped her hand around the door handle, and pulled.

📣 📣 📣

"The Spanish Civil War, World War II, and Vietnam," Cat said, showing Emmie a photograph of Martha Gellhorn on her phone. "All that was probably a cakewalk compared to being married to Ernest Hemingway."

Emmie scraped at the last bits of her banana yogurt. "She was Hemingway's wife too?"

"One of them. The only one to sneak on board a hospital ship to watch the D-Day landings in Normandy."

"Huh." Emmie pointed her spoon at Cat. "So that's what awe looks like."

Cat's cheeks grew hot.

"No, own it, Cat. It honors you both—her for all she did and you for having the ambition to want to do the same."

"Like you and Mrs. Torres? Have you met her?"

"Once. She broke her heel right before a speech. I got her a new pair. I'm sure I looked worse than you just did—like a heart-eyes emoji. That's probably the same way I'll look when I leave for college."

"And you're applying to Harvard?"

"I'm *going* to Harvard." She said it with such confidence, Cat was sure she would. "And you?"

"Northwestern?" Emmie raised her eyebrows, and Cat tried again. "*North. Western.*"

"That's it." Emmie flicked her spoon at Cat and accidentally dropped it. Cat offered up her own. Emmie almost accepted but instead grabbed a new one, which she first cleaned with a sanitizer wipe. "I know, I know."

"No judgment . . . except—"

"Shaking hands and kissing babies?" Emmie cringed. "Universe has quite a sense of humor, doesn't it?"

Their easy conversation carried them through a half-priced refill and then another before they finally exited onto the street where, instantly, Cat's phone buzzed with a Twitter notification.

"Did *The Shrieking Violet* publish a new story?" she asked.

"Sorry, I'm not following it."

"It must have. *The Red and Blue*'s been tagged in a tweet: 'Investigate. *Shrieking Violet* says Angeline's bogus. Shouldn't even be at Acedia.' Bogus? What does that mean?" Without waiting for

Emmie to respond, Cat plugged in the website. She read the head-line, and something twisted in the pit of her stomach.

"Read it," Emmie said. "Or I can pull it up. What's the address?"

"No, it's okay." Cat swallowed and began to read:

Angeline Quinn's Darkest Secrets Coming to Light

With so much hallway flutter about our dear Ask an Angel and her Mary Poppins bag of bribes— nay, "samples"—it's time for some transparency. Before casting a ballot in the StuCo election, voters deserve to know the truth about presidential candidate Angeline Quinn. But voters have homework. And band practice. And little brothers and sisters to ~~torture~~ babysit. With active accounts on Snap, Insta, Twitter, and, apparently even Facebook (cultivating the wrong seniors' vote there!) on top of her YouTube channel, knowing all there is to know about Quinnie falls to The Shrieking Violet.

We gathered our pumpkin spice popcorn, put up our bunny-slippered feet, and sat back to watch every single episode of Ask an Angel. For you.

Research matters, folks. Don't say The Shrieking Violet isn't serious. Or is that "isn't not serious"? We get confused with all the shrieking around here.

Anyhoo, what did we learn?

From those red lips in episodes 18, 22, and 31, we can confirm that rumors of Quinn being a succubus are some percentage true.

Of greater concern, however, is Quinn's very position as a student at this school. Not only should she not be running for elected office, but she *shouldn't even be allowed at Acedia since she lived outside the charter region when she applied for the lottery!* 😮

Shriek with me, folks!

Cat set down her phone. That twisting in her stomach coiled into knots. Because the article wasn't entirely false. Succubus aside, the bit about the charter school region contained a modicum of truth.

It was the summer after their dad had left. Their move into the current apartment, though planned, had yet to be completed. They were living with one of her mom's friends a couple of towns over when they'd both applied.

Details Cat had never shared. She'd bet the Fit to Print award that this was a secret Angeline would entrust to only one person.

Leo.

Which meant he must have been feeding stories to *The Shrieking Violet*.

Which had an ad from the bowling alley underneath the article.

This was all Angeline's fault.

"I have to go," Cat said.

"No problem." Emmie's eyes filled with concern. "I wouldn't worry though. No one in their right mind would take that seriously."

The notifications kept coming on Cat's phone. People asking *The Red and Blue* to confirm the claim.

"You forget, this is high school," Cat said. "'Mind' barely applies, let alone 'right.'" She started walking. "See you in school."

"Sure," Emmie said. "Or text me later."

Cat nodded as she clicked on *The Shrieking Violet*'s account. The original tweet linking to the story had comments like:

Rules *are not* made to be broken!

Expel!

Succubus are wicked cool. Vote for the succubus!

The likes were pouring in. Everyone was reading *The Shrieking Violet*.

And waiting for a response that *The Red and Blue* couldn't give. Cat couldn't investigate a somewhat true, mostly false claim that affected not just her sister but herself.

Angeline had put her in an impossible position by being so selfish. If she hadn't betrayed Leo, none of this would have been happening.

Cat charged into their apartment, and her mom lifted her head from Evelyn's *Girl, Talk Like Everyone's Listening* book.

"Cat, I was just about to make lunch. Are you—"

"Not hungry." Cat marched through the living room. *The Angeline show. As always.* Cat ripped the ribbon off the knob and flung open their bedroom door.

"Hey! I'm filming!" Angeline popped out of the desk chair. Half her face was covered in what looked like strawberry jelly, and the room stunk of rotten fish and sour milk. "Cat, you know better!"

"Me, what about you?"

"Oh, what evil have I managed to do to you now? I'm not the one trashing you in *The Red and Blue*."

Cat's face reddened with anger as she lifted her phone.

"Cell phones?" Angeline grabbed a towel off the end of her bed and leveled it under her chin. "I know you're a total Luddite, but honestly, Cat, I'm not responsible for the ills being done to our society by smartphone technology."

"But you . . ." Cat couldn't concentrate what with Angeline's half-bloodied face straight out of a horror movie. "What is that?"

"Wine-soaked, macerated seaweed facial. Natalie Goldberg's mom's apparently a budding entrepreneur in skin care."

"And you're promoting it?"

"Testing first. Hence the one side."

Cat pinched her nostrils. "Whatever she's paying you, it's not enough."

Angeline shifted the towel to catch a glop falling from her cheek. "She's not paying me."

"Then why are you . . . Oh, you really are unbelievable! Is this all for a vote? That's . . . that's just . . . how could . . ."

"Use your words, Cat."

Cat swiped her palm across Angeline's face. The foul, sticky concoction coated her fingers, and she shook her wrist. Red globules dropped onto the white carpet.

"Cat!" Angeline fell to her knees and dabbed at the stain, only spreading it wider. "I swear you're trying to sabotage me."

"Funny, that's what I came here to say to you."

Angeline stood and wiped the rest of the gunk off her face. "Natalie's vote comes with that of the whole swim and tennis teams, not to mention band and the hippie artist crowd."

"How very well-rounded of her," Cat said through clenched

teeth. "But you'll have no need of votes at this rate."

"Are you talking about that ridiculous thing in *The Shrieking Violet*?"

"That ridiculous thing that's getting more reads than anything I've written except for my story on the Frankengirls? That ridiculous thing that's stealing my advertisers? What's going to keep my paper going when *The Shrieking Violet* pilfers them all?"

"Why does this have anything to do with me? I'm not responsible for it."

"But you are. How did they get that story?"

"How should I know?"

"Think, Angeline, think. Who else knew?"

"You, and I'd think you were the snitch except you're a terrible actress."

They stared at each other.

Cat's heart pounded in her throat, and she wanted to smear seaweed in Angeline's eye. "Leo? Did Leo know?"

The way Angeline drew back confirmed it.

"Then he's doing this!" Cat said. "He's giving them these stories."

"Leo? No way. He'd never. He's too . . ." Her thoughts trailed off, and Cat saw doubt enter her sister's eyes.

"Too what?" Cat said. "Moral? Good? He was all those things before you. Before he became a mini Tad. And now he's not just hurting you, he's hurting me. If you don't belong at the school, neither do I."

Angeline stiffened. "We both belong there. We didn't do anything wrong. Our application will show—"

"Don't you get it? It doesn't matter what's true or not, it matters what someone makes someone believe is the truth. Haven't you been paying attention to anything that's been going on for the past few years? Ms. Lute said Acedia was a microcosm, and she's one hundred percent right."

Everything Cat had done, everything that was finally on the verge of paying off, all right before her, and now, because of her sister, she might lose it. Lose the award, lose Northwestern, and then what? Everything she'd worked for would be replaced by the deep dark hole of everything she'd given up to get it: fun and friends and bonfires and boys—*yes, boys*—a love life, *any* kind of life outside the newsroom.

Angeline sighed. "What would you have me do, Cat? Quit?"

"What if I said yes?"

Her sister's eyes shifted away from Cat's. "The thing is, I've already sent Evelyn the deposit and signed the confidentiality agreement."

"Then why even ask?"

Cat stormed out and straight into the bathroom. At the sink, her pulse raced as she washed off what she imagined the regurgitated supper of a seal felt like.

She dried her fingers with a towel, refusing on principle to acknowledge the softness of her skin.

18

When Cat Watches Grady

Grady: Video's uploaded to server.

Cat: I'll watch soon.

Grady: Now soon?

Grady: 🙏

At the desk in her bedroom, Cat rolled her eyes. But she set aside her essay for government on protest marches and opened the shortcut to *The Red and Blue*'s server.

"Testing, one, two, three, testing. And action . . .

"I'm standing outside the entrance to the boys' bathroom in the west corridor where the first images of the Frankengirls were seen at the start of the school year. In that short time, while the climate outside these walls gradually transitions from summer to fall, inside has been experiencing a glacial shift. The question is, how did we enter this AF era—that's 'After Frankengirls,' by the way. A question I hope to answer.

"Welcome, I'm Grady Booker, *Red and Blue* staff reporter and your trusted guide for this special online video report. Come with me as we venture forth from this iconic spot and travel through the halls of Acedia. Our journey chronicles the student council election, from its first sign-up sheet at this bulletin board outside Ms. Lute's classroom to the primary election that kicked off our Battle of the Exes in the auditorium, which we'll visit in a bit.

"That battle has become an all-out war in the weeks since. It started small, with cheeky campaign posters and messages on marquees. The all-in-good-fun feel continued when Quinn pulled her car sporting a three-foot-tall halo into the parking lot, only to be overshadowed, literally, by six-foot-high devil horns on half the cars of the football team, including Tad Marcus's. Then there were the pink cozies snuggling over every football, basketball, and baseball bat in the equipment room. That was soon followed by the text messaged 'round the school with photos only Torres had access to take of the expensive wardrobe in Quinn's closet, completely at odds with her dress code promise; the dozens of *Finding Nemo* stuffies strangled with plastic straws creepily dangling in unsuspecting corners of the school, challenging Torres's 'stop telling us what to do' platform; and the corridors covered in bubble wrap, mocking the 'safe space' Quinn advocated for.

"But I'm getting ahead of myself. For now, with less than two weeks before the election, let's center on Angeline Quinn. As many voters know, Quinn's eligibility to run was called into question by *The Shrieking Violet*. After a visit from Quinn's mother and an unearthing of her student file, she was given the all-clear. The confidentiality terms that prevent us from showing the evidence may be the reason skepticism remains.

"Exhibit A."

"As you can see, Quinn's campaign poster has been vandalized by someone in need of a grammar check, but that unfortunately doesn't narrow down the suspect pool. But look closer as I zoom in . . . is this the zoom? I don't know how to use this thing, which is old AF, and not in the After Frankengirls way . . . cheese and crackers . . . where's the . . . okay, okay, there we go . . . note to self: edit here . . . and . . . action.

"I hope you can see that all over Quinn's poster are words of support like this one, 'Ash for Ang 4Ever,' as well as the outline of lips. Girls have been coming by and planting kisses. Wait, here comes someone now . . . And zoom back out . . . ooh, ooh, here she comes. Sonya Robins. God, she's hot. I mean, not hot, I mean attractive. She's a lovely girl. Lady. Person. Who I'd give my left pinkie to plant my own lipstick kiss on . . . And note to self, cut."

Grady landed the camera on Sonya just as Riley met up with her. "Here we have Riley Donovan and"—Grady swallowed—"and Sonya Robins. Sonya, can you tell us what you are doing and why?"

Sonya started to respond, but Riley interrupted. "This for *The Shrieking Violet*?"

The camera swung back and forth.

"Good, that rag has a vendetta against our Angeline." Riley unspooled a lipstick. "Which is why we're here."

Sonya took the lipstick and circled her lips three times. She kissed Angeline's poster, leaving behind a perfect imprint.

"We're showing Angeline our support," Sonya said.

"Who's 'we'?"

"The girls," Riley said, edging her way into the frame.

"The girls?"

"In the school," Sonya said. "We're all behind her."

"Fluttering our wings!" Riley said.

The camera angle widened but remained squarely focused on Sonya as she and Riley walked down the hall.

Sounds of a throat clearing.

"*All* the girls may not be entirely accurate, but a hefty portion of them . . . don't say 'hefty,' that's not right . . . large . . . a large portion . . . uh, not all the girls but many of them . . . *yes!* . . . many of them are behind her. This sign with both the anti-Angeline comment and the lipstick smooches is representative of what we'll see during our tour on at least half a dozen of her individual posters, incidentally painted by the uber-talented Sonya Robins, and even on what remains of the half-stolen mural, which is printed with images from her Ask an Angel YouTube channel. A channel that some say she's using to unfair advantage. A Reddit post in particular has accused Quinn of offering freebies and promo spots to voters. Scratch that, *allegedly* offering.

"But if the girls are behind Angeline, the guys, the jocks, and the wannabe jocks, they're behind Leo Torres, offering up negative criticisms of Angeline's 'more regulations' campaign and allowing Leo to remain above the fray. Yet Torres is not without his own critics."

"Now . . ." The camera zoomed in for a close-up of Grady's fingertips caressing the poster. "Presumably the professional design and high-quality paper of Torres's campaign posters are causing doubt as to whether he's made them himself or relied on members of his mother's campaign.

"The posters and their defacing are one element that speaks to the divisiveness of this student council election. But another can be seen not in these halls but online."

The camera centered on a phone logged in to Instagram.

"I'll read a few comments that are representative of what's being posted on all forms of social media by students and, increasingly, nonstudents.

"'Rules of succession don't apply to chicks!' one says, even though this is an election and not a monarchy. And even then I'm not sure that's true anymore. Here's another: 'Frankengirls didn't point to Angeline's brain.' They snipe at Torres too, with more than a few citing his tendency to follow the lead of friends like Tad Marcus. 'Look close and you can see those puppet strings!'

"Whether this is indicative of a student body that cannot find common ground or a bunch of kids trying to be what they think is funny, it's dividing the school, and it's being seen as hurtful to many, not just Quinn and Torres.

"Though Quinn is taking another hit. This one even more personal than the last. According to *The Shrieking Violet*, sources say when Angeline's father said he was getting remarried, she was pissed, thinking if he had another kid, she'd lose her inheritance. To get back at him, on the eve of his wedding, Angeline turned arsonist, setting his fiancée's house on fire with her future stepmom and her prized cockapoo inside. The four-alarm fire reportedly cost the town nearly a hundred thousand dollars, and the smoke clinging to Angeline was so strong that she was stripped of her role as flower girl.

"That explains the latest hashtag: #HotheadQuinnCantWin. With as many trolls fueling it as supporters—including women's groups outside the school—denouncing it. Now, on to the cafeteria, where the first spontaneous debate over vegan bacon occurred . . ."

📢 📢 📢

Cat turned off the sound and tucked her feet under her on the desk chair in her bedroom. Grady had begged her to expand into more multimedia reporting. She'd given him this chance to prove himself.

As usual, the latest *Shrieking Violet* story had more fiction than fact. Angeline *had* gone to their dad's house. She'd brought a wedding gift: a photo of the four of them, her dad in the center with his guitar slung across his back. It was the first year his band had played a set at Heritage Days, the annual festival celebrating the founding of the town, and he'd never been happier.

Angeline thought the picture would remind him of where he belonged. Instead, she got the reminder. Because from the front steps of his fiancée's house, she spied her dad through the window—smiling just as wide as in the photo—helping his fiancée glue daisies onto boxes of wedding favors with the cockapoo's muzzle on the side. That was why Angeline wasn't a flower girl—Angeline or Cat. The cockapoo was. He'd chosen it—*he'd chosen Botox Wife*—over them.

With tears welling, Angeline had turned to leave. She noticed wisps of smoke coming from the side of the house where a charcoal grill was heating up. The sight of the bag of marshmallows—

as homey as the hot glue gun and the perky fiancée and the cutesy dog and so unlike the dad she knew—was what did it. Angeline gathered as many leaves and twigs as she could find. She even yanked out handfuls of grass. She lifted the lid and dumped it all onto the grill. As the flames roared, she tossed the framed photo on top and bolted.

Her hair did hold on to the odor, just a little, even the next day.

Cat: You really want to post this?

Grady: After my edits, it'll be perfect, Chief. I'm a whiz with editing software. No worries.

Cat: Talk to Angeline. You need to give her a chance to respond.

Leo knew the whole truth. But he hadn't used it in that story in *The Shrieking Violet*. Cat was both glad and not.

Cat: Make the edits and show me again.

Cat: And you might want to make your crush on Sonya less obvious.

Grady: Crush? I don't . . . I'm not . . .

Grady: Yeah, okay.

Cat pushed her phone to the side, planted her feet on the floor, and dragged the play button back to that "#HotheadQuinn-CantWin."

Her breathing became shallow, and she let herself be drawn to her sister's bed, where she'd found Angeline that long-ago night, curled into a fetal position, tears streaming down her cheeks, her long hair still wet from the shower, clutching the angel-embroidered pillow she'd just gotten for her then brand-new YouTube channel. Cat had approached slowly, pausing in the space between their two twin beds, surprised when Angeline reached for her. Cat clasped her sister's hand, sat on the edge of the bed, and folded Angeline's arm into her chest, unable to remember the last time they'd been that close.

And then Angeline inched toward her and rested her head in Cat's lap. "He's really gone," Angeline had said, because she had yet to learn the lesson that Cat had internalized in fourth grade: she'd never be enough for him. *They'd* never be enough for him. For his hopes and dreams remained so wrapped up in the person he wanted to be that he couldn't see the person he was—the person he should have been. No amount of attention-seeking from either of them would tear off his blinders. And so Cat had stroked the tangles out of her sister's hair and told her it was going to be all right, but all she'd thought was *good*.

She'd been glad he was gone. Most days she still was.

Cat rested her hand on the angel-embroidered pillow and heard a crinkle. Underneath were two issues of *The Red and Blue*. Cat had never seen her sister reading her paper. Not once. And yet the issue with her first Frankengirls story had markings in her sister's handwriting including underlines and hearts in the margins. A lump swelled in Cat's throat. She returned the pages, fluffed the pillow, and picked up her phone.

The Shrieking Violet was calling her sister—*Leo* was calling her sister—a loose cannon. Too emotional to be president. How would he like the same sexist comments to be made of his mom?

Cat texted Grady.

> **Cat:** Those female-empowerment comments on Angeline's feed? Maybe add one or two. Helpful to see specifics.

> **Grady:** Good idea, Chief. Support comments for Leo too?

He should. To be fair. Cat glanced at the notebook Leo had given her. Leo, who no longer cared about fair.

> **Cat:** One. Only if there's time. We don't want it to go too long.

Acedia Confronts Its Inner Sloth: Controversy Surrounding Student Council Unprecedented in Charter School History

Coverage by rival newspapers *The Red and Blue*, which began to employ new ways to reach its audience by increasing its online presence, and *The Shrieking Violet*, an exclusively online publication, flamed interest in the student council election within the walls of the school.

Quinn's platform of more oversight sparked support from those who felt the administration was not properly addressing complaints, including harassment and cyberbullying, as well as from students wanting to free the school from what many saw as an unequal, hierarchical culture. Eliminating things like prom court, blocking texting in school, and tightening the dress code to forbid extravagance gained steam with a large percentage of voters. Yet a near equal number of students endorsed Torres's campaign seeking fewer restrictions. Citing the dress code as archaic and biased, Torres found favor with those wanting the freedom to express themselves with clothing choices that defied expected societal or gender roles.

All of these issues begged for debate, but that Acedia's

student council election permeated beyond the walls of the school came courtesy of the Frankengirls. The salacious nature of the photos made them primed for social media sharing and engagement. And with no one to hold accountable, one voice of outcry became two, which became four, and so on in a social media spiral that reached hundreds, then thousands, and culminated with live television coverage of Quinn standing beside the statue of Major Mushing on the front lawn of the school.

Quinn, as an influencer popular mostly with young women, had a built-in platform that situated her well for encouraging and promoting calls for more action, particularly with respect to schools.

The Frankengirls shined a spotlight on the fact that schools are not—and many believe cannot be—immune to the discussions surrounding gender and diversity that have taken hold in the wider landscape in recent years. In fact, drilling down through simple fury and venting and "I'm with her" or "I'm with him" social media posts brings one to a core argument: the need for awareness and tolerance to be instilled from an early age in order to set patterns of behavior.

Torres himself remained largely silent as the online storm brewed. But a "no comment" attitude that may have worked in an earlier time does not stand now. Silence equals complicity, and Torres was hit with a landslide of feminist attacks. And so the Battle of the Exes that had once been stunts and pranks escalated in the online world, with some of the more vocal supporters on Torres's side, including *The Shrieking Violet*, poking at Quinn.

But, some say, Quinn poked back. With near deadly consequences.

"Blue. My man could've slipped inside a Marvel comic, he was so blue," Baker said of Torres. "Switched my vote after that. No way I was gonna test that witchy-woo mojo."

Click for more: 3 of 6

19

When Angeline Becomes a Hashtag

#HotheadQuinnCantWin was trending.

Locally.

But still.

Trending?

Wasn't everyone on Snap or Insta anyway? How was this much of Acedia on Twitter that #HotheadQuinnCantWin was trending?

Angeline defiantly strode down the hall to her locker, employing the deep-breathing exercises Sonya had helped her to learn from that meditation app. She'd trained herself out of blushing the same way she'd trained herself out of sweating. Her mind controlled her body, not the other way around.

Then she reached her locker. And the picture. Her head jammed onto someone else's body, wearing an orange prison jumpsuit.

Her breathing grew short and fast.

So juvenile.

She pressed her hand against the metal door.

Pathetic cowards.

She tore off her cropped white denim jacket even though her #ad said she'd be wearing it today.

Who were voters.

Goddammit, that deposit was nonrefundable. This had better not make her lose—

Viewers.

That was how #HotheadQuinnCantWin was trending. It wasn't just Acedia.

Oh my God, has Evelyn seen?

Her blood boiled, and her sweat glands defied her, and she couldn't stop it, and she couldn't breathe, and—

"Assholes."

Leo surprised her by tearing the picture off her locker. "I'm sorry, Ang."

"You should be," she spat out.

He tore the photo in half. "You think I did this?"

"You didn't have to do that, specifically, to be responsible. You're spilling my secrets to them. It. Whatever. *The Shrieking Violet.*"

He set what she used to think was his trustworthy square chin straight. "No way."

"That's what I told Cat. I almost believed it too. How naive was I to think you couldn't be the 'source who says'? Tell me, who's writing it, anyway? Least I can do is give her a name."

"I can't tell you because I don't know. Maybe Baker or . . . who's that guy who was opposite you in the school play last year? Doesn't he do podcasts?"

"Ash? We're friends. And I'm pretty sure he's had a crush on me since freshman year. Bad choice for a scapegoat. Besides, this is all about access. You have it. *Had* it."

Two guys passed, and the one wearing a DON'T BE SEXIST (CHICKS HATE THAT) tee called, "So how much is the inheritance, Angel? My uncle knows someone who can do more than light a match."

180

Angeline's chest inflated, and she felt herself about to unleash a rant that was sure to go viral. She settled her breath and leaned against her locker. "So we should all believe everything we read?"

The guy shrugged.

"Because stall three in the girls' east corridor bathroom has a whole book written about you." She lowered her voice. "And I'm no expert, but you might want to see a specialist."

His jaw fell open, and his buddy put two feet between them.

And Leo . . . Leo laughed, full and deep and real.

It threw her. "Careful. Can't appear to be consorting with the enemy."

Leo's head shook slightly. "You're not my enemy."

"Does your campaign manager know that?"

"He's not really my campaign manager."

"Again, does he know that? Because he seems to be pulling your strings. Strings that are all for guys wearing gross shirts like that."

"And who's pulling yours? Cell phone restrictions and no limos to prom? You'd hyperventilate without your phone for five minutes, and you've wanted us to go to prom in a limo since our first date."

"Actually . . ." The truth danced on her lips. A truth Leo could use against her. Whatever, let him. She was tired of all of this. "I wanted us to go to prom. The limo was so it looked better on Instagram. Which is pretty pathetic when you say it out loud."

"Yeah, well, is there an application process to join that club? 'Cause I'm there with trying to defend that asswipe's right to wear that shirt." He frowned, but his dark eyes reached out to her. Though that was their only contact, Angeline felt held, as she always had with him.

They fell into step on their way to government. Down the hall, the same two guys were cornering a petite freshman girl, the taller one wiggling a cell phone above her head. The girl clutched the sides of her skirt with one hand and stretched toward her phone with the other.

Her faint smile said, *I'm a good sport*. Her forced chuckle said, *I'll play along; it's just a game*. Her sweaty forehead said, *I'm the butt of some inside joke*. Her crimson cheeks said, *I'm mortified*. But it was her eyes that had the most to say: *I'm afraid, afraid of having no control, afraid that anything could happen*.

Two male teachers hovered outside their classrooms, arms crossed, eyes glazed, staring straight at the scene before them but not seeing it—or not seeing it for what it was.

This was how they got away with it. So routine that it didn't register. And the girl wouldn't log an official complaint for the same reason.

Angeline remembered the research she'd done into peer juries. In most, anyone could file a grievance. Anyone could start an inquiry.

One of the guys said, "You got a prom date yet, sweetie? I'm taking backups if my girl boycotts because of this stupid no-limo shit. Forget 'I'm with her.' You can just direct those pretty blue eyes my way and say, 'I'm with him.'"

Leo slipped his sling over his head. "Hold this for me?"

She took it, wrapping her hands in the warmth that was Leo's.

He strode over. He told the guys to stop. He told them to give the girl her phone. They elbowed each other and laughed and said he of all people, he of the Franken-donut, should know this was all in good fun and raised the phone higher, winking at Leo as if he were playing the game too.

Leo clenched his fist, and Angeline rushed forward. She'd never seen Leo fight—he'd never even consider it with his mom's focus on their image—but the anger on Leo's face was something

182

she'd only seen once before: that night in Maxine's screening room. With super fast aim, Leo shot out his arm, and his hand connected with the guy's torso. And *tickled*. The phone fell, and the girl caught it in two hands. She gave a quick thanks and started to run off.

"Report them," Angeline said.

She mumbled an "It's okay," to which Angeline said it wasn't. None of it was.

Ignoring the "Hey, man" and "Can't take a joke," Leo approached and introduced himself.

"Olivia," the girl replied sheepishly.

Leo gestured to her phone. "Can I?" She handed it to him, and Leo punched at the screen. "That's my number. Text or call or anything if you want to talk. Or if it happens again."

Her eyes were wide and grateful, and Angeline and Leo walked her to ELA, two doors down from their own classroom.

Just as Angeline and Leo were about to enter, a "*Hothead Quiiiinnnn*" rang out.

Angeline ignored it. "Well, here's something. If that girl tells her friends what you just did, you'll be a hero and have this election locked up. Maybe I should just drop out now."

"Then they win."

"And so do you."

Leo slipped his arm back through his sling. "Listen, if you want to quit because you don't want to do this, that's your right. But don't quit because they're trying to make you."

An earnestness infused his expression, but could she trust what she saw in his eyes? Was it proof that he wasn't behind *The Shrieking Violet*?

He gently touched the heart on her ring before wrapping his hand around hers. He was only an inch or two taller than Angeline, but one wouldn't know it from his hands. Wide palms, long fingers, always warm around her always cold hands. That was proof too, his touch, strong and sure and right.

She wished he'd never let go.

He did.

But his eyes remained on her.

"Stay," he said.

And Angeline let herself pretend he meant more than in the race.

📢 📢 📢

"Accountability," Ms. Lute said. "That's been bandied about in this student council election by both of your candidates. Let's take a closer look at that today but with respect to this."

The screen on the projector flashed to the home page for *The Shrieking Violet*. The headline: "Voters, Be Warned! Track Record Shows Quinn Betrays 100% of HS Boyfreinds: You Could Be Next."

"Hilarious," Josh Baker said.

"Gets my attention," from someone else.

Tad slapped the top of his desk. "Spot on."

Silence followed, broken by Sonya. "Typo aside, it's technically true, but without context, it's not the whole story."

Angeline gave her a grateful smile.

In her front-row seat, Emmie raised her hand. "It challenges us."

Angeline jerked her head. "In what? Our ability to spot typos and the lack of actual facts?"

"Maybe," Emmie said. "Or maybe in how we have a responsibility too."

Ms. Lute smiled. "I like this, Emmie, continue, please. Responsibility for what?"

Emmie rested a finger on her ratty friendship bracelet. "At leadership camp, we're taught that when we enter positions of authority, we have a responsibility to be honest and accurate. Because those who hold higher positions are automatically perceived as more trustworthy. There's a bias toward those in charge, that they should be believed."

"Meaning political leaders?"

"Political, corporate, the media, all of it. Authority commands an inherent level of buy-in for a lot of people."

Leo leaned forward. "Which is why it matters when they lie. Everybody wants to be somebody. No matter the fallout." Angeline's body tensed, but then he turned to her and said, "But the problem with lies and exaggerated truths is that sometimes people follow because they're too weak to trust themselves. We're all responsible at some point, for something. For not questioning or for not standing up or for taking the easy way out."

"Essentially, being accountable," Ms. Lute said. "Whether it's your student council election or the national one, whether it's *The New York Times* or the local TV news, Twitter or Facebook, or whatever's to come, the question is what responsibility do not only purveyors of information have but also consumers? Especially now, when social media gives a platform to anyone who seeks it. An anonymous platform, if they wish, like *The Shrieking Violet*. What responsibility do we have when we don't have a face or a name to hold someone accountable?"

Ms. Lute clasped her hands around the projector remote and looked out at the class.

"So . . . are you going to tell us?" Josh said. "What responsibility do we have?"

Ms. Lute flicked off the projector. "I've said it before. My job is to teach. But some things you have to learn and decide for yourself."

Principal Schwartz waited outside Ms. Lute's classroom. "Miss Quinn, Mr. Torres, may I have a word?"

His stern look was a sharp contrast to the one on the back of his phone. The photo case showed him on a boat, beaming like the foot-long striper in his hands was the size of a great white. Even in that suit in need of serious tailoring, it humanized him.

Which was why it was that much more jarring when he said, "This administration has a limit, and you two are butting up against it. We can't have such negative attention brought to the school. And we can't have more of these." He kicked at a box by his feet. Inside, a dozen or so bubble wrap mailers lay torn open, and spilling out were . . . wings. Angel wings.

Angeline lifted a pair. "Is this hand-knitted?"

And could she offer the pattern online?

"And likely teeming with moths. We can't have an infestation." Principal Schwartz pursed his lips. "When I saw you two had signed up to run, I mistakenly thought it would be beneficial to this school. I thought you stood a chance of getting the student body engaged, but this is not the kind of engagement we want." He held out his phone screen. "These comments are only getting worse. It's not just our students anymore; we've got students from other schools in Massachusetts, Connecticut, New York . . . this one's in Oregon. Not to mention the organizations of adults weighing in. My wife follows this Evelyn character, and she keeps telling me she's favoriting Acedia tweets."

Angeline's heart skipped.

"How does someone in Oregon and some minor celebrity know about a student council election on the South Shore of Boston?"

First, *minor*? Second, was that a rhetorical question?

"Well," Angeline said, "that's basically the point of social media. It breaks down barriers and brings people closer." That it was a stock answer didn't mean it wasn't true. But what Ms. Lute had been talking about was also true. Hiding behind an avatar and a quippy screen name released the darkest parts for many. Parts that were calling her "Hothead Quinn."

"Apparently not here." Principal Schwartz reached over their heads and popped a section of bubble wrap that Leo's supporters had glued to the wall. "Voter engagement and loyalty is one thing, but we have a zero-tolerance policy on bullying, and this is starting to cross the line."

"*This?*" Angeline blurted out. "I'm sorry, but this is absurd considering what just happened with—" She stopped herself. It wasn't her place. She couldn't go against Olivia's wishes.

Principal Schwartz waited, eyebrow raised. When she didn't continue, he said, "We're getting calls from parents." The yellowy-green bags under his eyes seemed to hang heavier. "Over a student council election. All these rumors circulating about Miss Quinn, these unfortunate Frankengirls, this 'he said, she said' squabbling . . . it's making the school seem out of control. You both need to shut this down, or we'll be forced to."

Leo raked his hand through his hair. "What do you want us to do? We can't stop other people from going online or messing with posters."

"You can start by being better role models going forward. Turn this around and run a clean and positive campaign. We've got a little over a week. Use it."

20

When Cat Enters the Watch Yard

Cat ran into Emmie in the girls' bathroom after school.

"Finish the issue?" Emmie asked, washing her hands at the sink as if she were scrubbing for surgery.

"Just. You need a lift home?"

"Thanks, but I've got at least another hour of debate practice. I'm showing my team pointers from Mrs. Torres's speech last night. Her husband introduced her, which was a nice personal touch, but I didn't see Leo or his brother there, which seems strange."

"Oh? Does it?" Cat pressed the automatic dryer to hide her lying face. Leo wouldn't have been there because of the deal he made with his mom. "Homework, maybe?"

"Couldn't keep me away if one of my dads was running."

"Are they interested in politics?"

"One's an immigration lawyer and the other works for an LGBTQIA for teens nonprofit."

"So just a smidge." Cat grinned. "Is that where you get it from?"

"In a way, though they're more into activism than running for office." Emmie dried her hands with a paper towel and pointed to the automatic dryer. "You know those things only spread around E. coli."

Cat eyed her hands suspiciously, and Emmie squirted hand sanitizer into them. She opened the door with her elbow. "I assume the story about Leo's above the fold?"

"Leo and Angeline. The latest polling data, and I've got a story on Maxine's security measures for the voting app and—"

"No. About what happened today. In the hall?"

"You mean with that girl and her phone? It was cool of Leo." And nice to see that version of him—the one Cat knew—hadn't completely disappeared under Tad's thick, gross thumb. "But it's not really a story."

"Sure it is. Especially since Angeline was there and did nothing. From the things you've told me about her, I know you wouldn't shy away from calling her out. The whole situation speaks to their character. The voters should know."

Cat had gotten to know Emmie well enough not to be surprised by her strong opinions, but Cat had her own—especially when it came to her paper. "Well, I wasn't there, but I'm not sure it's accurate to say Angeline did nothing. It must have been a mutual decision to send Leo over since he's a guy—and taller."

"Even so, if that's true it cuts into her whole girl-power thing, doesn't it? Either way it's a story."

Seemed more like clickbait to Cat. Not to mention something that would only embarrass the girl further, which Cat thought Emmie should understand. "I'll look into it."

"Let me know if you need help." Emmie headed toward the auditorium.

Cat hiked her backpack higher, but instead of going straight to the exit, she took a lap through the empty halls.

Emmie was smart and knew a lot about politics. Was it possible she was right? That this was a story? And Cat's connections to Leo and Angeline were making her miss it?

The unexpected sound of a door closing led Cat farther down the hall to the alcove beyond the school's grinding server room. There was an exit she'd never noticed before. She peeked through the small pane of glass to see Ravi. She pushed the door open.

"Hey," she said.

Ravi tucked his sketchbook under his arm. "Hey, Cat. Come to pay your respects?"

Cat awkwardly slipped her thumbs through the loops of her backpack straps. "Uh, sure, okay."

"You have no idea what I'm talking about."

"Well, I . . ." She sighed. "No, I don't."

"Here, I'll show you." He led her down the narrow sidewalk that wound around the building to a dead end, where a low rock wall stretched along the whole far side of the school. Beyond it, scattered among the tall grass and weeds, were little signs. Some on rocks glued to sticks, some on paper, faded and wrinkled, some on wooden two-by-fours stuck in the ground.

WE'RE WITH YOU!

NEVER FORGET.

THANKS FOR WATCHING OVER US.

"What is this?" she said. "Like a graveyard?"

"A watch yard." Ravi pointed to the roof of the school.

"I'm not sure what I'm looking at."

Ravi filled the space beside her. He plucked his pencil out from behind his ear and used the tip to direct her gaze upward. "See, there, right at the edge?"

A grayish mop-like thing hung slightly over the side. Not moving.

Ravi's bare leg brushed hers, and she felt her spine go rigid. "I heard they used a ladder and a fishing rod to nab the lawn chair, but they couldn't reach him. Probably figured no one would ever know since this exit's hardly used anymore. They blocked the path that once led to the parking lot a while back. So they just left him. All alone."

"You mean, that's . . ."

"Slothy." He exhaled a long sigh. "Poor little dude. Kids couldn't stand the thought so . . . the watch yard. Like graveyard but with less chance of ghosts."

Signs and flowers and plants and stuffed walruses and octopuses and a giant bear lay strewn throughout the overgrowth. A memorial to a stuffed sloth.

Cat laughed. "I told Ms. Lute not to bother with StuCo. That this is what got Acedia engaged, and I was right."

"Not so fast. This is one of the coolest things I've ever been witness to, but it's not the only thing that's gotten our school engaged. This election wouldn't be anything without you. And *The Shrieking Violet*."

Cat narrowed her eyes.

"Destroy any rakshasa with that look? Yikes." Ravi shivered. "But I'm serious. The competition helped. Got everyone interested."

The Shrieking Violet did what she couldn't on her own. With lies. She could never be grateful.

Ravi sat on the rock wall and opened his sketchbook.

"Are you including this in your novel?" Cat asked.

"Yeah, I need inspiration for a scene honoring the rakshasa. Trying to finish this to send with my Emerson application."

"Oh, you want to stay close for school?"

"Close enough to see my little sister on her birthday but not so close as to have to go to every one of my brother's violin recitals." He winced. "You?"

"Northwestern. Maybe. I don't know."

"Don't know if you want it or if it'll happen?"

"That second one."

"You can only concentrate on the first. So want it, Cat. Do what you can, and then . . . see what comes."

"You make it sound so easy. To not, like, obsess."

"Eh, you haven't seen me with my stack of Marvel comics. My parents being into books meant I was plenty indulged. Camp sucked in all ways but one. 'Cause all it took was my art teacher to say I had talent, help me get a couple of drawings into a kids' magazine, and my parents were hooked. Now they think I'm going to be the next Stan Lee."

Cat smiled weakly. "Hard when there are expectations." *Especially when they're your own.*

"But they come with all sorts of encouragement. My mom's got the aunties asking me when my books will be made into movies. I just don't want to disappoint them."

"So you're here, in the watch yard, searching for inspiration."

He paused and looked straight at her. "And finding it."

A tiny electric shock sparked through her, and suddenly Cat wished for her sister. Because not only would she know if Ravi was flirting, she'd be able to tell Cat how to flirt back.

21

When Angeline Hits the Sweet Spot

Angeline met him at the lighthouse. Free of his sling for the first time, Leo gingerly clasped his hands in front of his stomach.

"Remember when you couldn't go up?" Angeline said.

"Only because you like to remind me."

"We'd already bought the tickets."

"It was five dollars."

"Ten, together. But not enough to push you past your fears."

"Of falling to certain death? My podcast says falls are the second leading cause of accidental deaths in the world. I'd like to think my life is worth more than ten dollars."

"This with inflation or without?" She grinned, and he gave a crooked smile, and it felt like no time had passed since they'd last been here during Heritage Days. When Leo's fear of heights meant he couldn't follow Angeline up to see the view from the top of the white stone lighthouse, which was built in the early 1800s. It was only open a couple of times a year. Fear held him back in the way it never did Angeline.

For the first time, instead of thinking his way was wrong and hers was right, she wondered if there wasn't something in between.

They walked the circular path, past the monument to the warship that ground just offshore during a blizzard in the 1950s, heading for the long jetty that stretched into the Atlantic. It curved in toward the harbor like an elbow, protecting the shops and homes as best it could. Which was all one could ask, really.

Their words flowed with familiar ease, talking about Ms. Lute's class and the incident with Olivia and shying away from the election. The whole time she wished she could read him, to know if he was here solely because of Principal Schwartz, because he needed to win or wanted to win or . . . or maybe something else.

The late afternoon sun warmed Angeline's skin, and she breathed in the sulfur smell of the harbor at low tide. "It's different here. From Eggshell Beach." Eggshell was their beach. Which was why she'd chosen to meet him here—more neutral ground.

"Which, I'd like to mention, has a terrifying mountain I've repeatedly risked my life to climb."

"It's a dune."

"It's steep," he said. "Been since the bonfire?"

"Not much time." And too many memories.

"Shame."

"Sweet spot," they said at the same time.

Leo laughed. "Better that they don't know."

"They" being most of their fellow New Englanders who started writing off the summer at the end of August, readying themselves for walls of snow and puffy parkas. All the fuss buzzed about June, July, and August. But the secret that Angeline and Leo shared was that September was the perfect month for beachcombing. Tourists and summer people had packed it in, school and birthday parties and sports practice kept the little kids away, and the ocean was warmer than it ever was in June.

Especially at Eggshell Beach. The curve of the shoreline offered protection from the wind, and the flat, oval rocks that littered the sand and gave the beach its name radiated heat from the sun. Warm enough to lounge on the boulder-sized rock that was their favorite. She could picture its deep green, hear Leo saying how it reminded him of her eyes, feel the tender pressure against her lips as they shared their first kiss. Three Septembers ago.

September was the sweet spot, all right.

"Really is too bad," Leo said. "I miss looking at the stars."

"Me too." Angeline waited for him to say more, like if he missed looking at them with her, but Leo simply pointed to one of the flattest rocks on the jetty about halfway out.

They sat, and Angeline slipped her tote bag off her shoulder. She drew out two pairs of knitted angel wings she'd snagged from Schwartz's box and set them down as placemats, making Leo laugh. On top, she laid out a container of sushi, a thermos (*free with purchase of three pounds of fair-trade coffee beans with the AngelsAreFair promo code!*), and two reusable plastic cups.

Leo screwed off the top of the thermos and sniffed. "Riley?"

"Naturally. She's thinking of going to the juicery with this one. Wants to know what we think." Angeline set out the sushi, and their arms brushed. Goose bumps. Instantly.

"So, any ideas?" Leo asked, getting down to business. "Or should we follow in George Washington's footsteps and just spend our entire campaign budgets on booze for the voters?"

"Seriously?"

"It was before he was running for president. Just state legislature."

"Oh, well, that cleans it all up, then." She and Leo had made a pact to end the dirty campaigning, but it wouldn't matter if no one followed their lead. They needed an initiative, one to work on together, to get their classmates to cool it on the whole Battle of the Exes. "Blood drive? Clean the beach?"

"May as well ask them to nap in class," Leo said.

"Now that would engage them."

"Would be totally nonpartisan, though. Speaking of, can I really expect Maxine's voting app to be fair?"

Angeline feigned shock. "Whatever are you suggesting?"

"Uh-huh."

"It will be. Promise." She expected him to say something about her promises, but all he said was, "Okay."

"Okay." She tilted her cup to taste Riley's drink. Sweet and savory and felt like fall, the color a mix of yellow and orange and red, like leaves changing color. She felt Leo's eyes on her as she set down her glass. Lifting her head the barest of inches, she glanced up at him.

He was staring at her. In a good way.

Very, very good.

He quickly looked away, but a grin crept in, and he sipped his drink to cover. His tongue circled his lips in satisfaction, and Angeline pretended that she hadn't seen what she'd seen. Him looking at her like he did before everything happened.

Leo shifted forward, closing the gap between himself and Angeline. "How about we take a photo? Show Schwartz we're trying at least."

"Good idea." Angeline leaned into him, against him, and her heart beat in her temples. He snapped the photo, set down his phone, and lifted his cup for another sip—then stopped. His cup slipped from his hand, and reddish-orange liquid spurted in the air as it landed with a shallow thud against the rock. His hands clawed toward his throat.

Angeline reached for him. "Are you okay?"

His lips puffed, starting to double in size.

Angeline sucked in a breath. "What's in this?" She whipped out her phone and voice-activated it to call Riley while she wrapped an arm around Leo's waist.

"So, whaddya think?" Riley asked.

"What's in it?" Angeline half screamed.

"No, it might bias you, I need to know—"

"Riley! Leo's turning blue! What's in this? It's not . . . it can't be beets?"

"Yes! It's beet. For color."

"He's allergic to beets!"

"He's what? I've never heard of someone being allergic to beets. Peanuts, I'd have warned about, but beets . . ."

Angeline yelled for Riley to call an ambulance to the lighthouse. She carefully guided Leo onto his side. He wheezed, and his skin devolved into a sickly shade.

"EpiPen?" Angeline asked fruitlessly. She could see his pockets, which weren't deep enough for the large syringe. She started to leave to run to his house, but he grabbed her hand. She swallowed past the golf ball in her throat. "I'm here."

And she waited, Leo in her lap, sirens in the distance, the lighthouse high above her, feeling the fear Leo must have felt when he imagined going to the top.

The paramedics allowed her to ride in the back instead of the front after a brief exchange in which they assured her that Leo was fine and she assured them that that was wonderful but she wasn't letting him out of her sight.

"Doing okay?" she asked him.

Leo's eyes were closed, but he nodded gently. Under the blanket, strapped to the stretcher, he seemed smaller than he was, only adding to Angeline's guilt that her wanting to be bigger than she was had led them here.

The medics had given Leo an injection and hooked him up to an IV on-site, but he still needed to go to the hospital. She'd asked Riley to call Leo's mom. Leo might have been the one turning blue, but Angeline could barely speak. Even parting her lips to wet them with her tongue now threatened a torrent of tears.

Leo.

He was fine. She knew he was going to be fine. But she clung to his hand like it was a life preserver and she'd been thrown overboard. Easy to do since that was exactly how she'd been feeling since the day they broke up.

That night, in Maxine's screening room, she'd held his hand like this, almost as tightly.

A horror movie had been about to begin. She hated horror movies, same as Cat. Her dad loved them. Cat couldn't even watch the opening credits, but Angeline and her mom would sit beside her dad, clutching each other's arm and leaping off the couch at every jump scare, no matter how predictable.

Angeline could never sleep after. Her mom would pull out pints of ice cream and sit on the floor with Angeline. That was how Angeline had learned her mom had wanted to be a photographer but had given it up in favor of a career with a more consistent salary so her dad could keep playing his music. That was when she'd first seen pictures of a young Grams and Gramps dancing in an Irish pub in Southie. That was when she'd told her mom she wanted more. "More what?" her mom had asked. Angeline hadn't known then. She just knew whatever more was, she had to have it.

The night of Maxine's party, sealed off in the windowless screening room, she'd held Leo's hand because she loved him more than she hated scary movies. And she'd thought, maybe her mom wouldn't mind some ice cream when she got home.

But the instant that projector had shut off and the image of Leo's face filled the enormous screen, playing the capture of her live-stream, Angeline knew she'd rather watch a thousand horror movies than see what was to come.

Clicks and likes and a road to fame had superseded everything for so long. When Evelyn had liked her video featuring Leo, Angeline planning another wasn't a decision so much as an effect.

Cause = twenty thousand thumbs-ups.

Effect = Angeline sweeping right and wrong under the rug.

She thought he'd be okay with it.

Well, not okay, but that he'd understand.

That he'd forgive her.

That he'd get past it.

That it'd be worth it.

In the back of the ambulance, Angeline brought his hand to her lips and kissed his skin. She drew back at the cold. Then, she gave up her fight against the tears and wrapped both of her hands around his.

📢 📢 📢

"Did you tell Riley we loved it?" Leo asked after the nurse had left.

"No, of course not." Angeline rose from the chair at the end of the hospital bed, a pair of angel wings in her hands. The curtain quartering off his ER stall hung mostly closed, but she tugged it the rest of the way.

"Too bad, pretty sure it's killer."

Angeline watched his dimple carve into his cheek and let out a small bubble of laughter for his sake. "You're ridiculous. And what happened to agreeing to carry your EpiPen after that night at your mom's fundraiser last year?"

"Relax, I smelled that Santa-swirl cabbage-beet slaw from across the room. Food allergies give you a heightened sense of smell."

"Apparently not." She gestured to his current situation, skin pale, head woozy from the drugs, shirt replaced with a washed-out hospital gown. The hives around his lips had retreated, but the image of his hand reaching for his throat would never leave her. Angeline tried to breathe normally, but each intake plunged a thorn in her chest.

"Hey." He tried to sit up higher.

"Don't." She moved to him instead, resting carefully on the edge of his bed.

"I won't break." He tilted his head toward his shoulder. "Again."

"This isn't funny, Leo."

"It wasn't. It is now. Beets in a mixed drink? Who would have thought?"

Angeline felt her eyes burn, like more tears might come.

"Ang, it's okay. This has happened before, you know that. Tomorrow, I'll be tired, but I'll be back to myself in no time. You'll see."

"Will I? Because tomorrow we're back to Battle of the Exes, aren't we?"

"No, we're not."

"Battling? Or exes?"

He closed his eyes. "Angeline, I . . ."

She shifted off the bed. "Sure, I get it."

"No, wait . . . just give me—"

Metal scraped metal, and the curtain tore back.

"Leo!" Eliza Torres, a short woman with dark hair in a sophisticated but not trendy bob and eyes that demanded one's attention, strode to the bed, edging Angeline out of the way.

Angeline retreated to the front, where Sammy appeared, his red shirt around his waist, a cup of ice chips in his hand.

"How did this happen?" Mrs. Torres said. "Was there a label? We will have your father talk to the lawyer and see what recourse we have. Did you see a specialist? Where is the nurse?"

"Mom, take a breath. No lawyers, no specialist." Leo must have noticed the fear on Sammy's face, because he sat up higher and said, "I can't be beet-en down, right, Sam-o?"

Despite his nervousness, Sammy casually shrugged. "Beets me."

Leo grinned. "I like to be up on things, but I've been thinking, might not be so bad to miss a beet."

Sammy set the ice chips on the pink plastic tray by Leo's bed. "Tell me what you really think, bro. Stop beeting around the bush."

"Enough, you two," Mrs. Torres said, but her tone had softened. She set a hand on Leo's forehead. "I have a thing for symmetry, you know. Pictures would be completely lopsided if you weren't in them."

Leo's chest expanded. "Mom, I . . ." Tears crept into his eyes, and Angeline's throat tightened.

The nurse from earlier appeared. "A tad crowded in here, folks. Let's have a couple of you in the waiting room, 'kay?"

As if she remembered they weren't alone, Mrs. Torres shot up straight and directed a nasty look at Angeline.

Leo mouthed a "Sorry," but Angeline simply offered a feeble,

"Feel better," before heading toward the stiff plastic chairs in the waiting room.

She'll never forgive me.

Angeline hugged the angel wings to her chest, watching cars turn into the lot in front of the hospital.

If she wouldn't, did that mean Leo couldn't?

Slowly, Angeline eased into one of the blue chairs, her back straightening as Sammy approached. "Hey, hey," she said, playfully waving the angel wings.

"I don't like you anymore," he said.

She wanted to fold in on herself. "I know."

"He does. He pretends he doesn't, but he does."

Angeline tried to push her heartbeat back down to her chest.

"So I might have to learn to like you," Sammy said.

Angeline carefully said, "Okay."

"This . . . you being with him. I'm glad . . . I'm glad he wasn't alone." His face was so round and his skin so smooth. He might have been a freshman in high school, but he was barely fourteen, had a birthday right before the school year started. "He really going to be okay?"

"He really is." Her heart pinched thinking of Leo and Sammy and how close they were despite their age difference. Or maybe because of their age difference. One of them got to be the big brother and one of them the little. She and Cat never knew what it was like to not be in lockstep with the other.

Sammy shuffled forward and sat beside Angeline.

She let the silence become uncomfortable, ensuring his relief at having her break it. "So, here's the thing. I've apologized to Leo, but I realize now that I never apologized to you. I shouldn't have done what I did. I'm sorry I hurt your brother. But I'm sorry I hurt you too."

Sammy's eyes narrowed and then relaxed. "Apology accepted."

"Really? I mean, thanks, Sammy. That's really mature of you."

"Eh, I've been considering it for a while. Just haven't done anything about it. But that's what makes doing nothing hard— you never know when you're done." He smirked, and Angeline realized how much she missed him. She started to say as much when he added, "Besides, enough tension at home, don't need it in school too."

"What's going on at home?"

Sammy tugged at an already raw cuticle.

"It's okay, you don't have to tell me if you don't want to. Leo mentioned something about your mom, so I get it."

"He told you?"

"Nothing specific."

He shifted to face her, and all she could see was Leo. He was there in the angle of Sammy's chin, the broadness of shoulders yet to fill out, the appearance of perfection masking the cracks everyone had but the Torres brothers weren't allowed to show.

"She's under a lot of pressure. The race is the biggest she's ever been in. She's hardly around. And even when she's around, she's still not really around, you know?"

Angeline nodded. Cat used to say the same about their dad.

"She and Leo are barely speaking. It's been weird. More weird. Ever since she had that emergency meeting with Principal Schwartz at the end of last year."

"Schwartz?" Leo never said anything to her. "Meeting about what?"

Sammy shrugged. "Beats me." He laughed at his unintentional pun.

Heels clicked on the hard, sterile tiles, and Mrs. Torres aimed for the reception desk. Angeline stood.

"Not sure I was supposed to say anything," he said, spine rigid as if he were suddenly balancing a book on his head. "Don't tell anyone?"

"I won't. You're a good brother, Sammy."

She left because she couldn't stay. There wasn't a place for her here anymore.

Outside, the sky clung to hints of blue and yellow and muted pink—that in-between-day-and-night sky, where without any context, time could play out in either direction.

She hadn't thought to call for a ride-share. This wasn't Boston, and the wait could be twenty minutes. She headed toward a bench when a sputtering resounded from the parking lot. A silver hatchback inched out of a spot two rows over and pulled up in front.

Their silver hatchback.

"Is everything all right?" Cat asked.

No. But at least now she could admit it.

22

When Cat Considers
the Merits of Butterscotch

Cat unlocked the door to their apartment. Her sister had been quiet on the ride. Not texting or watching YouTube or recording memos to herself for her next video, just fingering that pair of white woolen angel wings she still had in her hands.

"Mom wrangled Gramps into having a salad at the gastropub," Cat said as Angeline sunk into the couch instead of immediately disappearing into their bedroom, claiming the space as hers like she normally did when it was just the two of them. It unnerved her.

Angeline bobbed her head, facing the coffee table where Cat's notes for the next issue, her "EIC" notebook, and printouts of last year's Fit to Print winner were spread out.

It was like being caught naked.

Cat quickly went to gather them up, and Angeline set her hand on one of the front pages.

"*Red and Blue* totally trounces this," she said.

Cat froze. "Yeah, well, Ravi's really talented."

"Don't do that. Not take credit. Without your stories, he's got nothing to work with. And you've given him a lot to work with lately."

"You've been reading my articles?" Cat tried to sound nonchalant.

"A few." Angeline lifted her legs off the floor and drew them into her chest. She then let out a long breath and added, "Fine, all of them."

"But why?"

"Because they were about me, obviously." Angeline gave a wry smile.

Right.

"Okay, so truth?" Angeline said. "I did start reading your stories to keep tabs on how you were portraying me. But I kept doing it because . . . it was sort of like knowing what was in your head."

Cat tentatively sat on the couch opposite her sister, waiting for some joke about what she found in Cat's head.

Instead, Angeline continued, "Leo and Sammy are super close. So, whatever, we've never been. There's no rule that we have to be just because we're biologically linked."

Cat gave a half nod, half shrug. She stretched out her legs, and from the other end of the couch, Angeline did the same. Their jeans touched—Angeline's high-waisted, spray-painted-on pair and Cat's straight leg that sat squarely on her waist. Cat wore one of her long-sleeved black T-shirts, while Angeline had on a short-sleeved linen shirt with buttons along the sides—black too.

Cat pointed to their unintentional matching outfits. "Mom would love this."

"Irish twins," Angeline said.

Cat had nearly forgotten people used to call them that, seeing as how they were less than a year apart. A familiar nickname on this stretch of coastline known as the Irish Riviera due to so many residents having ancestral ties to Ireland. Their mom had indulged it, getting a double stroller, dressing them alike, attempting to style their hair the same, even though Cat's would never cooperate.

She and Angeline acted like they'd always hated it when they got older, hindsight attaching feelings of the present to the memories of the past, warping it as much as bringing it into perspective. But they'd tied those matching ribbons in each other's hair before Easter egg hunts in the backyard, rode matching white bikes with yellow baskets to Lighthouse Beach, and made their communion together in the same church just across from where they sat now. Angeline had dropped out of Sunday School first, not reaching confirmation, and Cat had followed.

Cat said slowly, "That's not technically true. That we've never been close. Before Dad left—"

"You look like him, you know?" Angeline said suddenly. "At least the him I remember—in person, not through one of Botox Wife's sepia or sunset or happy-day filters."

"No, you look like him. You've got his hair, at least minus the red. While I've got . . ." Cat ran her hand through her bob, and when she pulled it free, pieces stuck straight out to the side. "I mean, is this part glue or what?"

Angeline popped up and kneeled on the couch. She swatted Cat's feet. "Turn around." When Cat didn't move, Angeline lowered her voice. "Trust me, okay?"

No teasing hid in her sister's tone, so Cat swung herself around.

"You're using the wrong conditioner." Angeline started to brush Cat's hair with her fingers. "I set that butterscotch hair mask in the shower weeks ago, but you never even opened it." She pulled back Cat's bangs. "Your hair is coarse. It needs the moisture."

"Why didn't you tell me to use it?" Cat asked.

"Figured if I did, you'd be less likely to."

"You're probably right," Cat whispered, lulled by her sister's deliberate movements.

"So pretend it's from Emmie and use it. Along with the coordinating butterscotch shine I'll put in with the hair dryer."

Cat jerked her head. "What?"

"Butterscotch. Really, Cat, you need to let yourself have a signature scent anyway."

"No, not that."

"Emmie? Emmie Hayes? You two are friends now, aren't you? That's who you've been texting with?"

That sensation of being naked returned. She and Emmie had settled into a friendship, their texting letting Cat open up in ways she hadn't to anyone in a long time. And that was supposed to be hers, alone. She started to sit up. Angeline held her and switched out her fingers for an actual brush from her tote bag on the floor.

"It's okay," Angeline said. "At least you waited until after the primary. Doesn't look so bad."

Cat's senses piqued. "An endorsement? Is that what you're after? You didn't have to butterscotch me up, you could've just asked."

"Oh, I wasn't . . . that's not why I . . ." Angeline fell back on her heels. "Why is this so hard?"

Cat already missed the feel of her sister's hands in her hair. She retreated to her end of the couch and grabbed the stupid pair of angel wings. "I don't know."

"Listen, truly, Cat, I'm just glad you have someone to talk to." She gestured to the angel wings. "Someone to be your wing girl with Ravi."

Cat's eyebrows shot up. "My what?"

"You're into him."

"Into—"

"It's okay, Cat in the Hat." Angeline's eyes lit up. "He's cute.

Totally got an artsy surfer soccer player vibe going. And he's into you too, I can tell."

Cat's face burned, and she wanted to brush her off, but instead blurted out, "You think?"

Angeline nodded eagerly. "That drawing he made of you? Total love letter."

"That was just so I'd let him put editorial cartoons in the paper."

"Last week's with Slothy behind the voting booth curtain was hilarious. But, sorry, still not buying it."

Cat traced a line of tweed on the couch. Her sister knew more about this than she did, but she wasn't operating with all the facts. "Even if he was, he's not anymore."

Before she could stop herself, Cat told Angeline about Ravi's text and the trip to Boston and Natalie Goldberg.

"Aha, that's why you were so upset about the seaweed thing."

Was that why? Cat had never really been interested in someone before to know if she was the jealous type.

Interested. Was she?

"I don't . . . I guess . . . Maybe? . . . But I also thought . . ." This was the longest conversation she and Angeline had had in months, maybe longer.

"Go on. I want to know what you think."

"Really?"

Angeline nodded again, and a warmth spread through Cat's chest. "Well, you've just got all these people, all these women, behind you, outside of school. The things you've been saying about girls being treated with respect, you're like this role model or something. You don't need to cheapen it by covering your face in regurgitated seaweed."

"Macerated."

"So not the point."

23

When Angeline Gets It

Angeline shifted on the couch across from her sister. "Fine, I get it." Maybe this was a mistake. She didn't even know what she was doing.

Her and Cat.

Talking?

"Forget it," Cat said. "I didn't mean anything. You need votes, right?"

Angeline set her gaze on the coffee table, on all the work her sister was putting into the thing she loved. But when it came to Angeline, Cat had a blind spot as big as a black hole.

"I work hard too, Cat. Maybe not in a way you respect, but I do. And, yeah, when the election attention first hit, I did and said things because those hashtags about female empowerment were just ripe for the picking."

Cat played with the tip of an angel wing. "I never said I didn't respect you."

"You didn't have to . . ." Angeline paused. Because something had been brewing inside her ever since the donut breakfast. Then

210

with the way those guys were teasing Olivia . . . those hashtags started to become something other than just a road to more likes. She might not really know what she was doing, but she sort of wanted to try. "I'm starting to think that Emmie was right. About having a voice. That Ask an Angel app I promised was just a ploy for votes. But maybe it shouldn't be." She sighed. "Or maybe I'm just exaggerating my reach. Blame too much time around Riley. You know how she is."

"Not really."

"But that was your choice." Cat had never hung out with Angeline and her friends, even before her friends were Riley and Sonya and Maxine. She was a year older, and everyone else was beneath her. Including Angeline. She'd made that clear in fourth grade after the school play. Angeline had given her a wish rock as a peace offering. She'd said that "Fraidy Cat" in the moment, a joke to lighten the tension, and everyone laughed, and she'd thought it was all good. She never once thought the name would follow Cat around for weeks, months.

She'd scoured the beach for the roundest, most perfect wish rock she could find. She gave it to Cat, saying, "Now you can wish not to be afraid." Cat looked at her like she'd given her a handful of live bees. She went straight to the bathroom and flushed it. The whole bathroom flooded. Angeline was done. She'd tried to apologize. And Cat hadn't cared. So Angeline didn't either. That was how easy it was for habits to form.

Cat began to pile up the papers on the coffee table, but Angeline wasn't ready for this . . . whatever this was . . . to end just yet.

"Leo's mom had some emergency meeting with Schwartz at the end of last year," she found herself saying, sharing what Sammy had told her in confidence.

"Strange, I agree," Cat said, shifting to the edge of the couch. "Don't take this the wrong way, but are you sure about trusting Leo? Because it really does seem like he's behind all these rumors and fake stories. And if it's not him, who is it?"

"I don't know . . . Baker? Maybe Tad." Angeline didn't really believe that. Baker cared too little and Tad too much—his ego would never let him be anonymous for this long. "I just know it's not Leo. You should have seen him today, Cat. He was . . . we were . . ."

"Like you used to be? Is that really what you want? Still?"

Angeline hesitated. Because this election had shown another side of Leo. But they'd both done things they shouldn't have.

Cat stuffed her papers into her backpack. "I always liked Leo. But the evidence is there, Ang. You might be too close to see it. Just be careful, okay?"

Later, lights off, under her white comforter, listening to Cat's heavy breaths of sleep, Angeline spun her claddagh ring around and around. Because more than the election, more than the YouTube channel and boot camp that had gotten her into all this, she wanted Leo to be the same person he'd always been, because that way, they'd have a chance.

(Well, maybe more than her YouTube channel is a stretch. As much? Yeah, as much.)

24

When Angeline Becomes a Witch

The cold penetrated the lace back of Angeline's salmon-colored tank. Yet she couldn't trust her legs to support her without help from the metal partition in the bathroom stall. In what had become her morning routine after arriving at school, she'd been checking *The Shrieking Violet*. Better to learn of an ambush alone. Today, she was, and she did.

Somethin's Brewing in Quinn Coven!

Hide your broomsticks and eyes of newt! Sources say some mojo of the witchy-woo kind's swooping through Acedia.

Toil's trouble, caldron's bubble, potions that look like lotions, we're chanting all things pointy hats today with the news of a certain student council presidential candidate's recent poisoning.

(Spoiler alert! It's Leo!)

Today, we leave no wand un-swished as we dig deep into the case of Angeline Quinn and the Sorceress's Smoothie . . .

The whoosh of flushing in the adjacent stall was quickly followed by the same farther down. Doors creaked, and then a girl's voice said, "Poisoned."

"Totally a woman's weapon."

"Could've been a spell or something."

"Sources say she's got the birthmark to prove it."

Giggles from both, and Angeline retreated onto the toilet lid, floating her feet in the air.

The sound of water running nearly covered the girl with the nasal voice saying, "Have you seen the mark?"

"Not even at Maxine's party," her vocal fry friend said. "That super cute gold bikini was to die for." A gasp. "And Leo almost did."

"No wonder she doesn't recommend thongs."

On the wall beside Angeline's head, *No thongs* was written in permanent marker. It came in third on the rundown of her top Ask an Angel tips, right after *Be your own motivational quote* and right before *Gastrointestinal issues are TMI*. It grew each week. It was why this was her favorite stall in school.

"Everyone would've been able to see," Vocal Fry said.

Wait, what?

"Totally. A thong couldn't hide the shape of a lightning bolt on your left butt cheek."

Oh my God.

"Went around telling people she was Harry Potter and mooned them when they didn't believe her?" Vocal Fry snorted.

"No wonder her ass wasn't in any of the Frankengirls pics."

"How lucky are we to have *The Shrieking Violet*?"

"If only someone could have warned poor Leo . . ."

The outer bathroom door groaned open.

Jagged, sure. A bit of a zigzag, really. But she'd never called it a lightning bolt.

Angeline hopped down and quickly skimmed the rest of the ridiculous article before texting Maxine.

> **Angeline:** The Shrieking Violet?

> **Maxine:** Bogus to the bogus max. I mean, if they're going for witchy, broomstick maybe. But lightning bolt? Who'd come up with that?

One person. Who knew how much she loved Harry Potter. She felt sick.

> **Angeline:** Can you hack into it? Need to know who's behind it.

Because it can't be who I think it is. It just . . . can't, Angeline thought.

> **Maxine:** Give me the day.

📢 📢 📢

Ms. Lute adjusted the star-speckled headband in her dark hair. "Before the Revolutionary War, votes were cast by voice, often at local carnivals. Does anyone know what that means?"

"Clowns voted for the president?" Josh Baker answered.

"Not quite," Ms. Lute said. "Since prior to the Revolutionary War, there was no office of president to vote for."

"Hundred percent trick question," he said.

Ms. Lute's eyes fixed straight ahead as if she were using all her strength not to let them roll. "Two things. One, votes were cast under varying states of sobriety, and two, voting was easy to corrupt."

If Leo were here, he'd be sharing his fact about George Washington.

Ms. Lute transitioned into a discussion of voting security, while

Angeline studied the empty seat in front of her. Was Leo actually home recovering from his allergic reaction or using his time to concoct more stories about her for *The Shrieking Violet*?

Angeline had often wished her sister to be wrong but never more than with this.

Emmie raised her hand. "How do we know our votes in the student council election won't be corrupted?"

Ms. Lute smiled. "Checks and balances. Thanks to Maxine Chen, we'll have a brand-new voting app to use, but we'll also be employing traditional paper ballots. An experiment to allow us to discuss the flaws and benefits of each, which share a common trait: secrecy. Today, no one has to know your vote unless you tell them. Not parents, partners, friends—"

"Witches," Tad Marcus taunted underneath his fake sneeze.

Angeline bit the inside of her cheek.

Emmie again raised her hand. "That can help. I saw it with my grandmother. One of my dads, his father never fully accepted that he had a gay son, let alone that his gay son could get legally married. Took a lot for my dad to stand up to him, but my grandmother never could. She told me after he died that he'd sit down at the kitchen table with her before every election and tell her who to vote for."

"And did she?" Ms. Lute asked.

"Not once. She's the reason why I got into all this. I want to help people stand up for themselves."

"Thank you for sharing, Emmie. That's a good example of why anonymity has come to be thought of as imperative for our democratic process."

Sonya wrinkled her brow. "But it also lets people make a choice without having to stand behind it. They can lie about who they voted for, in polls, to their families, whoever."

"True," Ms. Lute said. "An unpopular opinion can gain traction under secrecy. Privacy versus open debate, that's what we'll be discussing today . . ."

Angeline's phone vibrated.

> **Maxine:** Got 'em. Not even a challenge. Like they wanted to be caught.

> **Maxine:** But . . . are you sure you want to know?

She already did.

Anonymous though it might be, she'd heard this voice loud and clear.

📢 📢 📢

Later, after dinner, while her mom made a PTA phone list, Gramps and Cat flipped through one of the oldest scrapbooks that Grams had made. He'd written some of those stories sixty years ago. Angeline tried to listen but couldn't focus on anything but what Maxine had confirmed.

She set aside the mountain of angel wings that continued to arrive at school and scooped up Tartan. Once she settled herself on her bed, her pillow propped behind her and the cat purring in her lap, she texted Leo.

> **Angeline:** Feeling okay?

> **Leo:** Except for the stomachache from the undercooked arepas Sammy made me.

Maybe she deserved it.
Maybe she didn't.

Angeline: Good.

Angeline: Oh, and by the way, you should learn to cover your tracks better.

Leo: ???

Angeline: IP addresses don't lie.

The Shrieking Violet and the Torres network were a match. Which Maxine discovered by digging into the paper's and Leo's email accounts.

Cat had been right. But Leo wasn't just feeding stories to *The Shrieking Violet*, he *was The Shrieking Violet*. Not only to dismantle Angeline's campaign, but to take her down—*her*, personally.

He'd wanted her to know it was him. There was no other reason for him bringing up her birthmark.

She should have been livid. She should have screamed at him in all caps.

Her breaths came quick, each one stinging deep.

How did they even get here?

She didn't bother to blink away her tears and texted through blurred vision.

Angeline: I know The Shrieking Violet is you.

Then she blocked his number and deleted his contact information, her body folding in on itself, her face buried in the soft fur of the purring cat, her heart heavy in her chest the way it had been only twice before: the morning that Cat flushed her wish rock and the night after her dad had left.

25

When Cat Wraps Herself in
Yellow Caution Tape

Cat passed by her bedroom door, closed more than an hour ago by Angeline. She helped Gramps return the scrapbooks to his closet and asked, "Think Grams would approve of me following in your footsteps?"

"Likely, though she'd steal your passport and stash it in the freezer." More nostalgia than usual dampened his smile. "Ah, she'd want you to be happy. That's all she ever wanted for any of us. But I swear she'd smack the back of your dad's head if she were here. Can't help but feel responsible. I raised him."

A tightness gripped Cat's chest. "Well, you raised us too, and I think we're mostly doing okay," she said while silently cursing her father.

"Not okay. Great." Gramps settled on the edge of the bed and gestured for Cat to sit beside him. "Both of you. Angeline's got your grams's verve and sass and isn't afraid to show it. But you know something, Cathleen, so do you. Maybe you use your talents differently, but you are just as brave and smart and witty and ambitious as your sister." He kissed her forehead. "Couldn't be prouder of you."

Love and appreciation for all her grandfather had done bloomed in her chest. If only her grams was still with them. Cat's chest tightened as her eyes fell upon the framed photo on his nightstand. Grams standing behind Cat and Angeline in matching rash guard shirts and cowboy hats on Eggshell Beach. Cat was holding a toy Woody, and Angeline, Jessie. They'd just jumped the waves, the whole time Angeline unafraid, which had made Cat unafraid.

"Sometimes we see what we want to see instead of what is," Gramps said. "And the danger is it becomes a self-fulfilling prophecy. But you know what's fortunate? Those who set the prophecy have the power to change it."

Change things with Angeline? Could she? Fill an Instagram with photos of the two of them on Eggshell Beach, in the hatchback, on . . . double dates? Would that be the life she wanted? All the things the Fit to Print award and Northwestern and her goal of being a correspondent never made room for?

She stumbled over Tartan, who scampered down the hall with Angeline's filming ribbon between his teeth with as much pride as if it were a giant rat.

Cat quietly opened their bedroom door in case Angeline was filming. They'd spoken since last night, but they hadn't spoken about last night. Now part of her was afraid to, like if they did, it wouldn't happen again.

As Cat peeked inside, she saw Angeline curled around the angel pillow on her bed, video chatting.

"No, I'm not sorry I asked you," Angeline said with an ache in her voice. "I already knew. Maybe I always did."

"The IP address proves your sister was right all along," Maxine's voice said.

"I guess I should have listened," Angeline said.

"Now what? Tell Schwartzy?"

"You think he'd get in trouble?"

"Oh no, you didn't say that. Leo writes all that crap about you in *The Shrieking Violet*, and you're worried about him getting in trouble?"

The Shrieking Violet.

Leo.

Cat's fists clenched.

And her heart sank.

She'd known it in her gut, yet she'd hoped, same as Angeline, that she was wrong. Cat pictured her sister's face when they'd gotten home from the hospital. Not just worried about Leo but lined with guilt. She could still feel Angeline's fingers in her hair, remembered, despite all the years in between, her own trailing through Angeline's wet strands that night she'd come home from their dad's.

No matter what Angeline had done, Leo had gone too far. And Cat hadn't gone far enough. She'd never once responded to one of the threads calling Angeline "Hothead Quinn." She hadn't defended her.

Angeline's voice lowered. "Maybe I should just bow out."

"Nuh-uh," Maxine said. "You're not dropping out. My polls have had you ahead this whole time."

"And now?"

"Did I tell you my voting app's nearly done?"

"Nice swerve. But, yeah, that's what I thought about the polls. I've seen the comments on Leo's Insta."

"Voters are fickle. Which means you can get them back."

Tartan ran across Cat's feet, hit the end of the hall, and darted back. Just as his paw landed beside her foot, she dropped and tugged the ribbon out of his mouth.

It was chewed up and wet. But she tightened her hand around it.

In the newsroom the next day after school, Ravi drew his latest cartoon: Acedia as the *Titanic*, Angeline on a raft, each limb stretched out to save a Frankengirl who was dangling in the water, her phone in her hand videoing herself, and Leo, his back turned, partying on another boat. The influences of the exhibit at the Boston Public Library showed in the pop culture reference and the one-panel scale. But he'd made it feel entirely his own. She wanted to say that, to compliment him, but she didn't want it to seem like she'd been spying.

She faced her computer, plugged in *The Shrieking Violet*'s website, and the urge to scream at Leo returned. She wanted to turn him in, but she didn't want to make things worse for Angeline. The article on her birthmark had left her more embarrassed than #HotheadQuinn. Maybe it was because the latter didn't have guys checking out her ass at every turn.

Cat would like to think the administration would discipline Leo, but even if it did, would some see him as a martyr? Would some claim Maxine, as the best friend, couldn't be trusted? Could it all backfire on Angeline?

Yet Cat needed *The Shrieking Violet* shut down.

If she revealed the truth in *The Red and Blue*, maybe she'd be able to control the spin.

She considered texting Emmie, but they hadn't been on the same page the last time, and besides, Ravi *was* right here. Maybe they could walk into the harbor and talk it through. Stop for frozen yogurt or scones or—

Ravi stood. "All right. That's it for me. Unless you need anything?"

She lost her nerve. "I'm good."

"See you tomorrow then, Chief."

He left, and Cat promised herself that she wouldn't stalk his feed later.

Reluctantly, she returned to the *The Shrieking Violet*:

It's A-a-a-alive! Maybe Inside You!

Oh, do we have a tail to tell, dearies!

We at The Shrieking Violet *love being green as much as the next information source. (Well, maybe not, considering said next information source still prints on paper! Gasp!)*

And so it is with great sadness weighing down our shrieks that we must advise against being environmentally conscious and filling a reusable bottle with water from Acedia's drinking fountains. For this is a green of the "ribbit" kind, one that will soon require a delivery of lily pads, which, come to think of it, might actually be trés chic and a substantial improvement in decor.

Absurdity had reached a new level. Tadpoles living in the school's water fountains. Leo was more creative than she'd thought, she'd give him that.

Though he'd done the same thing with the vegan bacon, taking a kernel of truth and spiraling it into a story. Earlier that week, two freshmen had gotten sick in front of the water fountain outside the gym—*after* mixing twelve packets of energy powder into a gallon of water and daring each other to chug.

Cat's mind churned with likes and comments and tadpoles and #HotheadQuinn and Leo and Ravi, and she needed air. She left the newsroom for the empty halls and almost immediately came upon a flash of yellow near the girls' bathroom. Caution tape. Three strands wrapped around the water fountain. An itch crept underneath her skin. She kept walking. Down the west corridor to the boys' bathroom and another water fountain, more yellow caution tape. That itch spread. She increased her speed and did a lap around the school.

More yellow.

More itching.

Every.

Single.

One.

By the time Cat had come full circle to the first, she wanted to claw her hair out. Every drinking fountain in the school had been covered in yellow caution tape. A petition signed by nearly a hundred students hung above each one, demanding the administration conduct testing and warning fellow students to avoid using until *The Shrieking Violet* confirmed the water was safe.

How was this even possible?

Leo had reach. Reach Cat didn't.

She tore off one of the strands. Static cling attached it to her, and each turn only entangled it further. She spun out of it, flung it to the ground, and stomped.

Reach that maybe Cat never would.

Stomp, stomp, stomp.

Or maybe never would like this.

She pulled out her phone and texted Grady.

Cat: Up for some investigative reporting?

He responded instantly with a series of thumbs-ups. She asked him to come back to school and kicked at the caution tape one last time. Her mind begged for her to return her phone to her pocket, but her heart disobeyed. She swiped open Instagram. Not Ravi's feed. Natalie's. She was at Eggshell Beach, sharing a pint of orange-colored frozen yogurt with Ravi.

26

When Angeline Takes an Ice Bath

Angeline shook food into Tartan's bowl. Cat was out, her mom had texted a thousand apologies that she'd be working late, and Gramps was watching the Red Sox at the Irish bar since none of them would curse at the umpires with him. Baseball was how Angeline had learned every bad word.

Every bad word now an adjective to describe Leo.

Tartan dropped the angel wing he'd taken as a toy and scurried to his bowl. Angeline grabbed a yogurt and reread back issues of *The Shrieking Violet*, now with the perspective of Leo as its creator.

The live-streamed streaking during homecoming had Tad Marcus written all over it. She'd seen his text begging Leo to help coordinate it for last year's junior prom. How had she not remembered that until now?

Jennifer Lawrence cousin? Sure. They'd watched the Hunger Games movies three times with Sammy, finding his crush totally cute. A descendant of George Washington? Angeline thought back to Leo's random fact about him at the lighthouse. Totally fit.

And Angeline and Cat living outside the charter school region when they'd applied? Like Cat said, Angeline had been the one to tell him. The grill fire, the birthmark—it all made sense now in retrospect.

Her secrets, entrusted to someone she thought would protect them like they were his own. She'd misjudged. She wouldn't do it again.

She clicked on the headline for *The Shrieking Violet*'s most recent story: "It's A-a-a-alive! Maybe Inside You!"

At least Leo had learned a thing or two from her about how to write a headline that demanded to be clicked. She read the full story, which was ridiculous but also creative.

Super creative.

Super creative *fiction*.

Leo had written a fiction story for an ELA assignment last year. It had taken her about thirty seconds to realize that he'd ripped off an old *X-Files* episode they'd watched—and gotten the twist wrong.

She scrolled back.

"Student council is yours because your students."

Leo might have needed editing help with his storytelling, but his grammar had always been rock-solid. The "your" and "you're" mistake was unusual. As were the "its" not "it's" and more than a handful of other errors and sloppy typos.

She dissected each article *The Shrieking Violet* had published with all of its sarcastically silly humor.

"Shriek with me, folks!"

Earnest, loyal, smart, that was Leo.

"Bacon from cows."

Funny? Leo wasn't this funny.

"Succubus, some percentage true."

Leo wasn't funny.

"The hard thing about doing nothing's that you never know when you're done."

But his brother was.

Dammit, dammit, dammit. Seriously, what were these loafers constructed from? Thorns? Needles? Razor blades? Each step of her walk to Leo's house brought a new and more brutal form of torture. She breathed through the pain and the nerves, unsure which was greater.

(The pain, it was definitely the pain.)

Leo's house sat on the block behind Frontage Street, but a straight route required climbing two fences and trespassing through a backyard with a prowling Satanic mutt. Leo had done it a couple of times when he'd stayed at Angeline's past curfew. She should have risked it if she was going to insist on wearing these damn shoes. She'd owed another endorsement and figured she'd get an action shot. Now it felt like she was *being* shot, over and over again. Less than ideal if her #ad came with a pic of her blood staining the gold fabric.

Angeline whimpered along until, finally, the slate-blue house came into view. Clapboard siding, black shutters, traditional neat and tidy New England colonial. The 1808 in black letters on the white placard by the door still instilled a sense of awe in her. The history of this town ran deep.

Yet glamorous it was not. Unlike NYC and London, where Evelyn split her time. It wasn't trendy either like Nantucket or Mallorca, where Evelyn vacationed. As an influencer, part of Evelyn's appeal stemmed from living—on full display—a life others wanted, so they'd want everything else she was shilling too. Her brand was her life.

If Angeline were to follow in her footsteps, this small town an hour from the nearest city couldn't continue to be called home. Yet Angeline belonged here, where she could smell the salt in the air and hear the croak of seagulls and walk to three beaches within ten minutes. Like she and Leo had done together for the past three summers.

She knocked on the door.

Leo answered. "Ang? What are you doing here?"

"First, your parents home?"

He shook his head, and his dark hair fell into his eyes. "Just me."

"Good." She stepped inside the house and gingerly removed her shoes, gasping as the edges scraped her raw skin. Her hand flew out, and Leo caught it, steadying her.

"I swear it wasn't me," he said.

She breathed heavily. "I know."

Confusion lined his face, and then his eyes widened in surprise, recognition, and guilt.

Seated on the edge of the bathtub, Angeline faced one way and Leo the other. Thanks to the four trays of ice he'd dumped in, her feet soaked in a freezing cold bath as she explained that the joke about doing nothing in *The Shrieking Violet* was the same one Sammy had made in the hospital. Which meant . . .

"Sammy all along," he said, defeated.

She nodded and swirled her foot in the water, but it hurt to move, so she stayed still.

"I'm sorry," they suddenly said in unison, to which Leo shook his head.

"Sammy's all my fault," he said. "He cracked his screen, and his phone's been temperamental, so I've been letting him borrow mine."

"With our texts."

"And photos. Of skinny-dipping."

"Oh God." Angeline's cheeks grew hot despite the cold numbing her lower half. "And he was there the night I told you about the charter lottery and going to my dad's."

"Faking sleep, it turns out." He shook his head. "I can't believe he did all of this."

"He idolizes you. And I hurt you."

"But that's not a reason to do this. It's so . . . elaborate."

"Like Franken-donuts?"

"Not the same."

"No, but maybe that's why he thought it was okay." Angeline realized the truth of this as she said it. "He thought he was helping you win. Which would help with your mom and everything at home."

"An election isn't going to turn our mother into someone she's not." He snorted. "Well, at least *my* election. Her own . . ."

Angeline didn't laugh, though there was a time when she would have. "I'm far from her biggest fan, but maybe you should cut her some slack. A Latina woman running . . . can't be easy."

"You sound like my dad." Leo breathed out a sigh.

The coolness of the porcelain tub permeated Angeline's leggings. "Now what?"

"I drop out. End this."

"Is that what you want?"

He shrugged. "Schwartz is right that things are getting out of control. This stuff with the Frankengirls kicked off something we didn't know was happening."

Angeline would have liked to have been able to say, "You didn't know," meaning the boys, meaning the administration that hadn't been paying close enough attention. But that would have meant that Angeline knew, and the truth was, she hadn't thought much about it before all this.

Leo picked up a bottle of eucalyptus bubble bath. "I said all that crap about not telling us what to do because it was the opposite of your strategy."

Knew it.

He picked at the edge of the label. "Neither of us got into this because we wanted to change anything. I'd have bet on Schwartz walking through the halls with Slothy in a papoose before I'd have said this school would care about anything. But now I'm learning things I never knew. Like how that thing with Olivia's phone has happened twice before. She told a teacher who said to laugh it off or it'd only get worse. And that Ash kid writing on your posters isn't just a suck-up on your campaign because he likes you—he believes in what you're saying."

"How do you know this?"

"He made some comments on my Insta that weren't mean or rude. Just real." Leo gave up on peeling off the label and set the bottle down. "Like how not being able to afford a limo for prom doesn't just make you feel left out and embarrassed, but makes parents feel like they let their kid down. Then this other kid, a sophomore, he came to me and said he didn't make the cut for basketball so now he has to stop playing. He asked how he's supposed to get the practice to do better in tryouts next year. He's not wrong. Other schools around here participate in an intramural league. Maybe leveling the playing field in a place that's supposed to be about learning isn't the worst thing."

"But it's not the real world."

"Maybe it shouldn't be yet. And maybe we should have more of a say, like with your peer jury. I've been reading, and other schools do."

"So why not Acedia?" Angeline said, without the sarcastic edge she would have a couple of weeks ago. "Though merging platforms would kind of throw a wrench into the whole Battle of the Exes thing."

"Yeah, about that . . ." He sat up straight, his back muscles tensing beneath his thin cotton shirt. "Maybe I *was* following Tad so the guys didn't think my balls were in your purse. But instead—"

"They were in Tad's."

"Which the current dress code wouldn't let him carry, by the way."

She smiled. While she'd been staring at the slope of his nose and the freckle on his earlobe and the side of his hair that needed a fresh buzz, he'd been fixated on the sink across from them. Now, he turned his head, and his eyes flickered between hers and her lips. She wanted him to kiss her as much as she didn't. He leaned in, and she stood.

"I should go, before someone comes home."

"Yeah, yeah, okay," Leo said with the tone of someone who'd just been rejected, which wasn't what she'd meant to do. So much had happened between them, she just didn't want to try to resolve it beside a toilet when they could be interrupted any second.

Is that really why?

She stepped out of the tub, and Leo eyed her claddagh ring. "I'll talk to Sammy, I promise. But do you think . . . could you maybe not tell anyone? If the school or . . . anyone . . . learned it was him, he'd get in trouble, and he's just a kid. He's got everything before him."

"So do we."

"Do we? Or have we ruined it?"

"Not yet." He sighed with the same relief she felt. "I won't say anything, but he has to stop."

Keeping the secret wasn't just for Leo or Sammy. She wouldn't risk Maxine getting into trouble for hacking into a student's email—even a student publishing that. But it meant she'd have to keep the truth from Cat. With how much Cat hated *The Shrieking Violet* and her annoying adherence to right and wrong, Cat might push to tell Ms. Lute to make sure it didn't happen again. So long as the paper disappeared, Cat would get what she wanted. She'd be happy.

While Angeline carefully dried her feet, Leo went to get her a pair of shoes.

She reached the living room first, where Leo's mom eyeballed her from the giant poster propped beside the stone fireplace, that same single photo of the family on Los Roques Beach, where they'd vacationed with both sets of Leo's grandparents two summers ago. Smaller yard signs rested in the corner, flyers on the coffee table, an extra TV on a stand where the rocking chair used to be. Though his mom had a campaign office, naturally things would wind up here too, which meant Leo couldn't escape it despite the deal he'd made with her.

A deal he'd break if he dropped out.

"She never wears these." Leo held up a pair of black canvas sneakers. "You can keep them, so you don't have to come by and return them."

"I'll return them." She relished the softness of the socks he gave her despite how weird it was to wear his mother's shoes, which were exactly her size. "On one condition. You don't drop out. I want to win, but not by default."

He stuffed his hands into his pockets. "That really what you want?"

She nodded. "Besides, it'll be hard enough on Sammy when you confront him about *The Shrieking Violet*. Let's not make it worse by you dropping out of the race too."

Silence held them together until the sound of a car interrupted. It stopped just past the house, so that only the back quarter was visible, along with its VOTE TORRES bumper sticker.

Angeline's heart thudded. "Did your mom get a new car?"

"No. It must be someone from the campaign dropping off Sammy. He went straight from school."

With a shout of "Much obliged, as always!" Sammy appeared from the passenger side.

"Uh, maybe I'll go out the back." Angeline picked up the shoes that might have forever ruined her for loafers. "Better if he doesn't think I pressured you into this."

"You didn't, you know."

"I know." She let Leo's hand graze hers as she moved past him, heading toward the back door, thinking of Sammy. He was a good kid. Which meant Angeline had become the type of person to make a good kid like Sammy do what he did.

27

When Cat Clicks and Baits

The five o'clock alarm trilled in Cat's ears. She tugged out her head-phones and quietly extracted herself from bed. She grabbed her backpack with her computer already inside and snuck out without waking Angeline.

Thanks to the floodlight in the adjacent parking lot, the apartment was bright enough that she didn't need to turn on any lights. She settled herself at the dining room table, opened her link to *The Red and Blue*'s server, and clicked on the file named "Grady's Secret Interviews." Nellie Bly would have been so disappointed. No more enlisting Grady in undercover operations without some serious training.

She'd sent him to conduct interviews with Leo's teammates and friends under the guise of a deep candidate profile. Meanwhile, she'd been reviewing every *Shrieking Violet* story and social media post. She needed to uncover at least one piece of evidence to back up Maxine's finding. That way, when she reported the story, no one would be able to deny that Leo had created *The Shrieking Violet* to take his rival down. So far, she had nothing.

She'd been hoping Grady had better luck, but standard blow-hard "Leo's the best, man" quotes filled her screen.

"There's got to be something," Cat muttered. She tucked her legs underneath her on the dining room chair, the beige microfiber flattened from use smooth against her bare skin.

She jammed the down arrow on her keyboard, skimming until she came across a quote from Andreas Costa.

"Leo's a big fan of cupcakes," Costa winked.

Cat resisted the urge to correct Grady's notes since one couldn't "wink" actual words. But Costa *had* winked. Why wink at Leo liking or not liking cupcakes?

Cupcakes? Really?

She was about to hit the down arrow when she remembered something: Leo didn't have a sweet tooth.

Which meant . . . was Costa not talking about the frosted kind?

The final spirit day at the end of the previous year began like always: lights out, music low, cheerleaders positioned in the center of the gym. Up went the volume and on came the lights to signal the start of their routine. Yet the lights had been replaced with black bulbs that revealed the word "cupcake" written in invisible ink across the back of the cheerleaders' uniforms.

The person responsible had never been found.

Cat looked more closely at Grady's notes. Costa was also quoted as saying, "Leo's like a Jedi master. He can make shit happen by force."

A bunch of stuff followed about him orchestrating plays and outguessing their opponents and rallying his teammates from certain defeat.

The conclusion was that his skill as an athlete and strategist made things happen. The implication went wider.

Leo was hiding his real motivation for running for student council president.

Leo was hiding his writing of *The Shrieking Violet*.

Leo was hiding his mom's visit to Principal Schwartz.

At the end of last year.

And ever since, things had been worse between him and his mom.

"No way!" Cat said.

She dropped her feet to the ground and loaded a blank template. Her fingers furiously hit the keyboard. This went so far beyond Leo lying about why he was running. Leo shouldn't even have been *allowed* to run; he should have been suspended last year for orchestrating the spirit week incident. *The Shrieking Violet* wasn't his first prank. She wrote what she was sure would be the Fit to Print award-winning story, and the apartment filled with natural light as the sun rose.

Finally, she leaned against the back of the chair and read over her article.

The adrenaline that had fueled her faded.

Circumstantial, all of it. So many questions remained. She started to delete, then paused. Because *The Shrieking Violet* would have an answer. A germ of truth that sprouted into whatever Leo wanted. She wondered how Angeline felt about Leo presumably learning such manipulation tactics from her. Skirting the truth was a core tenet of her YouTube channel.

Cat opened her browser and typed in "Ask an Angel."

I Had an Elephant Dung Facial, and You Won't Believe What Happened Next!

Three Out of Five Women Are Making This HUGE Gaffe
Every Day. Are You One of Them?

The Alternative to Sexting That's Got Everyone Hitting
Send!

Angeline could write a good headline, if you could call the titles
to her videos headlines. But Ask an Angel was entertainment, not
news, despite what a high percentage of her viewers thought.

Cat backed out to her home page, which she'd set up to compile
the top headlines from all the major news outlets.

Choice of Lingerie Predicts Who Women Will Vote For

What Democratic Candidate Says to This Elderly
Woman Leaves Everyone in Tears

The Oval Could Be Round If Republican Candidate
Doesn't Shed Pounds per Doctor's Orders

These were *professional news* outlets. Where journalists worked.
Where journalists were being laid off in droves.

And whoever was left behind was doing the same thing Angeline
was. Hinting. Exaggerating. Inflaming. Scare tactics. Clickbaiting
all the way. They said her generation got its news from social media. This was the alternative? Better? For how long?

She wanted to ask if anyone noticed, but perhaps the real question was if anyone cared. Maybe she really was the dinosaur Angeline always said she was . . . because she'd been taught by one. The
rules she'd been playing by, ones her grandfather instilled in her,
ones she saw in Nellie Bly and Martha Gellhorn and Katharine

Graham and Christiane Amanpour, were no longer how this game was played.

And maybe the only path for dinosaurs was extinction.

Cat set her fingers back on her keyboard. With her heart pounding against her rib cage, she stopped thinking and simply typed, laying down her suspicions without bothering to ensure they were backed up. With every letter she struck, she had to stop herself from hitting delete. But soon, she found the story reflected the essence of what she believed to be true. So she kept going, layering in more narrative, framing the quotes.

She found herself breathing heavily with each piece that came together as something plausible, something real. It was easier than she'd have thought. To create a thread made of the thinnest of fibers. To lead a reader to draw their own conclusions . . . conclusions such as Leo being behind the sexist "cupcake" stunt and someone letting him go unpunished.

She hinted, just like everyone else.

"Leo might not be able to make things happen by force, but someone else could."

She insinuated, just like everyone else.

"Someone else with more pull."

She gave just enough so her readers could surmise the rest. Then she gave a little more.

"Who in Leo's life holds such power?"

Her fingers trembled as she saved the article and followed the instructions Grady had left in the "Social Media!!!!!" folder. She published the article on *The Red and Blue*'s website as a breaking news exclusive.

Then she shut her laptop and stopped fighting the tears pricking her eyes.

28

When Angeline Drowns

7 DAYS TO THE ELECTION

Angeline couldn't help thinking about the time she almost drowned.

The summer after sixth grade, she'd spent nearly every day at the beach, searching for wish rocks that she'd drop in a plastic bucket each morning and scatter back onto the sand each afternoon. The tide would steal them overnight and redistribute them in a new spot for her to find the next day. She loved walking along the edge of the water, dancing with the incoming waves, letting her feet be buried by the sand until all she could see were her ankles and all she could feel was a heaviness pressing down against her feet. She'd yank herself free, delighting in the release of suction and dipping her toes in the pools left behind. And then, one afternoon, she pulled, and the sand pulled back.

At first, she relished the game getting harder. But as more waves rolled in, the sucking power of the sand increased, and she was buried deeper and deeper until her heart thundered in her ears and panic set in. She'd made it more difficult by refusing to drop her bucket, holding on to those rocks and those wishes yet to be made. It was bad luck to drop a wish rock without tracing the line around the middle.

Her struggle exhausted her so that when a wave twice her height barreled through, she had no strength left to resist its riptide. An invisible force pulled at her, the ocean a magnet and she the object in its orbit. She knew what to do, to float on her back and wait it out, swim parallel to shore until she could head back in. She had to let herself be bent to its will.

But her will was all she had left with her father moving out at the start of the summer. Her mom didn't seem to miss him; neither did Cat. Angeline became intent on training herself out of it. She could do anything she set her mind to.

So when the riptide tried to control Angeline, she'd been determined not to let it. Her legs kicked and her arms stroked and her head bobbed over, under, over, under the water until the salt stung her eyes and the echo of the waves muffled her ears and she swallowed so much water her stomach cramped. All along, her sandcastle bucket floated beside her, just out of reach.

Then she caught sight of a bright orange bathing suit in the distance.

Dad.

Orange to match his hair, he would say. It made him stand out, so no matter how far Angeline and Cat ran, they'd be able to turn around and always find their way back to him. She realized now that meant he didn't have to look up from whatever he was doing and find them.

But that day, she'd let her legs drift up and spread her arms wide. Head back, eyes on the puffy white clouds above, she'd floated and waited for him.

All that came was the cornucopia of rocks that lived at the end of the beach, right before the shoreline curved back out to sea. A rock scraped her arm, and she knew where she was. She knew how to save herself. So she did.

She hugged the next rock that came, her fingernails scraping against the slime of the seagrass and algae coating it. She steadied herself, reached for another and another until she was able to stand. She dragged herself all the way to the sea wall and lay down on top, running her tongue along her lips to rid them of the caked-on salt. When she'd caught her breath, she sat up, searching for her dad. But the beach had been empty.

That had stung deeper than all the rest of it.

She should have learned from all those wishes made on all those rocks that she couldn't will something into being.

But then Cat had appeared, a small float shaped like a flamingo clutched under her trembling arm.

That was what she remembered now, as she stood in front of her locker reading the story Cat had written about Leo.

Angeline's heart thundered, her ears muffled, her eyes burned, just like that day in the ocean, but here the riptide tearing at her was her sister. And still their dad was nowhere in sight to save either one of them.

Cat had betrayed her. Outright.

Angeline didn't care that the bell for first period was ringing. She barreled into the newsroom and flung her tote bag to the ground. "How could you do this? How could you use what I told you? How could you lie to me? How could you lie to yourself?"

How, how, how, how, how?

Cat held up her hands. "Take a breath, Ang. What are you talking about?"

"What am I . . . This." She lifted her phone. "I'm talking about this."

Cat skirted around Angeline and shut the door. "If you'll just calm down and let me explain—"

"Explain?" Angeline's fury nearly blinded her. "Explain away giving up everything you've claimed to believe in? Everything you claim I don't? For a story? To win some award that doesn't actually matter?"

Lines puckered around Cat tight lips. "This story *is* a story, Angeline. It deserves to be told not for me or for an award that *does* matter, but because it's the truth." The word broke as she said it. "Something's going on here. What Sammy told you proves it."

"But you don't know what." Angeline began pacing the room. "So you just guess? Speculate? Instead of finding the truth? What would Gramps think?"

Cat's hands shook, and she pushed them down into the pockets of that skirt she shouldn't even have one of but had three.

"It's just a line of inquiry to prompt the reader to think," Cat said. "It's no different than what everyone else is doing."

"And that's supposed to make it okay?"

"I don't get you. I can't win with you."

"No, you can't turn this around on me, not this time."

"But why do you think I did this? I did it for you."

Angeline snorted. "Yeah, you know, you really are a shitty actress."

"No." Cat's voice trembled. "Don't do that . . ." Her eyes welled with tears that were like a sucker punch to Angeline's gut. She couldn't remember the last time she saw Cat cry. Not even after their dad left. "I started writing the story because I wanted to help you. Leo . . . *The Shrieking Violet*, everything he said . . . did to you . . . to us . . . We couldn't just let him get away with it." Her voice weakened as she said, "It was mostly there."

243

"Leo? What Leo did . . . oh . . . *oh* . . ." Angeline felt that pull of the ocean, and she needed to sit.

"I wasn't eavesdropping. I-I-I didn't mean to be. Tartan had your ribbon, and Gramps had just said . . ." She focused on the cartoon version of herself on the wall above the computer. "I was heading to our room when I heard you and Maxine . . . I'm really sorry, Ang. I mean . . . it's Leo." Cat reached out as if to take Angeline's hand but stopped just before their skin touched. "He was like family."

"Is. He is." And once again she'd hurt him. "We were wrong. Maxine . . . well, she was right. The IP address does match his, but it wasn't Leo. It was Sammy."

"But that doesn't make any sense. Sammy couldn't possibly know all of that. Unlike Leo. I know how much it must hurt, but it's okay. I'll handle it. I'll go to Ms. Lute, and I won't involve you or Maxine."

"No, Cat, you can't. I went to see Leo last night. Sammy'd been snooping on his phone. He learned enough of what he didn't already know."

"You're sure? Absolutely positive?"

Angeline nodded.

"That means I . . ." Cat retreated until her back hit her "EIC" chair. "I've turned into—"

"Me?" Angeline said. "Irish twins. Wouldn't Mom be proud?"

Angeline rested her head in her hands, trying to figure out if she was madder at Cat or Sammy or Ms. Lute for pushing this whole election thing or whoever posted the Frankengirls or herself . . . mad at herself.

The door to the newsroom opened, and Cat's eyes widened at the sight of Leo. Angeline started to speak, but he pressed the screen of his phone with one finger, and sound emerged from the speaker as a video began to play.

"In a breaking 'and that's news to you' exclusive, we've learned that Congressional Democratic candidate Eliza Torres may be implicated in a scandal at her son's private high school."

"It's not private," Cat said.

Leo's sharp look silenced her.

"Questions have arisen regarding her son's involvement in a sexist prank last year. According to what appears to be an unnamed but reliable source, someone may have arranged for Leo to go unpunished. Speculation that his mother, Eliza Torres, knew or perhaps even facilitated such action herself brings a new round of attention on her character for serving for elected office. She's already been called 'aggressive' and 'hot-tempered' by many—"

"By you," Leo snarled at the video before stopping it. "Did you know in New Zealand you can't do this? Election advertising is banned, candidates can't be on social media, and loser talking heads like this can't make a projection let alone a single comment about a candidate's clothes or heritage or temperament. They've got kiwis and integrity."

Angeline's stomach twisted.

"I-I-I'll fix it," Cat said. "I'll print a retraction and—"

"If you really think that will fix it, you're not just two-faced, you're naive." The red coloring Leo's normally tawny cheeks hadn't faded since he'd arrived. It just bloomed with varying shades of intensity. Peak level right now. Yet his tone was even and calm. Which somehow was loads worse than if he'd charged in screaming.

Angeline wanted to go to him and instead said, "She'll be okay, she always is."

His hand clenched his phone. "No wonder we were together. I said the same thing to my dad when he reamed me out this morning. And you know what he said? He asked if I heard that 'aggressive' and 'hot-tempered.'"

"Leo, I didn't think . . ." Cat said.

"Well, maybe we all should start," Leo said, and Angeline knew what she'd ask for if she had a wish rock right now. To go back to that day in her bedroom when all of this started.

"I haven't been thinking, or paying attention, or whatever," Leo said. "But this is what they've been doing all along, isn't it? Throwing in racist stereotypes any chance they get? And here we all are, making things worse."

Cat cleared her throat. "I thought you were behind *The Shrieking Violet*. I thought you were the one going after Angeline—"

"Two wrongs make a right, then?" he said.

"But the cupcake comment. I mean, do you suddenly like sweets?"

He pointed to the notebook he'd given her, which sat on her desk. "Aren't you supposed to be an investigative reporter? What was Costa talking about?"

"You."

"And? Strategy? Plays?"

"You mean lacrosse?"

"Lacrosse." He faced Angeline. "The sport I played for her and stopped playing because of her. Nothing like starting a game with brand-new white lacrosse balls—cupcakes. Google it if you don't believe me."

"But . . ." Cat started. "Then why was your mom meeting with Principal Schwartz?"

"The election, media approaching campus, which I kept to my-self because it sucked that the only thing that'd bring her around

246

was herself. Also made me look like I was getting special treatment. But then this morning, my dad told me it was more. There was a threat against her—she was . . ." He tugged at his hair. "Afraid it might extend to me. Security for me. That's why she came."

Cat glanced at Angeline, looking like she wanted a shell to crawl into. Angeline longed to join her, regretting being so critical of Leo's mom.

"I trusted you, Cat," Leo said. "Gave you that interview when I didn't want to."

"I'm sorry, Leo." Cat's whole body shrunk. "I don't know what else to say."

"Just wait, soon as you sit at your keyboard, you'll surely come up with something." He reset his jaw. "Dad wanted to sue the school and you for libel. Guess you have my mom being so strategic to thank for our lawyer not being here now. She thinks the attention would only make things worse." He jutted his chin toward Angeline. "And tell Maxine that she's wrong about the IP address. Sammy swore he didn't do it, and I believe him. But thanks, because he now thinks I'm an ass for believing he might have done it in the first place. Do me a favor and find yourselves another pair of brothers to scapegoat." He pointed to Angeline's feet. "And I want those back."

The silence grew as they stared at one another, finally broken by static from the speaker in the hall. "Leo Torres, please report to the principal's office. Leo Torres to the principal's office."

He closed his eyes and laughed. "Thing is, I actually wanted to do this. It's been nice being thought of as more than just Eliza Torres's son and the jock dating the most beautiful girl in school." He headed for the door. "What's that phrase about fool and shame?"

"You're not a fool, Leo."

"That's always been the difference between you and me, Ang. I've always been able to admit when I'm wrong."

29

When Cat Clucks Back

Cat couldn't help thinking about the time she'd crashed into a chicken coop.

She was in eighth grade and had only been to her dad's new place once before. He and his then girlfriend had picked up Cat and Angeline, and he'd helped with dinner, unlike at home, cutting onions for the salad, not knowing or remembering or caring that she and Angeline hated raw onions. The house belonged to his girlfriend. Smaller than theirs, but somehow felt bigger. Maybe because it was just the two of them.

That day, with the girlfriend now his new wife, Cat had ridden her bike. Past the river, down the winding road lined with so many thick, tall trees it was hard to believe the houses tucked behind were still part of her town. The ocean wasn't in charge here. It had been then that she'd realized she could live somewhere else. That she wanted to. But the ride was longer than she'd expected, and the sky darkened with each rotation of her wheel.

She'd studied the map on the computer, and it was basically three lefts and a straight ride down one long road, but somehow, she'd gotten lost. Her mom hadn't yet caved on giving them phones despite Angeline's pleading.

The handlebars slipped in her clammy hands, and the burning in her legs begged her to stop, but the memory of Angeline curled into her lap after she'd set that fire in her dad's grill propelled her forward. If only she knew where to.

She pumped harder, and then she saw him. Her dad, behind the wheel of his new wife's small SUV, heading toward her.

She panicked. Every thought of what she'd planned to say disappeared out of her head, and she spun the bike in the opposite direction. She skidded in the gravel on the side of the road and rolled down the embankment, trying to steer herself to flat ground when chicken wire rose up in front of her.

She jammed on the brakes and flew over the handlebars and into the coop. Three hens clucked as if she were a coyote, and the rooster puffed out, lowered his head, and started hopping on his wiry toes.

Her fear of birds increased in direct proportion to their size. The jagged movements of their heads and their black cold eyes freaked her out. They clucked. She clucked back. She jumped up and scrambled over the bent chicken wire. Long scratches ran down her hands and forearms, and something on her head felt sticky, and she tried not to imagine if it'd come from her or the chickens.

Her bike lay twisted on the ground. She stood at the bottom of the embankment, looking up, expecting to see her dad.

But he wasn't there.

He hadn't seen her. His focus had always been somewhere else.

She untangled her bike from the brush and walked it straight to the house beyond the chicken coop, where she'd called her mom to come pick her up.

The next day, she'd written her father a letter with all the things she'd planned to say to him. She'd never sent it. She hadn't needed to. Turned out, he did the main thing she'd asked all on his own: stopped disappointing them. She hadn't expected him to do it the way he did, by running off to LA with his new wife, playing the music he loved more than them in any club that would have him and simply opting out. But that worked too.

She'd watched Angeline struggling with it, but that day, when he hadn't appeared on the road above her, Cat knew she wouldn't. Sometimes the thing you wanted didn't want you, and that was okay. Forcing it meant getting less than what you wanted, far less than you deserved.

She wanted this. The Fit to Print award. But she didn't deserve it. She closed the email with the submission instructions and once again watched the story about Leo's mom. She still couldn't believe her article had basically reached the local news. They hadn't attributed anything to *The Red and Blue* or her. They'd simply reported what she'd reported, with no effort to verify anything. This was how easy it was to make suspicions and rumors fact.

She began typing an email to the news station, directing it to the retraction she'd just posted online. But she knew they wouldn't pick it up. They'd moved on.

She shut off the lights in the newsroom and headed for the parking lot. When she passed the front office, she saw more packages of angel wings had arrived. As had Leo and his mom. His face was somber, hers wasn't angry exactly . . . defeated, that was it.

Or maybe Cat was projecting.

No deaths occurred save for *The Shrieking Violet*. In the last days leading up to the election, the online paper went dark, perhaps resting on its tadpole laurels (the petition and parental calls forced the administration to conduct testing, and it would be another two weeks before the water fountains were cleared for use). The void was filled by active engagement within the walls of Acedia as well as out. While Quinn maintained a steady lead in Maxine Chen's online polls throughout the campaign—a point of contention by many, considering the friendship between Chen and Quinn—with five days remaining before the election, Quinn and Torres entered a dead heat.

Whether accusations of Quinn being a witch were truly to blame, her supporters were more outraged than ever. The pacifist kisses they'd been planting on her posters were replaced with aggressive graffiti on Torres's. Using what students reported smelled like nail polish, those behind Quinn painted in bright red things like "Nepotism's not my prez" and "Fakers can't be allowed to prosper."

Despite *The Red and Blue*'s retraction, the story about

Torres receiving preferential treatment brought direct attention to Acedia. Twice, teams from news stations in Boston
camped outside, interviewing students about the climate inside the school, seeking to uncover whether those students
with influential and wealthy parents seemed to receive perks
not available to the full student body.

"I didn't tell them this," Andreas Costa said, "but always
seemed fishy to me that Marcus didn't have any classes
after noon on Friday. Stacked up three study halls one after
another, where he got to nap for, like, three hours before every Friday-night game, while I had P.E. last period. I begged
for just one study hall before game night. So, you do the
math."

Costa wasn't the only one with a story like that to tell,
but with one or two exceptions, the focus remained on Torres
and Quinn. Yet what had once been platforms with concrete
goals largely devolved into a male versus female fight.

As memes of each—Quinn, an animated Frankengirl riding a broomstick, and Torres, a robot programmed by his
mom—went viral, attention-seekers on the lookout for the
next cause to exploit picked up the "Battle of the Exes" to further their own agendas.

On Twitter, a vocal male-rights proponent started a
hashtag, #UnleashTheTorres, supporting Torres, and in response, a prominent feminist continued urging followers
to knit angel wings in support of Quinn. By election week,
seven hundred pairs of angel wings had arrived, and more

continue to arrive daily from as far away as Alaska and Singapore, where year-round temperatures above ninety degrees would seem to make knitting a less than popular pastime.

Despite this being a high school election, the "he said, she said" narrative struck a chord with a nation that had been having the same debate on a grander scale for the past few years, culminating in a presidential election where issues of minorities—especially women, LGBTQIA+, immigrants— had taken center stage.

Yet Acedia might have faded behind the next viral flash in the pan had it not been for what started it all: the Frankengirls.

"They're baaaaaaack!" Baker reportedly was the first to cry, directing students into the cafeteria during the exchange of classes four days before the election.

Huge blowups of all three original Frankengirls blanketed the lunchroom like tablecloths. Quinn arrived before Torres, leading some to question his dedication to the cause of investigating the responsible party.

While two female students from the junior class were seen ripping a poster to pieces, Quinn strode to the center of the cafeteria and carefully rolled the one on the table in front of her into a long cylinder. Even before Quinn spoke, witnesses say other girls were already mirroring her action and, instead of shredding the posters, calmly turning each into a large scroll.

Quinn's words were equally restrained. Instead of posturing and campaign promises, she simply said such action hurt.

Goldberg relayed Quinn's impromptu speech. "She said—and I remember it exactly because I got chills. And, well, yeah, because I videoed it: 'Imagine actually doing this to us. I mean, actually tearing us limb from limb and stitching us back together. Because that's what this feels like for us—all of us. If you still think this is one big joke, go ahead and laugh. And see if anyone's laughing with you. Respect us. Respect one another. What we need in this world is empathy. Because we are all so much More Than Our Parts.'"

Comments and cheers poured in on Quinn's social media accounts, and it seemed she'd be a shoo-in not just to win the student council election but to nab an interview with Oprah or a dinner invite from Emma Watson.

And then, a phone without a passcode, an angry ex, and one last shriek changed everything.

As Goldberg said, they should have seen it coming. "Football players, right? Everyone knows you can't trust a jock."

Click for more: 4 of 6

30

When Cat Hits the Big Time

4 DAYS TO THE ELECTION

Cat's hands wouldn't stop shaking.

"Let's hear it for *The Boston Globe*!" Ravi clapped as Cat entered the newsroom.

A goofy grin took hold . . . until Cat saw Grady's eyes, the disappointment made worse by his large glasses. He'd begged her to be able to write the story about the resurgence of the Frankengirls. The story that had just been linked to by *The Boston Globe*.

Her phone lit up.

The story that had just been retweeted.

Again.

And again.

"That's awesome, Cat," Ravi said. "Huge deal."

Grady's hands twisted something white and fluffy.

He'd wanted it so much.

"Not so huge," Cat said nonchalantly despite the fireworks ricocheting in her belly. "Really, just a lucky break."

"Um, radar?" Ravi's eyebrows lifted. "You apply for an internship or pitch a freelance article, you can namecheck it. Make sure you screenshot it." Cat gave the briefest of nods, but Ravi kept going. "Or better yet, you could be a special correspondent on this! You've seen the traction online, haven't you? No way they won't pick up the full story, especially after the accusations against Mrs. Torres and the statement she gave. Acedia's hitting the big time."

"Thanks to me," Grady blurted out, tossing down a ball of yarn and the angel wing he'd been knitting.

An angel wing? Really? So much for being objective.

Ravi turned to him. "Oh, did you get Cat quotes for the Frankengirls story?"

"No, she did that all on her own," Grady said.

Though he had no right to make her feel guilty, Cat said delicately, "Listen, Grady, we talked about this. You've been invaluable on so much, but with this one, there just wasn't the time. Besides, there was no way Mr. Monte was going to let you miss class in order to write it. I'm a senior; it's just different."

Angeline calmly rolling that huge Frankengirl poster spoke volumes in its quiet resistance. Videos had been going viral even as Angeline spoke. Not a minute could be wasted in getting *The Red and Blue*'s factual account of what had transpired out there, and Cat had a correct feeling that Ms. Lute would excuse her so she could write the story quickly. Without hers, the only reports would be ones framed by nonprofessionals.

A voice inside Cat scoffed: *Some nerve, lumping yourself into the professional category after what you did to Leo.*

"I'm good, Cat," Grady said. "I know a story when I see one."

"I know—"

"Do you?" He closed the gap between them. He always towered over her, but until this moment had never used his height to his advantage. "Ever stop to think how the news picked up your story about Leo and the cupcakes so fast?"

"I . . . well, all the followers Angeline has, and the original Frankengirls had gotten some attention in the local papers—"

"Me. It was me. I sent it to my cousin. Bo Booker was on it, like *bam*! He brought it to the producer. The story, the news stations camping out here after, *The Boston Globe* paying attention to you now—none of it would have happened without me."

Grady had started all of that? He wanted her to be grateful, but all she felt was even more responsibility for the fallout that had landed on Leo's mom.

"I'm your secret weapon, Chief. Use me or . . . or someone else will."

The indignation on Grady's face took her off guard in how much it hurt, like catching the tip of a finger in a drawer as it closed. She'd dedicated time to mentoring him. Had she gotten through at all? Or was he still aiming to be like his fame-hungry cousin?

"I am using you," she said. "I already said yes to you live-tweeting the election assembly on Friday. Do Snap and Insta too, okay?" He softened, and she added truthfully, "That's all anyone's going to pay attention to. By the time my story on the results runs, it'll be old news. I'm counting on you, Grady."

She glanced past him to Ravi, who nodded in encouragement and chimed in, "Me too. Could use some ideas for an election-week cartoon if you're up for it."

Grady thrust his shoulders back. "Yeah, well, I don't claim to be an expert, but I do have a thought or two." His phone rang. "Uh, yeah, hey, Mom . . . Yes, I have my retainer, and no, I'm not sending you a pic to prove it." He shoved his arms through the straps of his backpack and said to Cat and Ravi, "Orthodontist appointment. See you tomorrow."

And then, from the hall, came a "Sent, happy now?" in Grady's signature whine, and Ravi's face brightened with laughter.

"I know it's a bit much," she said. "But at least he cares. And right now he's got more connections than I do in the journalism world."

"Bo Booker, total gateway to the Pulitzer." He smiled as he leaned against the table with the ski pole leg. "Paper's really awesome this year, Cat."

She brushed her bangs out of her eyes. "Stavros and Jen wouldn't have made the mistakes I have."

"Probably not, but they'd have made others. We're all learning, Cat."

Nerves stirred in her stomach. "But I knew better." She cared what Ravi thought about her. She cared that this might change that. But lying fit her as poorly as her sister's loafers. She forced herself to look straight into his eyes. "Those connections I made in the story about Leo weren't done by mistake. I knew that what I was doing wasn't what I'd been taught." She breathed out heavily. "Right. Wasn't right. And I did it anyway. "

If Ravi was surprised or disgusted, he didn't let it show. "Why?"

"For my sister. I thought that Leo was the one going after Angeline in *The Shrieking Violet*."

"Not a crazy thought. Can't say I didn't wonder myself."

"Pretty sure now that it wasn't him."

"But you thought it was. I'd have done the same thing if I thought someone was going after my sister." He gave a wry smile. "My brother, on the other hand . . ."

Cat appreciated Ravi trying to let her off the hook, but she had to admit the truth to him as much as herself. "I was doing it for Angeline, but I was also doing it for me. I got swept up in the idea of breaking news, so much so that I made news to do it."

Ravi was silent for a beat longer than Cat would have liked. Finally, he said, "And you can't stop thinking about it, can you?"

She half nodded, half shrugged.

"You learn from it. You take it with you. Perfect is for landing planes and blending chai, my mom always says."

Cat allowed herself to release a small smile. "I think I'd like your mom."

"She'd like you right back."

Their words were about his mom, but it sure didn't feel like it.

He pushed himself off the table. "And to make sure she likes *me*, I better get to my shift."

Except he didn't head for the door. He looked like he'd stay if she asked him to. She wanted to ask. But not for the paper. And that scared her.

"Sure, you should go," she said. "Especially since it'll be a late one Friday after the election."

"Got plans after?"

"After the election? I'm getting a pass out of last period to start writing, so I'll have a head start before you and Grady get here."

"I meant after we're done. Got a bowling alley scene in my graphic novel, and I realized I need some research in order to make it authentic."

"Bowling alley at a summer camp?"

"Summer camp has a rakshasa trying to suck the life blood of a bunch of twelve-year-olds, and it's the bowling alley that you question?"

"Buy-in comes in the little details even more than the big."

"And you've just been hired as my editor." He paused. "So, Friday?"

She weighed the options: spending a Friday night watching Natalie Goldberg snuggle up to Ravi or spending a Friday night watching Tartan bounce off the walls. "I-I, sure, yeah, okay. Maybe I'll see if Emmie wants to come."

"Oh, then I'd need to make it a reservation for three, so let me know."

Three? Because otherwise it would just be . . . the two of them?

So much ran through her mind and jumbled her stomach that she did the only thing she could: she gave him a thumbs-up.

Cat walked the halls, using the silence that came after-hours to think. Corridors and classrooms empty, no bathroom doors creaking open, no fluorescent overheads buzzing, just the hum of the HVAC. The only exception was the gym, where after-school practice led to the squeaking of sneakers and the gushing of water through the pipes in the adjacent locker rooms. Usually she thought about her next article or what Northwestern would be like. Rarely about a boy. She didn't have time for it. Now she realized she also didn't have the stomach for it. Because hers was roiling at the idea that Ravi had kind of asked her out. And that she kind of wanted to go. But what was the point? It was senior year, and they'd each be off to separate futures soon.

She rounded the corner, and the thrum of activity spilled from somewhere new: the auditorium.

"I stand here?" Leo called from one side of the stage.

Ms. Lute turned around from the voting booth she was constructing out of a large cardboard box and a cloth curtain. "Left, Leo, figured that'd make it easier."

"Uh-huh," Leo said with a lack of enthusiasm.

Angeline made her way to the right side of the stage, notecards in hand. She tensed when she saw Cat hovering in the back.

But Ms. Lute waved her in. "Great! We could use another set of hands."

From the side of the stage, Emmie trudged out, her arms weighed down by a box with more curtains and long rods sticking out the top.

Cat's thoughts of Ravi were momentarily replaced by wonder.

Red, white, and blue streamers curled around the arms of the chairs running along each aisle, blue umbrellas speckled with the star stickers Angeline had always wanted hung upside down from the ceiling, mini flags sprouted out of buckets of sand all along the front of the stage.

"It looks amazing in here," Cat said.

Ms. Lute beamed. "What did I tell you? People care when someone makes them. And that someone's been you, Cat. Excellent work. I'm sure the Fit to Print judges will be just as impressed as I am."

A snort from Leo, which drew a glare from Angeline. A glare she then directed at Cat.

Ms. Lute handed Cat a roll of tape. "We need another box. I'll be back."

Emmie grabbed a small spade and dug into a bag of sand. She filled a bucket and passed it to Cat, who stuck in a flag from the pile on the seat behind them.

"It's big of you to help, Emmie, considering."

Emmie reached for more sand. "One has to believe in the system or it falls apart. Voters speak, all we can do is listen."

"But was it the voters?" Cat asked. "Ms. Lute's wrong. I didn't make people care, the Frankengirls did. Our candidates owe them. And so do I. I'd have had nothing to write about without them." Which made her feel like real live clickbait.

Onstage, Ms. Lute drew her hand up from her stomach to her throat. "Enunciate, candidates, enunciate."

Cat considered all that their new government teacher had done to engage the students. "I'm glad for Ms. Lute though. She'd have been crushed if the election were a dud."

"Dud might have been better than these two," Emmie said. "Did you hear Leo's speech?"

"No, I only just got here."

Emmie frowned. "It's all over the place. No consistent platform. I bet you his mom's speechwriter's going to take a crack at this later."

Cat's stomach lurched. "Didn't you see my retraction? I jumped the gun. The facts weren't there."

"Just because you didn't have them yet doesn't mean they don't exist," she quipped. Then, more quietly, she said, "I believed in her. I thought Mrs. Torres was someone we could believe in."

"She is—at least, I think she is."

"Well, the system will decide, won't it?"

Step Aside, Mary Shelley, a New Victor's in Town!

See what I did there?

No, of course you didn't.

You're Acedia. Acedia.

Lucky you can tie your own shoes. Though half of you still use the bunny ears method (yes, we see you, and no, it's not cute).

Anyway, we digress.

We're back from that early grave you believed us to be in, and we're SHRIEKING because we have news!

Quick, grab your phones and text "I Want to Know" to the following number, and an automatic ten-dollar charge will be billed to your phone.

1-800-I'M-JOKING!

And . . . digression.

So what's this news? What's this about Mary Shelley and Victor?

It's sure as sugar not your student council prez victor, because neither candidate deserves your vote. They're complete and utter frauds. Betcha already knew that, didn't you? You just got caught up in smooching on germ-infested posters and hollering insults and making noise out of the sheer and utter boredom and drudgery and monotony of high school.

(Could we use more adjectives?)

Our StuCo election is indeed a microcosm with our candidates being just as full of crap emojis as the main players.

Now just what are you getting at, Dear Violet, Dear Violet?

See for yourselves and click <u>here</u>.

For those with fingers still lazy from the hazy days of summer or internet connections from the

Jurassic era, we'll spell it out for you:

SCENE: INT. HOUSE ON THE CLIFFS. SUMMER

We pan down from the oh-so-original nautical chandelier to the it-cost-eight-thousand-dollars-to-get-this-lived-in-look sectional where a pair of drooling dudes whose lives will be defined by that pigskin they tossed in high school sit.

We are in the living room belonging to a Miss Maxine Chen at the end of the summer.

You heard us. Yes, it's THAT party.

Let's zoom in closer, shall we? And up the volume.

Because that right there is someone—not in the frame, aside from his occasional thumb over the camera lens, but audible as a seal off Lighthouse Beach—shoving pizza down his gullet and saying: "That's how I'd do it. Take Acedia's hottest chickadees, gimme a little of this, and ooh, ooh, ooh, a little of that right there, and, oh yeah, that, and that, and double to get a set of THAT, and boom, my dream girl. A perfect ten. Up high, bro!"

Two hands high-fiving, barely caught at the edge of the screen.

END SCENE

Shriek with me, folks!

Origin of the Frankengirls wallpaper in our school!

It's just a voice, you say? It is.

But it belongs to Tad Marcus.

Who we talked to.

After Tamara, his girlfriend (excuse us, ex-girlfriend), borrowed his phone without his knowledge

(PSA here, folks, always use a passcode!), discovered this video, and sent it straight to us.

"We were having fun," Tad Is Rad said. "It was a stupid joke. Those damn apple pie balls. They should really have a warning label."

(They do.)

"But I swear on old Slothy that I had nothing to do with those posters."

Putting aside that swearing on a stuffed animal carries as much weight as Angeline Quinn's Harry Potter butt cheek, when asked who might have been responsible, Rad Tad denied it was anyone on the football team.

"We care about girls too much to do that [bleeped] up [bleep]. We've got cheerleaders, man. You seen a pissed-off cheerleader? Not pretty. Well, I mean, dude, usually still are, but like, yeah, not something you want your balls anywhere close to."

So who else could it be, you ask? We did too.

"Torres was there," Tad the Rad (or is it "Rat"?) said.

Leo Torres? Student council presidential candidate?

"Yeah, Torres," Tad the Rat said. "He's smart and got that access to his mom's designer or printer or whatever, right? Just saying, might be worth looking into."

Huh. Might be. So we did.

Now, lazy fingers and Jurassic internet, this time GO, GO, GO to that link.

Watch.

Again.

Do you see it?

No?

Oh, come on. You can lead a horse to water . . .

All right, here's a clue:

The hand?

High-fiving?

Jutting out of a lime-green sweatshirt.

Now, who do we know loves himself some lime-green sweatshirt?

Ah, now you got it.

(Maybe you'll move past those bunny ears yet, Acedia!)

So you may be wondering why, just why Leo Torres would be compelled to turn this drunken rambling into reality.

One word: the election. (Okay, so that's two, but one main word, and . . . digression.) Torres needs you to vote so he can win. Because those were his mommy's orders. Yup, that's right, Acedia, your very fearful potential leader was acting on orders from his congressional hopeful mom to follow in her size seven footsteps and enter political life. That's why he's running. Not for you, not for off-campus lunches or straws or whatever else he's been spouting. He doesn't actually want to win. But he promised he would. And though he lies, he's loyal, or so sources say.

He likely didn't count on his ex, Angeline Quinn, being showered with hearts and fist pumps for her "impromptu" speeches.

Or did he?

Before we paint #HotheadQuinn as an innocent bystander, let's cue up a couple of Ask an Angel videos.

*Hmm . . . here we have Natalie Goldberg
prominently displaying her mom's macerated seaweed
facial. Natalie's, like, a five-degrees-of-separation
influencer in her own right at Acedia, bursting with
connections to students able to cast their votes.*

M'kay . . .

*What about this? Have you seen who's liking Ask an
Angel lately? Both YouTube and Insta?*

*None other than mega influencer Evelyn's Epic
Everyday. Rumor has it, Miss E is inviting baby
influencers to something of a help-me-help-you
scenario. And who's strapping on training wheels?*

None other than our Quinnie.

*But only if she follows her own mommy's orders
and does something other than slap poo on her surely
silicon-implanted cheekbones.*

Who knew mommies had such power?

Not us.

*So, let's review . . . Battle of the Exes? We
thought they were duking it out against each other
when all along perhaps it's been them against
us. See exhibit QT. Our "cuties" getting cozy on
Lighthouse Beach less than a week ago. In the
height of the election. Which means we've been fool
enough to swallow exactly what they've spoon-fed us:
Frankengirls. Conspiring to drum up interest in this
farce of an election.*

SHH! For harbor's sake, don't tell anyone.

Don't tell anyone any of this.

'Tis our secret, m'kay?

31

When Angeline Breaks the Rules

3 DAYS TO THE ELECTION

This.

Is.

Not.

Happening.

Angeline let go of the honey section she'd been weaving into her ombre braid in front of her locker as Sonya stopped reading. The horror on the faces of Sonya, Riley, and Maxine must have matched her own, and a hollow sensation gripped Angeline's stomach.

"A hypocrite," Angeline said. "This makes me look like a total hypocrite."

Maxine grabbed Sonya's phone out of her hand and scanned *The Shrieking Violet* article. "I can't believe he'd do this to you. I mean, you practically saved his life."

Angeline had never stopped believing it was Sammy, despite Leo insisting it wasn't. Any lingering guilt for pushing Sammy to do this vanished.

"It's not Leo," Angeline said, wondering why Leo was still letting Sammy use his phone, which gave him access to that photo of the two of them.

Maxine huffed. "You cannot keep defending him."

"I'm not." And then her breaths shortened. "Wait, did that say . . ."

Baby influencers.

Help-me-help-you.

Training wheels.

Her lungs seized, and her head swam with dizziness.

Sonya leaned forward. "Breathe, just breathe."

Beside her, Riley placed a hand on Angeline's shoulder. "From the diaphragm." She tucked her blonde hair behind her ear, pleased with herself for maintaining a straight face.

Angeline tried to ground herself by zeroing in on the slats of her locker, but her eyes refused to focus. "Evelyn," she whispered.

"No one believes this garbage," Maxine said. "Get on your Insta now and call this trash out."

"No." Angeline's voice trembled. "You don't understand. I signed a confidentiality agreement when I sent in the deposit. This violates it."

This cannot be happening.

How can this be happening?

She opened her eyes. Leo was heading straight toward her.

Leo, who'd just been accused by *The Shrieking Violet* of creating the Frankengirls.

Accused by Sammy?

This didn't make any sense.

Neither did seeing Cat trailing Leo, who had his green sweatshirt balled up in one hand.

Riley dismissively flicked her eyes at him. "Didn't take you for a perv. Your mom really print the Frankengirls posters for you?"

Leo's only response was his solemn face turning even graver. He addressed Angeline. "We need to talk."

Maxine stepped between them. "Think again. Whatever she says to you winds up in print, so not going to happen."

But then, Cat set her hand on Maxine's forearm. "It's okay. I've got her."

It was such a strange, unexpected comment from Cat that Maxine automatically moved aside. It was equally as strange and unexpected that Angeline's throat ballooned upon hearing it.

Cat led Angeline and Leo to the newsroom, and though they only numbered three, the space felt even more claustrophobic than usual.

Leo tossed his sweatshirt onto the table with the ski pole leg. "It's not me," he said with resigned defeat.

"Of course it's not," Cat said. "What would you have to gain by writing such things about yourself?"

"I meant in that video," Leo said. "At the party. I'm not sure I even went in the living room. First time I saw my good bud, Tad, who just ran me over with a semi, was in the screening room."

Cat snatched up the notebook Leo had given her. "Did you take the sweatshirt off? Where might you have left it? Did someone ask to borrow it?"

Leo shook his head. "I didn't even wear it to the party. It was humid as hell."

"He's right," Angeline said. "It was super hot, then freezing in the . . . the screening room. I remember wishing he'd worn it. I can vouch for him. On that . . . and on him being afraid of heights! Leo would never go to the top of the bleachers to tape down photos. And the hand in the video . . . skin tone's all wrong for Leo. That's it, Cat. We'll just go tell Principal Schwartz and—"

"No one's going to believe you," Cat said flatly.

Her tone set Angeline's teeth on edge. "Because of those

ridiculous stories? Then how about you write something to defend me, for once?"

"I have to remain objective."

"You didn't just say that."

Leo shoved his chair back. "Stop. Just stop. Whoever did this wants to get us in trouble—real trouble. My brother would never . . ." He looked at Angeline with a heaviness that pressed on her chest. "Once the media picks this up, they're going to be all over my mom. *Again*. And, turns out, I care about that. Actually, turns out, I feel really, really shitty about that."

A sharp rap on the door preceded the appearance of Principal Schwartz, his face lined like a discarded gum wrapper. He thanked Riley, who mouthed a "sorry," and Angeline nodded in understanding.

"Small fishing town, they call us, did you know that?" Principal Schwartz bounced his clasped hands against the buttons of his ill-fitting suit jacket. "Boy, do I love it. That first tug on the line, so slight that you could almost miss it. But it's the only warning you get, and you've got to act fast, planting your feet, gearing up for a good fight. Every day until the boats get pulled from the harbor, I try to get out there." He drilled his eyes into each of theirs. "That is, before you all decided to turn this school into a circus. Now, instead of the *ting, ting* of the ropes swaying against the mast, I'm deafened by the *ting, ting* of email after email arriving in my inbox, screaming at how we could be so inept. That sound's going to haunt me until next spring."

Cat cleared her throat. "The inability to find the culprit is hurting all of us. Does the administration have any leads?"

Principal Schwartz smiled. "Leads? Why, we have our responsible party. Mr. Torres, we've already called your parents.

Probably best if you come with me to the office."

"That's not fair." Angeline looked to Cat, who immediately stepped forward.

"Principal Schwartz," Cat said. "I'm confident that Leo is being set up. If we put all of our resources into finding out who is behind this sham of a newspaper, I'm sure it'll lead us to not just the person spreading these rumors but the actual perpetrator behind the Frankengirls."

"Uh-huh." The principal bent a finger toward Leo. "Let's go, Mr. Torres."

"You can't—" Angeline started.

"I can. And I can also do this: you're both disqualified from the student council race."

The air whooshed from Angeline's lungs. She sputtered an unintelligible response while searching Leo's already sucker-punched face.

Principal Schwartz continued, "Obviously this business with the Frankengirls takes you off the table, Mr. Torres. But you and Miss Quinn also managed to violate the honesty pledge by lying about your motivations for running in your campaign speeches at a school-sponsored event. In addition to breaking election rules delineated in the student handbook: Mr. Torres by having an outside professional service contribute to the production of campaign material and Miss Quinn by offering bribes in exchange for votes. So you're both gone, but you're leaving a legacy nonetheless. Congratulations on taking this election out of the hands of your fellow students."

Cat's brow creased. "But you can't cancel the election. Students have signed up to run for other positions. That's in the handbook too."

Angeline filled with pride.

Principal Schwartz cracked a smile. "You are entirely correct. But that handbook also states that if the student body proves unable to act within the behavioral guidelines of this school, the administration can step in. No more vandalizing and stealing posters. No more unsanctioned debates in the lunchroom. No more news vans and retweets and angel wings. We will choose the proper students to lead, because this student body cannot handle the responsibility that goes with participating in an election this year." He stood in the doorway. "And you can quote me on that, Editor Quinn."

Acedia Confronts Its Inner Sloth: Controversy Surrounding Student Council Unprecedented in Charter School History

But Acedia did trust a jock. In fact, it trusted many of them. Following the accusations against Torres, the administration interviewed the football players pictured in the now viral video in which Tad Marcus conceived of the Frankengirls. Marcus maintained his innocence pertaining to the enactment of his idea. With the two witnesses on Maxine's couch backing up Marcus that it was Torres in that infamous green sweatshirt, the guilty party seemed to have been found. Though Torres denied culpability, the administration, which had taken quite a bit of criticism from parents, social media, and the local news, seized on him, suspending him pending a complete investigation. A guilty finding might lead to him being expelled, but the fallout from the accusation reached great heights without it.

Media attention expanded outside the Boston metro area when CNN picked up the story, which sparked the usual copycat rounds on the rest of the twenty-four-hour news channels, morning talk shows, and even late night. Soon, "Acedia" and "Frankengirls" were rolling off tongues across the country.

For Torres, his reputation and impending acceptances to colleges were at stake, but reports also suggest criminal charges of child pornography were being contemplated. Such an outcome would fuel the mob already swarming around Eliza Torres. With her son accused of creating something that was such an affront to women, supporters of her far-left campaign struggled to defend her, while those already opposed pounced on her as a hypocrite. With the election mere weeks away, Mrs. Torres's team had a new battle on its hands. Yet she was not the only one.

The Frankengirls and the rights of female students had become a rallying cry. And Angeline Quinn, the once hero, was now tainted, believed to be a villain. What had started as a position on a charter school student council now threatened to derail the budding influencer's career before it truly began. She'd given a voice to many—a voice that, at least in her own backyard, was being suffocated.

That, some say, is what led to what happened next.

Baker, who had a prime position on the front lawn of the school that day, said this: "Man, it was like a box of red and blue Crayolas was dumped on the lawn and left in the sun—wall-to-wall reds and blues and ones melted all together into violet. Wicked scene, man, wicked."

Click for more: 5 of 6

32

When Cat Makes a Plan

Cat had been up before the sun, crunching on dry cereal at the round dining room table.

When they'd gotten home the night before, Angeline had been uncharacteristically quiet. Together, with Gramps and their mom, they'd watched the report that hit CNN. Acedia had gone national. Take a candidate for Congress, mix in a bad-boy son, add a dash of sex and a twist of misogyny, and the media had a gift-wrapped package it would tear open and exploit until the next scandal took over the news cycle.

Last night, as they watched, Ravi had texted.

You ok?

Was *she* okay? Vicious comments on social media were accusing Angeline of using the Frankengirls as stepping stones, but he wanted to know how she was doing. It was nice, knowing someone was thinking of her.

Too bad it had to come because of all this.

As much as Cat loved journalism, she hated this. Hated that this was a story. Her sister, Leo, her school. All because of *The Shrieking Violet*.

She hit play on the video from the party for what must have been the twelfth time. Using last year's yearbook, she'd identified two kids on the fringes and was working on a third. The football players weren't worth her time. They'd already decided to stick to their Leo story. Implicating him took the focus off of them. But someone else, someone new, might be able to prove that the hand sticking out of that sweatshirt didn't belong to Leo. If she could give another viable option, maybe she could at least slow down the school's inquiry long enough to conduct her own.

"Got 'em!" she said, pegging the third student at the edge of the video as Andreas Costa based on a glimpse of his lacrosse jersey.

Her heart pumped with adrenaline, just like it had when she'd hunted down the student selling the school's Wi-Fi password last year. This was the type of reporting she was good at, that she'd somehow let get lost in her rivalry with *The Shrieking Violet*.

Out of the corner of her eye, she caught sight of Leo and his mom on the television in the living room. The local news had rolled into one of the national morning talk shows. She didn't need to unmute to know what was being said.

She returned to her computer. By the time Angeline, still in her yellow-flowered sleep jumpsuit, came into the living room, Cat was ready. Though not for the red lining her sister's eyes.

Angeline yawned. "How long have you been up?"

"Long enough to have come up with a plan. I could use you, if you're up for it."

Angeline pulled out a chair beside Cat. "I'm all for helping Leo."

"And you."

"Me? I'm not the one about to be expelled."

"No, but you are the one who violated your confidentiality clause. Unintentionally, but still. Let's get ahead of it."

"It's too late, Cat."

"Maybe not." Cat spun her computer around and clicked on the email she'd drafted when she'd first gotten up. "You just have to send it from your account."

Angeline started reading. "Wait, you want me to admit to Evelyn's Epic Everyday that I let the boot camp slip?"

"Keep reading. You tell them the truth: that an invasion of your privacy led to the information being released. This way it looks like you aren't hiding anything. You'll provide definitive proof or you'll excuse yourself."

"Just drop out? And"—she pointed to the screen—"invite them to keep the deposit?"

"They were going to anyway. Offering it up shows how genuine you are."

Angeline scanned the email again. "You really think I should send this?"

"I know my judgment hasn't been entirely spot-on lately, but I think it'll help. At least I can't see how it hurts." She grabbed the television remote and hit rewind, pausing on the photo of Leo and his mom at that event in the harbor. "Not anymore."

Angeline's eyes clouded. "Imagine them watching this. After all his mom's done to get here, this is the thing people are going to be talking about. Even if you manage to clear Leo, it won't matter."

Cat tried to respond. The words filled her mouth, but releasing them felt silly, childish even. But she believed what she believed. And she wouldn't let this take it from her. "It will. The truth always matters. Even if it's not reported, it matters. And it won't be me who clears Leo, it'll be us."

Angeline smiled with an unexpected warmth. "Where do we start?"

33

When Angeline Encounters
a Green Ghost

Angeline's thumb cramped, and she took a break.

She'd been sitting at the small white table in the frozen yogurt shop scrolling through photos and videos from Maxine's party since school let out. Fortunately many of her classmates had used the #LastSummerBlastOnTheCliffs hashtag that Maxine had coined in her text invites. For each pic or video using the hashtag, Angeline noted who posted it and worked her way through that person's account from the night of the party through the current date to catch any later or throwback posts. As she went, she also marked who else was tagged in those posts and began running through their social media accounts too, finding more posts that didn't use the hashtag.

She still hadn't found anyone wearing a green sweatshirt.

Angeline flexed her thumb and returned to her phone. She didn't even realize Cat had arrived until her sister handed her a spoon to share what looked to be blueberry topped with granola.

"No luck yet," Cat said. "I spoke to all three, but none of the other students I identified in Tad's video remember seeing anyone in a green sweatshirt."

"And Tamara?"

"Waiting for her to text me back. What about you?"

"Never thought I'd say this, but social media is totally failing me." Angeline dug into Cat's yogurt. "Kid's a green ghost."

Cat grabbed Angeline's phone and began to scroll.

"Do me a favor, check my DMs," Angeline said. "I reached out to a few people who seemed to be in Maxine's living room the whole night. See if anyone wrote back. And ignore what the trolls are saying."

The haters that had come along with Angeline's potential involvement in the Frankengirls had turned her off reading comments for whatever was left of her influencer lifetime.

"Hmm," Cat said. "Yeah, I can see how 'You are an inspiration. Never give up!' is a tough one to swallow."

"Real funny, Cat," Angeline said.

"I'm serious." Cat began reading out loud:

> Saying good-bye to twenty years of yo-yo dieting and hello to healthy eating because we are all #MoreThanOurParts. I believe in you!

> I'm applying to med school because #MoreThanOurParts means #GirlPower and #BrainPower! My wings are fluttering!

> My school's adopting my peer jury proposal. Because of you! xxx

Angeline's heart lifted, then fell. Because these had to be the exception. "So a couple don't hate me."

"It's more than a couple. Haven't you seen all these heart emojis and prayer hands and—"

"It's corny as hell, I know." Angeline jabbed her spoon back into the frozen yogurt. She knew what Cat thought of Ask an Angel.

"Maybe . . . but *people* posted them. Your followers seem to care."

"In the way that can only exist in the vortex that is the internet, right?" Angeline reclaimed her phone. "It's fine, Cat. You don't have to pretend you believe in all this."

"But I don't have to believe in this to believe in you. I didn't treat this with enough respect. I'm sorry, Ang."

Angeline twisted toward her sister, surprise sending a tiny electric shock up her spine. "I . . ." She nodded slightly, a warmth spreading across her chest. She then read the comments for herself. Her followers did seem to care about her, and for maybe the first time she wasn't stretching the truth when she said she cared back.

Then, her phone dinged as a text arrived from Tamara.

Tomorrow. Lunch. You both owe me.

"So, looks like we're on," Angeline said.

"That's great. Though it's strange that she texted you when I'm the one who reached out to her."

"She texted us both." Angeline showed her the chain, then looked at Cat's phone. "No cell service. You need to get on the Wi-Fi."

"There isn't any in here."

"But I've been working all afternoon." Angeline opened the Wi-Fi settings. "See?"

Cat read the list of available Wi-Fi. "You're connected to Torres Extension. No froyo shop, so you must have been on Torres Extension the whole time. Leo's house is basically behind us, right?"

"If you don't mind getting mauled by a dog with the personality of a grizzly. To walk there you have to go all the way around, far enough to get blisters in crappy loafers."

"What happened to 'comfy as clouds'?"

"Didn't you see that little ad hashtag at the bottom?"

"I've so much to learn."

"Fortunately you have an excellent teacher."

Angeline wrote back to Tamara, whose reply came right away.

> **Tamara:** I may get arrested, but we gotta have each other's backs. I know you would.

And in the moment that Angeline should have felt pleased, all she felt was a deep fear that, if everything were on the line, she would always put herself first.

34

When Cat Thanks Slothy

Cat nearly dumped her iced tea all over Ravi's bare legs. He had on his green cargo shorts and a blue long-sleeved Boston tee he'd gotten on his trip to the library. Which she only knew because she saw the photo of him buying it from the kiosk. Social media was like a super creepy form of mind-reading.

"Sorry," Cat said. "I wasn't paying attention."

"No worries." He tucked a strand of hair behind his ear. "Got a lot to distract you."

Um, yeah, and one of those distractions was standing right in front of her in the cafeteria, with an absurdly sweet smile on his face, in need of a haircut that she hoped was way far down on his to-do list.

"Right, sure," Cat said. "Speaking of, thanks for your text last night. This sudden media attention is hard for my mom and grandfather."

"Course. And hard for you."

Cat's instinct was to deny it. "Yeah, me too." She shifted her lunch tray in her hands.

"I should let you sit."

"Okay." *Okay?* "You have one yet? A sit?" *Ugh.* "A seat, I mean."

"Mobile lunch." Ravi lifted his wrapped sandwich. "We definitely fueled the monster. Grady's all hyped up about an idea for a cartoon. I'm meeting him in the newsroom. Figured you'd be there too."

"Oh, well, I needed to talk to—"

"I'm glad you're not. Nice to see you out in the wild, Cat."

She gave him a quick, shy grin.

"So," he said, "probably take less time to put the paper to bed tomorrow without the election."

"Probably. Unless something changes." Unless *she* could change it.

"Maybe add pizza before bowling? If you're interested?"

"In pizza?"

"Pizza, bowling, all of it."

"But what . . ." Cat swiveled her head. "What about Natalie?"

"Nat? A friend. Always just a friend. And here's the thing, Cat: while I'd be a Lake Lookey Loo happy camper to have more friends, I'd be even happier to have something else." He started walking away, backward, keeping his eyes on her. "Just think about it."

Her stomach fluttered and her skin was hot and she thought maybe she was breaking out into hives or at least *hive*, and she watched Ravi until he disappeared out of the lunchroom, and then, finally, she forced her feet to move, yet her mind remained stuck on Ravi. Stuck on his *something else*. But she couldn't think about Ravi now . . . she couldn't think about Ravi later . . . because really what was the point of thinking about Ravi when she had so much else to think about?

Angeline waved from a table in the center. Cat nodded, flashing a five with her open palm. Jitters filled Cat, yet her sister appeared calm, pulling a metal straw out of her tote bag and dropping it into a chocolate milk. They were meeting Tamara in five minutes. But clearing Leo was only part of their plan.

For the second part, Cat needed Emmie. She set her tray down across from her, intent on brainstorming ideas for returning the election to the student body, when Sammy approached.

"Hey, Cat," he said solemnly, though his eyes brightened when they landed on Emmie. "And, oh, hey, Em. Next HQ overlap, maybe we swing by for froyo again before you drop me off. Heard they got pumpkin in. Your favorite?"

Emmie hesitated before nodding.

Sammy shifted his weight as his cheeks turned the color of cooked lobster. "Well, yeah, okay then, just wanted to say hi."

Cat watched Sammy dash off. "Someone's got a crush." She laughed, but Emmie's face had gone pale. "You okay? It's no big deal. Just don't show too much interest. I'm sure he'll get the hint. There's nothing else you really need to do."

"Yes, well, that's the thing, isn't it?" Emmie gave a weak smile. "Doing nothing's hard precisely because you never know when you're done." She quickly stood. "I just remembered I need a book from my locker."

"Okay, but—" Cat stopped when a hand pressed down on her shoulder. She turned to see her sister, her lips tight, eyes bugging.

"Text me." Emmie picked up her tray full of uneaten salad and headed for the exit.

Angeline squeezed. "That . . . did you hear that?"

"What? That Emmie forgot something in her locker? Nobody's perfect, even when they try to be."

"And she tries hard, doesn't she?"

"She's driven. Same as you and me."

"Uh-huh. Driven enough to stab her friends in the back?"

"What are you talking about?"

Angeline's eyes narrowed. She unlocked her phone and began scrolling.

Cat checked her digital watch. "We're going to be late."

Angeline raised a finger in the air, and Cat wolfed down her hummus wrap.

"Read." Angeline shoved her phone in front of Cat's face.

"*The Shrieking Violet*? Now? I've read it and don't care to again."

Angeline zoomed in. "Just this part."

Cat sighed. "'Tip for ya, dearies, the hard thing about doing nothing's that you never know when you're done. So take it from us and do SOMETHING.'" She looked up at her sister. "Are you trying to make a point?" And then Cat's stomach plummeted. "Oh. *Oh*. You don't think . . ."

"Freaking Emmie Hayes. Creator of *The Shrieking Violet*."

📣 📣 📣

As they hurried to meet Tamara, Cat's mind worked double-time, same as Angeline's lips.

"I remembered because that's the joke that made me think it was Sammy. He said it at the hospital. After it was in *The Shrieking Violet*."

"That doesn't prove anything," Cat said. "Emmie could have picked it up from the paper or even from Sammy himself."

"Wait, what? How would she have picked it up from Sammy?"

"She volunteers for Mrs. Torres. She gave Sammy a ride home at least once, because they stopped for frozen yogurt." The words had barely left Cat's lips, and the pieces were already falling into place. "Frozen yogurt. They stopped for frozen yogurt."

286

"Where there's no Wi-Fi."

"But there is the Torres Extension."

"If Sammy gave her the password . . ." Angeline whooped. "That's why the IP for those *Shrieking Violet* emails matched the Torres network. I knew Maxine was right! She was covering her tracks and framing Leo at the same time. Has to be! Except I don't get how Emmie knew so much."

Cat's legs filled with lead. She knew how. Because she was the one who told her.

📢 📢 📢

Sweat dotted Cat's brow as she waited in the watch yard amid the shrine to Slothy. When Maxine arrived, Angeline filled her in and then sent Leo a text, asking him to confirm what they suspected about Sammy and Emmie. Meanwhile, Cat scrolled through her own texts, confirming what she knew to be true about herself.

She'd texted with Emmie about how small this town was and how they each wanted more. Cat had mentioned living somewhere else for a while. Was that enough for Emmie to research the rest?

That first day when they'd met in the frozen yogurt shop . . . *when Emmie was probably posting her latest article* . . . Cat had told her about Angeline making fun of her in fourth grade. She'd been upset. She'd been venting. To a friend. Never in a million years did she think any of it would come out. Had she actually said anything about the grill fire? In one of her stream-of-consciousness rambles? *Had she?*

She tried to remember everything, but she didn't need to.

There was enough.

Same as there were enough clues in *The Shrieking Violet*—at least in hindsight: *Who knew mommies had such power? Not us.* Emmie was being raised by her two dads. One article called the posters "germ-infested," and Emmie was a self-declared germo-phobe. There'd been something about Mrs. Torres's size seven shoes—a size Emmie would know, having once gotten her a new pair.

Emmie—can it really be Emmie?

The door to the watch yard opened, and Tamara stepped outside.

"He never carries it to lunch," she said, handing over a back-pack and a sheet of paper with Tad's locker combination on it. "Return it before the period's over. And try not to get caught."

Cat said, "No matter what, you had nothing to do with it. Promise."

"Just nail him," she said.

Maxine grabbed the bag. "My pleasure."

As Maxine plopped herself on the grass and searched for Fran-kengirls evidence on Tad's computer, Cat's body became riddled with nerves.

"Anything?" Angeline asked.

"No photo editing or layout software," Maxine said. "No large enough image files from the time of the first incident on here or uploaded anywhere. If he created the perfect tens, he didn't do it on this."

"Damn," Angeline said.

"I've got the video, but it's the same length as what was posted online," Maxine said with disappointment. She kept working. "But . . . wait . . . what do we have here . . ."

"You found something?" Cat asked. At least if she helped to exonerate Leo, then maybe the rest of it wouldn't be so bad.

"Deleted photo. Metadata shows it was taken right after the video. Probably by accident. It's just the corner of my front door and someone's back." Maxine grinned. "Someone's lime-green back."

"No way!" Angeline and Cat huddled around Maxine.

In the photo, the person's hood was up, so they couldn't even tell what color their hair was. Maxine zoomed in and out, searching for some detail to identify their former green ghost. Who was actually a green giant.

Green.

Giant.

The person's head was just shy of reaching the top of Maxine's surfboard, which rested by the door.

Cat's heart gained speed. "Leo's not—"

"That tall," Angeline finished. She pulled up a photo of her and Leo entering the party. Neither of their heads came anywhere close to hitting the top of the board. "This has to prove it, doesn't it?"

It was good, Cat had to admit. But she wasn't sure it was enough. And then Maxine zoomed in once more. "Wait, stop. The arm of the sweatshirt. It's all pushed up, but it looks like there's writing on it. Can either of you read it?"

Maxine sent the photo to herself. "No, but I can enhance it when I get home."

Angeline bounced beside them. "But we don't have to be able to read it. Schwartz took Leo's sweatshirt as evidence. There's no writing anywhere on it. That along with the photos showing his height has to be enough to clear him, doesn't it?"

Cat nodded. "At least cast serious doubt. Force the administration to expand the investigation."

Maxine returned Tad's computer to his backpack. "You know what this calls for?" She lifted her hand in the air, and the three of them met in a high-five.

As Cat looked up at their joined hands, she caught sight of Slothy on the roof of the school. Slothy watching them. Watching anyone who came in or out. She walked to the door, her eyes searching. "No camera."

"You're right." Maxine moved to Cat's side. "And I've never found the door locked. Keyhole's so rusted probably can't be anymore. Makes this the perfect place to come and go unseen."

"Maybe. Except for that." Cat grabbed Maxine and Angeline's hands and drew them back. "Look up."

"Slothy's not exactly the biggest chatterbox," Angeline said.

"No, but he's got a camera—an all-weather one. At least he did last year." Cat turned to Maxine. "Think the webcam still works?"

"I'll find out," Maxine said.

"Damn, we make a good team, don't we?" Angeline said.

Cat smiled. "More than our parts."

35

When Angeline Goes Campaigning

Angeline had often walked through the harbor overcome by a sense of calm. It was comforting to live in a town small enough that the routines of others were as familiar as your own. That same long-haired guy in a wet suit hanging out at the cafe, fresh from his morning surf. The same eclectic antique shop owner watching her toy greyhound chase dust bunnies through the store. On Friday nights, the same set of Red Sox–capped tradesmen drifting into the Irish pub for dollar oysters and two-dollar drafts. Saturdays, the same moms and dads and dogs and strollers making the loop around the lighthouse.

She knew them, and she liked to think they knew her too. Knew she picked up a latte every Friday after school to energize her for that night's party. Knew she met Maxine, Sonya, and Riley every Saturday morning at the bagel place to rehash said party with a round of whatever questionable hangover cure Riley had made. Knew she'd be the last one cuddled under a blanket on the beach in October, Leo beside her.

And if they knew all that, they also knew that the very last place she'd go was Eliza Torres's campaign headquarters.

(Avoiding confrontation can be a form of self-care. See Ask an Angel's "If You Don't Care, Why Should We?" video!)

Her nerves were already rattled by the email from Evelyn's Epic Everyday, who wasn't only "disturbed by" the boot camp leak but "deeply offended" by the negative attention Angeline had been bringing to Evelyn, especially after she was "gracious enough" to show Angeline support online. As if someone like Evelyn did anything online that wasn't directly related to furthering her own brand. Angeline had been the same. Evelyn was exactly who Angeline thought she was, letting nothing stand in the way of her success; it was why Angeline wanted to learn from her. But then why did it sting so much?

Angeline arrived at the pop-up space in the harbor, inhaled a breath, and pushed open the door. She was greeted by a large blooming orchid on the front desk and . . . Leo's mom.

"Angeline," Mrs. Torres said. "Thank you for coming."

Her tone was clipped but not entirely cold.

"Of course." Angeline's eyes searched among the brochures and posters and boxes of campaign pins for Leo. He said he'd meet her after he changed the Torres Wi-Fi password, which Sammy had confirmed he'd given to Emmie.

Mrs. Torres caught and held Angeline's gaze. "You were expecting to see my son?"

Angeline's bottom lip folded between her teeth. Mrs. Torres had a way of making her feel stripped down—down to her basest self, without the flash of her ombre hair, the perfect dewiness of her makeup, the thousands of fans hitting thumbs-up after thumbs-up—to someone who wasn't anyone, no matter how hard she was trying to be.

Angeline's heart beat in her throat. "Is that really so bad? That we want to see . . . that we want to be together?"

Mrs. Torres tilted her head. She was a woman of firsts. First female state senator for her district, first Latina town council president on the South Shore, first anyone to challenge the long-term incumbent in this congressional seat. A hard road, which Angeline must have always known, somewhere in the back of her mind, in those few instances when she could consider Mrs. Torres as the Mrs. Torres everyone else did and not as the woman trying to stand in the way of her and Leo. She understood the drive to keep going in spite of it being hard—maybe because of it. Mrs. Torres left casualties in her path the same way Angeline did. But Angeline wasn't sure Mrs. Torres could see that. For all Mrs. Torres's strength, was she just someone trying not to be just anyone too?

"Or do you not even know that?" Angeline said. "That he's always wanted me in his life. And that I'm good for him."

Mrs. Torres frowned, but then she straightened her lips into a thin, flat line. "Tell me."

Angeline's eyebrows lifted. "Tell you what?"

"Tell me how you're good for my son."

Tell her? What could she say that this woman would understand? That Leo helped Angeline with all the things she couldn't do: test beard softeners, warm her cold hands, make her family feel whole. That Angeline helped him focus on his homework, prune a rosebush, feel like he mattered for who he was and what he thought and not the role he played in someone else's life.

At least, she used to.

She looked at Mrs. Torres and said simply, "Because I love him."

293

Angeline showed Mrs. Torres the photo from Tad's computer and explained what she, Cat, and Maxine had found. She sent her the evidence and accepted her thank-you—more sincere than the one she'd given upon Angeline's entrance.

As Angeline walked past a whiteboard with the latest polling statistics, she heard Mrs. Torres on the phone, already setting up a meeting with Principal Schwartz for the next morning. With any luck, Leo would be back in school for first period. And on the way out, Angeline got a little luck of her own.

"Can I borrow this?" Angeline asked one of the aides.

"So long as you bring it back. We like the interns to be well-versed in how to care for our plants."

"Good to know." Angeline scooped up the book that stacked one more piece of evidence against Emmie and left to meet Cat.

Angeline laid *Stop the Shrinking: How to Make Your Orchids, Birds of Paradise, and Violets Shriek with Delight!* on the Formica table in the frozen yogurt shop. When Emmie showed up right on time wearing her plain-Jane flats and lace-fringed button-down, she couldn't miss it.

"I want to talk to Cat alone," Emmie said flatly.

Cat's eyes were full of resignation—and hurt. "No, I don't think so."

Emmie's strawberry-blonde hair trailed her collarbone as she swiveled her neck to check out the other two customers—a grandmother and toddler. "The book? That's what gave me away? Not that it particularly matters." She pursed her lips. "Now what?"

She wasn't even going to try to deny it. Or sound remorseful.

Angeline's nostrils flared. "Do you even care what you've done?"

"Oh, that's precious coming from you."

"Emmie—" Cat started.

"No, Cat, I've got this." Angeline marched past the toppings bar and looked down at Emmie, who was even shorter than Cat. Clearly not their giant, but definitely green. "Jealousy, is that it, then?"

"Do you think I'm that petty?"

"I don't know you enough to think anything about you."

"Then ask your sister."

"You mean your 'friend'?" Angeline longed to squirt hot fudge all over Emmie's white shirt. "No wonder you don't have many if this is how you treat them."

"I don't hear Cat complaining." Emmie said in a softer tone, "Cat, let's go somewhere else and let me explain."

Cat remained silent, intentionally or not letting Angeline direct the conversation.

"Explain what?" Angeline said. "You flat-out lied."

"So did you."

"You used people."

"So did you."

"You betrayed people's trust."

"This could go on all day, Angeline. I'm assuming you have a point?"

Angeline hadn't expected such a formidable response. "What about Sammy? Did you really take advantage of his crush on you?"

"You think I got things about you from Sammy?"

And from Leo's phone, which Sammy had made his own.

Emmie shot a look across the empty bistro tables at Cat, who had sunk into the blue metal chair. "Sure, yes," Emmie said.

Barely audible came Cat's, "Just, why?"

Emmie's eyes finally showed some emotion. She angled around Angeline, sat across from Cat, and whispered, "I honestly thought you'd be glad."

"I never said—"

"No, but I heard what you left out."

"But we were friends." Cat gestured to Emmie's bracelet. "Which I thought was important to you."

"It is," Emmie said. "And friends help one another, especially with things they can't do for themselves—or won't. Though perhaps being an only child means there are some things I can never understand." She turned to Angeline. "But I also believe in treating people with respect—when they deserve it. You don't. You said and did whatever you needed to in order to win that primary for reasons that had everything to do with you. You didn't care about the election or the school or your classmates. You don't care about anyone but yourself. That election was supposed to be mine."

Angeline snorted. "That's not the statement of someone with altruism in their heart."

Instead of lashing into Angeline, Emmie continued to address Cat. "Representing others is a responsibility. Even at Acedia. Because if we treat it like a joke or a popularity contest or as something that can be bribed now, don't think it doesn't become instilled in us later." Emmie became more animated as she spoke. "Cat, you know I'm the one who's been working on actual ideas to make things better in the school. Ideas your sister twisted when they were mine and then stole to be hers. At first, I just wanted Leo to win. With a mom like Mrs. Torres, how could he not be better? So I gave a little push, and yes, I pushed the envelope. Just like Ms. Lute talked about in class. Newspapers used to do this thing all the time. It's actually a useful lesson for students about being gullible."

"Don't blame this on Ms. Lute."

"I'm not. I own what I did."

"But you don't," Cat said. "You hid what you did. You used anonymity to say whatever you wanted without consequences. And all those mistakes? You put them in purposely to throw off suspicion. Those aren't the actions of someone proud of what they're doing."

"I'm proud of the end result. It's part of the game. And it's not like this kind of thing doesn't go on at Acedia all the time. Is it worse because I'm a girl?"

"Of course not," Cat said. "But don't you see, Emmie? You can't use the level that others stoop to in order to justify what you do. You're no better than the people you're trying to stop then. Believe me, I know."

"Do you mean Leo? His mom covering up the cheerleading thing? That wasn't true?" Cat shook her head, and Emmie winced as if she'd just been pricked by something sharp. "But, Cat, how could you do that to Mrs. Torres?"

Hypocrite. Total hypocrite. "Please, you didn't just say that."

Emmie ignored Angeline. "But you made me believe she wasn't who I thought she was."

"My story? That's why you went after Leo?" Cat looked like she might be sick.

Damn you, Emmie.

Though Emmie seemed truly shaken. She slumped, the first time Angeline had ever seen her posture wane.

"She was my role model," Emmie said. "Strong and smart and from our town, *my* town. It meant what I wanted wasn't silly. But then, reading that about her, I felt duped. When Tad's girlfriend sent that video to *The Shrieking Violet*, I used it. When Sammy said Angeline and Leo were getting closer and showed me that picture on Leo's phone, I really did think they were trying to fool everyone and that neither one of them deserved to win."

Angeline gave a derisive laugh. "You got your wish. At the expense of the election itself."

Emmie set her hands on the table, right in sticky yogurt residue, and looked about to jump out of her skin, but she stayed put. "I never wanted that. I never thought things would go this far. I got swept up."

Angeline knew the feeling, and the expression on her sister's face meant she did too.

Emmie slid her chair back and held her sticky hands in front of her. "Principal Schwartz rendezvous in the morning, then?"

Cat stood. "No." Angeline cocked her head, but Cat continued, "I trusted you, Em."

"This doesn't have to change that. This doesn't have to change us being friends."

"No, I guess it doesn't have to. But it will." Cat sighed heavily. "The truth is, we all played a part. No one's innocent here. Not even our classmates. The Frankengirls, the angel wings, the hashtags, the parents calling—it's all drowning out what actually matters."

Emmie nodded. "What Ms. Lute's been trying to make everyone see. Our school election and our votes teach us not just how to do this but why."

Cat lips thinned. "And all they'll learn is not to bother being engaged because someone with more power will say when enough is enough and make their decisions for them."

"Just like my grandfather," Emmie said.

Angeline had never particularly liked Emmie, and this wasn't going to help. But knowing her history humanized her, a little, same as Principal Schwartz's fishing photo. "What can we do to change that?"

"First," Cat said, "*The Shrieking Violet*'s over, Emmie. Deal?"

"I'll shut down the website tonight," Emmie said.

"Not just yet." Cat flipped open the notebook Leo had given her. "You have one more article to post. We need our collective reach and more for . . . for Operation Red, Blue, and Violet."

36

When Cat's Alive with Butterflies

1 DAY TO THE (NOW CANCELED) ELECTION
THE NIGHT BEFORE OPERATION RED, BLUE, AND VIOLET

Alone in her room, Cat reviewed the information from Ms. Lute, who'd been generous enough to respond to Cat's email after-hours and careful enough not to question why Cat needed such information after-hours.

She incorporated the necessary details and finished the article she, Emmie, and Angeline had collaborated on earlier. A shared goal overcame their differences even if it couldn't erase the hurt. New as her friendship with Emmie had been, it was a friendship. At least to Cat. The sting of betrayal eclipsed the hollow feeling that came with losing Emmie as a person in her life, but surprisingly not by much. Cat hadn't realized how lonely she'd been until Emmie had made her feel less so.

Emmie had apologized, though Cat could tell there was a piece of her that didn't think she had to. That believed her cause was worthy enough to justify her actions. She thought that was something Cat would understand as a journalist. The idea of getting a story no matter the cost. Maybe Cat wasn't cut out for this after all.

The threads of shame latched on to Cat not only for what she'd done to Leo but for what she'd done to Angeline. Venting to Emmie had given her everything she'd needed, filled in the pieces that Sammy's own hurt ramblings and Emmie's snooping on Leo's phone—especially in his photos—when Sammy wasn't looking had left out. Emmie had skillfully pressed them for dirt on Angeline, Cat could see that now. Yet Angeline only knew about Sammy.

Cat should tell her. She knew she should. And she would. After. Because this—Operation Red, Blue, and Violet, which would go live the next morning—needed all of them in order to work.

The article detailed everything they'd discovered about the Frankengirls perpetrator. They left out Emmie and *The Shrieking Violet*. Cat didn't want to distract from Operation Red, Blue, and Violet. She also didn't want to give Emmie more attention than she deserved.

She attached the article to an email addressed to Angeline and Emmie and clicked send. Between *The Red and Blue*, *The Shrieking Violet*, and Angeline's social media, they'd reach the full student body.

She sent a copy to Grady, asking him to forward it to his cousin Bo, with a special note she'd written for the news station. It was time for Grady to prove he could be as useful as he seemed to think.

There was only one thing left to do. She loaded her web browser, logged in to the Fit to Print site, and retracted her award application.

At the gentle knock on the door, Cat blinked back tears.

Gramps poked his head into her room, and that was it. She couldn't hold anything back anymore. She sprang out of her chair and fell into his arms.

With a box of Gramps's favorite Irish soda bread cookies open on the dining room table, Cat told him everything she'd been keeping from him. He didn't hide his disappointment in her. But he also didn't dwell on it.

"You don't need me to tell you what's right and wrong," he said. "Your insides must be black and blue from how you've been beating yourself up. Mistakes are how we learn what to do as much as what not to do."

Cat softened a little, thinking of Ravi. "That's what my friend said."

"I'd like to meet this friend, as it would seem she's up to snuff in the intelligence department."

"He."

"What?"

"*He's* up to snuff. My friend's a he."

"Then I demand to meet this . . ."

"Ravi."

"Good. Now tell me, why hasn't he been around?"

Cat squirmed and snatched a cookie.

"Is he not interested?" Gramps asked. "Give me his number. I want to know what's wrong with this boy's head."

"I'm pretty sure he's interested."

"Didn't doubt it for a second. Then what's the problem?"

Cat played with the edge of the cookie.

"Ah, you're the problem," Gramps said. "What is it? He not smart enough for you?"

"No, he's super smart."

"Doesn't make you laugh?"

"No, he does."

"So he's not a looker, huh?"

Cat's stomach flipped, and her face blazed crimson.

"Okay, so he is," Gramps said. "Then what am I missing?"

Cat set the cookie on the dining room table. "It's just . . . what if . . ." She brushed crumbs off her hands. "What if we go ahead and do something together, and we realize we don't really click that way. And then we're both still working at the paper and in the same physics class and lunch, and then it's super awkward, so then we start avoiding each other in the hallways and skipping lunch, and he leaves the paper for yearbook, and then I have to find a new designer, and how will I even start that now and how many issues will we miss? And then there's Grady, and I like him, but I don't really want to do this just with him, and it's senior year. I mean, it's *senior year.*"

She picked up the cookie. "Then again, what if we do something and realize we *do* click, like, really click, and we spend all this time together, which naturally means the paper's going to suffer, and then I'll never have a shot at Northwestern, which I probably don't anymore anyway without the Fit to Print award, so I stay here and live here and go to community college, which frankly I probably want to do anyway because I don't want to leave him and he doesn't want to leave me and then here we are in this same town probably living in this same apartment complex twenty years from now." Cat shoved the cookie in her mouth and said between chewing, "Um, so, yeah, there's that."

Gramps jiggled his head. "That we share the same blood is perhaps the only reason I followed that. But humor me. This boy ask you to marry him?"

"Geez, of course not, Gramps."

"What did he ask exactly?"

"Bowling."

"Bowling. He asked you bowling, and you got all of that?"

Cat curled her feet underneath her on the dining room chair. "If I'm a bit of an overthinker, I have you to blame."

"Blame accepted. Because without the ability to think and analyze, you couldn't be the journalist you need to be."

"What kind is that? Unemployed? They don't need us, Gramps. And more than that, they don't want us. No one cares about the truth. Social media's the new evolution. Weeding out anyone with a conscious or independent thought."

"When did you become so cynical?"

"When *The Shrieking Violet* got more readers in a day than I got in three years. Fake news does such a good job of pretending to be real, the only way we can compete is to write everything in listicle form."

Gramps pressed his hands to his belly. "I can't pretend I'm not worried. As a society, we are running the risk of losing touch with what truth is, but that doesn't mean it no longer matters. When figuring out what's true gets this hard, it's almost understandable that people just go on and believe the lies. It's easier to find sources that reinforce existing ideas rather than challenge ourselves by seeking an objective truth."

"Ms. Lute talked about that. The responsibility consumers of information have."

The wrinkles around his green eyes deepened. "True, but we can't let journalists off the hook. The news isn't static, and neither is the industry. We've gone from newspapers being political megaphones to prizing objectivity because, at least at first, bias meant half your readership bought another paper. Not so good with advertisers looking to reach as many wallets as possible." He spread his hands wide. "So, change. I saw it with television. Its immediacy with breaking news meant we had to offer something else. So we implemented the series and deep investigative reports that would take us weeks and months. Now it's social media's turn."

"Making journalists entertainers with fruit juice and sustainable underwear sponsors."

"Grams's sass." He smiled approvingly. "Still, I don't believe the ethics and standards of journalism need to change, but the methods might have to. Let's use our platforms. Let's boast about our fact-checking, legal reviews, source confirmation. Show how we're different. Show how we do what the others don't. Help consumers choose us."

Cat considered what he'd said. "But we probably also need to adapt." She thought of the changes both Leo and Angeline were proposing to a school stuck in the past. "We can't push an old system onto a culture that expects something different."

"See? This is why it's not so bad to be an overthinker."

"It won't be the same."

"Probably not." He split a cookie, giving her half. "Ah, Cathleen, we can never replace what we've lost, but we can create something new, maybe something even better. In life, in family, in love. We just have to pivot."

📢 📢 📢

Cat waited in front of the hardware store. She tucked her hands in the pockets of her khaki skirt to wipe away their clamminess. She should have changed. She'd worn the same long-sleeved black tee that she'd had on in school. He'd seen her in it, and not just today, all the time. Plain, no frills, so not Angeline.

And he liked her anyway.

Ravi came from the direction of the parking lot behind the store. He hadn't changed either. Same green cargo shorts, same Boston tee, just with a gray hoodie over it. His hair fell in his eyes, and he swooped it back—knowing, Cat suspected, exactly how cute he looked doing it.

"The draw is that strong, huh?" he said. "Just couldn't wait even one more day."

Cat tucked her elbows tight against her somersaulting stomach.

"It's the shoes, isn't it?" Ravi said.

Cat's brow furrowed at his plain tennis sneakers. "Uh, well, they're okay. Nice, and I guess they do make your feet look slim." Her eyes widened. "Not that you need to look slimmer. You look fine. Good. You're—"

"The bowling shoes," Ravi said. "A joke? Maybe slow down and take a breath?"

From the diaphragm.

So she did. Super deep inhale. As she exhaled, she skimmed her sneaker along the sidewalk, running it over a mussel shell encased in the concrete. She could stay right where she was and feel okay, good even, with Ravi as her friend, sharing the newspaper for the rest of the school year, same as she'd done with Stavros and Jen for the past three. They might not become as close as Angeline and her friends, but their mutual interest would sustain them. It'd be a good senior year.

She thought of her sister, of the senior year her sister had expected with Leo. The one of homecoming and prom and parties and nights of pizza and corn hole at the outdoor restaurant that stayed open until the first snow, of Saturdays walking the jetty, searching the ocean for seals, of being in this town where they'd lived as a family their whole lives.

The town where their father had left them.

The town Cat was so sure she wanted to leave.

Was that why?

Was he why?

Why she poured herself into the newspaper and surrounded herself with Gramps and Jen and Stavros, who were interested in what she was interested in so she didn't have to open herself up to anything else, anyone else? Why she didn't take chances like she'd done when she'd stepped onto that stage in fourth grade despite her heart booming in her ears and her mind screaming at her that she couldn't do it, that she shouldn't even try?

But she'd tried, and she'd failed, and life went on—narrower in scope. But it didn't have to be. She controlled her dreams as much as her reality. And she didn't just want good. She wanted great.

So she stepped up. Stepped closer to Ravi. She rested her hand on his arm, fingering the soft cotton of his sweatshirt. He pressed his hand on top of hers, and a rush of adrenaline made her dizzy.

"I've wanted to ask you out since last year," he said, his breath hot against her cheek.

Last year? He'd liked her since last year? She could have had this, her heart pounding, her skin tingling, and her whole body alive with butterflies, since last year?

Regret threatened to dampen the feelings overwhelming her. But last year she wouldn't have been ready. Without everything that had happened since, this moment would have never become this moment.

So she embraced it all, the excitement and the fear and the way her stomach pitched with surprise and her mind filled with wonder as she brushed her lips against his.

37

When Angeline Rock Climbs

1 DAY TO THE (NOW CANCELED) ELECTION
THE NIGHT BEFORE OPERATION RED, BLUE, AND VIOLET

Angeline and Leo scaled the steep incline, securing each foothold among the small, flat rocks on the uppermost layer of the dune. When they reached the top, they could see the foaming white-caps in the moonlight, the waves meeting their end against the shore. Though it wasn't an end. Not really. The froth simmered and eased, dissipating into waters the tide would reclaim and energize once again. The crash was simply a stage in the transition to something else.

Hoping to ease his fear, Angeline extended her arm toward Leo at the same time as his reached for hers. They clasped hands and supported each other as they navigated down the other side of the dune, the clatter of rocks mixing with the thunder of the waves until they hit the beach.

On the ride over, after Leo had again thanked her for finding evidence that might exonerate him, they talked about Emmie. Angeline would have liked to say she was surprised that it was Emmie behind *The Shrieking Violet*, but it took time to really know someone, to know what they'd do and not do, to know the kind of person they were.

To understand what it meant when that person betrayed you.

They skirted the edge of the water, the occasional spray dancing against their legs. The rock they both thought of as theirs lay just ahead. The destination in each of their minds without having to be voiced.

The flashlight from Leo's phone lit up the sand, and Angeline spotted the white line of a wish rock right in front of her. Beige. Like the one she'd given Cat all those years ago. She pocketed it and fell back into step with Leo.

They climbed the large green rock whose small, flat top forced them to sit close. Their arms and legs brushed against each other, and Angeline could almost convince herself that it was two months ago, on a crisp summer night, when the beach roses still bloomed and all that lay ahead was more of the same, not an upending of everything.

Leo shut off the flashlight, and Angeline's eyes adjusted to the darkness. Stars previously invisible began to emerge.

"Bear," Leo said, pointing to the sky.

"Gemini." Angeline lifted her own finger beside his.

When they'd first starting coming here three years ago, the only constellation they could identify was the Big Dipper. Using an app on Leo's phone, they'd discovered more, quizzing each other on each visit until they no longer needed the app.

Angeline realized she hadn't looked up in weeks. Hadn't looked at herself for far longer than that. Her life had been all about looking ahead, to a future post, to a future video, to a future she had spent so much time and energy crafting to make a reality. She would never apologize for being ambitious, for having goals, for wanting success. She had that in common with Leo's mom.

The consequences of such drive had always been so clear when it came to Mrs. Torres. Leo and Sammy feeling less important, more like set pieces than an integral part of a whole, of a family that existed independently of their mother's grander desires. The intentions or actual feelings of Mrs. Torres mattered less than how her sons interpreted them.

The same was true with Angeline and Leo. She'd been blind to the pitfalls her own demands had laid in their path.

The more success she found, the more thumbs-ups and likes she received, the more she craved. She was supposed to be the influencer, but the truth was, she'd been letting them influence her. Their validation pushed her forward, and it didn't matter what she actually believed, be it flesh-eating loafers or no limos to prom, she said what she said to gain more. She took for granted that she could do anything in service of her goal and her followers and supporters would applaud using every emoji that existed. She'd allowed it to skew her judgment. And she'd alienated the one supporter she cared the most about.

She laid her hand on his knee. His muscles pulled taut, and she drew back, but he caught her hand and enveloped it in both of his. The warmth spread to her toes.

"I'm sorry," Angeline said, straight out, no buildup, only the honest truth.

"I know," he said back, just as simply.

Her heart pounded even though it wasn't the first time she'd said this. Yet it seemed like the first time Leo was truly open to hearing it. "I never set out to hurt you, Leo. But everything that's happened since, with us, with the election and the Frankengirls and Emmie and *The Shrieking Violet*, all of it . . . it's made me realize something. When I planned that live-streaming, it wasn't so much that I thought the end result would justify the means, it's that I was self-centered enough to think the means wouldn't matter."

"That I'd just be okay with it?"

Angeline breathed in the smell of seaweed and brine and wanted to have an answer that was different from what it was. "Yes. Because what I needed mattered more."

Leo rubbed the skin on the back of her hand with his thumb. "I almost was—okay with it. Because how could I hate you for anything? And yet, those things I said . . . about missing my mom, missing her knowing me, afraid she never would. Gutted me to say them out loud and to just let the tears come. The reason it was all okay was because I was saying them to you."

Angeline's stomach clenched. "And I broke your trust. Just like she did."

He pressed his hands harder against hers. "Yeah, but that's it, isn't it? Like you said, I was partially blaming you for all I kept bottled up about her. About thinking she put everything before us, before me. And then it was like you were doing the same. So I followed Tad's lead and acted like an ass to get back at you both. Maybe partly even to fit in, back to that kid in elementary school who was afraid to speak up. The worst part is that you didn't set out to hurt me, but I can't say the same. I'm really sorry, Ang."

Her heart ached, and she almost made a wish on the rock that was to be Cat's—for all of this to have never happened. But it had. And she'd learned so much she didn't want to forget. "We both did things we shouldn't have." She looked into his eyes and was flooded with how much she missed him. "But I'm tired of fighting, Leo."

"Me too." They sat in silence, and she let him just breathe, just be, beside her. Then he shifted to face her. "I've been thinking about it ever since you came over—not fighting anymore. Us and the school. Say the election's suddenly back on and they vote for one of us. That's it? One of us has a say and screw everyone who feels differently?"

"It actually doesn't feel very democratic when you put it like that," Angeline said. "Which, though I hate to say it, makes Emmie's idea about everyone having a voice seem like a good one. Maxine finished the voting app last week, but I never actually asked her to go forward with the Ask an Angel one."

"She should. That's what our school needs—to be heard. Everyone does, right? I guess that's why my mom does all this. To help that happen."

"I almost wonder if that's why she wanted you to run in the first place. So you could see what it's like, maybe have something to share." Being a politician herself, Mrs. Torres probably knew her son would be good at it—because he was. He *had* been speaking up. And kids at school had been going to Leo more than to Angeline. He was better at it because he'd become more invested. Her first allegiance would always be to Ask an Angel. "Do you still want to run?" Angeline asked suddenly.

"It's over, Ang, not going to happen for either of us. Even if you and Cat find out who really did it, they're not going to change anything."

"That's not what I asked."

"Okay then. Do I want to be on student council? Yeah, I do."

"Good, because Cat and I need you."

"Oh . . . is that why we're here?"

When they first broke up, Angeline had an almost desperate

need for Leo to forgive her, to prove she wasn't the person she'd become. But she'd proved that all on her own. Which made it easier to concentrate solely on what she wanted.

"No." She slid her claddagh ring to the end of her finger, the point of the heart facing out. "I'm here because what I want is you back in my life."

A sharp inhale preceded his whisper. "I want the same thing." He eased the ring back onto her finger with the point of the heart turned in.

A wave crashed on the rock below. They'd been so focused on each other, they hadn't noticed the tide coming in.

Leo brought his head in line with hers, his lips a breath away. "And maybe a small dinghy."

Angeline and Leo held hands as they walked through the door of her apartment, a detail that drew a smile from Cat. Yet her sister's nervous face and proximity to Ravi made Angeline suspect—and hope—that she wasn't alone in advancing her love life that evening.

After a round of awkward "hey"s, Angeline sat on the end of the couch. "Leo's in."

"Even though I don't know the details," Leo said. "How's that for rebuilding trust?"

Angeline winked and grabbed his hand. She couldn't get enough of touching him. She had so much lost time to make up for.

Cat's face lit with excitement. "We're going to advocate for the election to be returned. Hopefully with you two as candidates, but we'd accept without. Is that okay?"

Leo said yes without hesitation, despite earlier admitting he wanted it. Angeline loved him for it.

"Ravi made us graphics," Cat said. Words that shouldn't have made someone blush but totally made her.

"Happy to help," Ravi said. "Even if that means ranking below Slothy on Principal Schwartz's hit list." He sighed. "Poor Slothy."

Leo bumped Ravi's fist in solidarity. "But—and don't take this the wrong way, because I'm all for speaking up about the election— but I don't think Principal Schwartz is going to listen to the four of us."

"Maybe not. But he doesn't have to listen to us. He has to listen to them." Cat showed them a drawing Ravi had made of the Acedia front lawn crowded with artfully rendered stick figures beneath a marquee that read: FIGHT FOR YOUR RIGHT: THE RED, BLUE, AND VIOLET PROTEST NEEDS YOU.

Leo cocked his head. "Like a rally?"

"A walkout," Cat said. "During fourth period, right on time for the midday news, if Grady comes through."

Leo released Angeline's hand and pushed himself off the arm of the couch. "Students demanding their vote? The media will definitely pick it up. After all the attention on Acedia, it can't not."

Angeline stood. "Which means your mom will see. If you don't want to be a part of it, we understand."

His eyes filled with gratitude that tugged at Angeline's chest, then dropped to the notebook he'd given Cat. "No, let's do this. I mean, what better optics for a politician than her son fighting to preserve the right to vote?" He nervously shoved his hands in his pockets before adding, "Never thought I'd see the Quinn sisters so in sync. Looks good on you both."

"Yeah, it does." Angeline smiled at her sister, whose face faltered for a split second before reciprocating. "Okay, so about us as candidates. I've got something I'd like to run by you all. And we're going to need Maxine."

Acedia Red and Blue @TheRedandBlueAcedia • 2h

Fight for Your Right: Students to Take a Stand Today. http://www. achsma.com/redandbluenewspaper #RedBlueVioletProtest #AcediaHigh #FrankengirlsNoMore #Walkout #ElectionRights #VotingRights

Reply 12   Retweet 25   Like 180

Show this thread

The Shrieking Violet @ShriekWithMe • 2h

Color us ready! Are you? Make sure you're wearing red, blue, or (our favorite) violet! Yes, that means purple. http://www.shriekingviolet.com #RedBlueVioletProtest #AcediaHigh #FrankengirlsNoMore #Walkout #ElectionRights #VotingRights

Reply 25   Retweet 40   Like 290

Show this thread

Angeline Quinn ✔ @AskanAngel • 2h

What use are wings if you don't take flight? http://www.youtube.com/ user/AskanAngel #RedBlueVioletProtest #AcediaHigh #FrankengirlsNoMore #Walkout #ElectionRights #VotingRights

Reply 50   Retweet 78   Like 456

Show this thread

Leo Torres @LeoTorres2002 • 2h

Replying to @AskanAngel

We can't be part of the conversation without a voice. It starts here. #RedBlueVioletProtest #AcediaHigh
#FrankengirlsNoMore #Walkout #ElectionRights #VotingRights

Maxine @MaxineChenontheCliffs • 2h

Replying to @AskanAngel

In. Who's with me? #RedBlueVioletProtest #AcediaHigh #FrankengirlsNoMore #Walkout #ElectionRights #VotingRights

---

Nat @NatGberg • 2h

Replying to @AskanAngel

Me. #RedBlueVioletProtest #AcediaHigh #FrankengirlsNoMore #Walkout #ElectionRights #VotingRights

---

Dipti P. @drp98 • 1h

Replying to @AskanAngel

Me. #RedBlueVioletProtest #AcediaHigh #FrankengirlsNoMore #Walkout #ElectionRights #VotingRights

---

BakedBaker24/7 @Josh Baker • 30m

Replying to @AskanAngel

Getting out of physics? 100%

Jay Choi Is Tweeting @J_Choi • 10m

Replying to @AskanAngel

THERE for it. Join me rallying for write-in votes to count!

Acedia Charter School @AcediaCHSMA • 4m

Replying to @AskanAngel

This is not a school-sanctioned event. Participants will be subject to disciplinary action.

Jay Choi Is Tweeting @J_Choi • 3m

Replying to @AskanAngel

Eh, make me a maybe.

38

When Cat Protests Just Enough

THE DAY THAT SHOULD HAVE BEEN ELECTION DAY
THE DAY THAT IS OPERATION RED, BLUE, AND VIOLET

The bell signaling the end of third period rang. Cat shot out of her seat like she'd been stung by a bee. The whole government class looked at her, and she almost sat back down. Then Ms. Lute gave a barely perceptible nod.

Cat took a deep, shaky breath and returned the same gentle acknowledgment of what was about to happen.

What Cat hoped was about to happen.

She exited the room, her mind abuzz. Ravi was waiting for her, just as they'd planned. He looked as anxious as she felt. As they passed the newsroom, she considered peeling off, dragging Ravi inside, and hiding out until it was all over. Let Angeline and Leo handle it. They were the stars of this anyway. Cat had done her part. She'd come up with the idea, used social media to spread the word. They didn't really need her.

But she'd roped Ravi in.

And she wanted to see it through.

Not for a story or an award but for herself. She didn't only want to report on the world, she wanted to be a part of it.

"Think it's going to work?" Ravi asked.

They watched Leo leading a group of male students toward the side exit. After the meeting with Principal Schwartz and his parents, Leo's suspension had been lifted pending a complete investigation—one that Cat's hunch, Maxine's hacking, and Slothy's camera might end.

"Something's going to happen," Cat said. "What? I have no idea."

"Well, we're in it together," he said.

Cat stole a glance at him, those dark eyes she could get lost in, which scared her as much as it intrigued her.

"All together," Angeline said, meeting them at the exit. She'd layered her red Acedia short-sleeved tee over a long-sleeved white one. Her jeans were dark blue, and a purple ribbon secured her long braid. A beach rose, the last from the plant in their room, was tucked behind her ear. Cat had borrowed a blue sweater but wore her own khaki skirt.

Behind them, feet shuffled and murmuring spread. A collective shift as if from a gust announced Principal Schwartz's arrival, his too-large suit jacket making his shoulders seem broader. Cat wondered if that had always been his goal, to appear more imposing than he actually was.

The first bell for fourth period rang, silencing conversations and gluing everyone in place. Ravi brushed his finger against Cat's, hooking it around hers, not pulling her back but also not urging her forward.

She didn't look at Angeline. She simply laid her hand on the door and pushed.

Students followed, slowly at first. Maxine, Sonya, and Riley, who'd coordinated to each represent a color: red, blue, and violet.

Then came Natalie Goldberg, Dipti Patel, Josh Baker, Chelsea Anders. And Emmie. Emmie came. She didn't have to. That wasn't part of their deal.

They were all juniors and seniors, and more of their classmates made up the first wave. It wasn't long before sophomores and freshmen joined. Soon, the green grass was obscured by students wearing red, blue, and violet. Red was the most popular, with many in their Acedia-issued red athletic tees for gym. But as Cat looked around, the picture became the one Ravi had drawn, the one she'd seen in her head. Down to the poster painted by Sonya announcing the Red, Blue, and Violet Protest, hung over the marquee by Grady.

Angeline and Cat stood on the concrete mound beneath it. Leo came to Angeline's side, Ravi settled a step behind Cat, and Emmie was before her, her blue eyes anxious but determined.

Seventy, eighty, maybe even a hundred students filled the lawn, turning in unison at the rumble of one news van, then another. Cat gave a silent thanks to Grady for sending her note, in which she'd asked the reporters to delay their arrival as long as they could. Though the administration would see the activity on social media, she didn't want it to realize just how big this might become.

As it was, Principal Schwartz had had time to prepare. He claimed a spot by the flagpole, megaphone in one hand, watching as students trickled out of the building, probably waiting so he could saddle as many as possible with disciplinary action.

Cat nodded to Maxine, who'd added protest streaks of red and violet to the already blue tips of her hair. Before homeroom, Cat, Angeline, and Leo had downloaded an app that would turn their phones into mics. Maxine had tested it using Cat's phone. As Maxine pressed the power button on the Bluetooth speaker in her hand, a light glowed green and through the tiny holes came: "Now connected to Cathleen Quinn's phone."

And everyone looked at her.

Her.

But it was Angeline who was supposed to speak. Not Cat.

She went as rigid as a rabbit caught in an open field. Angeline whispered, "Give me your phone" just as Grady shouted from the far edge of the lawn, "Go, Chief!"

The buzzing echoed in Cat's ears. A few shouts rose above the hum: some more "Chief"s and a couple of "Cat"s. Despite the increased readership of *The Red and Blue*, she was surprised that so many were able to connect her face with her name. She tried to wet her lips, but the throng of students before her and the reporters and cameras rushing closer made her tongue go numb.

Her heart pounded and her mind spun and she wondered how she could ever expect to lead anyone at any paper, at *anything*, with spots dancing before her eyes.

And then she remembered something she read about one of her idols: Katharine Graham, who transformed *The Washington Post* into a leading newspaper by going against the advice of her male colleagues, trusting her instincts, and publishing the Pentagon Papers. When asked how she did it, she said she put one foot in front of the other, shut her eyes, and stepped off the edge.

And so Cat closed her eyes, imagining herself alone in front of her computer, her fingers stroking the keyboard, and let the words come. "Today on the lawn of Acedia Charter School, hundreds of students have gathered to protest the administration's decision to select the members of the student council itself, stripping from the student body a responsibility that previously belonged to it."

She opened her eyes to a sea of blank stares. A few students looked to be sleeping standing up. Some were eyeing the main entrance. And Principal Schwartz smirked.

Angeline nudged her, and Cat began to pass her the phone. But instead Angeline placed something in Cat's free hand: a beige rock with a single white line encircling it. "You got this. Just be yourself."

Cat's eyes widened in surprise. Slowly, she ran her finger around the rock and, for the first time, made a wish instead of watching Angeline do so. *Please let this work.* Her pulse beat faster, but she squeezed the rock and tried once more. "Thank you for coming."

What is this? A birthday party?

Someone snorted, and someone else said, "Still better than a calc quiz."

Cat paused, trying to find her place in this story. But it wasn't just her story. It was her sister's, her sister's friends', Leo's, Emmie's, Ravi's. And they were all there. Trusting her. Believing in her. Being in front of all these people was so far out of her comfort zone that she was in another zip code. But this was a story worth telling.

She gripped the phone and stepped off the edge. "You're here because you follow *The Red and Blue* or *The Shrieking Violet* or Ask an Angel. Or maybe you were curious or wanted to get out of class or maybe saw these news vans . . ." Cat waved.

Oh God.

She cleared her throat. "Maybe you thought it was your chance for a few minutes of fame. Or maybe you're here because you're angry."

"Pissed off!" Natalie shouted.

"Exactly!" Cat said, emboldened. "Frustrated by everything that's happened since the school year began. We've had female students degraded, we've had rumors being spread by an untrustworthy and unverified source, we've had two candidates for student council president antagonize each other, rile up the student body—"

"Cat," Angeline cautioned.

"Right. Yes, well, so, maybe things got heated, but at least it did what no other election at this school has done in years: it got us engaged. And then what? We're rewarded by having it all taken away because someone else says we can't handle the responsibility?" Boos pushed Cat to continue. "No matter why you came, I hope you stay because you realize that you have a voice. Our generation has more eligible voters than any other. But change only happens if we make voting a priority. How will we learn to do that if we don't start here?"

Cat lowered the phone, and Angeline reached for her hand. The students had multiplied as Cat had been talking, and it seemed the entire student population filled the lawn.

Principal Schwartz pressed the button on his megaphone, and with his first words of "Very well, Miss Quinn," that entire student population erupted.

Cat didn't hesitate to give Angeline her phone. "Guess I warmed them up for you," she said over the roar.

"And made a hard act to follow." Angeline's tone and smile were so genuine that pride swirled in Cat's chest.

Then, there under the marquee, Angeline and Leo buried the Battle of the Exes.

They held hands. They faced their classmates. And they apologized.

Leo first. "The climate in our school has gotten toxic. Something for which I accept responsibility. I followed at the same time as I was asking you to let me lead. Not anymore." He pushed his shoulders back. "I own my role in hurting you, hurting our school, and hurting Angeline Quinn." He glanced at her and turned back to the students. "Now I need you to do something. Own your role in all of this. Because I may have let you take things too far—"

"We." Angeline added her voice to Leo's. "We let you."

Leo nodded appreciatively. "We egged you on with things we only half believed, and we watched as bandwagons were hopped on. That's not to say that you shouldn't stand behind what you believe. But Angeline's right about the need for empathy, something the world hasn't given us the best role models in lately. Because standing behind shouldn't mean tearing others down." He eyed the news vans. "What it should mean is getting engaged, and Cat's right that we have. But a lot of us are only deep in slacktivism. A like, a thumbs-up . . . maybe, if we're really feeling generous, a share or repost. We think we've done our part by using a hashtag, so we don't do more. And we let the trolls go wild."

"And that's a spring break vid I definitely don't want to see on YouTube," Angeline said, impressing Cat at her perfect timing for lightening the mood.

And then Leo showed just what a good team they could be by adding, "Do you know there's a law that if you live in Texas, you can vote from space? So our astronauts don't miss out on their rights. How's that for a role model? If we let them drown us out now, we send the message that they can keep doing it. We need to show them that we won't stand for it. And that we can come up with something even better. A new approach."

"No president," Angeline said, engendering gasps and a few boos.

Then someone shouted, "Sure 'nuff, angel, you can be my queen!"

Angeline's response came quick. "Hey, hey, now, as much as I'd rock a tiara, we want more students to have a say, not less. Which is why we propose to eliminate all the traditional officer roles and replace them with a committee."

She gave the phone to Leo. "This committee will consist of an elected delegate from each grade and three volunteer representatives from each class. The committee will randomly choose the volunteers from the pool signing up, rotating every four weeks, so more students have the opportunity to have their voices heard."

Angeline nodded, then accepted the mic. "And because Maxine Chen and the Girl Coders Club are total geniuses, they're transforming my campaign-promised Ask an Angel app into Acedia Speaks. Have feedback on a broken toilet? A sticky locker? A couple of hallway bullies? Open, click, and speak. And tune in during the live-streamed committee meetings to speak up in real time. Total transparency for you and us—no hiding behind anonymity."

Despite being in the room when Leo and Angeline had hammered this out last night, Cat was struck by her sister. This was a new Angeline, one taking the focus off of herself, but also the same Angeline, doing what she did best by employing social media as a way forward. Like Cat and Gramps had been talking about for the future she was still determined to have, even if the form wouldn't be what she'd thought.

"And yes," Angeline said, addressing Principal Schwartz, "the student council allows for such modifications. All that's required is a vote by the student body."

Eyes frowning, Principal Schwartz lifted the megaphone. But before he pressed the button to speak, Ms. Lute carefully tipped her head toward the news cameras. If Principal Schwartz's shoulders slumped, his oversized jacket hid it well as he said, "Acedia supports students making their own choices."

Maxine whooped and grabbed Cat's phone from Angeline. "Here we go, Sloths. Let's ramp things up. Because today is election day at Acedia! If you haven't already downloaded my voting app, first, what's wrong with you, and second, do it now."

Cat was too short to see over Maxine's shoulder. Immediately, Ravi stepped forward. She inched closer, eliminating any space between them, despite being able to see his phone fine right where she was.

On the voting app was a brief description of Angeline and Leo's proposed new system with a button for yes and a button for no. The entire lawn of red, blue, and purple moved as one: heads lowering, thumbs swiping, fingers tapping. Voting out in the open, not exactly a town fair like Ms. Lute had talked about, but being all together, watching one another act had the same accountability for participating.

Maxine added, "And anyone without a smartphone, step right up! I'll ensure your vote's counted."

A reporter and cameraperson approached Jay Choi, who let them zoom in on his phone.

As heads began to lift, Maxine checked the results. "Isn't democracy grand? A resounding ninety-eight percent say yes to Student Council 2.0!"

"That's not what we're calling it," Angeline whispered.

Maxine flung her long hair over one shoulder. "My app, my rules." Then, to the crowd, "We'll have to hold a new signup period to elect the officers from the rest of the classes, but since we happen to have two seniors on the ballot who've already campaigned, let's go ahead and vote in our senior class officer right now."

"No," Leo said. "It should be brand-new for everyone to have a chance."

Maxine sighed. "Isn't he just the cutest? Sorry, babe, this is happening. You two started this, it's got to end with one of you." She jutted her chin to the students whose heads were lowered once again. "Kinda understanding the power trip you've both been on of late. I mean, look what I did."

Angeline shushed Maxine and jerked her head toward the news vans. She then straightened her spine and shifted to offer what Cat knew she thought was her better side to the cameras.

Her sister was who she was. And Cat loved her because of it as much as in spite of it.

Maxine gave a one-minute warning. When time was up, her entire face frowned and she swore.

That was how they all found out that Leo had won.

39

When Angeline Becomes News

THE NIGHT AFTER THE STUDENT COUNCIL
2.0 ELECTION

Must have been the World Series, Angeline thought, when the Red Sox were in it. The last time the four of them had crowded onto the couch in front of the TV like this. And that had only been for the first pitch.

Beside her, Cat hit play, and the reporter with her hairsprayed helmet of a bob began summing up all that'd happened at Acedia since the school year began. Weeks of anger, hurt, fear, and triumph reduced to a twenty-second intro.

Angeline watched herself, angling to show more of her good side, as the reporter asked how she felt about Leo winning the race for student council president.

"Officer," she'd said in the news segment. "Student council officer representing the senior class."

"In Student Council 2.0," the reporter said.

Angeline then watched herself flinch. *Maxine.*

"Are you surprised you didn't win, after all the attention you've received?" The camera panned down to the boxes spilling over with angel wings that they'd staged at Angeline's feet.

328

"Surprised in a good way." Angeline remembered how it felt for the words to spill out of her, her own beliefs, without her usual crafting to stay on-brand. "It means students are making a choice independent of media attention or hints of celebrity. Which is hard enough for adults to do, isn't it? That's a good thing. A great thing. Don't you think?"

"I don't think, I'm simply reporting."

"Uh-huh," Angeline said knowingly on-screen, and Cat snorted on the sofa beside her. "Thought you'd appreciate that," Angeline said to her sister, noticing a look passing between Gramps and her mom.

On TV, Angeline pulled Leo into the frame. "Leo Torres deserves this win. His loyalties are one hundred percent with his constituents, something he learned from his mother, who's the hardest working woman in politics I know."

Cat snorted again. "And the only one."

"Still true."

Another look.

The reporter glanced at Leo as if she should address him but instead asked Angeline what was next for her.

Cat leaned into their mom. "This is my favorite part."

Because during the live report, Angeline had wiggled her phone. "We have what's next for me right here. Evelyn. You know, from Evelyn's Epic Everyday?"

The reporter instinctively smoothed her nest of dark hair. "Evelyn . . ." her voice trailed off.

Angeline had smiled. Right after the protest, she'd sent a direct message to Evelyn, "hinting" about all the good press about to come Angeline's way and how advantageous it might be for Evelyn's Epic Everyday to be seen leading it.

Angeline began, "As some sources have said, I do have a

connection with Evelyn. She's actually just reached out, asking me to read the following statement: 'Hey, Boston! Evelyn's Epic Everyday has her epic eye on you! We at Evelyn always knew our Angeline would never betray her sisters by having inside knowledge of those Frankengirls.'"

Gramps paused the report. "This is the phony you want to spend a week with, Angeline?"

Her mom recrossed her legs. "I tend to agree. Despite some solid advice in her book, is this really the person you want to be mentored by?"

Angeline nodded.

"Not without a thorough background check," Gramps said. "I've got a buddy on the force who owes me a favor."

"Gramps, it's fine," Angeline said, but he was already sending a text. Her heart swelled.

Back on the news, Angeline read: "'And now everyone else knows she's innocent too! Social media is blowing up—a thousand sticks o' dynamite in support of this one! You want to know what's next for our Angel, well, I'll tell *youuuu*!'" Angeline had pointed to the phone. "Lots of *u*'s here." She continued, "'I hereby announce Angeline will be my special guest at my very first inaugural Evelyn's Epic Everyday Boot Camp.'"

"'Inaugural' means 'first,'" Cat and Gramps quipped at the same time.

Excitement—and a touch of unfamiliar fear—had preceded Angeline's next move. She lowered the phone and spoke directly to the camera. "Since Evelyn's telling secrets, I may as well share one of mine. Hope it's okay, Evelyn!" She flashed a mischievous smile. "While I didn't win this election, I received an even greater reward. Getting to see how people responded to the #MoreThanOurParts hashtag. Something that, thanks to Evelyn's boot camp, I'll be taking wider under Ask an Angel. I'm going to enlist my followers to not just use the hashtag but embody it by donating, volunteering, and mentoring young women. I'm confident, knowing Evelyn, that she'll do the same. *Bring. It.* And flutter your wings, my angels!"

Angeline and Cat high-fived, and Gramps said, "Nicely done, granddaughter!"

Because Angeline had perfectly manipulated Evelyn into supporting Ask an Angel's new initiative. Her mom tried not to look pleased but failed entirely.

The rest of the segment played out, with the principal promising to ramp up investigations into security, parental influence, and, of course, the Frankengirls. Footage rolled of Cat addressing the student body, and again, Angeline felt a surge of pride for what Cat had accomplished.

Gramps shut off the TV and moved to his favorite armchair beside the couch.

Her mom slid from the sofa onto the coffee table, leaving Cat and Angeline side by side. "Let me see if I have this right. You not only didn't win, you basically did away with the office of student council president? I underestimated your ability to finagle your way out of a deal."

"Wait, what? No, Mom . . ."

She smirked, then let it evolve into a genuine smile. "I'm so proud of you, Angeline." She looked at Cat. "And you. But I'm especially proud that you did this together." The silence grew along with the glistening in her mom's eyes. "I was starting to think I'd made a mistake."

"But you're the one who forced me to run," Angeline said.

"*Suggested,*" she teased. Her mom's eyes swept over Angeline and Cat, holding them both equally. "I meant a mistake in letting you figure this out on your own."

Something tingled beneath Angeline's skin, and Cat nervously laughed. "What? How to almost get an entire school expelled?"

"Not exactly." Her mom reached for Angeline's hand. "That you're stronger together than you are apart." She then took Cat's hand and joined them as one. "I never wanted to push."

"I did," Gramps said.

"Almost wore me down too." Her mom smiled gently. "But I didn't think more interference was what you needed. Time was. To find each other again, to start to undo the damage done by your dad."

Angeline felt Cat stiffen and watched as she slipped her hand free and secured it under her thigh.

"Sometimes I wonder what would have happened if I'd been the one to see that this life wasn't for him. If I could have prevented the wedge he drove between you."

"Dad?" Angeline said, extracting her own hand. "But he didn't do anything—"

"Exactly." Her mom sighed heavily. "Which meant you both spent so much time competing for attention he couldn't give. You stopped being a team. My two girls, so strong on your own, but so perfect together. Supporting each other, helping each other, accomplishing great things togeth—"

"Stop," Cat said softly. "Just stop . . ."

Her mom eyed Cat quizzically and set a hand on her knee, but Cat brushed it off and sprang to her feet, scaring Tartan into their grandfather's lap. "I didn't do that, any of it. It's the opposite. This, all this . . . it's my fault."

"Cat, hey, it's okay," Angeline said uneasily. "I understand why you wrote the story about Leo."

Cat wove around the coffee table and paced in front of the TV, her cheeks shining red.

Angeline raised an eyebrow at her mom and shrugged before adding, "Cat, listen, I get it. It's actually kind of, I don't know, nice? You thought you were helping me."

"Helping?" Cat came to a halt, kneading her hands in front of her stomach. She then blurted out, "Emmie. *The Shrieking Violet* didn't only learn things from Sammy."

"The shrieking . . . what?" Angeline's mouth felt dry, like it was stuffed with cotton.

Cat kept on kneading. "I was watching you, everyone reacting to you, and I was, I don't know, upset, maybe jealous? And she was there. She listened." Cat swallowed. "She was using me, I see that now, but then, I was . . . lonely, I guess. I wanted us to be friends. I wanted her to like me and—"

"Like you?" A match flamed inside Angeline's chest as she realized what her sister meant. *Cat's the one who told Emmie? Told her everything?* "You did all this . . . *to me* . . . because you needed someone to *like* you?" Angeline gave a harsh laugh. She ignored the "Calm down" from her mother and the "Now, just wait" from Gramps and tore past Cat, heading for their room and the door she could slam and the phone she could snatch up to tell Maxine all about this. All about what her dear sister had done to her.

The sharp pain that ricocheted through Angeline's chest stopped her.

Maxine. She had to talk to Maxine.

About Cat.

Her instinct. A habit ingrained.

Angeline spun around and faced her sister—the sister she'd been complaining about to her own friends for years. Now she was on the other side.

Realizing how wrong that was.

And how much it hurt.

She stepped closer, struggling to take a full breath, smelling the butterscotch of Cat's hair, feeling their closeness and their distance at the same time. She then looked at her sister. Really looked. At those bangs growing longer, now perfectly framing her face. At her khaki skirt and black shirt and the ease with which she wore them, not trying to be something other than who she was, doing what she loved. What she was good at. And Angeline had mocked her for all of it.

The pain in Angeline's chest seared deeper.

Made her dizzy.

Made her remember.

Fraidy Cat.

That joke. *Her* joke. Something said in the moment, without thinking of anything but making people laugh. *Making people* like *me.* And Cat had been teased for weeks, months. All those years ago, Cat must have thought Angeline was rubbing it in when she gave her that wish rock and told her not to be afraid. Even now, she remembered Cat's bright pink cheeks, her own clenched fists, the anger and fear and sadness brimming in them both. And their dad there, mopping up the overflowing toilet.

He never even asked what'd happened. Her mom was right. And not. Because he might have been the one to let that wedge slide in, but Angeline had hammered it into place.

"I should have been a better sister," Angeline said.

Cat's face sagged. "No. I'm sorry. This is all my fault."

Angeline shook her head. "Our fault, can we at least agree on that?"

Cat nodded, guilt still clouding her eyes. "But from now on, we protect each other. We don't have to always like each other while doing it, but we still have to do it."

"I'll like you," Angeline said, but the heaviness of the moment made another instinct kick in. "Well, most of the time."

Relief spread through Cat's smile. "Bring. It."

Something warmed Angeline from the inside, and she longed to reach for Cat, but her mom rummaging inside her worn messenger bag interrupted. She pulled out a packet of tissues, handing one to Gramps before taking one for herself.

"I guess you were right," Angeline said to her. "Dad left us a long time before he moved out, didn't he?"

Her mom blew her nose. "It's true. Someone doesn't need to physically leave in order to be gone." She balled up the tissue and hesitated before tossing it to the side and again digging into her bag, sending it to the edge of the coffee table as she drew out PTA schedules and flyers for SAT prep courses. "Same way they don't have to be physically present to be here." She found her phone. "Your dad saw the news reports. He wanted to call you both."

"But he doesn't have our numbers," Cat said. "We didn't have phones before."

"I'm giving you his," her mom said. "He'd like to hear from you, if that's something you want."

Angeline sought out Cat, who glanced down at her feet. And so Angeline turned first to her mom, then Gramps. "And that's okay with you?"

Gramps responded first. "Of course. Missing your dad's nothing to be sorry about."

Angeline thought back to that day at the beach when she wished with every rock in her bucket that her father would be there for her. Something she never told anyone. Something she tried so hard to forget. "But I was. None of you seemed to miss him, so I didn't think I should. Could."

"Oh, sweetheart." Her mom hopped up and placed a hand on each of Angeline's shoulders. "That's on me. You were both so young and never asked about him much, so I guess I thought *out of sight, out of mind*. But maybe that was to protect myself more than you."

Angeline started shaking her head. Because it was true that she didn't ask about him, didn't seek him out, ignored Botox Wife's social media smiley faces, sent the requisite Father's Day cards in response to his requisite birthday ones. And still, she'd spent her whole life trying to get his attention, even now, racking up as many hearts and likes as she could from everyone else because she couldn't get them from him. She hated him. She missed him. And she needed both of those things to be okay.

The creases around her mom's eyes were the only evidence of how heavily this all weighed on her. She always put Angeline and Cat first, and Angeline loved her with every cell of her being for it.

"People can disappoint you," her mom said. "They can also surprise you. Only you can determine if the risk is worth it. You each decide what you want, okay?"

Each of them—separately, like they'd been for years. Finally, Cat lifted her head. Angeline looked into her sister's eyes. "Or maybe we could talk about it? Together?"

Cat beamed. "I'd like that."

As their mom stole another tissue, her bag slumped to the floor. Angeline picked it up, felt the threadbare fabric, and suddenly said, "You need something new, Mom."

"Don't start. Replacing it would be like replacing you two."

"But that's the problem. Ever since Dad left. You've made us your everything."

"I didn't *make* anything. You *are* my everything. If only I didn't have to go to work, I could be here all the time."

"That's not a good thing," Angeline said, and her mom's face fell. "The sentiment is, but you need more. Especially now. Like you said, everything will be different next year. You've taught us to put all our energy into what we love. But it's okay for you to love more than us. I want you to."

"Me too," Cat said. "Though I want Gramps to vet him."

Angeline nodded. "Sure, that, date. But also . . . maybe cut back on PTA and take some photography classes?"

Her mom's brow knitted.

Gramps leaned forward in his armchair. "That studio in the harbor has a sign in the window for a leaf-peeping retreat. What do you say? Early Christmas present?"

She shook her head. "Ganging up again, huh?"

"Would you like to go?" Angeline asked.

"A little. And I do have plenty of vacation days . . . so maybe I should think about it? Would that be—"

Cat tackled her in a hug, reached out with one hand, and drew Angeline into it, where she stayed, finally letting herself be held by her big sister.

40

When Cat Freelances

Cat waited for the fireworks to explode and bring the newsroom down to rubble. They'd come close before.

There really should have been a warning sign on the door. A ribbon or a flashing light or maybe a tiny electric shock, something to alert them when Emmie was inside and Angeline was about to enter or the other way around. They'd both become fixtures in Cat's newsroom since the completion of Operation Red, Blue, and Violet.

Today, thankfully, Angeline and Leo were just leaving as Emmie came in to grab the camera to take photos for her latest story. Angeline patted Cat's shoulder, and Leo fist-bumped Ravi, whose artsy surfer soccer player vibe held its own against Leo. They looked good together, the four of them in front of the table with the ski pole leg, in the first and still only square on Cat's Instagram. For now, it was the life she had and the one she wanted, and it was enough.

Emmie smiled softly as she tucked the camera in her backpack and left the newsroom.

Cat didn't trust her. She wasn't sure she ever would.

When Emmie had first come to Cat, asking to work on the paper, Cat's gut had told her to say no. But Angeline had given Cat a second chance and vice versa. Was that only okay because they shared the same DNA? Or did everyone deserve a take two?

Angeline didn't like Emmie working on the paper, but she'd supported Cat's decision. Maybe because Angeline actually believed in second chances more than Cat.

She'd texted their dad. Cat wasn't ready.

So now Emmie was a reporter, being schooled by Grady, whom Cat had promoted to assistant editor; he was in charge of all their social media accounts after he did a surprisingly stellar job reporting on the protest, live and in print. While Leo dug deep into every idea that reached Student Council 2.0, a name that had stuck no matter how much it made Angeline itch, Angeline had rebranded her #MoreThanOurParts to the less salacious and more empowering #MoreThan. And she was at Leo's side when his mom nailed her interview with *The Today Show* and all but secured her congressional win.

Still Angeline found time to collaborate with Cat. Testing new online formats, like Instagram-style micro news stories and enhanced articles with links to source material so readers could see the evidence directly. Maybe journalists needed to meet readers halfway and evolve like the press had been doing since its inception. What better place for Cat to experiment than here, in this community she knew so well? And it had the makings of a kick-ass essay for her college applications.

Cat loved seeing the newsroom bustling again—no, not even again. With Angeline and Leo, Grady and Emmie, and Ravi—Ravi, who was at her side now, drawing letters on her forearm with his index finger, totally distracting her from the story she was editing—it was fuller than it had ever been.

This semester's Fit to Print award was long gone, but they gave out another next semester. Cat wouldn't be able to put it on her Northwestern application, but if she won, it wouldn't just be hers, it'd be all of theirs.

Ravi treaded farther down Cat's arm until the tip of his finger grazed the back of her hand. He flipped it over and traced.

"Uh, think I'm going to need that," Cat said, goose bumps erupting under her skin.

"You're so greedy. Seriously, isn't two hands to type overkill?" He continued drawing. "I'll stop when you guess right."

She had so much to do: editing this article, writing her own, plus homework and cooking dinner because it was her mom's photography class night, and yet this was a priority too. So she closed her eyes and concentrated.

"I'd love to go to Boston with you." She faced him, seeing the book on female journalists of the modern era on the shelf behind him. He'd given it to her on their first date, remembering how she'd lingered on it during her first visit to Harbor Books. "Any exhibit you want."

"Whoa, that was just *Boston, question mark*. The rest of that is wishful thinking." He pressed his lips against hers. "Find me at the bookstore later? There's a new beanbag chair that could use some serious breaking in."

Cat's temperature spiked. They'd been "testing" the chairs to find the most comfortable one each night as she helped him close. "Are you sure you can't stay until the pizza arrives?"

"Mom's got chauffeur duty for my sister and brother all afternoon. Bring me a slice."

He walked out backward, and Cat inhaled, deep from the diaphragm, to steady herself.

She returned to Grady's article on the peer jury system, which was the first thing Student Council 2.0 had acted on. It was scheduled to hold its introductory meeting before Thanksgiving break. She continued her edit until she came to the placeholder Grady had left for a comment from Principal Schwartz.

She texted him.

> **Cat:** When are you coming back?

> **Grady:** Mom's dropping me off now. Sorry, ortho took forever.

> **Grady:** Stupid retainers.

Cat set down her phone, and the smell of cheese and grease wafted into the newsroom. She turned, and the hairs on the back of her neck rose at the flash of green.

The green sweatshirt, worn by a guy holding a Frank's Pizza box.

"Nine fifty," he said.

But all Cat could concentrate on was the FRANK'S PIZZA written on the arm of his sweatshirt.

His lime-green sweatshirt.

"Right. Sure. Okay." Cat fumbled for her wallet. This was the same guy she'd seen when she'd gone to Frank's looking for the security camera footage. Except then he'd been wearing the wrong uniform. "You, uh, go to school here?"

"Not anymore. Graduated last year. But this is just a side gig. Once my gamer channel takes off, I'm sticking those cheese sticks to Frank."

"Right. Sure."

He left, but Cat's mind stayed with him. With that lime-green sweatshirt. With the writing on it. Like they saw in Tad's photo. Coincidence? Had to be.

Her phone buzzed with a text.

Maxine: Slothy is mine!

Cat: You got into the webcam?

Maxine: In and found this.

It was a photo, time-stamped around six in the morning on the day the Frankengirls photos appeared. Someone in a lime-green sweatshirt with the hood pulled low over their forehead, carrying a package from PosterPrinters.com. Cat couldn't make out a face, but this time, the writing was clear. And exactly the same as the delivery guy's.

Frank's Pizza.

No one remembered seeing someone in a green sweatshirt at Maxine's party because that someone wasn't a guest. That someone had been delivering a pizza.

Maxine: Looking for more.

Cat: I might have a lead.

Cat was grabbing her bag to go after the delivery guy when she heard a "Dude, missed you" from the hallway.

"Devon? What are you doing here?"

It sounded like Grady. Cat peered around the doorway to see him tugging at his dark curls.

"Delivery. And, dude, you ever wanna make some bank like you did this summer, you can be my runner again. Same deal. I drive, you pop in, we split the tips."

"Uh, yeah, maybe."

"I'll text you."

Cat's heart beat double-time. *Grady had worked at Frank's Pizza?*

He entered the newsroom, sweat dotting his upper lip that belied his nonchalant nod.

Grady? *Grady?*

He was tall, as tall as Tad Marcus.

His skin tone was light, like the hand in the photo.

He was a whiz with editing software.

But Grady, really?

Cat needed more. She breathed heavily as she exited the newsroom, rested her back against a locker, and called her sister.

"Just caught me," Angeline said from behind the wheel of their hatchback. Cat moved farther down the hall for more privacy for their video chat. "I stopped by my P.O. box, and we were just about to head back out. Want me to swing by and pick you up?" Angeline set the phone in the holder on the dash, freeing her hands to open a package and extract something gold and shimmery.

Cat squinted at the screen. "Please tell me that's not another bigger is better?"

"Okay."

"Okay it is or it isn't?"

"Okay I'm not telling you."

Cat sighed. "Just don't leave it in the back seat."

Angeline peeked inside. "Certainly not. It needs the dark of a closet."

Course it does. She refocused on the task at hand. "You helped Maxine clean up after her party, right?"

"Naturally, good friend that I am. Why?"

"Do you remember pizza boxes?"

"Loads. Frank's. What's this about?"

"Let's just say I've got a hunch."

Angeline's eyebrow lifted. "Must be a good one. Touch base when you're un-hunched?"

Cat nodded and hung up. She reentered the newsroom and attempted a casual smile, but Grady's eyes barely darted to hers before shifting back to the computer. With trembling fingers, he punched in his password, and Cat committed the numbers to memory thanks to the skills Gramps had taught her years ago.

She worked and waited, said a "Sure" to Grady's "See you to-morrow, Chief" when he pushed his chair in. Then she closed the door and logged in to Grady's email.

Bo's name, a few freshmen Cat recognized, his mom—a lot. She moved to his trash, the emails the system had yet to delete. In it was a receipt from PosterPrinters.com. A PDF proof, showing three images . . . one of each of the Frankengirls.

She heard the creak of the door, a gasp, and a "Cat?" in a whine she'd come to know—and like. .

"I can explain, Chief," Grady said. "It's not what it looks like."

A tightness gripped her chest. "Grady—"

"No, wait, just wait." His glasses fell down his nose, and his eyes shone with guilt. "We needed a story—a big story. And I was reading your series from last year on all those pranks and started thinking. It was just supposed to be the one time and then . . . then you wouldn't let me cover it, but I figured the next time, you'd see . . . you'd have to let me."

He wanted to cover the big stories. And she wouldn't let him.

Nellie Bly's editors hadn't let her cover the big stories either. Inventing one would have been a lot easier than ten days in an insane asylum. But truth mattered then. It mattered now. It would always matter. Without truth, people shouted past one another simply to be heard. Everyone became noise. And so they stopped listening. They stopped caring. Everyone was in everything only for themselves. That wasn't the world Cat wanted to believe lay in her future.

"No. This isn't on me, Grady. Your actions are your own. Same as the consequences for them."

He protested the entire way, begging her not to say anything, and then, the closer they got to the principal's office, to help spin it for him. A piece of her heart broke as she left him.

It looked like that peer jury system was going to have to kick into gear sooner than planned.

When Cat returned to the newsroom, she sat down, placed her fingers on her keyboard, and started to write.

Acedia Confronts Its Inner Sloth: Controversy Surrounding Student Council Unprecedented in Charter School History

---

A SPECIAL REPORT

Part 6 of 6

The monthlong suspension of Grady Booker from Acedia Charter School marked the end of the Frankengirls and the first recommendation by the Acedia Peer Jury. The responsibility and accountability that had been missing previously was embraced by a student body finally pushed to its limit. Whether it was a move designed to steer clear of blame for the outcome or not, the administration's decision to let the jury determine Booker's fate allowed students to send a strong signal that they would not go easy on offenders, as one might assume.

"Why shouldn't we decide?" said Goldberg, who is a member of the current jury. "This is our community. We feel the effects more than anyone. We know what's actually hurting the school. And this did. It's right up there with the vegan bacon. I mean, the way it impacted the election. Not the vegan bacon itself. There's nothing wrong with vegan bacon. Some of my favorite foods are vegan. Eggs and cheese . . . Really? Those aren't vegan?"

That sense of community was reinforced when a second protest brought students to the front lawn, this time in shades of gray.

"No way Slothy was leaving that roof, man," Baker said. "Me and Jay Choi, we had the whole thing planned. They didn't listen to us, we were gonna do that tree hugger thing and chain ourselves to him. Except we needed to find some chains. And a ladder. And fill a cooler because dudes gotta stay hydrated, right? So, yeah, had the whole thing planned. He commands that roof like a boss, and no one's taking Slothy down."

The protest succeeded in protecting the stuffed sloth, which remains on the roof, with its webcam streaming the watch yard. It's become something of a confessional, with students entering and baring their souls to Slothy. With no audio, their secrets remain such, but students claim feeling a sense of freedom that Slothy knows. Because in the end, that's all anyone truly wants, whether it's accomplished through the knitting of angel wings or the clicking of a thumbs-up or a tiny heart or the sharing of posts or pics or video or the continuing solar battery of a stuffed sloth's camera: to be seen.

We see you, Acedia, and you're looking fine.

INBOX: New Message
From: cquinn@TheRedandBlueAcedia.com
To: editor@bostonglobe.com
Subject: A Special Report

Following up on our phone conversation from yesterday, please find attached the first draft of our agreed-upon freelance correspondent article: "Acedia Confronts Its Inner Sloth: Controversy Surrounding Student Council Unprecedented in Charter School History."

I look forward to your thoughts. Per your suggestion, I've submitted my application for your summer internship. Thank you for the opportunity.

Best,
Cathleen Quinn
Editor in Chief, The Red and Blue, Acedia Charter School

the end

Acknowledgments

I've had editors since middle school. I've been an editor since high school. Both make me more than qualified to know not just a good one, but an inspiring one. That's what I've been fortunate to have across two books with my editor, Jessica Harriton. When I brought the idea behind *Sources Say* to her, she was an immediate champion for it and helped craft it into the story it became. But neither of us would have been able to bring these characters and their important story to life without the impressive team at Razorbill and Penguin Young Readers Group. I'm especially grateful to Bree Martinez for her creative publicity efforts, and to Theresa Evangelista for the fun, bold, eye-popping jacket design. I'm positive I had a shirt that color in middle school. (And yes, it's much better suited for a book cover!)

My agent, Katelyn Detweiler, continues to deserve my utmost respect as a story genius and savvy strategist as well as my awe and gratitude for making me feel like the only client deluging her inbox. She works tirelessly to make my writing sing and my spirits soar. An author could have no better home than with you and Jill Grinberg Literary Management.

If this book had a masthead, it would include the names of so many authors I admire, starting with Chelsea Bobulski and Natalie Mae, who were invaluable in the early shaping of the story. For the cheerleading, discipline, and commiseration, I am indebted to my talented confidants, Alycia Kelly and Chandler Baker. I'd have never met my daily word count goals without either of you (and what a lonely place my texts would be!). Thanks also to the many professionals and friends who helped flesh out the ensemble cast, especially Jose and Pamela Ardila.

As always, I'm grateful to my parents, Denise and Frank; my in-laws Martha and Steve; and my Marangos and Goldstein nephews and nieces (oh yes, and their parents too!).

Rounding out my masthead is my husband, Marc, who got a big promotion on this one. Thank you for being my sounding board (and knowing when to listen, when to offer advice, and when to stop me from chucking my laptop off the balcony). Especially, thank you for being my partner in all things. A partnership that began, fittingly enough, in the newsroom.

This book, more than any I've written, has its roots in my personal life, because I had that editor in middle school and was one in high school, thanks to newspapers. While always drawn to the written word, my writing career began in journalism. I worked on every school newspaper through college, where I began as a writer, moved on to become features editor, and, eventually, editor in chief. Though stashed in the dark, dingy, musty basement of the university center, the newsroom was electric. It's an energy that's never been matched. The camaraderie of what was the strongest team I've ever been a part of, the adrenaline rushes of landing "*the*" quote, and the bleary eyes of the twice-weekly late nights (*cheers upon hitting the hour of pi, i.e., 3:14 a.m.*) formed the student I was, the work ethic I developed, and the writer I became. This book is an homage to those people and that time, including my former professor Jack Lule, who I'm honored to still have in my life.

But this book is also a reflection of where we are in terms of journalism and the media and where we will go. Both the spark of the idea and the actual writing of this story came when the world was a different place than it is as I write this now and than it will be when the book publishes. But whether we are dealing with "fake news," a political landscape that challenges and blurs fact and fiction, or a pandemic that alters our daily life, I fundamentally believe that truth matters. Truth is not pliable. I offer my deepest thanks to the journalists who continue to fight for truth in reporting and who will be integral in shaping what that means for this generation and the ones to come.

Check out

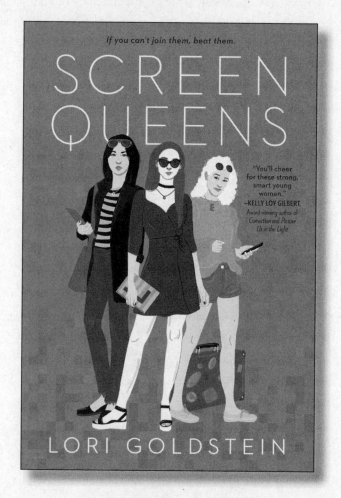

Turn the page
for a sneak peek!

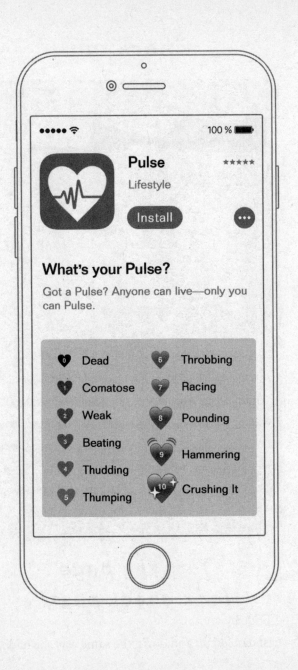

ONE

FOUR. *STILL*. ONLY FOUR.

Lucy shifted in the hard wooden chair across from her mom's desk and clutched her phone tighter. She swiped up and down with such force that her Caribbean Blue Baby fingernails would have scratched the glass had she not been diligent about using a screen protector.

Twitter, Instagram, Tumblr, Snapchat, Facebook . . . *Swipe, swipe, swipe.* The likes, favorites, followers, friends . . . she had enough. Enough for her ranking on the Pulse app to be higher than four.

Four?

Swipe, swipe, swipe, swipe.

The pink plastic bracelet the bouncer had secured around Lucy's wrist danced up and down the same way she had last night, after name-dropping her way into the hottest new club in San Francisco's Tenderloin District. The fact that she didn't actually *know* Ryan Thompson, founder of Pulse, was a technicality that would soon be remedied.

Her ❤ OUR FINGERS ARE ON THE PULSE ❤ tee only given to Pulse employees opened doors closed even to most of Silicon Valley's elite. She'd snagged it from a hipster-preneur six months ago at a party in Fremont. He was so busy claiming he left Pulse of his own accord (*uh-huh*) because his eco-friendly (*read: non-profitable*) idea was going to change the world (*i.e., drain his bank account*) that he scarcely knew what he'd lost. All it took was a deftly spilled cocktail, an exorbitant dry cleaning bill, and Lucy's favorite tank (*note: pomegranate margaritas don't come out of silk*), but it was worth it.

Soon she'd have one of her own.

And she'd no longer be a 4.

Really?

The likes on her Instagram story from last night alone should have bumped her up to a 5. Thumping. But here she sat. Still at 4. Still Thudding.

She stared at the string of hearts on her Pulse profile, knowing that, somehow, this was all because she was wait-listed at Stanford.

And *that*, Lucy knew the exact "how" of: Gavin Cox.

Freaking Gavin Cox.

She shouldn't have done it, but her blue fingernail moved on its own, navigating to his profile.

Level 6. Throbbing. Gavin Cox was Throbbing and she was Thudding. If only she possessed a male member and a wingspan like Michael Phelps, she'd be Throbbing too. But now that high school was over, winning state would no longer be a crutch for Gavin, and his Pulse would plummet. He'd be lucky to be Beating—a measly 3.

Lucy was tempted to knock her mom's expansive cherrywood desk. But Lucy Katz didn't believe in luck. Lucy Katz didn't hope. Lucy Katz didn't dream. Lucy Katz did.

She knew what she wanted.

And it wasn't this.

Thudding and wait-listed and this drab third-floor office in this mud-brown building in this sad little Sunnyvale office park.

So it wouldn't be.

Tired of the edge of the chair digging into the soft underside of her knees, she scooted forward until her wedge sandals reached the floor.

Her mom was twenty minutes late.

As usual.

Lucy knew enough to show up for their scheduled lunch a half hour after its start time, but she was on time.

As always.

Lucy planned like other people breathed.

Which was why she wasn't nervous about Stanford. It was a blip. A minor inconvenience. Nothing that an internship at Pulse wouldn't wipe away like a hard reset on her MacBook Pro.

She stared at the gently tanned skin of her exposed ankles and wiggled her toes, enticing circulation to resume after being dangled two inches off the floor despite her heels. She pulled her pink-and-white-striped notebook onto her lap and leafed through the pages, refreshing herself on all the notes she'd taken thus far on ValleyStart, the summer tech incubator program she was about to begin. The five-week competition ended with one team winning an internship at Pulse. If she succeeded (*please*), she'd spend the rest of the summer at Pulse with Ryan Thompson. And Pulse, well, not even Stanford could ignore a pedigree that included Pulse.

Satisfied it was all already committed to memory, she closed her notebook and stared at the shiny gold *L* floating on the center of the cover—the only Hanukkah gift she'd received last year, sent in a FedEx envelope from her mom's assistant.

She tucked it under her arm and stood, passing by windows that looked out on row after row of blue, red, black, white, and green hybrid cars lined up like Crayolas in the parking lot, the closest the office came to having a pop of color. A four-by-six double frame propped beside her mom's three monitors was the only personalization in the room.

One side held Lucy as a baby, swaddled in her mom's arms with her dad looking off to the side, toward the London office he'd soon head. The second photo once again displayed the three of them, this time on graduation day, just a few weeks ago. Her dad had scheduled a week of meetings before and after in order to attend.

Two milestones in Lucy's life, as if nothing had happened in between, with the frame leaving no room for anything to come.

The graduation photo hung crooked in the frame. She could just see her mom hurriedly shoving it inside with one hand, typing an email with the other, while on a conference call with Singapore, Melbourne, and Dubai.

Lucy set her phone on the desk. She pulled off the cardboard backing to straighten the photo, and out fell the slip of paper behind it: a smiling baby—not Lucy, simply the picture that had come in the frame. How long had her mom kept that other child beside Lucy? Long enough to forget to print one to take its place, long enough to no longer notice that she should.

On the desk, Lucy's phone vibrated and lit up with a text.

ValleyStart: Team assignments are in! Meet Your Mates!

Lucy's arm shot out like a rattlesnake, and her notebook fell, knocking into one of her mom's monitors.

"Lucy!" Abigail Katz entered the room and rushed forward in her expensive flats.

"Got it!" Lucy's tennis-trained reflexes saved the monitor before it took down the others like dominoes.

Considering Lucy had read and reread the acceptance packet about a thousand times and been waiting for the past two months to see who she'd be spending the next five weeks with, her restraint in not jumping on the ValleyStart portal instantly was extraordinary.

It's actually happening.

Her pulse quickened, and she was almost dizzy as she circled one way around the desk, back to the hard chair. Her mom rounded the corner from the opposite direction, adjusted the tilt of the monitor, and sat down in front of it.

With the seven-inch height difference between them, Lucy could only see her eyes. And the tiredness in them.

Lucy would never deny that Abigail Katz worked hard.

But that was all she did.

"I'm sorry, Lucy." Abigail smoothed the ends of her chin-length bob. The barest hint of gray dusted the roots—a constant battle, waged every three weeks as she colored it back to brown. "They needed some guidance in a branding meeting that wasn't on my schedule."

"Right," Lucy said.

Abigail reached into the top drawer of her desk and pulled out two protein bars. "Just a quick lunch, then, okay?"

Peanut butter. Lucy hated peanut butter. "Sure." She peeled back the wrapping. Not even peanut butter could ruin her ValleyStart high.

"All set for tomorrow?"

"Packed the car this morning." She bounced (*just a little*) in her seat.

Abigail stopped chewing. "Not an Uber or Lyft?"

"It's ten miles."

"Right. *Ten.*"

Half the number of fender benders Lucy had been in. *Who has time to spend learning to be a perfect driver?*

"Fine. Whatever." Lucy pretended there was no judgment in her mom's question and forced a bite of the peanut butter. "I'll leave the car."

"Better plan. You won't need it anyway." Abigail set her own half-eaten bar down. "You have to focus. Palo Alto High School may have been competitive, but ValleyStart's in another league. The top startup incubator for high school graduates in the country with only sixty accepted out of—"

"Three thousand applicants, I know." An acceptance rate of only two percent. *Two.* Stanford's was four. The sole explanation . . .

Freaking Gavin Cox.

The only other applicant from her high school to make it into ValleyStart.

Lucy pushed her heels into the floor and all thoughts of Gavin where they belonged—in the past.

"I've been focused, Mom. I'm certainly not going to stop now." Top ten in her class, 4.8 GPA, tennis all-star, two marathons under her belt, and still a lecture on being "focused." Lucy regretted the bite as her stomach churned.

"Nothing wrong with reminders," Abigail said, just as one dinged on her computer and phone in unison, the sound as familiar to Lucy as the squeak of her bedroom door.

Lucy stood.

"Wait. It's just . . ." Abigail's eyes slowly drifted from her three monitors to Lucy's expertly draped off-the-shoulder tee and perfectly cuffed dark-wash jeans. "I've always given you freedom because you've shown that you can handle it. Up until now."

Now meaning not getting into Stanford.

"But with this, with this new world you're entering, well, I just want you to be aware of the pressures and the importance of how you present yourself."

"Present myself? I'm not a poodle in some dog show."

"That's not what I meant."

"Then what do you mean, Mom?"

"Letting off steam in high school is one thing, but now you're an adult."

"So I've heard." Her mom had repeated the same phrase ad nauseam since Lucy's eighteenth birthday three months ago.

"Believe me, Lucy, it's no secret how little you've wanted to heed my advice lately. If and when that changes, you know where to find me."

Right here in this same baby-poop-brown office you've lived in since I took my first steps . . . which, naturally, you missed.

Heat rose in Lucy's chest, and all she wanted to do was give her mom a reminder: that the phrase was "work hard" *and* "play hard." And the playing bit could yield the same—if not better—results as the working. Connections made things happen. Just ask her Pulse tee.

"Sure, Mom." Lucy brushed her hand through her long dark hair, forgetting she was still holding the brick of peanut butter. She picked a crumb off a strand by her chin and watched as her mom slipped on her computer glasses and turned the world right in front of her eyes crystal clear, blurring everything else beyond—including Lucy.

Lucy headed for the door. "Just one small thing . . . in order to give me freedom or anything else, you'd actually have to be around."

She didn't wait for her mom to look up; she simply wrapped her hand around the metal knob and closed the door behind her with barely a sound, making sure she "presented herself" properly.

How am I even related to her?

Lucy only made it halfway down the hall before she slowed, leaned her head against the crap-colored walls, and tried to stop her heart from racing.

Level 7. Seven hearts was Racing.

Like everyone her age, like everyone in the world, Lucy knew the Pulse levels as well as her home address. "What's your Pulse?" were the first words off anyone's lips upon meeting, the first background check determining worthiness for everything from friend to blind date to party invites, probably even job offers.

The brainchild of Ryan Thompson when he was only a year older than Lucy, the app amalgamated an individual's likes, favorites, views, thumbs-ups, and more from every major social media platform, translating it to a simple Pulse level, ranking you from zero, Dead, all the way to ten, Crushing It. Over time, as the app evolved, Level 10s became top influencers, the people everyone wanted to be or be seen with. Advertisers and the entertainment business soon realized that Level 10s' smiling faces could increase sales and media coverage. Now 10s got complimentary everything, from the newest iPhones to dips in Iceland's Blue Lagoon. To be a 10 was to live with all the perks.

Once Lucy and her team won the ValleyStart incubator, Pulse would be her second home for the rest of the summer. The prize of an internship at the most successful tech company in the past ten years was worth more than any amount of money.

She'd use it to her advantage. Starting now.

Lucy opened the Stanford portal and did what she'd wanted to do for weeks, since she was accepted into ValleyStart. She requested a second alumni interview. She knew it was irregular, but she explained that she had new information she was delighted to share—namely the incubator.

Lucy then lifted her chin higher and straightened her top. As she passed by the largest office—a suite—she ran her finger along the three little letters on the nameplate: *CEO.*

Pulse would secure that future.

At the elevators, Lucy logged in to the ValleyStart portal to find not just the names of her teammates but her assigned mentor: Ryan Thompson.

For the first time since arriving at her mom's office, Lucy smiled.